Julie Anne Lindsey is an obsessive reader who was once torn between the love of her two favourite genres: toe-curling romance and chew-your-nails suspense. Now she gets to write both for Mills & Boon. When she's not creating new worlds, Julie can be found carpooling her three kids around northeastern Ohio and plotting with her shamelessly enabling friends. Winner of the Daphne du Maurier Award for Excellence in Mystery/Suspense, Julie is a member of International Thriller Writers, Romance Writers of America and Sisters in Crime. Learn more about Julie and her books at julieannelindsey.com

Former naval intelligence officer and US Naval Academy graduate **Geri Krotow** draws inspiration from the global situations she's experienced. Geri loves to hear from her readers. You can email her via her website and blog, gerikrotow.com

Also by Julie Anne Lindsey

Deadly Cover-Up
Missing in the Mountains
Marine Protector
Shadow Point Deputy
Marked by the Marshal
Federal Agent Under Fire
The Sheriff's Secret

Also by Geri Krotow

Her Christmas Protector
Wedding Takedown
Her Secret Christmas Agent
Secret Agent Under Fire
The Fugitive's Secret Child
Reunion Under Fire
Snowbound with the Secret Agent
Incognito Ex
Colton's Deadly Disguise
Colton's Mistaken Identity

DANGEROUS KNOWLEDGE

JULIE ANNE LINDSEY

COLTON 911: IN HOT PURSUIT

GERI KROTOW

MILLS & BOON

First Published in Great Britain 2020
by Mills & Boon, an imprint of HarperCollins*Publishers*
1 London Bridge Street, London, SE1 9GF

Special thanks and acknowledgement are given to Geri Krotow for her contribution to the *Colton 911: Grand Rapids* series.

ISBN: 978-0-263-28055-5

1120

MIX
Paper from responsible sources
FSC™ C007454

This book is produced from independently certified FSC™ paper to ensure responsible forest management.

For more information visit: www.harpercollins.co.uk/green

Printed and bound in Spain
by CPI, Barcelona

DANGEROUS KNOWLEDGE

JULIE ANNE LINDSEY

To Jack,
my home-building hero.

Chapter One

Katlin Andrews adjusted her sweaty grip on the steering wheel, smiling wildly as she navigated the dark roads in the worst part of town. She'd single-handedly nailed down the story of a lifetime tonight, and she couldn't wait to see her boss's face when she proved it. He thought she was too young and inexperienced to know a real story if it bit her, but he was wrong. And she hadn't just nailed this one down, she'd blown it wide open.

The thrill of victory rushed through her veins as she made the final turn out of the run-down neighborhood, thankful to be on her way home. Only a few more blocks to the highway, then she'd work until dawn. Put all the puzzle pieces together and tie up every loose ends. The findings from tonight's outing were going to change her life. She was sure of it.

A set of headlights flashed in her rearview mirror, distracting her thoughts and eating up the dark road behind her. Katlin pushed the gas pedal with renewed purpose, her intuition spiking. No one out at this hour, in this area, could be up to anything good, and she certainly didn't want to think about the reason a car was racing after her tonight.

Didn't want to think that maybe she'd been caught.

Katlin wet her lips and divided her attention between the dark road before her and the glaring headlights behind her. Maybe she was wrong. Maybe the car would just pass by. Maybe she was overreacting. She certainly hadn't seen anyone watching as she'd crept through the decrepit basement window and snooped around the overfilled space, taking photos to prove her suspicions.

Still, the headlights drew nearer rapidly, until they became one blinding spotlight that caused Katlin to squint and swerve. She urged the pedal lower, a sheen of sweat forming on her upper lip. With a mighty roar of the engine, the assailing car nudged her little sedan's rear bumper and she skidded sideways along the desolate road.

Katlin screamed and her heart raced as she struggled to regain control of the vehicle. She didn't know how, but she'd definitely been caught. The maniac behind her surged forward again, bumping her harder this time and causing her to clip an orange-and-white construction barrel beside the freeway's entrance.

She steered her vehicle back between the lines, then fumbled for her cell phone. The birthday card she'd been carrying with her for nearly two years fell from her purse in the process, but she didn't need the card anymore. She'd long ago memorized the number inside. Her brother had trusted Jack Hale with his life, and that was all Katlin needed to know. She worked to dial the number while staying on the road and keeping watch over the car advancing and retreating behind her. Taunting her in maddening waves.

The call connected then rang, with long, infuriating pauses between. Katlin's eyes blurred with tears of desperation. "Come on," she whispered. "Pick up. Pick up. Pick up."

"You've reached Jack Hale," a low, authoritative tenor announced. "Leave a message."

"Dammit." Katlin ended the call and immediately tried again.

The pursuing car slid into the empty passing lane then sailed effortlessly into position beside her. Its sleek silver paint made it look like a bullet in the night.

"You've reached Jack Hale…"

Katlin ended the call and redialed. One more time, then she'd leave a detailed message. That would be better than nothing. In the event she didn't survive the night, at least someone she could trust would be able to relay what she knew, and the son of a gun trying to kill her would be punished.

The silver car swerved sharply in her direction, and Katlin pulled hard on the steering wheel. Her fender nicked the guardrail with a hellacious screech and a jolt that nearly knocked the phone from her hand as she pressed Call one last time.

"Come on," she whispered. To the phone. To the universe. "Come on."

She smashed her toe against the gas pedal, steering wildly and one-handed as she raced along the narrow berm, dirt and pebbles flying into the air behind her. "Please," she begged. "Pick up, Jack. I need you. Pick. Up!" A lump formed in Katlin's throat as she listened to the slow, tinny rings.

"You've reached…"

A bone-jarring thump knocked the phone from her hand. The assailing car pressed against her door, forcing her farther off the road. She stomped the brake pedal and pulled the steering wheel hard, shoving back against the attacking vehicle and away from the thin metal guardrail.

The silver car relented for one fleeting heartbeat, then returned with a teeth-rattling *whack*!

And Katlin careened over the road's edge.

Airborne and plummeting toward the river below.

THE PHONE BEGAN to ring again as Jack stepped out of the shower. Being the last man on-site at Fortress Defense, the private protection firm he'd started with his brothers-in-arms, made catching a nap, having a meal and apparently taking a shower nearly impossible. Office hours had ended well before his evening return, and he'd just wrapped his last case only hours before, but duty, it seemed, never stopped calling. Jack had anticipated some quiet time while he filed paperwork, hit the agency's gym and caught a shower, but that hadn't happened. Especially odd since the emergency line was set to go to Sawyer's phone tonight. Instead the ringing had persisted off and on, from the minute he'd finished his postcase workout and started the shower until he'd stepped out and wrapped a towel around his hips. Now, barefoot in jeans and hunting for a shirt, the ringing had begun again.

He grabbed his cell phone and read the screen. Seven missed calls. Three from the same unknown number, a little over an hour ago. He'd missed those completely. Probably while he'd been working out. And four more calls from the blocked number calling in now.

"Fortress Defense," he answered, gripping the phone to his ear in one hand and knocking water from his hair with the other. "You've got Jack Hale."

"Mr. Hale, this is Detective Reihl from the Campbellsville Police Department," an unfamiliar woman's voice explained.

Jack stilled, a tendril of dread curling in his stomach.

Civilians called when they needed protection. Law-enforcement officers called when it was already too late. "What's this about?" He strained to recall a client who lived or worked in Campbellsville. Where was Campbellsville? East? South?

"This is about a car accident on Highway 68 tonight," the detective answered. "Near an exit downtown. Are you familiar with the area?"

"No, ma'am," he said, finding and tugging a T-shirt over still-damp skin. "Was a Fortress Defense client involved in the crash? Is everyone okay?" He selected a pen from the mug on his desk and poised it over a pad of paper, ready to take down the details for whichever one of his teammates was about to get bad news. It wasn't him. He'd never had a client from Campbellsville.

"Well, I'm afraid you're going to have to tell me," Reihl said. "The driver called your number repeatedly in the final minutes before her car left the road."

"My number?" Jack asked, setting aside the pen. His gaze landed on the silent cell phone on the charger across the room. The company phone. The phone pressed against his ear was his personal device. "And you said the crash was tonight?" he asked, recalling the other set of missed calls. Three from the same unknown number. "About an hour ago?"

"That's right," Detective Reihl said, a note of curiosity in her tone. "Any idea what that was about? Why she would've called you so many times while racing along the highway? Angry girlfriend, or an ex, perhaps? Maybe the two of you had a fight and she was all worked up?"

Jack shook his head, stretching socks over his feet and stuffing them into unlaced boots. "No girlfriend." The only woman he'd ever loved had died in a training exercise over Somalia four years ago. He wasn't interested in knowing loss like that again. "Who was she?" he asked. "The woman in the accident." Whoever she was, she'd wanted to talk to him, and he wanted to know why. "She's okay?" he asked, realizing the detective hadn't answered him before.

"Okay is subjective," Reihl said. "Kentucky driver's license says she's Katlin Andrews. Know her now?"

Jack felt the air press from his lungs. "Katlin Andrews?" he asked, his ears ringing. He was certain he'd heard wrong.

"Uh-huh. Twenty-six, blond hair, brown eyes. Stop me if I'm ringing a bell because she clearly knew you and really wanted to have a chat."

Jack forced back the ache of emotion and rising bile. Katlin was hurt. She'd called him for help, and he hadn't answered. "Where is she now? Can I see her?"

"I suppose," the detective answered. "Doctors seem to think she's fine, or that she will be. Hard to say for sure. She's been out cold since she got here. I can't talk to her, so I thought I'd talk to you. You do know her then?"

Relief flooded his limbs and lightened his head. "Not really. She's my best friend's baby sister, and I suppose I'm her unofficial guardian."

"So the brother is her next of kin? Can you tell me how to get in touch with him?"

"No, ma'am," Jack replied, then cleared his throat. His muscles stiffened in preparation for the coming words. "Griffin Andrews is dead." Lost during a reconnaissance mission three years back. "He and I were stationed abroad together for four years. We were family. For all intents and purposes. When I lost him, I gained her. You understand?"

"Like a replacement brother?"

"Yes, ma'am." Though he'd been a lousy one so far. Not such a great one before, either. The first time he'd seen a photo of Katlin he'd whistled and complimented Griffin on his smoking-hot girlfriend, then barely dodged a blow aimed at his nose. The way Griffin had spoken about her before that, Jack had expected Katlin to be in middle school, or even kindergarten, not in daisy dukes and cowgirl boots on Griffin's arm at a country-music concert.

Griffin had laughed when he'd missed his mark. "That's my sister," he'd warned, a very serious threat in his eyes. "You touch her over my dead body."

Jack's heart tightened at the memory. *Over his dead body.* What Jack wouldn't give to have Griffin back. Nothing. There was nothing he wouldn't do.

"I'm sorry for both your losses," Detective Reihl said finally. "Losing a sibling isn't easy. Neither is losing a friend."

Jack pocketed his keys then grabbed his sidearm and holster.

"Do you know how we can get in touch with Miss Andrews's next of kin? A parent or other blood sibling, perhaps?"

"Her folks are stationed in Austria. They're hard to reach. Sometimes impossible. Griffin was her only sibling."

Katlin was on her own in the States. Had been for a long while. And Jack had vowed to look after her for Griffin as he'd taken his last breath. Jack had promised, but he'd never gotten up the nerve to call or stop by her place. He didn't want to be a catalyst to all the emotions that came with the loss of a sibling, especially one as close as Griffin was to Katlin. Instead Jack had just kept sending useless holiday and birthday cards. He'd written his number in every one. Letting her take the lead and decide if she wanted to meet him or not. "It's just me," he said. Unfortunately for Katlin. "Will I be able to see her? Talk to her?"

"You'll have to work that out with the hospital," Detective Reihl said. "I'd like to talk to you in person, if you've got time. Feel up for a trip to Campbellsville tomorrow?"

Jack tugged a plain black ball cap over still-damp hair and threaded eager arms into his trademark leather jacket. "Yep."

He was already on his way.

Chapter Two

Jack made it to Campbellsville in significantly less time than the GPS had predicted. He'd ignored speed limits and taken liberties on the quiet country roads outside town. If there was an upside to the late-night call, it was traveling while everyone else was in bed. Traffic was something he didn't have time for tonight.

The hospital loomed tall and bright above the sparse cityscape, impossible to miss as he navigated through the sleepy town. He chose a front-row parking spot, then headed for the emergency-room doors. The woman behind the check-in desk looked up as he approached.

"I'm here for Katlin Andrews," he said. Images of the beautiful, healthy blonde swept into mind once more. Pictures of her and Griffin with family and friends. At the beach, on a boat, at concerts and graduations. The familiar prints had hung from his best friend's locker for years. Photos Jack had packed up to send home following his tragic loss. "She was in a car accident. Detective Reihl called me about two hours ago."

The nurse appraised him. "You family?"

"Yes," he said, having rehearsed the story on his way in. He and Katlin weren't blood-related, but Jack had made a vow to watch over her, and he couldn't do that if he wasn't allowed to see her.

"Third floor," she said, satisfied with his lie. "Trauma ward, but—"

"Thank you." Jack didn't have time to stick around for cautions or warnings. He needed to be present when Katlin woke. No one should be alone after what she'd been through. He jogged toward the stairs with renewed purpose.

"Visiting hours are over," the nurse called as the stairwell door swung shut behind him.

He took the steps two at a time, the sounds of his footfalls echoing off the stark white walls. Memories of another hospital pushed to the surface of his mind. Losing the only woman he'd ever loved had nearly cost him his sanity. Griffin had sat with him then, one protective arm around his shoulders while Jack fought the blinding tears of a gut-wrenching heartache. He gritted his teeth and willed away the memory. This wasn't a military base and Katlin wasn't another soldier. Jack's heart was no longer broken and would never be left unguarded again.

He exited the empty stairwell into a just-as-quiet hallway, the air tinged with bleach and latex. Pale green walls and a speckled tile floor led him to the nurses' desk, where a pair of women in scrubs were speaking in hushed tones over steaming coffees and an open laptop.

The women started when they noticed him.

"Sorry," he said softly, raising his palms in a movement he hoped would put them at ease. "I didn't mean to startle you. I know it's late, but Katlin Andrews was in a car accident tonight. I came as soon as Detective Reihl contacted me."

The nurses' postures and expressions relaxed by a

fraction. The little blonde, whose name tag said Julia, worked up a polite smile. "Of course." She stood and moved a clipboard in his direction. "We keep a record of all the visitors on this floor." She gave him a searching look, then a pen. "Visiting hours don't begin again until eight a.m., and we limit those to family only. It's my understanding that Miss Andrews's family lives abroad."

"They do," Jack answered on instinct, then kicked himself for forgetting his lines. "I'm Jack Hale. Katlin's… fiancé." The final word tasted like betrayal, a nonsensical affront to his love for Cara, but painful nonetheless.

Julia clutched her hands to her chest and her bottom lip jutted out. "I'm sorry. No one told us she was engaged."

"It's fine," he said, glad to put the lie behind him. "It's been a hard night. A lot's happened."

The second nurse's brow furrowed. "Katlin Andrews wasn't wearing an engagement ring."

"It's new," Jack improvised, officially disliking Nurse Two. "We've talked about marriage for a while, but we haven't made it official. *I...*" he amended. "*I* haven't made it official, and I should have. I need to get her a ring."

"Darn right you better," Nurse Two said. "She could've died without ever knowing you were serious about that ringless proposal."

"Absolutely," Jack agreed. "I'll make it right as soon as I can." Those words came easier. They were true. He would make things right for Katlin when she woke. He'd do whatever was necessary so that she would recover fully and fast. He owed Griffin that.

Julia smiled. "Miss Andrews is still unconscious, but we do rounds regularly. We'll let you know if anything changes." She pointed at the clipboard. "If you could just sign in before taking a seat, you're welcome to wait."

"Thanks." Jack lifted the pen, then checked his watch. "Any chance Detective Reihl is around?"

"Doubtful," Julia said, "but I expect she'll be back."

Good. Jack had about a thousand questions for the detective, beginning with the basics. How fast was Katlin going when she crashed? Were there any witnesses? Could she have fallen asleep at the wheel? All things he hadn't thought to ask until he'd been well on his way to Campbellsville. He raised his eyes to the waiting nurses before him. "Have you ordered a tox screen?"

Julia nodded. "We should have the results back later today."

"Can you tell me anything about the accident?" he asked.

"Sorry, but no. I suspect Katlin is the only one who can do that, and she's been unresponsive since her arrival."

Nurse Two folded her hands on the desk and leaned toward him conspiratorially. "I heard the detective talking to an officer when Miss Andrews was first admitted. The officer said her car was at the police impound lot, and there was some damage to the driver's side and rear bumper. Strange for a car that went headfirst toward the river. That's on the right side of the highway."

Jack widened his stance and crossed his arms, clipboard pinched between a thumb and forefinger. "You think someone hit her? Forced her off the road?"

Julia shrugged. "We've speculated. She was outside a pretty rough part of town. Could be she was nicked by someone who wasn't in any condition to drive."

Jack certainly preferred that to the possibility Katlin had been driving under the influence, but why would Katlin have been in a seedy part of Campbellsville? Why was she in Campbellsville at all? He'd been sending her cards to Stanford, at least an hour away. "Detective Reihl said she was near an exit when she crashed. Do you know which one?"

"One-nineteen," Julia said. "It's the only place where the river runs along the highway."

"And the impound lot?" Jack asked. "Do you have an address? I'd like to pay both a visit."

Julia wrinkled her nose. "Impound lot's on Main near the police station. It opens early, but you've got another couple of hours before sunup."

"Right." Jack looked around the empty waiting area behind him, rubbing his palms along the sides of his pants. "Care if I stay here until visiting hours begin, or until Katlin wakes?" he asked. "You'll let me know if she does? Even if it's before eight?"

"Sure." Julia smiled sweetly. "You can take a seat. We won't tell if you don't. I'm going to make my rounds now. If she wakes, I'll let you know."

Jack lowered himself into a chair beside a large window, angling for a view of the desk, elevator and stairs. And fought the urge to follow Julia down the hall to Katlin.

KATLIN SQUIRMED AGAINST an uncomfortable ache in her side and a slow pounding in her head. The world was too bright, her eyes scratchy and dry. Her limbs were heavy. Her thoughts awash. She squinted at the fluorescent lights overhead. Where was she?

"Oh!" A perky voice sounded nearby, drawing her attention to a petite blonde wearing blue scrubs and a smile. "Hello, Katlin." She moved closer and reached for Katlin's wrist. "You've been sleeping a long while. We were beginning to wonder when you planned to wake up."

Katlin resisted the urge to pull her arm away. She scanned the room instead. A hospital. And a nurse. The badge on the woman's chest said Julia.

Why was she in a hospital? She raked her memory, but came up with nothing. She didn't recall being hurt, yet her limbs ached and her throat was painfully dry. "I've been sleeping a while?" she croaked, not recognizing the voice that resulted.

"Several hours," Julia said. She released Katlin's wrist, then reached for a notepad in her pocket and made a note. "You were in an accident last night. Do you remember?"

"No." She cleared her throat several times, unable to remove the strange thickness inside. "What kind of accident?"

Julia's sharp blue eyes snapped to meet hers. "A car accident. Honey, you ran off the road on Highway 68. Nearly landed in the river. We're still not quite sure how you walked away with so many minor injuries."

Katlin's heart rate spiked and a vague sense of foreboding wiggled over her skin, raising gooseflesh in its wake. "What happened?"

"We were hoping you'd tell us." Julia played with the machines arranged near the head of Katlin's bed, a mischievous smile spreading her thin lips. "What I do know is that your dead-sexy boyfriend is in the waiting room, and he's determined to find out how you got hurt. He's a little intense, and I've got to be honest. I feel bad for anyone he thinks might've been involved. But he's sweet, too. Worried sick about you and ready to go charging into the night in search of justice for his honey. He'll be thrilled to hear you're up."

"Boyfriend?" Katlin tried and failed to recall having

one of those. Then, she tried and failed to recall anything at all, and a fresh surge of panic welled in her.

"It's just not fair," Julia mused. "Where on earth did you find him? I want one. Hell, every woman I know wants one."

Katlin shook her head. None of this was right. She didn't have a boyfriend. She didn't have an accident. She needed to leave. To move. To hide.

But from what? From whom?

She raised a hand to her temple and froze when an IV line came into view. "What is this? I don't want this."

Julia pressed Katlin's hand gently down. "It's fluids and medicine for the pain. You need both."

"I want to go home." Another flare of panic lit in her core. *Where was home?* Surely she had a home. Didn't she?

The nurse watched her carefully, narrow eyebrows pulling tight. "Honey, it's okay to relax. You're going to be just fine. Your vitals are strong. You only needed a few stitches and a little observation. You'll probably be released this morning."

Katlin's chest constricted further and her tongue seemed to swell. *Released to go where?*

A soft knock sounded against the doorjamb, and a man in his late twenties peered inside. He wore a black ball cap and leather jacket, nice-fitting jeans, boots and a pained expression on his brutally handsome face. The scruff on his cheeks suggested he hadn't shaved in at least a week, and the fear in his eyes said he was worried. About her? Was this her boyfriend?

If not, she had an idea of where Julia could find herself a smoking-hot man.

Whoever he was, Julia could have him. Katlin needed

to get out of there. The pooling sense of dread had filled her stomach and was quickly spreading through her limbs and into her pounding heart. She might not remember how to get home, but she was certain she shouldn't stay here.

"Hey," he said softly, hazel eyes fixed on Julia. "How's she doing?"

Julia glanced at the nearby machines, where Katlin's climbing heart rate was being broadcast. "She seems a little confused, but certainly glad to see you." She hooked a thumb in the machine's direction and cast him a knowing smile.

His gaze flickered briefly in the direction she indicated, then fixed on Katlin's face. A strange mix of emotions raced across the rugged features. Fear? Dismay? Urgency. She was sure about the last one, not as much about the others. And maybe it was all just the projection of her jangled nerves.

"How soon can I leave?" she asked, refocusing on Julia.

"I'll page Dr. Kraus and be right back," she said, stepping into the doorway where the man lingered. "You can go on in."

He waited for her to pass before crossing the threshold with an apologetic smile. "Hi," he said, removing his hat and clutching it to his chest. "I'm Jack Hale."

Katlin stared. "That's a strange way for a boyfriend to introduce himself."

He smiled. "Right. Sorry about that. How are you feeling?"

Awful. Achy. Terrified. "Okay."

"Do you remember me?" he asked. "Recognize my name?"

She shook her head, unwilling to admit the truth. Not

only did she not remember this man's name, but she also couldn't recall her own. "What happened to me?"

Jack moved closer, taking slow, calculated steps. "That's what I plan to find out." He stopped at the bedside, staring down at her as if she held the answer to something she couldn't fathom.

"So you're my boyfriend?"

A mischievous half smile tilted his lips. "Hospital policy says only family can visit you, and since your family isn't here, I figured it was okay for me to tell a little white lie. No sense in you being all alone when I was right outside."

"So you're not my boyfriend," she said, flatly, only interested in facts. "Then who are you?" Katlin ran a quick internal inventory, searching for signs she should fear him, but found none. Instead, there was an odd familiarity.

His eyes narrowed, crinkling the tanned skin at the corners. "Did you think I might be your boyfriend?"

Katlin sank her teeth into her bottom lip, eyes stinging with nonsensical emotion. "The nurse said..."

"And you assumed? You don't remember?"

Katlin shook her head.

Jack ran a hand over his shorn sandy hair, then gripped the back of his neck. "You would've gone home with anyone who showed up and said they were your boyfriend?" He crossed his arms and frowned, working out the thing she hadn't yet been brave enough to say. "What do you remember exactly?"

Her clogged throat seemed to tighten. "Nothing," she whispered.

Jack eased onto the mattress by her knees and turned intense, soulful eyes on her. "Did you tell the nurse?"

"No."

He pressed his lips into a thin line and gave one stiff dip of his chin. "All right." His tone grew composed and compassionate. "You need to tell her when she comes back. Tell the doctor when he gets here."

"Who are you?" she asked, pushing her chin higher. "You're not my boyfriend, and you said I don't have family here. So why should I listen to you?" Not that she didn't agree with him or think it was logical to confess all of any patient's symptoms to the medical team in charge of his or her care. It just didn't feel like the right thing to do in her case. In fact, the only thing that seemed like the right thing to do now was leave. The notion was intense and instinctual. She didn't want to ignore it. *Couldn't* ignore it. "Answer me so we can leave."

He cocked his head, considering her a moment. "My name is Jack Hale. I was your brother's best friend until his death three years ago. You remember Griffin?"

"No."

Jack's lips turned down, disappointment briefly coloring his cheeks. Then he regrouped. "I promised him I'd look after you, and I'm trying now, but this is the first time we've met."

She blinked. "We've never met?"

"No, but I know you, through your brother. The same way you know me. And I send you cards on your birthday and Christmas. I write my number below my signature and figure you'd reach out to me if you ever needed anything or wanted to meet. According to a local detective, you were calling me around the time of your accident. I can only assume that means you were in trouble."

Katlin tried to process the heap of information while battling her growing urge to flee. "Why would I call you and not the police if I was in trouble, and you and I have never met?"

"The detective says you were speeding. Maybe whatever you were running from had to do with the police. I'm not sure, but I will find out. I started a private protection firm called Fortress Defense with some of my military brothers, and I think that might be why you called."

"I needed protection."

"Maybe." He nodded. "You and Griffin were close. He trusted me, so you would, too."

She didn't remember having a brother, but something about Jack put her mind and muscles at ease. His face and voice didn't hurt the cause. "That's why the nurse said you were going to investigate. It's what you do at your protection firm?"

"We do whatever it takes to protect our clients," he said simply. "Knowing all the facts helps. You can't provide them, so I'll have to get them myself. I'll come back for you when I finish. I can drive you home after you're discharged." Jack stretched onto his feet and made a move for the door.

"No!" Katlin's hand snapped out, curling desperate fingers around his wrist. "Don't leave me. You have to take me with you. Get me out of here." She loosened her grip when he turned back in her direction.

"Why?"

"I can't explain it, and I don't remember the details of what happened, but I think you're right. Someone tried to hurt me. And maybe it's the pain meds or the trauma talking, but I feel strongly that I should get out of here before whoever it was finds me again. I don't want to stick around hoping I'm wrong."

Jack grimaced. "How do you know I'm not the one you should be afraid of?"

Katlin laughed, a hearty, unplanned sound. "If you are, then I'm in more trouble than I thought. My instincts are the only things I've got to keep me alive right now."

His expression softened a bit. "Not true," he said, pulling a wallet from his back pocket. "You've got me, and you can trust me. I can keep you safe." He flipped open the wallet and removed a well-worn photo, then passed it to her. "This is you and your brother when you were small. Griffin carried it with him everywhere, but it was left behind when they shipped his body home." Jack's Adam's apple bobbed, the movement long and slow. He cleared his throat before powering on. "I've carried that picture with me for three years so I could give it to you one day. Griffin saved my life more than once and in more than one way. I owe it to him to protect you, and I will. Whatever it takes, I'm your man."

Katlin sat straighter, his words an inexplicable balm to her nerves. She might not have her memories, but everything he'd said rang true in her heart, if not familiar in her mind. As a bonus, everything about Jack Hale indicated he was fully capable of keeping his promise, and every part of her was interested in seeing that come true. "Help me find my clothes?"

Chapter Three

Jack turned away in search of Katlin's things, thankful she'd chosen to trust him. What could he have done otherwise? Attempted to protect her from afar? All while trying not to be arrested for stalking? The thought itched in his mind. Why had she called him instead of the police last night?

He cast a furtive look in her direction. What kind of trouble was she in that she wouldn't want the police involved? And what could make anyone want to hurt her? She seemed so small and breakable, especially now with her chin and arms peppered with scrapes and bruises. The fact she'd nearly been killed only hours before tightened a knot in his core and set his jaw on lock. That she was holding herself together, looking determined and confident despite the pain she must be in, without her family or memories to support and guide her, suggested the petite woman he'd sworn to protect was far tougher than she appeared.

He circled the room in search of her personal things, glad to put some distance between himself and Griffin's little sister. Seeing nothing that looked as if it might belong to her, he ducked into the attached restroom for a peek there.

The bathroom was empty. No shoes or clothing. No purse or phone.

Jack took a beat to center himself before returning to Katlin. There was something about her that confused and unsettled him. Not the kind of sensations he wanted to deal with right now. He blamed the lack of sleep and back-to-back cases, something he normally avoided. He needed downtime to stay sharp, but he'd have to do without for now. It was already 6:00 a.m. If they wanted to slip away from the hospital before the sun was up, they'd need to get out within the hour. The sooner, the better.

"Knock, knock," Julia chirped, drawing Jack back through the bathroom doorway as she sashayed into Katlin's room. "Look who I found just starting her morning shift." She swung an arm wide, like a game-show hostess, to indicate the woman in a white lab coat at her side. "It's Dr. Kraus, and she has excellent news."

"Miss Andrews," the doctor said, barely glancing away from the computer in her hands. "You took quite a spill last night. We're glad to see you up. How are you feeling? Mind if I take a look?" She set the device on the nightstand before Katlin answered either question, then began a physical examination.

Jack moved to Julia's side. "Katlin's asking for her things. Do you know where they are?"

Julia smiled. "Sure. I have them in a bag at the nurses' station, but the clothes are a mess. Blood," she said, whispering the last word. "She can wear a set of my scrubs home, if she'd like. It looks like she's about my size." Julia headed for the hallway.

Jack followed, unsure how much he had a right to know about Katlin's care and condition now that she was awake and able to speak for herself. He hoped she'd take his advice and tell Dr. Kraus about her memory loss. He didn't want to snitch and make an enemy of her already, but he wasn't above doing whatever it took to be sure she was okay.

"Here you go," Julia said, returning a moment later with a pair of large zipper-sealed bags. "That's everything they took off of her at Admissions."

"Thanks."

"And here are those scrubs I promised." She stacked a set of powder-pink nurse attire atop the bags with sneakers, a purse, jacket and other clothing.

He dipped his chin in thanks, then passed the doctor on his way back into the room.

Katlin was seated on the bed, a grimace of discomfort on her face. "She said I can go."

Jack set the pile of items on the bed near Katlin's hand. "What did she say about your head and the memory loss?"

"She says I'm fine. Discharge paperwork is being processed. I'm supposed to take it easy for a few days and let her know if my pain becomes unbearable, or if any new symptoms develop." She pushed aside the scrubs and dug into the plastic bags, then frowned at the bloodstains on her clothes. She gave the pink scrubs a second look, then fanned out her stained jeans in front of her and slipped her feet into the leg holes.

Jack spun around, allowing her some privacy. "Okay, but what did she say about the amnesia?"

"She says it isn't uncommon following a trauma."

Jack peeked over his shoulder. "She doesn't want to keep you for observation?"

"No, and I think that's for the best." She stuffed her bare feet into sneakers, having already pulled the jeans over her hips and fastened them. Her expression fell as she gave the bloodstained shirt a second look. She stuffed it back into the bag with a sigh and lifted the pink scrubs top with a frown. "I think we should get out of here. I've had a lingering feeling of dread since I woke, and I don't think it's a coincidence or strictly a result of the accident. I want to go somewhere I can think and try to remember what's going on."

Jack turned back to face her. "We should start with your apartment. Maybe something there will kick-start your memory."

She nodded, then raised a tentative hand in his direction, her cheeks suddenly tinged with pink. "Okay. I just need to finish getting ready."

Jack followed her gaze to the pink top and a lacy red bra, barely concealed beneath it in her other hand. An image of Katlin in the bra alone rushed into his mind, unbidden, and he rocked back on his heels, reminding himself of the long list of reasons he needed to tighten up.

"I'm back!" Julia reappeared with a digital tablet and a wheelchair. "Just a few signatures here, and you're free to go." She handed Jack the tablet, then detached Katlin's IV and other monitors. "Would you like a set of pain pills before you go?" she asked, smoothing a Band-Aid over Katlin's hand where the IV had been. "It's better to stay ahead of the pain. There's a prescription for more with your discharge papers."

Katlin blushed, the shirt and bra still clutched in her free hand.

Jack sighed. "Give us just a minute." He reached for Katlin and pulled her onto her feet, then guided her across the floor to the bathroom. "You okay?"

She closed her eyes, then shut the door between them in answer.

He did his best not to ask if she needed any help in there.

KATLIN FINISHED DRESSING, then splashed water on her face and finger-combed her hair while searching her empty head for a memory. *Any* memory. Something to make her feel real and anchored instead of adrift like a two-dimensional drawing snipped free of its paper. A fresh wave of emotion slapped into her, and she gave in to it behind the closed door. When the tears had gone dry, she washed her face, squared her shoulders and lifted her chin, then returned to the unfamiliar world outside.

Jack stood at attention beside the wheelchair, clearly awaiting her return. He scanned her carefully, then reached for her hand. "Let me help."

Katlin steered out of his reach as she climbed into the waiting wheelchair. "I've got it, thanks." She was sore and shaken, but she was tougher than all that, and Jack didn't need to know what a mess she truly was. He was her lifeline. Between the two of them they would figure everything out. As long as she made it out of the hospital.

Jack took the hint and gave her some space. He passed the black motorcycle jacket to her that had been with the pile of her things. "Everything okay?" he asked. "You were in there a while."

Katlin fixed him with a warning look as she threaded her arms into the cool leather. "I'm fine. Just moving a little slowly. Where's the nurse?"

He moved into position behind her, taking the handles of the chair in his hands. "Called away. We're completing the discharge process at the desk now." He turned them in the direction of the door and wheeled her into the hallway. "Maybe you should spend the day recuperating instead of investigating. We can always start tomorrow."

"No." She groaned, trying to get comfortable in the chair. "I don't think we have that kind of time. I need my memories back before whoever came at me last night comes again."

"No one's coming for you on my watch," Jack said.

Katlin appreciated the confidence, but she wasn't so sure. She tried again to access the lost memories. They seemed to hover just outside her reach. Like vapor, she could see and sense them, but not get a hold.

A gray-haired nurse smiled at them over the big wooden desk as they approached. "Ready to go home?"

"Yes," Katlin answered enthusiastically, realizing too late that the question had probably been rhetorical.

"Then let's get started." The nurse turned a digital tablet in Katlin's direction, then guided her through the discharge process before handing her a sheet of printed care instructions and a prescription for more pain pills.

A young woman in scrubs and a volunteer tag came to relieve Jack of his duties. "Hospital policy," she said cheerfully, her gaze raking appreciatively over his lean, muscular form. When her eyes met Katlin's, she blushed.

Jack walked at Katlin's side down the corridor to the elevator, his attention constantly swiveling to take in everything around them. His arm swung wide to stop the wheelchair as a door opened on her opposite side.

Dr. Kraus stepped through the doorway and frowned, dragging her gaze briefly from the laptop in her hands. Her expression deepened at the sight of them. "I didn't know you were still here," she said, fixing her gaze on Katlin. "I just sent your brother out to the parking deck looking for the two of you."

Katlin's breath caught as she swung her attention to Jack. He'd said her brother was dead.

The stiff set of Jack's jaw and cold glare in his eyes sent a shiver down her spine. "Her brother is dead," he said sharply. "What did this man look like? Which way did he go?"

The doctor's mouth opened and shut. Her attention lifted and stuck to Jack for a long moment. "I don't know," she finally answered, clearly baffled.

Jack set his massive hands against his sides and glowered. "Well, that's fantastic and extremely helpful. Thank you." He dismissed the doctor, then took the helm at Katlin's wheelchair, effectively discharging the young volunteer, as well. "I've got it from here. Thanks."

He rushed Katlin to the elevator and jammed his finger against the small button to call the car. When the doors opened, Jack maneuvered her quickly inside. "I don't know who came here looking for you, but it wasn't your brother," he said sternly. "I saw the doubt in your eyes out there, and I want you to know—you have no other family in this country that I'm aware of, none Griffin ever mentioned, anyway. Regardless, anyone who knew you would have known Griffin is gone. I think it's fair to say your instincts were right. We need to get out of here."

Fear chewed at Katlin's gut, constricting her breaths and heating her chest.

"We'll have to walk to my truck," Jack continued. "I hate parking decks. I took a spot on the street around the far side of the building, where visibility is good and we can pull away quick. I can carry you if you aren't feeling up for the walk."

Katlin raised her chin and didn't speak. She'd already told him she was fine, and given the unknown man who was now looking for her, she didn't want to risk her voice cracking or quaking while she tried to set Jack straight.

"Don't say you're fine again," he said, interrupting her thoughts. "You could've been killed last night, and whatever you did to your head knocked your memories out. None of that is good, and I'm not joking about carrying you."

"I can walk," she snapped, unsure it was true. Getting dressed was tough enough. How far away was his truck? "And memories don't work like that," she went on, venting the tension through her words. "I'm not a faulty flashlight. You can't just whack my head again and the light will return. It's a trauma thing. I know the memories are there, I just have to figure out what I can do to trigger them."

Jack gave a puff of air behind her, a soft derisive sound. "Are you trying to convince me? Or yourself?"

"Shut up."

The quirk of his lips reflected in the shiny elevator doors.

She forced away her eyes. Was this normal for her? Did she typically become enamored with any handsome man who was nice to her? She didn't think so, but how could she know? The thought brought another disturbing possibility to mind. "What if I have a real boyfriend?"

The doors parted and Jack hesitated before pushing Katlin out of the elevator. "What do you mean?"

"Well, won't he be mad that you showed up to play hero? Steal his thunder. All that."

Jack parked the wheelchair near the sliding hospital doors, where at least a dozen other wheelchairs were lined against a wall. He moved around to face her and offered her a hand up. "If I was you, and there was some guy out there claiming to be my boyfriend who hadn't bothered to come to the hospital or look for me when I didn't call to say I'd made it home safely last night, I wouldn't care if he was mad. I wouldn't even know he was mad because he'd be out on the curb."

"Harsh." She pressed onto her feet without accepting his hand. "Kick him to the curb? That's your philosophy? No opportunity for explanations?"

Jack shrugged, then matched her tortoise-slow pace along the sidewalk, away from the hospital. "I'm not an easy guy."

"Fair enough," she said, passing men and women in suits and scrubs headed to and from off-site parking. Apparently it was time for a shift change. "Do you hold your girlfriend to the same rules?"

"No." He slid cool hazel eyes in her direction quickly, then returned them to the circuit he seemed to be making—scanning the street, buildings and folks around them. "No girlfriend."

Katlin opened her mouth to ask how that was possible, but the words were interrupted.

"Katlin Andrews," an unfamiliar voice called, making her turn around.

A dark figure peered down from the top floor of the open four-level parking deck. In one swift movement, the figure raised an arm, and the unmistakable sound of gunfire rang out.

Chapter Four

"Get down!" Jack called, grabbing Katlin and tucking her against him as he began to run. "Shots fired!" he screamed at the smattering of confused onlookers, who were taking phone calls and cigarette breaks around the property's edge.

Another shot rang out, and the sidewalk cracked in front of them, sending a tiny puff of dust into the air.

Behind them, people screamed.

Katlin struggled against Jack's protective grip. "I'm okay!" she yelled, pressing him back with her elbows. "Let's go!"

Jack released her, and she bolted for his truck.

He fumbled for the key fob, remotely unlocking the door a heartbeat before they dove in.

"Get down!" he yelled as he cranked the engine. It had been several seconds since the last gunshot, and Jack had lost sight of the shooter. He could be taking aim, reloading or on the ground by now and headed their way. "How'd you know where to go?" he asked, shifting into gear and craning his neck to check for pedestrians. She'd shoved him off of her and made a beeline for his pickup, a vehicle she'd never seen before. How was that possible?

"What?" Katlin grappled for her seat belt as they lurched into the empty street.

"My truck. How'd you know which was mine?"

Katlin rocked and tipped on the bench beside him as he wheeled around the nearest corner, tires barking and engine roaring.

He dared a glance at her as sirens blared in the distance.

She twisted for a look at the chaos erupting behind them. "You said you had a truck. You said you parked on the street behind the parking deck. This was the only pickup in the direction you were running, and it has a US Army window cling. Your dog tags are hanging from the rearview mirror."

He glanced at the tags and window cling—he barely noticed either these days. "You saw all of that? While being shot at?"

"I guess so." She spun forward and flopped against the seat, pressing a palm to her chest. "Holy cow. I think we can cross off the possibility I was running from a crazy ex, unless I have some seriously awful taste in men."

Jack's lip quirked and a short bark of laughter burst free. "You really are your brother's sister." Griffin had been impossibly calm in every manner of circumstance, right up to the end, when all he'd cared about was that Jack looked after his baby sister and made sure she knew Griffin loved her.

He forced the wedge of emotion from his chest and made a series of quick turns down neighboring streets until he was certain they hadn't been tailed. Then he settled onto the highway to collect his thoughts and make a plan. "I don't suppose being shot at roused any memories?"

She shook her head and rubbed her palms over the

tops of her thighs. "Someone tried to kill me last night." The quiver in her voice drew his attention.

He glanced her way, unsure if a memory was resurfacing or if the weight of it all was finally registering.

"Someone didn't just run me off the road in the middle of the night and leave it at that," she said, turning wide brown eyes on him. "They sent a gunman to a hospital to finish me. What the hell did I get into?"

That was what Jack planned to find out.

KATLIN WATCHED THE strangely foreign scenery race by her window as Jack followed Highway 68 west, toward downtown. He'd left a voice mail for a detective once they'd put some distance between themselves and the hospital, then settled into an unnerving silence.

She rubbed sweat-slicked palms against her jeans and hoped she was right to trust him. In a world where she knew no one and had already been shot at, it seemed ridiculous for her to trust anyone, and yet she did.

He took Exit 119 then crawled to a stop at the bottom of the ramp. "This is the exit where the nurses say you crashed. Any idea why you were here?"

Katlin scanned the area. The neighborhood was seedy and run-down with the kind of atmosphere that screamed high crime and low morale. She shook her head. "None of this is familiar. Do I live near here?" If so, what was her life like? Did she run with a rough crowd?

"No." Jack took a left and circled a few blocks, pausing to look both ways at the intersections, his features set in a frown. There were bars on doors and windows. Sneakers hanging from power lines. "Stop me if something rings a bell."

She crossed her arms and rubbed the chill from her

skin as irritation crept into her thoughts. Did he think she might regain her memory and not mention it? That she would see someone or something she knew, and just keep it to herself? She furrowed her brow as she stared across the darkened cab. She didn't remember the specifics from her life, but she was certain she hated being treated like someone with a diminished IQ.

She refocused on the sketchy world beyond the window. "Why would I be somewhere like this?" Why would anyone? Nothing good came to mind. "This looks like the sort of place where people go to find drugs or prostitutes."

"Agreed."

"The hospital staff didn't mention any drugs in my system, and I don't feel like someone dealing with an addiction." In fact, aside from the bumps and bruises, she felt pretty good. Healthy. Fit, even. "I don't think I'd need a prostitute, either," she said, regaining her humor. "People our age just go online or to a bar when they want to hook up, right?"

Jack slowed at the next stop sign and gave her a thorough once-over that sent heat straight to her core. "I don't."

She laughed, a bubble of nervous energy breaking free. "Well, I doubt you have to go searching for a hookup, so you don't count."

Jack turned his eyes back to the road without comment and reentered the highway on an eastbound lane. He leaned forward, scanning the road, and Katlin matched his posture.

Skid marks peppered the pavement, illuminated by the beams of his headlights. The marks were sporadic at first. Then more frequent, growing thicker and darker until they left the road completely, ripping parallel tracks through the scraggy grass beyond the shoulder.

Katlin's stomach tightened with instinctual fear and the phantom sensations of plummeting. Her mind ached to remember the moments her car had left the road and the events immediately before, but the thoughts were locked just outside her reach.

Jack eased onto the road's edge and shifted into Park. "I want to take a look. I'll only be a minute." He activated his emergency flashers, then got out to examine the crash site.

Katlin followed.

The rutted tracks, presumably made by her tires, were visible beneath a path of broken tree limbs over the hill beside the berm. The tracks ended abruptly at the river's edge. Hitting the trees' trunks at highway speeds would have killed her, but she'd hit a network of limbs that had bent and broken, probably saving her life. And they'd kept her from reaching the water, where she would have surely drowned.

Jack pressed broad palms to narrow hips and stared into the early morning. "You should be dead." He shook his head and sighed. "The fact you're standing here, no worse for wear, is a flat-out miracle."

She moved to his side, feeling the truth of that statement in her soul. "That makes twice now. I guess I have a guardian angel."

There was sadness in his eyes as he turned back for the truck and opened the door for her. "I should've called," he said quietly as she climbed inside. "I sent cards, but I should've called. Maybe you wouldn't have come out alone last night, and I could've protected you." He shut the door and rounded the hood, back to his position behind the wheel.

"You're here now," she said. "And I could've called you sooner. You said you put your number in the cards."

He turned his phone over in his hand, unresponsive to her rebuttal, and swiped the screen to life before starting the engine.

"Did we learn anything from the crash site?" she asked. "Besides I'm lucky to be alive?"

"It's still too dark. I'd like to get a look at your car if you're up for it. Then we'll head over to your place so you can rest."

"I've been out cold since the crash. I'm rested and amped up on adrenaline," she said. "So..."

Jack smiled. "Okay. Let's go see the car first." He set the phone in his cup holder with the GPS app open and merged back onto the highway. "Sun should be up soon. We can circle back to the crash site after you get some real rest in your own bed."

"What about you?" she asked. "When was the last time you slept?"

He grimaced and gripped the back of his neck with one hand. "I don't sleep much."

Katlin bit her lip against a volley of questions and folded her hands to keep them from reaching for him. How could someone look so thigh-clenchingly sexy and be so unfathomably lovable at the same time? Or was that just her head injury talking?

"What?" he asked, flicking his gaze in her direction. "What's that face?"

"Nothing." Katlin redirected her attention to the window at her side. She willed her thoughts to refocus and wondered instead about the kind of car she drove and who she was before she woke in the hospital. Not that it mattered now what she drove. Whatever it was had surely been totaled.

JACK PARKED ACROSS the street from the impound lot, in a more habitable part of town than the crash site. Reputable businesses and homes with fresh-cut lawns and tended flower beds lined the curbs. The police station, courthouse and town hall were only a few parking lots away.

He waited for Katlin outside her door as the sun rose higher on the horizon. "Ready?"

She nodded, and Jack reached for her hand. The electricity that coursed through her at his touch curled her toes inside her sneakers.

He cast a furtive look in her direction as they began to walk, and she couldn't help wondering if he'd felt the delicious charge, too.

According to the posted hours, the lot opened at eight. No one would be there for another hour. Jack stopped at the locked gate and took a look at the security cameras pointed at the street. A warning sign about a guard dog was posted front and center. "Any idea what you drive?" he asked.

"Nope." But the place was thankfully small, with a limited number of impounded vehicles, which would make it easier to identify Katlin's car.

Jack released her hand as they walked the perimeter of a tall chain-link fence. The rectangular guard booth was dark. No dog visible. "This place could use my team's help with security," he said, pausing to evaluate things further. "I'm not sure who *can't* break into this setup."

"Are we breaking in?" she asked.

He laughed, then stiffened.

Katlin's senses went on high alert, seeking the source of Jack's sudden tension.

A low, unidentifiable sound reached her ears.

"Probably the guard dog," she whispered. "Which car do you think is mine?"

He waited a beat before answering. "Something with significant front-end damage. Severely scratched paint from the broken tree limbs and maybe mud-caked tires. Possibly rear corner and bumper damage, as well."

"Wow." Her gut twisted again, responding instinctively to things her mind couldn't recall.

She strained her eyes, scanning the lot for a vehicle that fit the bill. Eventually, a familiar symbol came into view on the rear window of a navy blue sedan two rows away. She raised a hand to point it out, and her heart gave a healthy kick. "Look." Below the US Army symbol, six bold words declared "Proud Sister of a Green Beret."

Jack accessed his phone's flashlight app and pointed it at the car, still bathed in shadows.

Her heart seized at the sight of the damage. The front end was smashed. The windshield broken. The left side aggressively dented from the door to the rear bumper. No wonder she'd been unconscious for so long after the crash. Maybe she really did have a guardian angel.

The beam from Jack's phone landed on the rear window, and a silhouette appeared inside.

The dome light flashed on, and the passenger door swept open. A broad-shouldered figure dressed in black stretched to his feet on the far side of the car.

Jack extinguished the light and reached for Katlin. "That's not good."

She stepped back, bumping against Jack as panic

rose in her bones. "That was my car, right? He was in my car?"

The figure raised a gun and took aim before Jack could answer.

"Run." He grabbed her hand and jerked her away from the gunman, back into the street.

They threw themselves into the truck as the first bullet connected with his tailgate.

Chapter Five

"What is happening?" Katlin screamed as the pickup fishtailed away from the gunman. Her heart pounded and her ears rang. Emotion clogged her chest and throat. "Who am I?" The words ripped through her, followed by a sob she hadn't meant to let go. What kind of person had a life like this? *Not a good one*, she thought, hating the parts of her she didn't know.

"Change of plans," Jack said quietly, his breaths quick and audible in the silent cab. "We can't stay at your place with people shooting at you every few minutes. And I need a new vehicle. This one's been seen twice. We need to swap it out, and honestly, the police might want to take it somewhere to process. I think we were hit."

"I know we were hit," Katlin said. "Where are we going? To the police station?"

"No." Jack watched the rearview mirror as he navigated the giant pickup out of town. "I'll call in the gunman and update Detective Reihl again, but we're going to Fortress to regroup."

Katlin deflated against the seat back, hot tears blazing trails over her cheeks unbidden. Her leaden arms and hands were weights at her sides. Her reeling mind brimmed with awful thoughts about who she was before the crash. How had she gotten mixed up with a killer and why? Surely she was smarter than to have made choices that would lead her into a life of crime or the world of criminals. Wasn't she? *Clearly not.* Disappointment mixed with fear in her core and pressed the air from her lungs.

Jack reached for his cell phone. He left another voice mail for the detective, then called the police to report the shooting. Finally, he called someone named Cade and let him know he and Katlin were on the way.

He dropped the phone back into his cup holder and lowered his visor to block the now blinding sun before them. "Cade's meeting us at Fortress. He'll get the coffee on and make up a bunk, where you can rest a few minutes while we set a plan and swap the truck for a company vehicle."

"Is that safe?" she asked. "Trading your personal truck for a company car? What if the shooter got a look at your plates? If he can name you, it won't take long to link you to Fortress," she said, alarm ricocheting through her. "If he looks into Fortress, he'll find the vehicles registered to the company. Then everyone driving one will be in danger."

Jack frowned. "We only drive the fleet as needed, and no one has one out right now, as far as I know. Even if they did, my guys wouldn't be in danger. Whatever hornet's nest you kicked is no match for them, their training or their fortitude. When I tell you that you're in good hands now, I mean it."

She bit her lip and stifled the urge to point out she'd been shot at twice while in his care. Bottom line, she supposed, was that she hadn't been hit and she probably would have been without Jack at her side. "How long will we stay at Fortress?" she asked. "I don't want my presence to cause anyone else injury." *Or worse.* "Unless Fortress Defense is located on an island, there must be other people nearby, other offices or neighborhood residents who will be in danger if the shooter finds me there."

"We're only staying long enough to form a plan and gather necessities. From there we'll choose a safe house."

Katlin considered his words, attempting to make sense of what would happen next. "So the shooter will track us to a secondary location instead of the office?"

"No." He cast a curious look in her direction. "The shooter isn't going to find us. I'm trying to keep you away from the danger, not bring it to your doorstep."

She huffed. Didn't he know no place was safe in this day and age? "Anyone can do a title search for properties owned by your company and find us. If I'm not at my place when they come for me, they'll go to yours. They can find your address through your truck title. Once they link you to your company, it's an easy jump to assume you're hiding me at another location."

Jack scoffed. "What kind of amateur operation do you think we're running?" Offense dripped from his words and darkened his expression. "It's not like our safe houses are listed in a directory somewhere. The cars and the homes are all owned by an LLC and the link between that dummy corporation and our company is buried pretty deep. It's not impossible to make a connection with time, but we're hoping to get this wrapped up before it comes to that." He stole glances at her as they picked up speed outside town. "This isn't our first rodeo, Katlin. You're going to have to trust us."

She fought a shiver as he rolled her name off his tongue like a caress.

"Worst-case scenario," he said, forcing a small smile, "we leave the country to keep you safe and let my men finish the job. How does Belize sound?"

With Jack? Belize sounded pretty darn good. "You're joking."

He shrugged. "A little. But we will keep you safe. You can count on that."

She inhaled deeply, then released the breath. Jack hadn't failed her yet. And she couldn't do much on her own without her memory. "Okay."

"You ask a lot of deep questions for someone who can't remember their last name."

"It's Andrews." Katlin crossed her arms, then rolled her eyes. "It was printed on all the release papers at the hospital."

Jack barked a laugh. "Smart. Quick. Observant. You're going to be just fine, Andrews."

She could only hope he was right.

JACK PILOTED THE pickup into the underground parking area at Fortress Defense, squinting briefly as his eyes adjusted to the dimmer light. He saluted the security camera as they motored past. The lot was larger than the team needed, easily accommodating staff and guest vehicles, plus the small fleet of company trucks.

"This whole building is yours?" Katlin asked, sitting taller as Jack slid into a spot near the door.

"Yeah." His team had gotten lucky. The company who'd designed and built the building had been foreclosed on, and Wyatt, the one who came up with the idea for Fortress, purchased the place for two-thirds its value. The previous owners had a solid security system already in place: network cables, cameras and receivers.

Fortress only had to update and personalize things, then set up shop for business.

He climbed out and headed for Katlin's side of the truck.

She met him there, already closing the passenger door behind her. "I didn't realize you were such a large operation. Do you use the whole building or is there a lot of empty space?"

He smiled. The building was single-story with parking beneath, and Fortress made use of every corner. "There are only four of us now, but we're growing. The waiting area and offices occupy the main space. Aside from that we keep a fully stocked arsenal and extensive equipment lockers. Plus, each team member has a private bunk space for times we're on call or crashing between jobs. And there's a kitchen, gym and shower area." He swiped his key card then tugged open the etched glass door for her. "Bulletproof," he said, rapping his knuckles on the sparkling surface as they entered the underground foyer.

There was a mosaic tile floor, simple gray walls and a large Fortress Defense logo on the central elevator doors. A security camera in the corner tracked their progress as they crossed the room.

Katlin took it all in with a soft "Oohh."

"Like it?" he asked, uncharacteristically tense as he waited for her response.

"Yes. This is impressive." She turned in a small circle, taking in the area, then traced her fingertips over the logo on the shiny elevator doors.

Katlin stepped aboard when the car arrived, and an odd wave of pleasure swept through Jack at her approval.

She turned to face him as he pressed the button, commanding the car upward. She tipped her head back for a direct look at his face. Her brown eyes were warm with sincerity. Her expression was vulnerable, something he got the impression didn't happen to her very often. "I haven't thanked you properly for coming to get me at the hospital," she said. "I'd probably be dead by now if it wasn't for you. You've been kind, patient and heroic. You probably don't hear that enough in your line of work, so I want you to know. I'd also like to thank you for your service. Both things mean a lot to me."

Jack's gut tightened at her words. It'd been a long time since anyone had thanked him for his work. He supposed that was par for the course. He was hired to protect people, so it was expected. Still, knowing all that Katlin was going through, the fact that she'd taken the time between crises to acknowledge him did something to his core. "Thank you."

The doors parted, and Katlin turned away, stepping into the waiting area before him.

"Jack?" Cade's voice boomed through the space as his steady footfalls echoed down the hallway in their direction.

"Yeah. We made it," Jack answered, setting a palm against Katlin's back and steering her toward the couches.

An ensemble of overstuffed seating options was arranged on a carpet in the room's center, with a smattering of side and coffee tables around. Wyatt's and Sawyer's wives had added brightly colored throw pillows to the couches and chairs, then topped the tables with realistic-looking fake flowers. The women had made a weekend of fussing over the space and had even added a selection of flavored coffee creamers to the drink bar. While they were at it, they'd also replaced the plain white disposable cups the men had purchased in bulk with an assortment of colored mugs and napkins.

"Hey." Cade appeared a moment later with a laptop and a smile. "Sorry. I was doing some research in my office." He rocked back on his heels at the sight of Katlin, then flipped his gaze to Jack. "This is Griffin's baby sister?"

"Yep." Jack knew what his teammate was thinking, and jealousy pinched nonsensically in his chest. Katlin was nowhere close to a baby. She looked like a freaking pint-size pinup model, and Jack was supposed to somehow stay as close as possible to her while keeping his thoughts PG-rated. It didn't help that she was kind and confident. Sassy and smart. The perfect combination to steal any man's heart, if Jack's hadn't already been irreparably broken by Cara's death, and the bombshell in question wasn't his best friend's kid sister, whom he'd sworn to protect.

Cade snorted out a laugh, then approached Katlin with one hand extended and a fierce grin on his lips. "I'm Cade Lance. One of Jack's partners. It's nice to meet you. I had the pleasure of meeting your brother briefly several years back. My older brother, Wyatt, another of our partners, knew Griffin from basic training."

Katlin looked to Jack.

Cade quirked an eyebrow. "Did I say something wrong?"

"Nope," Jack said with a sigh. "Katlin has amnesia." He'd saved that detail to share at a time when they weren't running for their lives, and this was the first opportunity since they'd met. "She doesn't remember Griffin, or anything about herself or her life before waking in the hospital last night."

Cade grimaced and rubbed his fingers hard across his brow. "Well, that makes things more complicated." He took a seat on the sofa and rested the laptop on the table. "I guess you should tell me everything you know about what happened, and I'll see what I can do from there."

Katlin lowered herself onto the seat across from Cade and rested her hands in her lap. "To be honest, I'm not even sure about everything that's happened since I woke up in the hospital. Aside from being shot at twice in a matter of hours."

Cade's mouth opened then shut. He leaned forward to rest his elbows on his knees. "Jack?"

Jack started at the beginning. He relayed the missed calls, first from Katlin then the detective, and went from there. He rehashed every detail he could remember, then waited while his partner processed the information.

"All right." Cade nodded thoughtfully. "I'll start by tracking Katlin's life through her social-media accounts and see what I can find. Who are her friends, what she's been up to lately… And with whom. Then I'll see about cracking her passwords so she can close or suspend the accounts. Anything I can find out about her, the shooter can, too. With the accounts closed, the information will still be out there, but it'll take more work to find."

Katlin's knee bobbed wildly as she took in the explanation. "That buys us more time to figure out who's coming after me before they turn up again. Like getting a replacement truck and staying at a safe house."

"You got it." Cade stretched onto his feet and headed for the hallway again. "I'll be right back. I almost forgot. My fiancée sent some clothes for you. We didn't know your size, so she sent some of those stretchy clothes she jogs in. You've got to be ready to change out of that scrubs top and bloody jeans."

Katlin looked down at herself then cringed.

"You okay?" Jack asked.

"I forgot how awful I look. There's blood on my pants." Her eyes glossed suddenly with unshed tears. "It was really kind of Cade's fiancée to think of me like that," she said. "I hope I was that nice before." She swiped a renegade tear and batted the rest into submission. "Based on everyone wanting to kill me, I'm starting to think I was awful."

Jack crouched into a squat before her. "Hey," he said softly, drawing her eyes to meet his. "The fact you're worried about being awful tells me you weren't." He set a gentle hand over hers and leveled her with his most sincere stare. "You're going to get through this, and you're going to be okay. I won't leave you until I know you're safe and you want me to go. Okay?" And to be honest, he wasn't sure he'd want to go then, either. He traced her porcelain skin with his eyes, noting the feminine lines of her jaw and cheeks, the enticing curve of her neck.

She wet her lips, and Jack allowed himself the indulgence of trailing the path of her tongue with his heated gaze. He allowed himself one moment to imagine the taste of her smooth pink lips under his.

"Jack," she whispered, the sweet sound tightening his muscles impossibly further. "What if I don't remember?"

He forced himself back to the moment and gave her small hand a light squeeze. "You will. You're smart, and you're strong. Once we clean up and get a little rest at the safe house, we'll visit your apartment. Something there might be exactly what you need to access your memories. And we still need to meet with Detective Reihl. She might have more information we can use, too."

"Okay." Katlin turned her soft hand beneath his, aligning their palms until a jolt of heat and need lanced through him. She spread her fingers, allowing him to slide his between. "Are you sure we've never met?" she asked, searching him with seemingly all-knowing eyes. "Because you feel so familiar."

He agreed. He'd felt it, too.

Cade whistled his way back into the room. "I think this is everything. She sent a bunch of travel-size shower stuff, too."

Katlin released Jack with a blush and a start.

He stood to take the bags from Cade's hands. "Thanks."

Cade smirked, his attention flipping from Jack to Katlin, then back. His smile widened.

Jack moved to the broad reception desk and snagged two sets of keys from the pegboard on the wall. "I think we'll go ahead and get set up at the safe house, then call in and work out an action plan. See what you learn from her social media, and try to get a number where we can reach her folks."

Katlin said goodbye to Cade, then met Jack at the elevator. They stepped inside and watched Cade slowly disappear behind closing doors.

"Good luck," Cade called, a wicked gleam in his eye.

Jack swallowed a groan. He was definitely going to need it.

Chapter Six

Katlin's eyes grew heavy as Jack drove along the scenic country road toward the safe house. The pain medication she'd been administered at the hospital was wearing off, and her aching head and limbs longed for rest. The cab of their new truck was immaculate, had probably been detailed recently. An antiseptic scent of cleansers hung in the air, sharp and uninviting. She much preferred the hints of spearmint and aftershave that had lingered in the fabric of Jack's truck's seats. Otherwise the company truck wasn't bad. Standard size, a few years older than Jack's and in a boring shade of gray. There were no dog tags on the rearview mirror. No window clings spouting army pride. This truck was impersonal and utterly unremarkable. Easy to overlook in a lot or on the road.

The sound of crunching gravel pulled her eyes open sometime later. She hadn't realized she'd let them close. Farmland stretched to the horizon beyond her window. A cloudless blue sky arched overhead.

Jack guided the pickup down a winding lane, pitted and pocked from age and wear, toward an old white farmhouse in the distance.

Katlin straightened to admire the obviously historic home. Detailed scrollwork adorned the window frames and rooflines. A broad wraparound porch and stained-glass transoms showcased the front door. "Wow."

"You like it," Jack said, a note of pride in his voice.

"It's beautiful." The paint was chipping and the flower beds were all overgrown, but the bones of the home were magnificent. The roof was straight and the porches level. "This was probably a mansion in its day."

"It was," Jack said. "The original owner made a mint farming wheat, corn, oats and tobacco. The home was passed down by legacy until there were no more living heirs and it went to sheriff's auction."

Katlin smiled. "And the thrifty, resourceful team at Fortress Defense saw an opportunity to make a deal." She curled her fingers around the door handle, eager to take a closer look. "What's the inside like?"

"Utilitarian," Jack said, parking the truck behind the house. "Clean, dry and stocked with necessities, but very basic. The place isn't used often enough to leave anything of value. Plus, it's a prime location for vagrants or mischievous area teens who might notice no one's living here."

"Security?" she asked.

"No." Jack pocketed the key from the ignition and opened his door. "The monthly fees associated with ongoing service aren't cost-effective. We set up temporary networks as needed then take them down when we leave."

Katlin stretched gingerly onto her feet outside the truck and inhaled the brisk autumn air. Winter was coming. It wouldn't be long now.

"Come on." Jack appeared at her side, the bags from Fortress, plus a couple that had come with the truck, on his shoulder and in his hands. "I think we should get some rest first. Make a plan second, with clear heads. Then go out and look for your memories after we eat." They walked around to the front of the house and headed up the porch steps. Jack slid a key into the dead bolt.

Katlin followed, her stomach groaning at the mention of food. Her limbs, however, begged for sleep.

The front door opened to a small entryway with a staircase to the second floor.

Jack moved into a living area and tossed the black duffel bags onto a couch, then turned an odd expression on her. "How about a quick tour? Then you can clean up or nap, unwind, whatever you need. But there's only one bathroom. We'll have to share while we're here."

"Okay, but how many bedrooms?" She grinned, attempting to be witty, but suddenly regretting the choice.

Jack blanched.

"I didn't mean…of course, we aren't going to…" She motioned between them, then pressed a hand to her mouth in an attempt to shut up.

He turned and left the room, angling his head over one shoulder, indicating she should follow.

The rooms were beautiful but mostly empty and well-worn, like treasures in need of a little polish. Faded wallpaper clung to aged plaster and intricate woodwork lined ceilings, windows and floors.

Narrow beams made up the hardwood floor underfoot, each grooved and stained from wear. The living area had a couch, chair and coffee table. The kitchen had a small four-seat table, coffeepot, stove and refrigerator. The cabinets were tall and spacious, stretching to the ceiling along the far wall. A small hall led to additional rooms and the back porch.

"The parlor and study have been set up as bedrooms on this floor," Jack said, pushing a set of pocket doors wide. “This was the parlor. The study is across the hall. First-floor rooms are easier to defend and easier to exit in the event of an emergency.”

Katlin stepped carefully into the room, hyperaware of the gorgeous wrought iron bed against the far wall. Its thick eyelet comforter and a multitude of pillows called to her. The entire setup was reminiscent of another time. For one silly moment, she imagined leading Jack there. If he was half the lover he was the fighter and friend, it’d be a night she wouldn’t forget.

Except, she had already forgotten too much, and she was worried about the person she might be. If her suspicions were right, based on what little she had to go on, she wasn’t the kind of person Jack deserved.

He cleared his throat and backed out of the room. “The bathroom is this way.”

Katlin followed him past an open door to a room across the hall from hers. That room had a simple full-size bed with a plain blanket and a single pillow. Jack’s, she assumed.

He flipped the light on inside a large room with a claw-foot tub and freestanding vanity beside a pedestal sink and toilet. “There’s aspirin in the cabinet. I’m sure you’re feeling the effects of your crash by now.” He set the bags Cade’s fiancée had provided on a small table in the powder room, then ducked out. “I’ll get the perimeter cameras set up,” he called, moving quickly out of earshot.

Katlin rubbed her forehead, humiliated by her earlier comment on the number of bedrooms, then locked the bathroom door. The weight of her life pinned her to the wall, and she let her knees buckle, taking her all the way to the floor, where she gave in to the tears.

JACK WHISTLED HIS way around the kitchen the next morning, flipping pancakes and sipping black coffee. He'd gotten three consecutive hours of sleep before dawn, thanks to the well-established security perimeter he'd set before bed. There was a lot to be said for surveillance cameras and a hot spot.

He'd worked into the night attempting to create a narrative for Katlin's precrash life, but he'd come up short on that front. She'd taken impressive measures to control the amount of information available on her personal life, and it had paid off. Something she'd likely learned from her brother, a master of discretion.

As far as Jack could tell, Katlin had one tightly managed Facebook account, and no other social media. Not even a profile on one of those professional networking sites. Her digital footprint was practically nonexistent, and Jack couldn't help wondering what that said about her, or possibly, her career.

Could she be in law enforcement? Maybe undercover?

The sound of her soft footfalls in the hall drew a smile across his mouth. He'd realized he missed her as he'd crawled into bed, thankful there were two rooms where they could sleep. He was only human, after all. "Mornin'," he called, pouring and delivering a fresh mug of coffee to the table. "How are you feeling?"

"Better." She moved into view, a shy smile on her lips. "Apparently Cade's fiancée is pocket-size."

He gave the formfitting black pants and clingy long-sleeve T-shirt an appreciative look. Several parts of him were certain they owed Lyndy a thank-you. "She's petite."

Katlin laughed. Her blond hair hung across her shoulders in waves, curling casually over her breasts and drawing his attention where it didn't belong. "Sorry I fell asleep yesterday. I only meant to rest for a few minutes, then I woke around midnight." She rolled her eyes. "I figured you'd hear me if I got up, and I didn't want to disturb you, so I read the books on the table near my bed and dozed off and on from there."

"You didn't have to stay in bed or worry about disturbing me," he said. "And you can thank Emma for the books. That's Sawyer's wife. She came out here with him this summer when he mowed the grass. She thought the guest room was sad and uninviting, so she tried to improve it."

"It's nice. You should thank her for me the next time you see her." Katlin shuffled to the table, where Jack had set the coffee. "Is this for me?"

"Yeah. And I hope you're hungry. You like pancakes?"

"Yes," she said, groaning the word. "I love pancakes. I could probably eat about twenty of them."

"You remember?" Jack asked, hopeful.

Katlin wrinkled her nose as she sipped her coffee. "No. It's more like an instinct than a memory. Sometimes, when I'm not trying to think of things, they just come to me. Like, I know I love to dance, but I can't actually remember dancing."

"Gotcha," Jack said. "Anything else?"

"Some little things. I'm pretty sure I prefer country music to pop, and would much rather be outside than in."

"Me, too." Jack ferried a heaping platter to the table, then delivered a bottle of syrup with place settings for Katlin and himself. "Help yourself."

Katlin took a pile of pancakes, then greedily dug in. "Thank you so much for this. I know I'm not pulling my weight yet, but I will."

"You're healing, and you don't need to do anything else. I've got the rest."

"I should be helping." She slid a bite between her inviting lips and let her eyelids flutter in pleasure. "This is delicious. I wonder if I can cook."

"I'm sure," he said. "It's not hard, and you're smart."

"How do you know?" She set aside her fork and raised her eyebrows in challenge.

He sipped his coffee, enjoying the quiet moment with her, happy to share the impressive news. "Griffin came home for your college graduation. I heard about it for weeks afterward. You were at the top of your class."

"Really?" She lifted the fork again, clearly considering the information. "Interesting. Where did I go to college? What was my major?"

Jack stretched his memory, easily recalling the photos on Griffin's wall, but unable to find the details. "I'm not sure."

"Bummer." She pulled her lips to the side. "Hopefully I'll learn more when we get to my apartment."

Jack nodded. "That reminds me. I went over your hospital discharge papers, and I noticed the address there didn't match the one where I've been sending your birthday and Christmas cards. When I spoke with Detective Reihl, she said the information was pulled from your driver's license."

"Probably," Katlin said. "I wasn't awake when the papers were filled out, but I've looked at the papers and my license. The addresses definitely match."

"Then I guess you've moved." He shrugged. *And Katlin didn't tell him.* He wasn't sure why the fact stung, but it did.

She froze, her fork midway to her lips. "You finally

got to speak to the detective? What did she say about the shooters? What did she know about me?"

"Not much." Jack felt his lips pulling low into a frown. In truth, Reihl had been skeptical. She'd made him feel as if he was hiding something or covering for Katlin, though she hadn't said what she thought was going on. "She's as surprised as we are by the gunmen and general chaos that unfolded after your crash. She wanted an address for the safe house, but I told her I'd prefer not to divulge that information yet. When I reminded her that you'd called me instead of 911, implying you had reason not to trust local law enforcement, she relented. But I can't say she'll let it go for long."

Katlin forked another bite of pancake and dragged it through the puddle of syrup on her plate. "There's also the possibility I was involved in criminal activity, and that's the real reason I didn't contact the police."

"I don't think so," Jack said, and though he couldn't say for sure, every instinct he had said Katlin was as honorable and just as she was dangerously tempting.

TWO HOURS LATER, he parked outside a set of apartments in a town thirty minutes from the place he normally sent Katlin's Christmas and birthday cards.

"This is it?" she asked, comparing the address on her license to the building beside them. "Yuck."

He didn't disagree.

"Maybe I did run with criminals," she said. "Because this place isn't much better than the area where I crashed."

Jack met her on the sidewalk as she grimaced at the somewhat run-down apartments. "This neighborhood is about one hundred times better," he said. "This building has just seen better days."

Katlin didn't look convinced as she dug into her purse and retrieved a key ring with lots of options. "Good grief. Why on earth do I have all these?"

Jack smiled. "Let's just hope one of them opens your apartment door."

They moved along the squat brick building to a door marked with the same number as her license, and Katlin tried the keys until one turned the lock. Her shoulders sagged with relief. "Sorry I didn't tell you I moved," she said before turning the knob. "That seems like a rude thing to do."

"To be fair, we'd never met," Jack said, warmed again by her consideration of him when her life was such a mess. "It wasn't as if we were friends." He waited while she opened the door and ushered him inside.

"We should've been," she said. "I think we make great friends."

Jack snorted. "That's probably because you don't know anyone else right now. Normally, I say as little as possible and stay out of everyone's way." This was different. *She* was different, he realized, then quickly pushed away the confusing thought.

Katlin flipped the light switch beside the door and paused to take in the sparsely decorated apartment. "I think the safe house had more furniture than this." She moved tentatively across the worn carpet, scowling her disapproval. "And it was homier, too."

"Maybe you haven't had a chance to settle in and decorate yet," he suggested, understanding her disappointment. He'd looked into the address where he sent the cards, even done a drive-by after his discharge and considered a knock at her door. He'd chickened out and gone home. That address had been a small bungalow with flower boxes at the windows and a rocker on the porch. Small, but postcard-pretty and obviously loved. The apartment where they stood now had a sad desperation about it. And he couldn't help wondering if something bad had happened to initiate her move. Had she lost her job? Been forced to sell her things and downsize?

A small sound broke the silence, and Katlin froze.

Jack set a hand on the gun holstered against his back.

"Tell me I have a cat," she whispered.

Jack gripped her elbow and pulled her behind him. He raised a finger to his lips, then pointed at the door where they'd just entered. He removed his truck key from his pocket and handed it to her.

She bit her bottom lip in hesitation.

A moment later, a small red dot appeared on her forehead.

"Get down!" Jack yelled, yanking her to the floor with him as the front window shattered.

Katlin screamed and covered her head.

His ears rang as he spun and took aim, prepared to fire. "Go!" he hollered, daring a glance at Katlin before making his way to the nearest doorjamb and bracing himself there for cover.

"Come out!" he called into the apartment. "Put your hands up where I can see them. Police are on the way." At least, he hoped that was true. Surely gunfire wasn't so commonplace in the neighborhood that no one had made that call.

Behind him, the front door opened and closed as Katlin found her will to escape. A measure of relief spread through him knowing she had the truck to carry her away if things went south in the next few moments.

"Put your weapon down and kick it out here where I can see it," he yelled. "Now!"

Something thumped against the ground.

Jack's eyes flicked to the object. A remote control, not a gun.

Three rapid-fire shots sent drywall and wood fragments into the air as the doorjamb he was using for cover ripped apart. Jack returned fire, and the front window burst into a confetti shower of glass as the next errant round shattered it. Katlin screamed from somewhere outside, and Jack's heart ripped painfully down the center as he returned fire and told himself she was okay. That she'd screamed at the sound of the gunshots, but hadn't been hit or kidnapped on her way to the truck.

He needed to go after her.

He couldn't go after her.

Not until the gunman was down. Turning his back would only get him killed, and then where would Katlin be? The impossible choice clawed and tore at his chest as he stepped out from hiding and moved methodically through the apartment in search of an intruder.

Until he found an open bathroom window with a trail of blood draped over the sill.

Chapter Seven

Katlin sat at the kitchen table inside her unfamiliar apartment while local police combed through the rooms, dusted for prints and collected a sample of the blood in her bathroom. Her hands trembled with the aftershock of yet another life-threatening scare. She'd been only a few feet away from the front window when a bullet had sent glass shattering into the air behind her. She'd dialed 911 and prayed Jack would be okay. She hated being useless to him while he'd put his life on the line for hers yet again.

Jack paced the space beside her—apparently he was indestructible—and relayed the details of the apartment invasion to someone at Fortress Defense by cell phone. He traded pointed looks with Detective Reihl every minute or two, though the two hadn't spoken since he'd given his initial statement upon her arrival.

Nothing about Katlin's life felt real. Everything was too raw and dangerous. Her heart said this wasn't who she was—not now, anyway. Was it possible to wake up with amnesia and a new personality? Because she couldn't imagine a world where this was really her life. The pathetic, unloved apartment. Only a handful of belongings. No framed photos on the walls or trinkets and snapshots taped to the bedroom mirror. The whole place felt like a larger and more expensive hotel room. Although, even junk hotels made the effort to decorate. Sure, her folks lived overseas, but surely she had friends. Everyone had friends, didn't they? If she did, there was no evidence of them anywhere.

She shot an envious look at Jack's cell phone, then a frustrated look at Detective Reihl, who'd kept Katlin's phone after finding Jack's number dialed immediately before the crash. Tech support was going through it for clues about what happened that night, making the only link to Katlin's personal life locked up in police custody.

The detective moved slowly around the kitchen and living room, scrutinizing everything and frowning often. The pretty brunette had arrived twenty minutes after the initial uniformed responders, looking exhausted and accusatory. She'd gotten the rundown from an officer who'd been dusting Katlin's front door for prints, then taken statements from Katlin and Jack. She'd made it clear she wasn't happy about the number of shootings in her jurisdiction since Katlin's crash, and she gave Katlin the distinct impression it was somehow her fault. Currently, she seemed to be conducting an unwarranted search.

Katlin stood and cleared her throat when the detective reached for a folded American flag in a small display case. "Excuse me."

Detective Reihl lowered her hand, leaving the flag where it was. "Your brother was in the military," she said, tipping her head toward the display. "I'm sorry for your loss."

Katlin raised her chin an inch, wishing she could remember Griffin, and feeling guilty she wasn't saddened by his death. "Have you learned anything about the man who's doing this?"

"We're following every available lead, Miss Andrews." She turned stiffly to face Katlin, head cocked like a puppy trying to understand something new and peculiar. Her gray pantsuit was well-tailored and emphasized a youthful and athletic figure. The tight bun she'd cranked her thick brown locks into seemed to imply she wanted to appear older and more severe. *Occupational requirements for a young female detective*, Katlin supposed.

The detailed train of complicated and somewhat judgmental thoughts stumped Katlin. It wasn't the first time she'd caught herself unwinding an intense line of suspicions and curiosities. Maybe that was what had gotten her into trouble to begin with. Maybe she'd seen or said something she shouldn't have.

Detective Reihl clasped her hands behind her back as she moseyed toward the kitchen. "It would be incredibly helpful if you could remember what you were doing before your crash or anything at all about who might be following you and why."

"No kidding," Katlin groaned.

"Detective?" one of the uniformed officers called upon approach. He and his partner moved in tandem down the hall, evidence collection materials in hand. "We've got things wrapped up here." He turned to Katlin with a sympathetic expression. "We'll take what we have to the lab and be in touch. You can get a copy of your police reports from the station or online."

Detective Reihl shook the officers' hands. "Thank you both. Let's touch base later."

The men left, and Reihl turned to Katlin, nudging a

hunk of destroyed doorjamb with the toe of her shoe. The splintered wedge spun on the floor among bits of drywall debris. She cast a pointed look at the shattered window behind her. “I suggest you stay with family until we figure out what’s going on.”

“My family isn’t in the country,” Katlin answered sharply, feeling the well of fear and frustration rise.

“That’s right,” Reihl said. “Your only known connection is Mr. Hale, a man you’ve just met.”

Katlin bit her tongue to keep from lashing back. The detective was only doing her job, and the situation was unbelievable. Katlin was living it and barely believed it was real—that it wasn’t a bizarre dream cooked up in her head while she was lying in bed at the hospital in a coma.

Jack moved into the space at her side, tall, strong and ever-protective. “Something on your mind, Detective?”

“Just making sure I’ve got your story straight.”

Katlin bristled at the implication she might’ve made everything up. “It’s not a story. This is my life, and I’m terrified. You don’t think I want to know who I am? Why I live here in this cold, empty apartment? Or why someone wants me dead?”

“Of course,” the detective answered. “Like I said—I’m just trying to keep things straight. I can’t seem to figure out why you live here, either.” She fished a business card from her jacket pocket. “Let me know if that memory of yours makes a reappearance. Or if anyone else takes a shot at you.” She passed the card to Katlin, then flashed a tight smile and let herself out.

Katlin fought the urge to scream. “She thinks I’m lying about my amnesia. Probably thinks it’s my attempt to hide all the awful things I’m involved in. And what do you think she meant by that comment about not understanding why I live here, either? There was a look in her eye. Like I'm lying about that, too."

Jack moved toward the broken window, watching her leave. "She's run a background check and she has your phone. Maybe she found out you just moved? Your other place was a lot nicer." He turned back with a smile. "You're not some career vagabond. You had a nice little place a couple towns over, and you lived there four years. This place could be nice with some TLC. Maybe you just hadn't gotten to it yet."

She appreciated the continuous encouragement Jack provided, but couldn't quite believe it herself. Something bad was going on here, and she had a feeling it had all started before she moved to this place, especially knowing now that she'd lived somewhere nicer for a long while.

"I got ahold of your landlord," Jack said. "He'll be here to board up the broken window in a bit. He thinks he can get the pane replaced tomorrow. Until then, why don't you pack some things and see if anything personal jars your memory."

Katlin turned on her toes and headed for the bedroom. If she had personal things, the bedroom seemed like the most likely place to keep them. She started with the half-empty closet of too-dressy things. "I can't believe I don't have more clothes than this. I feel like I enjoy and appreciate clothes, but this wardrobe doesn't support that. And most of what's in here is business wear. Am I a businessperson? Because I like the clothes I'm wearing better than any of these, and this outfit isn't even mine." She plucked the comfy T-shirt fabric at her chest. "And if I'm a businessperson, why didn't I rent a nicer place or spend a little money making this one more homey?"

"I don't know, but we will find out. Meanwhile, pack

as much as you want. We can take it with us and go through it at the safe house."

She lifted the lid off a box on the floor of her closet and smiled. A small stack of notebooks stood beside a pile of paperbacks. "I knew I liked to read," she said with a nonsensical swell of pride. She had strong reactions to various things and gut instincts about her preferences. That had to be a good sign. Surely the actual memories weren't far behind.

A quick flip through the notebooks revealed nothing obviously relevant or useful, so she moved on to examining her wardrobe.

"Learning anything over there?" Jack called as he poked through the adjacent bathroom.

"Yes. I like to read and prefer running gear to business attire. I'm also apparently completely broke and have terrible taste in apartments and furnishings."

Jack snorted. "We don't know why you moved yet. Maybe this is temporary."

"Yeah," she said smartly, "just until I go to jail for whatever heinous thing I'm involved in."

"That's ridiculous." He crossed into the bedroom and fixed her with a frown. "I might not know you, but I knew Griffin, and he adored you. According to your brother, you are smart, dedicated, hardworking, courageous and loyal, just to name a few of his favorite adjectives. If you were some wayward troublemaker, he would've said so. He didn't sugarcoat things and he didn't lie."

Katlin turned back to her closet and stuffed the most casual clothing options into a suitcase. Then she went to her dresser in search of socks and underthings. Twenty minutes later, she had everything she needed and two boxes of personal items, from miscellaneous photos and notebooks to power cords and an older-model e-reader.

They headed back through the kitchen together, and Katlin grabbed her brother's memorial flag. Her gut said it wasn't right to leave it.

"Do you need this?" Jack asked, lifting a messenger bag off a hook near the refrigerator.

"Maybe." She tucked the flag under her arm and went to see.

The bag was mostly empty and likely used to carry a laptop she hadn't found. She sifted through a collection of plastic cards tucked into one interior pocket. Local library. Gas card. Health care. "Hey." She turned a photo ID over between her fingertips. "Look." She spun the small ID badge so he could see it.

"'Fitch and Quintz, Attorneys-at-Law,'" Jack read the card with a smile. "'Katlin Andrews, administrative assistant.'"

She smiled. "Maybe my coworkers can tell me more about my life than this apartment."

JACK LOADED KATLIN'S things into the truck, then entered her office address into his phone's GPS for directions. She was holding herself together extremely well, all things considered. He wasn't convinced he could do the same in her situation. He had his memories, knew he was a good person and was still darn tired of being shot at. Katlin was trying to piece together who she was with next to nothing to go on, except the fact that a man kept trying to kill her. That had to be an impossible burden.

"Why do you think I live like that?" she asked, eyeballing the run-down building as he eased the truck away from the curb. "Everything about it feels transient and detached. Even the landlord didn't know anything about me, except I pay the rent on time."

The landlord hadn't impressed Jack. He'd covered the window with an attitude, as if it had somehow put him out to have to do his job. He'd had no interest in the break-in, beyond its impact on him, and zero information about Katlin for the police. In fact, the man's line of return questions made Jack suspect he was trying to figure a way to charge Katlin for the damage. Good thing she worked for an attorney.

"You said I have a degree, and I work at a law firm," Katlin continued, "so why does my life seem so lonely and sad?"

"Maybe you're scrimping on rent and general spending to pay down your student-loan debt. That's a real issue for a lot of people."

"Scrimping is one thing. I live like a homeless person. No, actually, I've seen homeless people with more stuff than I had in there."

"So maybe you're a minimalist," he suggested. "One of those new age, vegan hipsters who go around telling everyone to live simply."

She rolled her eyes. "Whoever I am, I'm in a lot of trouble, and I hate thinking I might be a bad person or maybe in debt for more than student loans."

Jack set his hand over hers on the seat between them. "You're not."

She stilled at his touch, and he pulled his hand back, mildly shocked and embarrassed. "Sorry, I didn't mean to..." He let the sentence hang, unsure exactly how to finish the thought. He hadn't meant to make her uncomfortable. Hadn't meant to overstep. Hadn't even meant to reach for her. It had been an automatic response, one he hadn't had in years, which meant he needed to tighten up.

He fixed his eyes on the road and gave himself a few swift mental kicks. It didn't matter if he was attracted to her or intrigued by her or even if he felt a sincere and powerful connection. She was Griffin's little sister and a client. Kind of. She needed him to protect her, not touch her at every opportunity.

Katlin set her hand on his, where he'd rested it on his thigh, then curled her fingers under his palm.

He turned to find a cautious but warm smile on her pink lips.

She tugged his hand back onto the seat between them and squeezed. "Tell me about your life," she said as she watched him intently. His cheeks warmed as he turned a hesitant smile back to the road. "I don't know anything about my life. Maybe knowing about yours will help."

"I live alone, like you. I work at Fortress, doing things like this as needed, though I've been shot at more in the last two days than I have since leaving the military. Some days I miss the military," he said, surprised by the truth in the words. "I liked making a difference and keeping people safe."

"You're doing that right now," she said softly.

"And I wouldn't change it."

She seemed to consider his answer. "Do you think you'll ever want a family? Mortgage, white picket fence and all that instead?"

Jack's heart pinched and his breathing slowed. "I did once." He dared a look at Katlin, hoping to make his stance on relationships clear in case she was thinking about him the way he'd been errantly thinking of her.

"She died. Griffin helped me through it, but I don't ever want to go through that again. I wish no one ever had to."

He took the next turn, following the GPS's directions through town, thankful to have said his piece about love. It was a good reminder for his own stupid heart.

"Well, thank you for hanging in with me while I figure things out." She released his hand. "I'm sure Griffin would appreciate it. I certainly do."

Jack gritted his teeth, hating the loss of her gentle touch but knowing it was for the best.

She pulled a bag onto her lap from the floorboards. "I found an e-reader in the nightstand. I'm hoping it has photos or links to my email and social media. If I'm lucky, I kept myself logged in. We can try it out when we're back on Wi-Fi."

"We can use the hot spot on my phone if you want to look while we drive."

She powered the device on and swiped the screen to life, then lifted and dropped her hand. "It has a data plan," she said dryly. "I live like a pauper, but I pay for data on an e-reader. Maybe that's my problem. I'm terrible with money. Maybe the attorneys I work for specialize in bankruptcy."

Jack laughed, glad the awkward moment had passed so quickly. Outside, the sun was brilliant and the day unseasonably warm. A vast and welcome contrast from the day before.

"I have the lamest social-media accounts ever," Katlin scoffed. "It's all generic. There's zero personal information on here. Just memes and famous quotes. Thanks to Griffin, you know more about me than I do. How messed up is that?"

"It's temporary," he said, slowing to the designated reduced speed.

The roads in town were narrow and lined with businesses, from cafés to comic-book shops. Brightly colored flowers and banners decorated light posts and corners. "This looks like a nice little town. People are out walking. The streets are well-maintained. Crime is probably low. Not a bad place to relocate."

She rested her head against the seat back, e-reader in her hands. "Hopefully someone at my office will be able to fill me in on things. They have to be wondering why I haven't shown up at work." Katlin looked his way and frowned.

"What?"

"What if whatever is going on with me has something to do with where I work? It is a law firm. Maybe I'm not a criminal, but I accidentally crossed one."

"Or you might know something you shouldn't."

She barked a humorless laugh. "How ironic. I could be on a hit list for knowing something I can't remember."

Jack cringed internally at the reminder. He slowed at the intersection and engaged his turn signal. "The office is on the next block, so we'll know soon enough. But for the record, I stand by what I said earlier. You're not a criminal. You're a good person. Anyone can see that."

She offered a bland smile. "No offense, but I'll feel more confident about your assessment if I can find a single other person who knows me and doesn't want to kill me."

"Fair enough."

Traffic slowed as they approached their destination. Street congestion created a one-lane situation he couldn't navigate around.

"What's going on?" Katlin asked, sitting straighter and craning her neck for a better view.

"Car accident?" Jack guessed, noting an ambulance and police cruiser along the curb up ahead. He swung the truck into an empty space and cut the engine. "We might as well walk from here. If someone else shoots at us, at least there are already police and paramedics on the scene."

Katlin laughed, and his heart lightened.

He met her on the sidewalk and fed the meter, then double-checked their surroundings for gun-wielding lunatics before turning in the direction of Fitch & Quintz.

Katlin hooked her arm with his and fell easily in step at his side.

They slowed as a line of yellow crime-scene tape came into view, and a uniformed officer exited a building up ahead. He held the door for a pair of EMTs pushing a gurney into the windy November day. The sheet on top covered a body bag.

The stately gold script on the window behind him read Fitch & Quintz, Attorneys-at-Law.

Chapter Eight

A cold sheen of sweat broke over Katlin's neck and face. Her stomach coiled in silent panic. "What happened?" she croaked, forcing the words through a tightening throat. Whatever it was, she was sure it wasn't accidental—not at her office, not after the last two days she'd had.

Jack set a steady, confident hand over her fingers on his arm, offering his strength. "Excuse me," he called, projecting his voice beyond the caution tape and through the white noise of a gathering crowd.

An officer approached and swept his hands before him, motioning them back. "Please step away from the tape." The man was young and pale with blue eyes and acne. The badge on his coat said Jenkins, and the collar of his shirt was too large for his skinny neck. He barely seemed old enough to be out of high school. How had he passed the service exam? How did she remember police officers took the civil-service exam and not her middle name? She curled her fingers to quell her erratic thoughts and building frustration.

Jack stepped back in silent obedience of the cop's request, towing Katlin with him. "Can you tell me what happened here?" he asked the officer.

"I'm afraid there was a shooting," Officer Jenkins answered. “The law office will be closed today and tomorrow. Appointments will be rescheduled in a day or two.”

“Who was shot?” Jack asked.

“That’s confidential for the moment. We need to identify the deceased’s next of kin before divulging the identity. Now, if you could please step back. Go home. Call and reschedule.”

“But...” Katlin croaked, raising her hand and pausing to clear her throat. She forced a calm expression over her face and did her best to appear less panicked and more professional than she felt. With enough luck, the heat creeping over her skin and rolling in her stomach wasn’t obvious to everyone who looked at her. “I’m not a client. I work here. I’m an administrative assistant.”

The officer lifted his eyebrows. “Is that right?” He removed a small notepad from his interior jacket pocket and turned the pages. “What’s your name?”

“Katlin Andrews.”

His eyes flicked up from the page, meeting hers with obvious recognition. “Why don’t you step inside, Miss Andrews? We’re interviewing employees.” He returned to the office building and pulled open the door.

Jack cast a questioning look her way, clearly unsure if she was up to being questioned by yet another lawman.

She wasn’t. But she wanted answers. “It’s okay,” she said, nodding and willing her feet into motion.

Officer Jenkins raised a palm to Jack. “Employees only.”

Jack looked at Katlin, his hand tightening over hers. There was caution and a measure of fear in his eyes. He clearly didn’t like the idea of sending her into the recent murder scene alone. How could she blame him?

"He has to come with me," she told the officer, shoring up her nerve. "He's my personal protection."

Jenkins furrowed his brow.

"Tell him," she whispered, suddenly unsure she could voice all the horrors she'd experienced since waking in the hospital. She met Jack's gaze with pleading eyes.

Jack filled in the officer on the wiki version of events so far, then explained his position with Fortress Defense. "She has a head injury, and her car's at the Campbellsville impound lot. I'm here to keep her safe. I can wait if you'd like, but I can't leave."

The officer looked from Jack to Katlin, then back. "And you're in contact with Detective Reihl about all this?"

Katlin and Jack nodded, and the officer sighed. "All right. Take a seat in the waiting area. I'll be in to speak with you in a few minutes."

Katlin crossed the threshold, mindful of officers and crime-scene personnel passing through the room's center, presumably on their way to and from the location where the body had been found.

The suite was small with a line of uncomfortable-looking wooden benches near the front window. A large oval rug anchored the space between the waiting area and two reception desks—one for each attorney, she presumed. Cherry wainscoting climbed the walls to a matching chair rail, hip-high, and a severe green-and-maroon patterned wallpaper stretched the rest of the way to the ceiling. The lamps and light fixtures were brass. The paintings were landscapes, with gilded frames. Two offices with heavy wooden doors lined the back wall, separated by a narrow hallway and flanked by a sign indicating the way to the restroom.

"Kat?" An older woman with gray hair and pearls approached, clutching the necklace to her breastbone. "There you are. Where have you been? We were worried when you didn't come in or call. And your phone number goes straight to voice mail. We thought you might've quit for some reason."

Katlin worked up a smile—she hated the nickname Kat, and was unsure what to say to the stranger. "Sorry. I was in a car accident and lost my phone. This is the first time I've been able to come in." All true, she told herself, thankful not to have lied to the only person who'd paid any attention to her at the office so far.

The woman gave her a curious look, then belatedly took notice of Jack. "I'm Marsha," she said, offering a small wave. "Kat and I do administrative work here."

Jack smiled cordially, looking impossibly calm and charming in the awful situation. "Jack," he said. "Nice to meet you. So, which attorney do you work for? Or is it a team effort?"

"I work for Mr. Quintz," Marsha said, pressing a wadded tissue to the corner of one eye. She pursed her lips briefly and her eyes darted to Katlin. "Kat worked for Mr. Fitch. He preferred interns over regular full-time employees. It was his way of giving a hand to the next generation. Providing on-the-job experience with excellent credentials for coeds with an interest in law. He was a nice man." Her voice cracked on the final few words, and she moved the tissue from her eye to her nose.

Katlin had a lot of questions about those statements, like why had Marsha called her a coed when she'd been out of college for several years. More importantly, however, was the tense she'd used when speaking of Katlin's boss. "Did you say I *worked* for Mr. Fitch?"

Marsha batted away tears as she tracked the nearest police officers with her gaze. She sniffled, then stepped closer to Katlin. "The cleaning crew found him this morning." She looked at Jack. "They come in at eight and clean before the office opens at nine. The police were here when we all started showing up for work around eight forty-five."

Katlin tightened her grip on Jack's arm. There was no way that was a coincidence. She wondered how long the attorney had been dead. Since Saturday night, when she was run off the road?

Jack moved to a large desk near the window, leaving her to stand with Marsha several feet away.

"Is that your boyfriend?" Marsha asked, peeking discreetly over Katlin's shoulder. "He's very…nice-looking."

Katlin's cheeks warmed at the thought. Silly. Juvenile. Oh, so delightful. "Jack's a close friend."

"I like your desk," he called.

Katlin spun, pulse instantly rising. *Her desk?* Her desk!

He lifted a business card between his fingertips. "Very nice."

"Thanks?" Katlin asked, unsure about his point. Although she admired his steady confidence and the intensity in his eyes, Marsha was wrong. Jack wasn't nice-looking—he was hot and everything about him called to her. Those teasing hazel eyes, the breadth of his strong, broad chest and shoulders, the way he looked at her as if she was a treasure to guard at any price. The way he touched her like it was an honor.

Jack wiggled the card, clearly waiting for something.

"I think he's beckoning you," Marsha said. "But you should tell him we aren't supposed to touch anything."

It took a minute for the words to register through Katlin's muddled thoughts. "Right." She hurried to Jack's side, leaving Marsha to return to the others, a trio in white coveralls. Likely the cleaning crew.

Jack nudged the mouse and Katlin's computer sprang to life.

She immediately took a seat in her office chair.

The air around them was brisk from the open door, scented with old books and new carpet. Outside, Officer Jenkins stood in front of the window. His hands moved quickly as he spoke with the gathered crowd—rubberneckers and lookie-loos.

Katlin set her fingers on the keyboard and willed the password to come to mind. When it didn't, she tried the only things she knew. Her apartment's street number. The birth date on her driver's license. Word and number combinations for everything in sight. The law firm's name. The office address. Nothing worked.

Beside her, Jack poked through the contents of her desk drawers with a pencil. "New-hire paperwork."

Katlin spun in her chair. "Where?"

He tapped the pencil against a set of papers inside her right top drawer.

"I just started three weeks ago," she said, reading the date and doing the mental math. "So I might've moved here for the job. Do you think it's weird Marsha called me a coed four years after I finished college?" Was she changing careers? Why?

"Not really. You look young. Maybe she doesn't know all the facts," Jack suggested.

Katlin set her fingers back on the keyboard and gave the password another try. This time she entered her start date into the password field, and the computer unlocked.

"Nice," Jack whispered, leaning over her shoulder for a closer look.

Katlin double-clicked her office email icon and scrolled through her inbox. Dozens of unread emails awaited. Many were sent from the local courthouse, public defender's office and police station. "How much do you want to bet whoever shot Mr. Fitch was a client?" Katlin whispered.

Jack closed the desk drawer, then pressed his palms on the desk and hovered beside her. "You might've seen or heard something you shouldn't have. Maybe someone wants to be sure you can't repeat it."

Katlin shivered at the thought. Her boss was dead and she would be, too, if it hadn't been for Jack. "We should look into Mr. Fitch. See what kind of cases he normally takes and who his clients are. Anything that can help us figure out what the shooter wants kept quiet."

"Miss Andrews?" Officer Jenkins strode in their direction. His eyes were narrowed and his jaw set. "What are you doing?"

"Checking email," she said, logging out quickly and standing. "I thought I should work until I was questioned. I didn't want to waste time."

"Step away from your desk, please."

She obliged, and Jack followed.

"I spoke with Detective Reihl, and I'd like to ask you a few questions before you go."

Katlin swallowed a groan, steeled her composure and answered his questions without losing her mind or shedding a single tear. Once the officer was satisfied that Jack had told him everything already, she and Jack were free to go.

Katlin fizzed with anticipation as they made their way

back to Jack's truck and her e-reader. She'd checked her boring social-media sites earlier, but she hadn't had time to check her personal email before their arrival at the law office. Maybe that was where she kept all her secrets.

JACK NAVIGATED THE truck back through town, keeping close watch on pedestrians and other drivers. It seemed possible the criminal causing all the trouble could be loitering nearby, or at least driving past the murder scene. If not in the hopes of finding Katlin, then to check on the cops and see which direction they were taking the investigation.

Beside him, Katlin had plugged the e-reader into his charger and was sifting through her personal email, which, according to her, was mainly junk. Not the treasure trove of information they'd both been hoping for.

He stretched his memory as he drove, eager for some detail about her life that could spark a memory in her, or at least something she'd be glad to know. She often went to concerts with Griffin and took trips around the world with her parents. Parents that Cade had yet to reach via the only contact number they could come up with. The one Jack had from the year Griffin had died. Katlin had a degree in something and lived in a nice cottage in another town until recently. None of those things were useful to their current situation.

"Wait." Katlin clutched his forearm, and his foot hit the brake.

Katlin rocked forward and the e-reader toppled. Behind him, someone honked. "What are you doing?" she asked, her voice rising an octave.

Jack gently pressed the gas pedal and waved in apology to the driver behind him. "You said to wait. I thought something was wrong. Maybe you saw something outside or needed me to stop or turn back for some reason."

She swiped the e-reader off the floor with a grunt, her hips held firmly in place by the safety belt. "No. I found a link to my monthly bank statement and followed it over to the bank site. So far I've been logged in to all my accounts on this thing. It's brilliant. And guess what's being automatically deducted every month?"

Jack turned curious eyes on her, carefully keeping up with traffic. "What?"

"My utilities. Two sets of them, to be exact. Why am I paying someone else's utilities? And who do they belong to?"

An excellent question. He couldn't think of any reasonable answers and didn't know anyone in her life. "What are the addresses?" he asked, double-checking his rearview mirror before taking the country road that led to the safe house.

"Hang on. I'm not sure if I can access a copy of the bill here." She tapped the screen and scrolled.

"You just started working at the law firm. If you just moved to the apartment, you might still have a final bill for your previous address. That's not uncommon."

"I'm in at the electric company," she said, caught up in her research. "They're charging me for usage at the apartment we visited earlier and someplace out of town. Twelve forty-two Julip Lane, Stanford."

Jack nodded. "That's your last address." He would know. He'd sent cards there for three years.

Katlin made a low humming sound as she continued to tap the screen. "It doesn't say this is my final bill anywhere."

Jack beat his thumbs against the steering wheel,

searching for an answer that made sense. "What if you didn't move?" he asked, a new theory taking shape. "It would explain why your apartment didn't look lived in. Maybe it's just a part-time situation, and you still live at the other place, in Pine Hurst."

"Why would I do that?"

Another excellent question. "I'm not sure, but we can drive over there tomorrow and see if I'm right. I'd like to spend the rest of the day following local news coverage on Mr. Fitch's murder and reading up on him and his clientele. The sooner we make a connection between you and one of his clients, associates or friends, the sooner we can put together a possible suspects list for Detective Reihl."

"Okay, I guess," she said. "Better to prioritize naming the killer than worrying about what's going on with my living situation. Hopefully I wasn't living with someone and going through a breakup." She twisted slightly in his direction. "Though that would explain why I moved out and didn't take much with me. Maybe the bulk of the decor and furniture was his. Could that be what happened?"

Jack grimaced. "I hope not." The words were out before he'd thought better of them. "It would suck to leave a place you'd called home with so little of your belongings." Jack refocused on the road, hoping the explanation was enough to make him seem less worried about the possibility she had a boyfriend. "You should see if the e-reader is linked to any cloud storage. Maybe you can access recent photos."

"Good idea." She refocused on the e-reader. "I do," she said a moment later, sounding both surprised and impressed. "And I have a lot of Word documents. Do you think I kept a diary?"

"That would be incredibly helpful," Jack said. "I'm not sure we have that kind of luck."

Katlin was silent for several minutes as they continued back to the safe house.

Jack played a variety of explanatory scenarios in his mind. What did everything they'd learned today mean?

"Jack!" She gripped his arm again, her voice filled with sudden enthusiasm. "These documents aren't diary entries."

"It's okay." He shot an encouraging smile her way. "We'll figure it out."

"No." She shook her head hard and fast. "These files are interviews and news stories." She bit her lip, eyes twinkling. "I'm a reporter!"

Chapter Nine

Jack heated chicken-noodle soup on the stove top and tossed a pair of soon-to-be-toasted cheese sandwiches on the griddle. Now that Katlin had discovered she was a reporter, he could vaguely remember Griffin mentioning her writing. The high-school newspaper. A scholarship-winning essay. Her brother had bragged about her so often, the reasons had begun to blur. And it seemed to Jack she might've been a communications major in college, but he wasn't sure, and she hadn't come across her college details yet.

She was curled on the couch with her e-reader, her back to the armrest, her feet on the cushions, devouring every detail she could find about herself. The small, nearly outdated device was their only link to her life before the hospital, and she was determined to unearth all its secrets.

He'd opted to make lunch while she got lost in the articles and documents on her cloud storage. He'd needed the break from her immediate nearness. After he'd carelessly set his hand on hers in the truck, she'd been reaching for him at every turn, linking their arms and sticking close to his side. It was comfortable, pleasant and deeply maddening.

Jack gave the soup a stir and adjusted the fire beneath his griddle. Did she mean the touches to be so sweet and intimate? Was she growing close to him in a romantic way? Was she bonding with him as if he was a stand-in brother? Surely she didn't cuddle up to everyone as quickly or easily. Did she? And the possibility she'd just broken up with a live-in boyfriend clawed at the back of his mind. How bad must the situation have been to make her leave all her things behind? If the guy existed, Jack wanted answers.

He flipped the sandwiches then swiped his phone screen to redirect his thoughts. He typed the dead lawyer's name into the search engine while the buttered bread slowly turned golden brown. According to the results pages, Mr. Nathan Fitch was a criminal defense attorney. He received his law degree twenty-one years ago from the local university. He was divorced. Two grown kids. A home in a nearby gated community. The handful of news articles where his name appeared were favorable. The bulk of his cases were white-collar and usually dismissed.

"How's lunch coming?" Katlin called, already on her way to his side. Her shiny blond hair fell over her narrow shoulders, and light from the window behind her accented her luscious curves.

Jack set aside his phone, then lifted the corners of his sandwiches with a spatula. "Not long now. I hope you like grilled cheese and chicken-noodle soup. I found bread and soup in the freezer. Butter and cheese in the fridge. Seemed like a no-brainer."

She grinned. "Both sound and smell amazing. It's really kind of you to do this. I can't recall anyone ever cooking for me before."

"Funny," he said, trying not to smile at her joke, and feeling proud of himself for pleasing her. He did his best not to imagine all the other ways he'd like to please her.

Katlin hopped up to sit on the counter beside the stove, her backside just inches from where he'd rested his hand. Her enchanting brown eyes were level with his now. Her feet dangled over the cabinets by his thigh.

Jack's determination to clean up his thoughts weakened, and he instantly imagined reaching for her. Skimming her cheek with his fingertips, gliding the pad of his thumb across her perfect bottom lip before guiding her mouth to his and parting her slender thighs to make room for him between them.

He stepped back, forced his attention to the sandwiches, then removed them from the griddle. He plated the grilled cheeses and ladled soup from the pot, then moved their lunches to the small dinette table. "Did you learn anything new from your files?"

"Yeah. I'm probably biased since the articles came from my brain, even if I can't remember them, but I think I'm a good reporter. The articles were fascinating. I had fun reading them. I might've been a freelancer because I found my byline in a few different papers. Katlin Griffin."

Jack smiled. "A pen name. Interesting." No wonder he hadn't found the articles when he'd searched for details about her online.

"Makes sense if I wanted to maintain some measure of anonymity. Or if I was writing things about people that could've upset them."

"I'm sure you're an excellent and scrupulous reporter," Jack said. "Hopefully a trip to your house tomorrow will restore your memories. I researched your amnesia last night, and most people recover. Occasionally, a trigger will bring it all back. More often it just takes your mind time to relax and let it in. Though, you may never remember every detail of the accident itself. But the rest will come."

The warmth in her eyes softened him, and he longed to pull her close. He shook away the unfair thought. She needed a lot of things right now, but he wasn't one of them. And Griffin would never approve. He'd made that abundantly clear with a thrown punch after Jack had only complimented the photo of a woman he'd assumed was Griffin's date.

He set two places at the table, then looked to Katlin. "The rest of your things should be at the house. We'll get everything we need tomorrow, then let Detective Reihl know what we find."

Katlin hopped off the counter and made her way to the table. "Smart. We can ask my ex-boyfriend all about my life when we get there."

Jack fought the sour expression tugging at his mouth and lost. "Did you learn something from your e-reader about that?" he asked, taking a seat on the chair across from hers and hoping she was joking. His already complicated feelings for her didn't need another kink in the works.

"If I have a boyfriend or an ex, he hasn't reached out via email. Maybe we should go to my other address today. Why wait? Time is obviously of the essence, and I want to know more about myself. I can't understand why I stopped being a reporter. Or why I took the job at the law firm. Was it part of a story I was working on? Was I undercover? Had I been fired? Or did freelance reporting just not pay the bills, so I had to find another source of income?"

"All good questions," Jack said, dunking one corner of his sandwich into the chicken soup. He worried most about her first guess. It made sense that a reporter could find herself in sticky situations from time to time, overstepping boundaries or digging up skeletons better left buried. Research for the juiciest stories had to be tricky. And he could easily see the job at the law firm being a place to access records and eavesdrop, especially given the dead attorney's white-collar-criminal clientele. The scenario was all too plausible, and frankly, he wasn't in any hurry to take her back into the open, where she might be shot at again. Plus, there was plenty of research for him, and healing for her, to be done right where they were. "Let's stay in today," he suggested. "I want to see what we can learn online about Fitch's clients and hear what the evening news reports say on the subject before we head out again. Information is power right now, and we don't have much. We should make our trips short and sweet. Provide whoever's after you with as few opportunities as possible to reach their goal."

Katlin sipped soup from her spoon, apparently considering his suggestion. "Okay. I have plenty of files still to read, and I could probably use the downtime. My head never stops throbbing, and I'm a little tired."

Jack looked more closely at her then, tense with alarm at her admission of physical pain. "Why didn't you say anything?" He hadn't noticed the heavy fatigue hidden behind her smile before, but he should have. Even he was exhausted after the craziness of the past few days, and he hadn't been in a serious car crash. "You should rest. We'll eat, research, make a plan, then start fresh tomorrow armed with all we learn tonight and ready to ask the right questions." Whatever they were.

She bit into her sandwich looking a little unsure. "So you want to just hang out here the rest of the day? And night?" Her cheeks darkened, and her dark eyes flashed. "That sounds…really nice."

Jack worked to keep his mouth from falling open and ignored the painful jolt of desire that pulsed through his chest and into his jeans. There was nothing he wanted more than to protect Katlin, but he was starting to wonder who would protect him from her.

JUST AFTER BREAKFAST the next day, Katlin stood outside an adorable, but unfamiliar, cottage-style home in an inviting section of another town. Jack was still and quiet at her side as she took in the moment. "This is where I've lived for the past four years?"

"Yeah." He cast a curious glance in her direction. "Do you remember it?"

The cold weight of regret pressed against her lungs. "No." Three days had passed since she'd awoken in the hospital not knowing who she was. Each day, her body healed a bit more. She felt a bit stronger and hurt a bit less. But the firm block in her head remained. The frustration was infuriating. The need to relax and wait it out went against her natural inclination to fight and tackle her problems. Regardless of effort, tears and prayer, the memories were beyond her reach and control. Jack had been an incredible comfort to her the night before, when tears of anger and desperation had broken free. He'd held her, encouraged her and made her feel as if she could accomplish anything, even this, no matter how discouraging it seemed. His belief in her helped carry her through the night without another round of vicious self-pity. For that alone, she owed him everything.

"Do you have your key ring?" Jack asked.

She dragged the ring with six keys from her pocket and moved up the porch steps in answer, then tried each key in the dead bolt until one fit. The tumbler rolled and so did her stomach. Hopefully she was right about not having an ex-boyfriend who lived here, but maybe there was a roommate. It would be nice to get details from a person who knew her personally, but not too personally, since she couldn't remember ever being romantically or intimately involved.

The house was dark and silent as they entered. Jack flipped the switch by the door when Katlin drifted past, drawn by intense curiosity and need. She held her breath, listening closely for signs of another intruder, but there was only the pounding of her heart and ticking of a nearby clock.

Jack lifted a palm in warning, indicating she should stay near the door, then walked away. He moved swiftly through the home, clearing the rooms, she realized.

Katlin scanned the inviting space. A warm beige couch and armchair sat on a braided multicolor area rug with matching coffee and end tables. The throw pillows were white with rows of black script across them. She wasn't sure how, but she recognized the text on one as the opening page of *Harry Potter and the Sorcerer's Stone*, another as *Pride and Prejudice*. The entire space smelled like apples and cinnamon, likely a result of the unlit red jar candles on the tables.

"All clear." Jack's strong and level voice registered a moment before he appeared. He rubbed his palms together. "Let's see what we can learn."

A powerful wave of relief washed through her, and her shoulders sagged. Knowing she was safe, having him there with her and loving everything about the unfamiliar home around her, conjured a rock of emotion in her chest. Her eyes stung, and she covered her mouth with one hand as the weight of the moment tried to level her. "I lived here." The words were shaky and the torrent of feelings was nearly too much. "It's charming." She sniffled as she made a slow circuit around the obviously loved and cared-for rooms. There were framed photos on the walls. Stacks of paperbacks on the coffee-table top. And a row of tiny succulent plants in little pots along a windowsill.

She wasn't some half-homeless person living in a rundown apartment without connections to anything.

She was a reporter with a dead boss and weird apartment in the next town.

Tears were replaced with purpose as she moved more quickly through the first floor, trying to make what little she knew add up. There were no boxes or packing materials to suggest she planned to move. The bulk of her things were at this house.

Maybe she'd find her memories here, too.

She paused at the artfully arranged wall of photos, recognizing herself in most, frequently alongside Griffin. He was older in these photos than in the snapshot Jack had pulled from his wallet, but it was undeniably him. The older couple in multiple shots were likely her parents, though she didn't see a strong resemblance. Of the dozen or so framed images, all were of her family.

Family was important to her. She liked that.

She moved on to the kitchen, then stopped as a small table came into view. The two-seater, covered in papers, sat beside a window overlooking the backyard. And there was a laptop.

A broad smile spread over her face as she approached. The table had obviously been her work space, and whatever she'd been working on was still there, waiting for her.

Jack whistled behind her. "Jackpot." He pulled out the chair nearest to her, and she immediately sat.

She scanned the table, then the room at large, elated and eager. "A cell phone!" She thrust an arm forward, thrilled to see the device on the nearby counter, plugged in to a charger. "This house is magnificent. It's full of gifts, and I never want to leave."

Jack returned her smile. "Understandable, but we shouldn't stay longer than necessary. Just in case we were followed or the shooter figures out you rent this place, too. We can always come back."

A note of sadness tried to find purchase, but bounced instantly away as a new realization dawned. She felt her eyes go wider than her smile. "The phone Detective Reihl has isn't even my real cell phone." She barked a laugh. It probably wasn't very nice of her, but Katlin was glad the presumptuous detective, who'd made her feel as if she might be a criminal, didn't have her main cell phone. Everything about a person's phone was deeply personal. Not intended for anyone, especially local police, to comb through and pass judgment on.

Jack's eyebrows rose. "I guess not."

"Good. I need this one for my memory's sake. Hopefully there are some recent pictures on it. Maybe those will spark a memory."

Jack plucked the cell phone from the charger and passed it to her. "We can always call and fill her in on whatever we find, if it's relevant to the case. Otherwise, I don't see why she needs this phone. It wasn't part of the crash."

"Thank you." Gratitude filled her, and she stroked the back of his hand where it lingered on the table's edge. When he didn't pull away, she raised her eyes to his and found an intensity there that warmed her in all the best places.

"We can take whatever you want with us and go through it together at the safe house like before."

She returned her attention to the paperwork before her, clearing her throat and doubling down on her focus. A printout from the local college immediately caught her eye. "This looks like a class schedule. Don't I have a degree already?"

He frowned. "Yeah. I saw the pictures."

She turned the paper to face him. "Then why am I registered at Centre College in Danville right now?"

Jack frowned. "The town where you work and have a second apartment." He scrubbed a heavy hand over his impossibly short hair, then rubbed his nicely bearded cheeks in thought. "Taking graduate classes? Maybe the second apartment is just a landing spot for nights when you've been to work and class and can't make it home?"

Katlin considered the suggestion. It seemed financially far-fetched, but who knew? After the last few days she'd had, anything was possible. "The schedule doesn't seem like graduate work, but I'll look into it. Why does every answer lead to more questions?" She tightened her lips against a building tirade. "Nothing makes any sense."

"We're getting there," Jack said. "We have your phone and laptop now. Those should help."

Katlin tidied the papers and folders into a pile, then

swiped the phone to life. Her fingertip fit nicely into the small depression on its front, and the phone unlocked.

The thrill of victory whooshed through her as she went for the camera app and flipped eagerly through the snapshots, selfies and candids. She looked so happy in every frame. And she traveled. The couple she'd guessed were her parents appeared in pictures with her in Paris, Zurich and Rome. There were road-trip pics of her and a small redhead with cat-eye sunglasses and ruby lips. Group shots inside a newspaper bullpen. Katlin hiked, biked, camped, skied. Her heart soared and plummeted. She had a full and happy life, and she couldn't remember any of it. Worse, nothing in the camera feed gave a single clue about how she'd gotten mixed up with a killer.

She returned to the phone's home screen, then tapped another social-media icon. She hadn't seen the app on her e-reader. Her home page was basic and showed only a handful of friends and followers, most also students at Centre College.

The messages were short and direct, written across a selfie or snapshot. Katlin flipped through photos of friend groups, shared pizzas, football games and college-campus scenery. One guy's image caught her attention. He showed up more than twice as often as anyone else, and his username was Dylan_242. Blue eyes, shaggy blond hair. A bit of a skater vibe. His preppy clothes didn't support that theory. A rich boy playing at rebel, perhaps.

"Find anything?" Jack asked, striding back into the kitchen.

"I'm not sure. I found a lot of correspondence with this guy on a photo-messaging app." She passed him the phone then stacked the papers on top of her laptop for easier transport. "Give me a few minutes to walk around, then we can head back to the safe house and take our time with all this." She motioned to the stack of materials on the table.

"Or—" he said, his eyes flashing with mischief "—we can visit the newspaper."

He raised one hand into view, a lanyard dangling from his fingertips. The press badge had her photo on it, along with the name Katlin Griffin and the words *Investigative Reporter*.

"I work at the *Covington Gazette*."

Chapter Ten

The *Covington Gazette* was housed in a tall whitewashed building beside the local radio station. Like everything else in Katlin's life, nothing about the place felt remotely familiar.

She stared up at the endless windows and shivered against the brisk autumn air. The chill running down her spine seemed appropriate, given she had no idea what awaited her inside. Or if she even still worked there. She rubbed sweat-slicked palms against her jeans and prayed no one would want to shake hands.

Jack beeped the truck doors locked and moved into position at her side. "Ready?"

"Not even a little."

He set his palm against the small of her back, and she felt the zing of electricity to her toes. They moved slowly to the door, and she swiped her badge against the reader. The door buzzed and the lock released.

"I guess you still work here," Jack said.

That was one question answered. They'd discussed a dozen potential scenarios on the drive over, including the possibility that what she was going through had nothing to do with being a reporter, because quite possibly, she wasn't a reporter anymore. The badge could've been old.

She might've quit or been fired, then gotten the job at the law office for income. Maybe even decided to go back to school for a degree that more easily translated into a career. Who knew?

Those theories were officially out the window.

They crossed a marble-and-glass foyer to a welcome desk where a woman was on the phone.

Katlin lifted her badge, and the woman motioned them past with barely a glance.

"Tight security," Jack muttered as they climbed the steps to the second floor, following signs for the *Covington Gazette.*

Jack extended a hand to the door at the end of a short hall with the newspaper logo on it. "Here we are."

Katlin swiped her badge over the scanner, and the door unlocked.

Her heart hammered as Jack turned the knob and accompanied her into the office. A bustling world of activity whirled inside. Voices of rushing people rose above the clattering of keyboards and ringing of phones. Cubicles lined the far wall of windows and a center space was made up of simple, interchangeable white desks, each with a chair and monitor. Most were occupied.

Someone barked orders behind a closed office door in the opposite corner, and Katlin's heart raced. "This feels familiar," she whispered, mind humming. She was almost afraid to say the words, terrified of jinxing the new sensation.

Jack curled his fingers against her back in a move of silent support. "Anything specific?"

"No. Not yet, but it's good. It feels less alien than anyplace else I've been." She pulled in a steadying breath then pointed herself toward a closed door with lots of yelling coming from behind. Instinct told her that was the editor's office. If anyone would know what she was most recently working on, it would be the editor.

"Whoa!" A petite woman with bobbed red hair and glasses rounded a corner. She had earbuds in and a back-pack on, but stopped short at the sight of Katlin. She yanked out her earbuds. "Oh, my goodness. You're here!"

Before Katlin could formulate a response, the redhead launched herself across the room at her. She wrapped Katlin in a hug that knocked her back a few paces and required Jack's assistance to keep them upright.

"I can't believe it. I thought you were dead!" She re-leased Katlin suddenly and frowned. "Why haven't you called?"

"Hello," Jack said, flashing a charming smile. "I'm Jack Hale. You must be..."

The newcomer swiped shaky fingertips beneath each eye, ignoring Jack as emotion overtook her. "I was so worried about you. I thought something awful might've happened. I gave you seventy-two hours. I planned to call the cops and report you missing tonight."

"Sorry," Katlin said.

The redhead cast a curious, but fleeting, look at Jack, then refocused on Katlin. "Who's this guy?"

"Jack," he repeated. He extended a hand. "Nice to meet you..." He trailed off, waiting for the redhead's name.

"Maggie. I work with Katlin. She's my best friend."

Jack brightened his smile. "Great. You must know a lot about her."

"I do. She's like a sister to me. How do you know Katlin?" She folded her arms and examined Jack more carefully.

"I'm a friend of the family," Jack answered. "She's

showing me around while I'm in town. Did you two ladies meet at work?"

Katlin chewed her lip. She didn't like thinking of Jack as a simple friend of the family when he was so much more, but how could she define it all? And why did it matter? She gave herself a mental shove back to the moment.

"We went to Plymouth together, both majored in communications and got internships here after graduation. We've known each other for years." She swung her gaze back to Katlin. "Which is why I can't believe you haven't called. I've been sick. I haven't eaten in two days. I lost three pounds. Thank you for that last part, but all the rest sucks."

Katlin laughed. It was easy to see how she and Maggie had been friends.

"Did you get the story?" Maggie asked, her small frame going still. "At least tell me whatever you were up to was worth it, and that there's an excellent reason you scared me half to death."

Katlin shifted her gaze to Jack, unsure how much she could tell Maggie. Could she be trusted? If so, would telling her put her in danger?

"You say you're like sisters?" Jack asked Maggie.

"Sure," she said, a mischievous smile on her lips. "Family's not always blood, you know?"

"I do." He locked eyes with Katlin and gave a nearly imperceptible nod. "Is there somewhere more private where we can talk, Maggie?"

Maggie frowned. "I guess." She looked to Katlin.

"Please," Katlin said.

Maggie turned and headed for an empty cubicle near the window. The neighboring unit was empty, as well, and the man at the nearest desk wore headphones. Maggie hopped onto the desk and sat on a giant paper calendar, dangling her feet over the drawers. She motioned for Katlin to take the office chair. "What's up?"

"I have amnesia," Katlin said, jumping into what was sure to be a confusing and bizarre conversation.

Five minutes later, she'd shared all the key points of her nightmare, and Maggie stared back, agape.

"So you really don't remember anything?"

Katlin shook her head, nonsensically ashamed. She'd researched cases of memory loss like hers over the last two days and knew she was likely to blame. Specialists believed patients intentionally blocked things they couldn't deal with. In Katlin's book, that equated to cowardice. It wasn't just her life on the line anymore. Jack was right there with her, and her subconscious still chose to protect itself over him. Was she so emotionally delicate she couldn't face reality? Was this kind of thing typical of her? Her stomach sank at the thought. It wasn't who she wanted to be.

"Nothing?" Maggie asked, sweeping a hand meaningful between them. "Your work? Your past? Your family? Me?"

"I'm sorry."

Maggie hopped off the desk and closed the space between them, then wrapped her arms around Katlin. "That must be so awful. I wish I could fix it."

Jack cleared his throat. "Maybe you can help."

Maggie released Katlin, a hopeful look in her eyes. "Anything. Name it."

"Tell us whatever you can. About her life. The story she's working on. Anything. Maybe something will trigger her memories," he suggested. "Or at least help us figure out who's been trying to kill her."

Maggie's expression was aghast before she looked suddenly delighted. "Come with me."

She led the way around the shared cubicle wall to the empty unit beside hers. "This is your desk."

Snapshots of Katlin and Maggie hung on the padded walls. "I have this one on my phone," Katlin said, pointing to a selfie of her and Maggie on a road trip. Photos of a man in his dress uniform, she recognized as her brother, and others of her with him on mountaintops and at concerts, littered the space above her monitor. She touched the corner of one image, wishing with all her heart to remember.

"You were working on a story about the upcropping of gambling rings near local college campuses," Maggie said. "You did a lot of the general research here. You can probably check the history on this computer and read up on the information you started with."

Katlin took a seat and booted up the computer, thrilled with the salacious detail. "College gambling rings," she mused. "That explains why I'm registered for classes when I already have a degree, and why I have a second, barely furnished apartment in the next town."

Jack moved in beside her chair and crossed his arms. "What else can you tell us?" he asked Maggie.

"About the case? Not a lot. About Katlin? Everything."

Katlin groaned at first sight of the log-in screen. "Any chance you know my password?"

Maggie lifted the desk phone and pressed a few numbers. "No, but I know how to get it." She winked. "Hey, it's Maggie at the *Gazette*," she explained into the receiver. "Katlin forgot her password. Great. Thanks!" She hung up and grinned. "Toby's our IT guy. He likes me. He's in the middle of something for someone else, but he's going to reset your password in a minute and call back to let us know it's done."

"Nice." Katlin gave her friend a high five. Meanwhile, she could go through her desk for clues. "Let's see what I keep in here."

Maggie pulled a photo off the wall. Griffin and a group of others in fatigues. "Is this you?" she asked, passing the picture to Jack.

Katlin turned to wait for his answer.

Emotion raced across his face and disappeared before Katlin could name it. "Yes. Griffin was my best friend."

Maggie's jaw dropped. "So, you're The Jack?" she asked, eyes wide. "Like Jack-Jack?"

"Yes?"

Maggie pursed her lips, but a little smile broke through. "Holy wow, and I suppose you don't remember him, either?" she asked Katlin.

"I just met him after the car crash," Katlin said, suddenly wondering if Jack had lied about that for some reason.

Maggie laughed. "Maybe not, but you're crazy about him. You talk about him all the time. He sends you cards every year on Christmas and your birthday, and he always leaves his phone number." She pressed her hands to her chest. "It's the sweetest thing ever, and you love it." She leaned closer to Katlin's ear and lowered her voice. "You saw him at Griffin's ceremony for something or other the year we met, and thought he was the dreamiest. You asked Griffin about him all the time, and Griffin hated it. You loved getting him going, so you teased him mercilessly about coming to visit him so you could get to know Jack better."

Jack chuckled.

Katlin's cheeks flamed hot. She sat taller and changed the subject. "I found a laptop at my house, but it's locked. I don't suppose I could bring that in here and have your friend in IT take a look?"

Maggie frowned. "No. They're always busy down there with help-desk stuff. And I don't know him well enough to ask him to look at it after hours. Did you try Griffin's birthday? You use that a lot. Or the number from his Green Beret group. Troop?" She turned her attention to Jack. "Platoon?"

Jack tugged the sleeve of his thermal shirt over one elbow and up his biceps. "This number?"

Katlin tried not to swoon. New personal discovery. She liked strong, muscled arms. And she loved that ink. "Thanks."

The desk phone rang, and Katlin jumped.

Maggie snagged the receiver off the cradle. "This is Maggie. Thanks!" She hung up and typed six zeros into the prompt on Katlin's screen. "He said to change it once you're in."

Katlin pressed Enter, and the screen unlocked. She quickly changed the password and began to search her mail and files.

"Did you find the Green Beret thumb drive?" Maggie asked. "Your story's probably on there. You were tight-lipped last week about progress, but you said it was getting really big. I guess you were right." Her voice grew sad on the final sentence. "I can't believe you were out getting amnesia and shot at, and I had no idea. I'm a terrible friend."

Katlin lifted a hand. "I'm sure that's not true. I didn't know to look for a thumb drive. Where do I keep it?"

"Around your neck on a chain usually," Maggie said,

her gaze dropping to Katlin's chest. "Your brother sent it to you. You guarded it with your life. You have to remember the thumb drive."

"I remember nothing," Katlin grumbled.

Maggie rubbed her back. "Sorry. It's just so weird."

"It's okay," Katlin said. Maggie was right. Amnesia was weird. "If I normally wore the thumb drive on a chain, I wonder if it could've fallen off in the car." She looked to Jack. "We should call Detective Reihl, and maybe check with the hospital." She sighed. "That's all going to take forever. Plus, we'll have to search two residences, and it's probably small enough to be almost anywhere."

Jack pulled his cell phone from his back pocket. "Hopefully that wasn't what the intruder was looking for when we interrupted him at the impound lot and again at your secondary apartment."

Maggie sighed, drawing Katlin's attention. "I hate that you're going through all this alone. What else can I do?"

Jack moved to the far corner of the little workspace and turned away as he pressed the cell phone against one ear. "Detective Reihl, please. This is Jack Hale."

"I'm not alone, and you're already helping," Katlin told Maggie. She pulled the cell phone from her bag and used her fingerprint to unlock it, then swiped to the photo-messaging app. "Now that I know I was looking into a college gambling ring, it makes sense that I'm registered for classes at Centre College. It also explains why I got a job and an apartment in Danville. I created a total cover." The story must've been truly huge to go through all that.

Katlin flipped to one of the many photos of Dylan_242, then turned the phone to Maggie. "Any idea who this is?"

Maggie smiled. "That's Dylan. You've been getting close to him because he's connected to the gambling somehow. He's invited you out for coffee a couple times, but you're still waiting for an invitation to play. You should open the message."

Katlin turned the phone back. A small icon indicated a new message. "That wasn't there before." She clicked the message with bated breath. Did Dylan know who she was and what she'd been up to? Was he the one who'd run her off the road? The one who'd shot at her?

The photo message that opened wasn't of Dylan, it was a snapshot of the river at night with a strange invitation written on the image. "He wants me to take the boat out with him tonight." Katlin wrinkled her nose. "It says the dress is black tie and I should tell the captain I can swim."

Maggie squeaked. "'Take the boat out' is code for their underground casino nights!"

"And the captain is what?" she asked. "The doorman?"

Maggie raised her shoulders to her ears, still smiling. "Maybe? Are you going to go?"

Jack tucked the phone back into his pocket and returned to her side. "No."

His low, authoritative voice mixed with her much higher one as she declared, "Absolutely."

Chapter Eleven

Katlin chewed her bottom lip. The prospect of attending an underground gambling night was terrifying, but if it meant understanding what she'd gotten herself into and who was trying to kill her, she had to check it out. At least she wouldn't be alone. She had Jack, and he had an entire team of former military men on his side.

She scrutinized her reflection in the safe-house mirror, hoping she'd chosen the right look for the night. Jack hadn't been much help. He'd taken her back to her place to find a dress, clutch and heels, but he'd been too distracted making plans with his teammates by phone to help her choose. He'd continued organizing with the team when they'd visited Fortress for his suit and tie. At least Katlin and Jack wouldn't be alone tonight, whatever happened, and she was immensely thankful for that. Two of the teammates were already on their way to set up surveillance outside the venue now, before anyone else arrived. By the time the party got started, all signs of the Fortress men would have vanished into the landscape.

Katlin sighed and twisted in front of the mirror as light reflected off the beads and sequins of her black cocktail dress. The material hugged her body, emphasizing all her curves, then stopped midthigh. The plunging V in back nearly reached her tailbone. Thankfully, the neckline was higher, lying modestly across her collarbone. Still, there was no way to wear anything comfortable underneath. She'd found adhesive bra cups and a barely there pair of panties among her lingerie. So far the pieces were all working, but only time would tell.

She'd had more fun than she'd expected putting on her makeup and was surprised to find she was good at it. The routine of liquid eyeliner, powder and lipstick was comfortable and familiar, as was the process of blowing out her hair and securing it into a neat chignon.

She turned at the sound of steady footfalls in the hall outside her room. A moment later, Jack appeared. He was stunning in a perfectly tailored black suit and tie. His shoulders seemed impossibly broader, his waist more narrow. He'd shaved the small amount of hair on his head and tidied his beard for the occasion. Her fingers curled at her sides, desperate to touch him.

"Wow." He moved slowly into the room, his gaze darkening as it slid over her from head to heels. When his sharp hazel eyes flashed back to hers, there was heat there she hadn't seen before.

"Too much?" she asked, turning back to the mirror and selecting a pair of simple gold hoop earrings.

He whistled long and slow behind her, and she caught his gaze in the mirror as it returned from trailing over the deeply revealing back of her dress. "You look stunning."

"Thanks." She secured the second hoop earring, then turned to face him, admiring his strong square jaw and kind eyes. It was easy to imagine that he was hers, and they were off to a night on the town, a friend's wedding or other normal celebration. One where he would hold her close and she could pull his mouth to hers, kiss him tenderly and often. "This could be it," she said, feeling both hopeful and afraid. Tonight's outing could hold the keys to all her secrets and end the reign of terror on her life. Tonight's outing could change everything. "We might get all our answers at this event." Much as she wanted that to be true, she still didn't have her memories, which left her vulnerable and unsure how to pick up with a life she couldn't recall. More than that, she wasn't ready to say goodbye to Jack. Would he leave her when the job was done?

"We can hope," he said. "My team's in place, so we can go whenever you're ready. My guys will have eyes on the venue's outside and be listening through a microphone on my lapel. If anything goes awry, they can call 911 and get help to us in minutes. In the event of an emergency, they'll beat first responders to our aid. Hopefully it turns out to be an uneventful night, and we can fill in Detective Reihl on whatever we learn tomorrow morning."

Katlin took a steadying breath and nodded. She'd called Jack, a virtual stranger, while being run off the highway, not the police. That had to mean something, so she wasn't ready to just give the address of the event to authorities and hope for the best. Not until there was an officer she trusted as much as she trusted Jack, and that night wasn't tonight. She lifted her chin and tucked her clutch under one arm. "We shouldn't keep the team waiting."

Forty minutes later, Katlin climbed out of Jack's truck at the docks and shivered against the cool autumn breeze.

Jack met her at the front bumper and reached for her hand. "Try to relax," he whispered.

She nodded, feigning calm until her teeth began to chatter.

The air off the water felt like ice on her exposed skin.

And the faint scent of brine and decay lingered forlornly in the air. Water lapped lazily against the docks, where a dozen cars and trucks were lined up in the shadows, including, she noted, one ratty-looking unmarked van. Presumably containing the Fortress team.

"Were you able to reach your parents?" Jack asked.

She shook her head, fighting nerves and trying not to chew her lip and ruin her lipstick. "I know parents would want to know what's happening, but I don't remember them. Every time I started to dial the number in my contacts, I hung up before hitting Call."

"Do you want me to call?" he asked, brow furrowed in concern. For her? For her folks? She couldn't be sure, but loved that even in this small task of contacting her parents, he was willing to be her hero.

"No." She smiled. "I'll do it." Just not tonight. She took a step forward, and Jack joined her, setting a warm hand against the exposed small of her back.

He leaned in close as they moved toward the only visible door on the nearby building. "Someone is likely watching the area, so we need to look like a happy couple on a date." His breath blew softly over her ear, sending shivers down her spine and causing heat to pool in her core.

He grazed his lips against her temple. "Now smile as if I'm the only man you ever want to take you home." The featherlight caress curled her toes in the black stiletto heels and a small moan dropped from her lips.

Her eyelids drifted shut to absorb every ounce of the moment.

The low bleating of a boat horn made her open her eyes, reminding her that this wasn't a date. It was a reconnaissance mission in the industrialized section of the docks. And finding the man who was after her was literally a life-or-death assignment.

A man in a black suit, shirt and tie opened the door as they arrived. Someone had been watching, Katlin realized, and her stomach coiled tight with paranoia.

"This is a private party," he said sternly, widening his stance and glaring at Jack.

"We're aware," Katlin said, forcing a frown and air of pretension she didn't feel. "I'm an excellent swimmer."

The man's scowl relented with recognition of the strange password. He raked his narrowed gaze over Jack, then stepped aside to let them pass. "Have a nice night."

Katlin clutched Jack's arm as they moved down a dark hallway into another world. The sounds of chatter, laughter and the shuffling of cards could be heard behind a dark curtain several yards away. The clanking of chips and glasses played the score.

Another man in a dark suit parted the curtain as they arrived, and he ushered them inside.

Mile-high ceilings soared overhead in the abandoned factory. On the floor, a perimeter of temporary walls had been set up.

Dozens of people filled the space that was ringed with gaming machines and makeshift bars. Multiple green-felt tables with serious-looking card players occupied the center. Roulette wheels spun between blackjack and poker tables with onlookers lingering at every turn.

Jack wrapped a protective arm around Katlin's back. "Not quite the outfit of craps and beer pong I'd anticipated for a college gambling ring," he whispered.

A size-zero waitress in a slinky black gown stopped before them with a tray of drinks. "Champagne? Scotch?"

Katlin drained a champagne flute, then returned it

and selected a second. She gave an apologetic smile to Jack. "Sorry."

His lips curved up in a grin. "Better?"

"A little." She wet her lips and concentrated on breathing. "I don't know how to gamble, and I really want to kick the former version of me who dragged me into this." She cringed. "That didn't even make any sense."

"It did," he assured her, curving his fingers against her side. "We'll get this sorted, then you can do yourself a favor and chase leads on community do-gooders and adopt-a-pet events."

"Deal," she said. "But I'm not sure what I'm supposed to be doing here and now."

"Just keep your chin up and your eyes open," he said. "Let that dress do the rest."

She wasn't sure what that meant, exactly, but she liked the look in his eyes when he said it.

They made a sweep of the room, discussed their gaming options and provided his listening teammates with a general layout of the place, just as they'd talked about in the truck.

They stepped apart when Jack spotted Dylan. Jack turned to watch another game while Katlin waved to the stranger and hoped she could make him believe she remembered him. Or anything.

It only took a moment before Dylan noticed her. He wound his way through the crowd, drink in hand. "You made it." He stopped to kiss her cheek, then checked her out. "Hot damn. That dress is smoking." He ogled a bit longer, and she struggled not to cross her arms over her chest. "No one will be able to concentrate with you here. I might be in trouble." He laughed. "I've got a few losses of my own to recoup."

Katlin smiled back warmly. "Thanks for the invitation. This is wild."

"It is." He sipped his drink, head bobbing as his gaze made a jumpy circuit around the room. A small tremor in his hand belied his cool demeanor. "These parties are a good time until you're losing."

She felt an icy stab of terror on his behalf. Owing money to this group wasn't good. She'd crossed them somehow and they were out to kill her. "I'm not much of a gambler," she admitted, "and I'm pretty broke."

"Don't worry about it," he said. "You're doing me a solid by coming. They like it when we can get women who look like you to stop by. The big fish enjoy the company and admiration. Then they come back. Maybe I can catch a break if they know I invited you."

Katlin stiffened. "I don't understand."

He nodded to a line of older men at the blackjack table. "They feel younger, surrounded by people our age, and it feeds their egos to show off with gorgeous women around to watch."

"Oh." She relaxed into a playful laugh. "Funny. And I assumed this was just a Centre party."

"Not even close." Dylan set his empty glass on a passing server's tray and swiped a full one.

The feeling of being watched returned to her and she fought to keep her smile in place. She hadn't just stumbled onto a thriving college gambling circuit. This was a massive operation, and she'd clearly been in so far over her head, she couldn't see up. Fear and regret for her former self twisted through her. She must've been completely terrified when she'd realized. Must've felt so alone. No wonder she hadn't shared any details with Maggie. Knowing would've put her in danger, too.

But why hadn't she called the police? The question scratched again at the back of her mind. Had she been waiting for an invitation like the one she had tonight? Was the plan to get the location of the next party, then send officers in to raid it? Was that what she should be doing right now?

Dylan's voice faded into the background as she searched for the cause of her growing internal panic. A few men raised their drinks and winked as she met their eyes, but they quickly turned back to their games. Bouncers barely noticed her. Waitresses didn't seem to see her at all.

And then she saw him.

A man in his thirties stood at attention near the edge of the space. His face was unfamiliar, but his stance and frame were burned into her mind. Instinctual fear clutched her heart and demanded that she move. Demanded that this was the shooter who'd come for her so many times already. "Excuse me," she said, cutting off Dylan from whatever he was saying. "I'm sorry. It's a little warm in here and I haven't eaten today. I'm going to get some air."

Dylan smiled, clearly unoffended by her interruption. "Finish your drink," he said. "I'll grab you some fruit from the bar." He turned away, and Katlin spun in search of Jack.

"I'm right here," he said, already reaching for her. "What's wrong?"

"I think the shooter's here, and I think he recognized me."

Jack's posture was tight as he scanned the room. He pulled Katlin into his arms and moving her toward the door. "Blue eyes, salt-and-pepper hair?" he asked.

"Yes."

"Got him. Let's move out. You guys getting this?" he asked, pressing a finger to his lapel.

Katlin craned her neck for a look behind them, praying she was wrong. "He's coming," she whispered.

"Keep smiling and moving toward the door," Jack said. "Once we're outside my men will offer cover. Any sign of trouble, and the police will be on their way."

Katlin's breaths came impossibly faster as they reached the door and bypassed the man she'd given her password to.

"Stop!" a deep voice bellowed as their feet hit the dark pavement and they launched into a sprint.

She dared a look behind her, and found the shooter, widening his stance and sliding a hand inside his jacket.

"Gun!"

Chapter Twelve

Adrenaline spiked in Jack's veins. Katlin's scream registered at nearly the same moment as the gunshot. "Run!" He gripped her hand as they dashed across the parking area, darting between cars for cover, past stacks of abandoned railroad ties and derelict dinghies.

Katlin shrieked and ducked as a second shot rang out, covering her head with her free hand and stumbling on her heels.

"Keep moving!" Jack called. He understood her instinct to take cover, but the truth was that once the shot was heard, it was too late to get out of the way. All they could do was keep moving and hope his team got their backsides in gear.

Katlin rallied, matching his pace, despite the constricting dress and ice-pick heels.

Several yards away, a set of headlights flashed on, and the silhouette of a van peeled away from the other vehicles. Its engine growled as it sped toward them.

"Your team!" Katlin cried, relief and joy in her breathless tone.

A third shot exploded the window of a nearby car, staunching her joy and making her fumble over her feet.

Katlin screamed once more, this time going down on one knee.

The damaged car's alarm rang out, its lights flashing, and voices erupted behind them. Gamblers rushed from the building to see what was happening.

Jack scooped Katlin onto her feet when she didn't stand quickly. "Are you hurt?" She hadn't been shot. The bullet had hit a car several yards to the left.

"My heel broke!" she seethed, her voice feral as the van tore past them in the night.

The tires squealed as his team changed directions, rocking wildly to avoid them.

Jack used the fob to unlock his truck doors, and Katlin dove inside. Jack joined her, gunning the engine to life as the sound of gunshots continued. Muzzle blasts lit the night as he wheeled the truck away from the scene—he hoped none of the gamblers or staff were injured in the cross fire.

Other vehicles quickly joined them in their escape, headlights bobbing and weaving in his rearview mirror.

Katlin rocked on the seat beside him, struggling with her seat belt and angling for a look behind them. "Someone's firing on the van," she cried. "Everyone's leaving the building. What if someone's hurt because of me?"

"My priority is you." Jack pressed the gas with more purpose, needing to put as much distance as possible between Katlin and the danger. His team could hold their own, and they'd likely called the police at the first sight of the gun.

Seconds later sirens wailed in the distance, and Jack relaxed by a fraction. When the emergency crews and police cruisers tore past them, clearly on their way to the docks, he took his first deep breath of the night.

Katlin doubled over.

"Hey." He gripped her bicep, pulling her upright. "What's wrong?" He scanned her small body for signs of blood or injury. "Everything's going to be okay. My guys are well-trained and the police will be there any minute."

Katlin turned wide, tear-filled eyes on him. Her cheeks were scarlet, her lips quivering. She had one high heel in her hand and slammed it against the floorboards. She bent forward again, levering the other shoe off while she cursed and Jack processed the complaint.

He'd been sure she'd passed out beside him, but she'd been taking off her broken shoe? She wasn't sick with distress or limp with fear? She was mad at her broken heel? A small chuckle broke across his lips. "I don't think those particular shoes were meant for evening sprints over concrete."

She glared in his direction, blinking in and out of sight as streetlights passed over them, casting her in occasional darkness. "That was no college gambling ring," she griped, ignoring his comment. "What the hell did I get involved in? There was big money in there. Armed guards. Who apparently have no problem shooting at their guests."

Jack worked to loosen his grip on the steering wheel, then changed lanes and headed for the next road out of town. "Hopefully the team got some photos of the people going in and out. Maybe the shootings haven't been about the gambling itself."

"Like maybe someone important gambles with this group, and I got the scoop that could ruin him or her?" she asked. She'd said something similar to him while looking at all the clearly affluent middle-aged men at the card tables. A ragged sigh escaped her, and she flopped heavily against the seat back. "Why do I chase stories like this? Why put myself in danger? For what?" she asked. "Nothing. And I'm sorry if it offends the woman I once was, but I don't want to be a reporter anymore. I want to get answers for the police on this case only, regain my memories as soon as possible and be done with all of this nonsense. It's crazy!" She swiped tears from her cheeks, looking more angry than sad.

He glanced between her and the road, unsure how to respond, or if she was in shock.

His phone buzzed, and he pulled it from his pocket, thankful for an excuse not to say the wrong thing and potentially meet the business end of her broken shoe. "Hale." He listened as Wyatt gave him a rundown on the situation at the docks, then hung up to relay the details to Katlin, who'd turned to stare out her window.

"Wyatt says everyone got out of there before police arrived. There was a mass exodus when the shooting began. The shooter went back into the building, but didn't come out, and the cops said the building was empty."

"Empty?" Katlin's face reddened. Her jaw set.

He reached for her hand on the seat between them and discovered a clenched fist. "Hey, breathe. We knew this wasn't an amateur operation. They cleared the people as soon as shots were fired and were probably already tearing down the casino as they fled. There were enough men and women staffing the event to accomplish a lot in a short time if they hustled."

She hacked a deep, throaty sound of disgust. "Hustled? They probably run drills for practice."

"Probably," he agreed. "You want to talk about all this yet?" He ran the pad of his thumb over the back of her hand, working to relax her fist. "I'm an excellent listener."

She rolled her eyes. "I'm angry and scared and about a dozen other things I can't even put names to, but mostly I want to slap myself for choosing this life. I don't want to be in danger or on the run like this. I should've turned everything I knew about the gambling over to the police and let them sort it. Instead, I probably wanted the glory for breaking some big undercover story, and look at all the trouble I caused. Mr. Fitch is dead because of my need to get this byline."

"You don't know that," Jack said, feeling a strange tug of possessiveness in his heart. The cavemanesque thoughts were piling up, deep and high. *No one talks about my girl like that*. Except, Katlin wasn't his girl. She was just a gorgeous, sassy, fearless woman he had the good fortune of spending time with until she was safe and her memories returned. She'd had a full life already in progress before they'd met. One without him in it. "We don't know anything right now," he said, nonsensically defending her against herself, "other than the fact you're in danger."

Her hand unfurled from its fisted position, and she turned her palm beneath his, spreading her fingers, allowing his to slip between. "The shooter is still out there. What if he never stops coming for me?" she whispered, sounding vulnerable enough to break his heart. "Whoever's behind the gambling is making big money, and I tried to get in the way. No amount of time is going to make someone like that drop the vendetta. And I'm not even the same person I was when I started all this. I can't even remember her."

Jack's heart twisted. "Your memories will return. You need to give it time. And cut yourself some slack. You've got to stop blaming yourself until we have all the facts."

She rolled her head against the seat, looking away from him. "I was nearly killed in the car accident. I lost my memories. I'm shot at daily. Living on the outskirts of nowhere," she said miserably, "practically in witness protection. And I've got no one to blame but me."

Jack released her hand in favor of the wheel and refocused on the long, dark country road ahead. The sharp edge of her words cut into him, and he cringed with an unexpected lance of pain.

It was clear and reasonable that she'd hate her current situation, but which parts were the worst, and were there any bright spots? Did she only loathe the truly ugly parts, or was he just one more nasty piece in an unwanted box set of awful?

And why did it hurt so much to think that might be it?

"I can't go back to work if I'm on the run," she said abruptly, seeming to catch a second wind. "Even if I get my memories back, I'll have to stay in hiding. If I can't work, how can I live? Afford my rent and bills? I can't even go into actual witness protection because I don't know anything. I've got no leverage."

"We'll figure it out." He cast a glance her way, hating that he hadn't been of more help to her yet, and that despite his best efforts, she was unhappy. "I'll help. Whatever comes, I won't leave you until this is all over and I know you're safe. It's understandable to be scared."

"I'm not scared," she snapped. "I'm angry."

Their eyes met in the dark cab, illuminated briefly by the there-and-gone flash of oncoming headlights.

Jack tensed, then laughed. "Fair." How was he so terrible at guessing her moods? How was she so good at surprising him when so few people ever did?

"I meant it when I said I don't want to be a reporter

anymore," she said, "but I also don't want to be a murder victim, so I guess this is my last story. Which means I have to finish it." She turned to look through the windshield, chewing her lip and working her jaw. "I need to see this through."

"All right, then let's start with a pot of coffee or tea and call Fortress," Jack said, the night's events replaying neatly in his head. "We can trade information and try to work out what it all means. That'll give us a bigger, clearer picture of what we're dealing with. Then we can decide what to do next."

"First, I want to go to the law office," Katlin said. "No one will be there at this hour, and I want to look around without being watched by Marsha, the cleaning crew or a cop. Maybe something there will kick my brain into gear."

Jack frowned, unsure. "I get that you want to be proactive, but I don't think breaking and entering is the way to go right now, especially if you're trying to avoid the police."

"Who's breaking in?" she asked, a sly smile forming on her pretty mouth. "I have a key." She lifted the law-office identification card from her clutch, along with her ring of keys.

Chapter Thirteen

The dark sky opened and rain poured down as Jack parked the truck behind the offices. It had been one hell of a night so far, but he reasoned that the shooter from the docks would be in hiding for a couple of hours while his team of criminals regrouped. “The locks might have been changed,” he warned. “If so, we leave.”

She nodded. “Got it.”

“If anyone’s inside, we leave immediately,” he continued. “We don’t want our names on any more police reports. And you stay where I can reach you quickly in the event things go south.”

“Deal.” She tugged her door handle, then slipped into the dreary night before he could add another stipulation.

As if he could stop her. He nearly rolled his eyes at the thought.

He followed her to the back door of the law office, vigilant for signs of potential witnesses or shooters.

She dashed through the icy rain expertly and on tiptoes, managing her broken heel like a champ. She swiped her badge, and the small red light flipped to green. The snick of a rolling dead bolt drew a smile on her face.

And an alarm wiped it off.

“Shoot!” Katlin bounded to the keypad beside the door

and punched in a code before he could pull her away. The alarm went silent.

They stared at one another in the aftermath, waiting for what would happen next. When nothing did, her shoulders relaxed and the broad smile returned.

"You knew the code," he said, a ribbon of awe and hope winding in him.

"It's the last four digits of my social security number." She shrugged. "They probably make the codes personal so the system can track who comes and goes."

He lifted his eyebrows. "You knew the code," he repeated, and she froze.

Her mouth opened and closed, then she threw herself at him. Her arms circled his waist, and she squeezed him tight. "I know my social security number," she whispered.

His arms curved around her narrow back on instinct. His tall frame curled protectively over her. "Told you," he whispered back. "You've got this."

She wobbled in his arms, and he let her go. "Sorry." She bent to peel off the mismatched pair of heels, one broken and one not. "We should hurry," she said. "Just in case anyone's tracking visitors here. I can see why they might after what happened to Mr. Fitch." She hurried toward the front of the office and the desk that held all her things.

Jack forced his eyes not to linger on the deeply cut back of her sexy dress or the miles of bare legs visible below a very high hemline. He tried not to imagine running his fingers along that hem, inching it up from behind while planting hot kisses down her bare spine. He didn't mean to wonder what it would feel like to pull her back against his chest and rid her of the little dress altogether…

She turned and caught his eye, a wicked smile stretching over her face. She'd caught him ogling her. Wanting her. And she knew it. "Everything okay?"

"Mmm-hmm." He cleared his throat and nodded into the darkened room. "What now?"

Katlin wet her lips, returning his appreciative gaze and allowing her attention to linger unashamedly in places that made him want to moan. "We think I moved here to chase the gambling story," she said a moment later, slightly breathless. "So I probably got the job here for a reason, too. Maybe for more than just proximity to the college. I could've worked at a fast-food place on campus if that was the only goal. Instead I went after the internship Fitch offered."

Jack nodded. "So what are you thinking?"

"That I was a schemer." She offered a self-deprecating smile. "Cunning, manipulative and possibly not a nice person."

"You were thorough, thoughtful and effective," Jack said. "You had a goal and you went after it. Griffin would've been very proud. It takes courage to do all the things you did to get to the truth."

She crossed her arms, looking pensive and a little uneasy. "My memories of him feel so close to the surface. Him more than anything else. Something tightens in me every time you say his name, but it's all completely out of reach. I hate it."

"I know." Jack stepped closer, leveling her with his most encouraging stare. "No one can blame you for the frustration, or for anything else you're feeling. You've been through a lot. Are still going through a lot. But Griffin thought you were fearless. He said you faced every trial with your chin up, and he loved that. I think he was right, and I know it helped him worry less about you being here alone in the States."

"It's funny," she said, looking inexplicably guilty and a little ashamed. "Because being afraid is nearly all I've done since I woke up."

Jack pressed his hands to his sides, willing them not to reach for her. To hold and comfort her. Griffin would absolutely not approve of that, and Katlin didn't need more complications in her already messy life. "Well, I think you've handled it all very bravely. Now that we're here, where do you want to look first?"

She released a long, heavy breath. "Right. I'm wasting time." She turned for her desk.

"That wasn't what I meant."

"I think we should look at Fitch's client files. According to the internet, he handled a lot of high-profile white-collar crimes. Mostly mild-mannered schmoes. They embezzled. Committed fraud. Tried to make themselves richer or more powerful. No murderers or career criminals."

"Those white-collar crimes are in-line with what we saw tonight," Jack said. "Fancy dress. Big money. Important people. Could one of his clients be behind the gambling ring?"

Katlin's mouth formed a small O. "That's an excellent theory. Why don't I go through my desk while you take a look in Mr. Fitch's office? We can divide and conquer. Take pictures of whatever you find so we can evaluate it all later, without having removed anything from a crime scene."

Jack smiled. "On it." He moved swiftly into the office where he'd seen officers swarming earlier. The bloodstained carpet was a gruesome indication that this was the right place.

He selected a pencil from the mug on the desk and used it to open and poke through desk drawers.

A small gasp drew his eyes to the doorway a few moments later. Katlin was leaning against the jamb. Pale and unsteady, a visible tremor racked her limbs.

Jack rushed to her side, reaching for her the moment he was close enough. "What is it?"

She accepted his touch, pressing her body against his as she shook. "I don't know. This office just..." Her voice quaked and her teeth began to chatter, cutting off her words. "I have this awful, icy feeling and it's telling me to leave. Now."

Jack rubbed his palms up and down the cool skin of her exposed back. "Here." He released her to slip out of his suit jacket and set it over her shoulders. Something he should've done long before. "We can leave as soon as you're ready."

She nodded, tugging the jacket more tightly around her and pinching it closed at her chest. Beads of sweat clung to her brow despite the visible chills. "I don't know what's wrong with me. I feel sick, dizzy and panicked, but nothing happened. I just walked in here to say my desk was clean. The computer's gone."

Understanding lit in Jack, and he folded her into his arms. He should've recognized the symptoms immediately. He'd seen them countless times. Even experienced them himself. "You might be having a panic or anxiety attack." He caressed her cheek with the back of one hand as he looked into her eyes. "Possibly PTSD. You could've seen something bad in this room. Maybe being here again triggered the reaction."

She sucked in a ragged breath. "What if I was here when Fitch was shot?" she asked, gaze fixed on the bloody carpet stain.

He took her by the hand as he stepped away. "We should go. There was nothing to see here. Fitch's computer is gone, too. Probably taken into evidence by the police."

She backed away from the office, and Jack followed, thankful that they were finally on their way home. *To the safe house*, he mentally corrected, not their *home*. Though a piece of him could see her in his home. In his arms. And in his bed.

"Wait." Katlin drifted into a nook with filing cabinets and storage boxes. She opened one and frowned at the contents. "Who keeps paper files anymore?"

"They could be backups or just old," Jack suggested. "From before everything went digital." He watched as she worked methodically through the drawers and boxes, flicking past names and sliding hanging folders along the narrow silver rails. She stopped at the third drawer of the second cabinet and turned wide eyes on him. "No *P*s." She stepped back to give him a clearer view.

The space inside the drawer, behind a tab with a bolded letter *P*, was empty. There were plenty of files behind the tab with a letter *O*, and lots more crammed into the space meant for files beginning with *Q*s and *R*s, but… "No *P*s," he echoed.

The grin that followed was cut short as a flash of light swept over her face.

Jack ducked into the shadows, pulling Katlin with him.

Beyond the glass back door, a police cruiser was patrolling the alleyway where Jack had parked the truck. An officer climbed out and shined a light into the truck's windows, then circled the vehicle, pausing on the opposite side.

"Did you lock the doors behind you?" Katlin asked.

Jack watched the officer closely as he circled the truck. "Yeah."

"What's he doing?" she asked, setting two small palms against his chest and drawing Jack's attention to her incredible warmth and nearness.

"I'm not sure." He had to force his thoughts away from the feel of her warm breasts pressed to his torso. When he returned his attention to the alley, the officer was inside his cruiser and pulling away.

"Good. He's leaving, and we should, too," Katlin said.

They stepped carefully out from hiding and made their way toward the back door at the end of the hall.

The jingling and clanking of bells on the opening front door hurried their pace. Katlin swiped her discarded heels from the tile floor, where she'd left them, without missing a beat.

Jack checked in both directions before pulling her outside.

For the second time that night, they hit the pavement running.

He kicked himself mentally for agreeing to bring her here. There was no telling who'd just come into the office through the front door. The police? A shooter? Had Jack put Katlin in harm's way again? Or put her in danger of being arrested for disturbing a crime scene? He had to stop saying yes to her every request like an idiot in… He stopped himself, pulling up short mentally as the final word circled in his mind. *Not like a man in love.* Jack had been in love before, and it hadn't been anything like this. For him and Cara, love had taken years to build. The intense and wholly complicated feelings he'd developed for Katlin were something else entirely. And he didn't have time to think about what they might be.

He beeped the truck doors unlocked as they ran toward the vehicle, now only steps away.

A small red flash beneath the truck slowed his pace, reflecting on a rain puddle near the front wheel. Jack's feet dug into the ground, and his forward momentum ceased with a jolt. Katlin stumbled as their connected arms snapped tight.

"What is that?" she asked, pointing to the crimson shimmer on the water's shallow surface. Her eyes flicked to his in fear and recognition. "Jack?"

A sick sense of realization coiled deep in his gut. His jaw locked and his tongue seemed to swell. He pulled her back, curling an arm around her middle and sweeping her off her feet as he turned for the sidewalk. He managed three or four long, pounding strides before—

Boom!

The truck exploded behind them.

Chapter Fourteen

The world seemed to shake around them. Jack's ears rang, and his vision blurred as he tightened his grip on Katlin and curled himself protectively around her small body. He thanked the stars for their vast difference in size, making it easier to shield her from the flame and debris. They crashed onto the sidewalk in a painful heap, half tripping, half thrown by the force of the blast.

He rolled quickly away from her, careful not to let his heavy and aching body crush hers. Knives of searing pain sliced through his back and shoulder as he pressed against the icy sidewalk, his limbs momentarily weak.

Above him, the night sky quivered with apparitions of heat, and orange flame licked into the air.

"Jack!" Katlin's panicked face appeared in his view. She hovered over him, pressing shaky palms against his beard, jaw and chest. "Jack!"

He pushed onto his elbows with a groan. "Are you okay?" he rasped.

"You're hurt. Bleeding." The terror in her tone sent a new ache through him. He longed to reassure and comfort her. But they needed to move. If the shooter came by now, they'd both be dead.

"I'm okay," he said, forcing himself into a seated position and squinting to straighten his vision. He needed to get his bearings, then get Katlin out of here. Somewhere safe, where they could call his team and wait for an extraction.

"Your back!" Katlin moved onto her knees for a better look at the damage. "Oh, my gosh. There's so much blood. What can I do?"

He shook his head. "Nothing. I'm fine. Help me up."

"You're definitely not fine." Her small hands pressed against his shoulders, anchoring him firmly to the sidewalk. "You need medical attention. We're staying until you get it."

He wanted to argue, but the fact that he hadn't regained enough strength to shake away her small hands suggested she was right.

The distant cry of sirens slowly carved through his mental haze, and the previous few moments returned to him like a slap. Someone had blown up their ride. Only seconds before they would have been inside.

His focus snapped to Katlin's dirty, scraped-up face. "Are you hurt?"

"No. You're hurt," she said, her voice frantic as she waved her hands helplessly near his shoulder. "Someone blew up your truck. We could've been in it. And your back is burned and bloody." Fear tightened her tone, and emotion colored her cheeks. "There's so much blood. I don't know what to do. How are you not upset? Are you in shock?"

Jack rocked onto one hip with a wince, then freed his cell phone. He pressed his finger against the screen to unlock the device, then passed it to her. "It looks worse than it is. Call Wyatt. Let him know we need a ride."

Katlin took the device and made the call, mumbling

under her breath about Jack not being able to see the wounds on his back. How would he know what they looked like? She returned the phone to him with a smug expression. "Wyatt's on the way. He said to make sure you see a medic or he won't let you in his car."

Jack frowned.

The ambulance turned onto the street at the end of the block and rolled slowly in their direction, accompanied by a police-cruiser and fire-truck tail.

Katlin retook her seat at his side, tugging the hem of her little dress as she arranged her filthy, beat-up legs in front of her. "The police are going to know I used my code in the law-office security system," she said. "I'm going to tell them about my amnesia and admit it was a poor decision on my part, but that I'd hoped being somewhere familiar would jar my memories." She leaned against him, and rested her head on his shoulder. "Do you remember how all those *P* files were missing from the drawer?"

He inhaled the unique scent of her, able to identify it even in the midst of chaos, in an alley thick with smoke from the fire. "Yeah." He breathed deeply, allowing the familiar and comforting scent to anchor him. Whatever else had happened, Katlin was okay. He'd protected her. The pride in that realization expanded his chest and refilled his sails.

"I didn't think of it before now," she continued, clearly unaware of the powerful connection and unexpected attachment his heart was revealing. "There was a note on my desk calendar. I was supposed to remind Fitch about a dinner meeting with Peterson on the night of my crash. That's not a coincidence, right?"

Jack pushed to his feet with a groan. "Nope." He needed to get his head in the game.

It was normal to feel attached to someone he'd shared so many near-death experiences with. It was the way he felt about his brothers at Fortress. His brothers from combat. He ignored the voice at the back of his mind that demanded he knew better than that. He'd only felt this way once before, and he knew full well what was happening.

A pair of EMTs launched from the ambulance, now parked at a safe distance from the burning truck.

The fire truck rushed in closer, firemen jumping immediately into action.

Katlin stood and gripped Jack's elbow when he swayed. "You should sit."

"No." He looked her way, his vision focusing and his mind racing. He was eager to leave his unexplored feelings for another time. "Any chance you know that kid Dylan's last name?"

"No, why?"

Jack shook his aching head, sending knives through his brain. "I read an article last night that mentioned the chief of police here. Thomas Peterson. He's got a kid at Centre College."

"Dylan," she whispered.

"Maybe," Jack said, moving slowly to meet the EMTs. "Find out, but don't say more than you have to when the police get here."

"I won't," she agreed, keeping pace easily at his side. "There was a police cruiser out here just before the explosion."

He locked her in his gaze as the EMTs arrived. "I know."

They were in much deeper trouble than he'd imagined.

KATLIN EASED ONTO the couch beside Jack, careful not to jostle him as he rested. His back and shoulders had been singed and cut by bits of flying glass and debris. The paramedics had confirmed what Jack had told her. The wounds looked worse than they were. Lots of blood from multiple fairly shallow lacerations. They'd cleaned and bandaged the worst of it and given him an over-the-counter medicine and a prescription-strength one, then let him go at the scene. Meanwhile, she'd been completely unharmed. A few scrapes and bruises from their awkward landing on the sidewalk, but nothing that needed sutures or a medic's attention. Thanks to Jack.

Her heart warmed as she offered him a cup of steaming tea. "It's good for easing tension," she said. "You have to relax for optimum healing." A sudden idea of how she might aid him in his relaxation popped into her mind, and she felt her cheeks flush hot with the dirty visual. She'd been learning quickly how many things amnesia hadn't caused her to forget, like the impact physical desire had on a daily routine. Vivid intimate images of her with Jack had interrupted more serious moments and conversations than she would ever admit.

And when Jack had told responding officers that he and Katlin were out enjoying the night together as part of their date when the bomb went off, she'd been shocked at how badly she wished that was true.

Jack hiked an eyebrow. "Katlin?"

"Hmm?" She pressed her lips tight. She'd done it again, wandered into a shamefully lustful daydream while Jack was hurt and miserable. "Sorry, what?"

He shifted for a better look at her, and his broad, muscled arm brushed hers. His skin was warm and flushed from a recent hot shower and the scents of soap and shampoo clung to his clothes, a mere T-shirt and sweatpants. "I said I spoke to my team and researched the chief of police while you were in the kitchen." He handed her the tablet from his lap. "Wyatt and Sawyer are following up on what happened at the docks. Reviewing footage collected from the scene while the place emptied and reaching out to local police contacts for any other information they can get. They're going to call in a few minutes and bring us up to speed."

"Great." Katlin examined the article on the tablet's screen. A family photo of police chief Peterson, his wife and his son, Dylan, anchored the small write-up. Dylan was younger in the photo and dressed in a private-school uniform, but according to the article, he'd been accepted to Centre College. "So we were right. I'm attending Centre to get to know Dylan and grab the scoop on the gambling ring. I didn't call the police because Dylan's dad is the chief." She looked up. "Do you think that means I didn't want his dad to know I was investigating, or that I thought his dad wouldn't listen if I tried to alert him?"

"I don't know." Jack sipped the tea and grimaced. "This is terrible."

"It's not." Katlin laughed. "It's chamomile."

He nodded in mock understanding. "That's another word for awful?"

"Stop." She shoved his shoulder gently, enjoying the moment of levity before resting against his side. Her gaze landed on the fireplace mantel across from them. Her brother's memorial flag had been placed at the center.

"I hope that's okay," Jack said, following her gaze to the flag. "I saw it with your things and thought it should be displayed."

"Of course." She warmed further to him, even while

kicking herself for not having taken the time to put the flag on display. It didn't matter if she remembered Griffin. He'd given his life for her freedom, for their country. He deserved to be remembered, and his memory deserved to be respected. "I look at that flag and something in me tightens," she admitted. A foggy sense of patriotism, or memories for Griffin just out of reach? She couldn't be sure. "I know how important it is and exactly what it means. I wish I could remember him."

"You will." Jack reached for her hand. He curled his strong fingers over hers. "All of this will be over soon, and a year from now it'll probably feel more like a dream than reality, but it will be over."

"Thanks for saying that," she said, her heart expanding impossibly further in appreciation. "I couldn't do any of this without you." She shifted on the cushion for a better look into his sincere hazel eyes. "I'm sorry your truck was blown up. And I hate that you're hurt."

"Thankfully, I'm not nearly as delicate as I look," he said, the corners of his lips curling into a rueful smile.

She rolled her eyes and smiled back. As if anyone looking at Jack Hale could think he was anything less than lethal. The newly shaved head, sexy hipster beard and eight-pack abs screamed dangerous. Add the Green Beret tattoos, and prowling way he moved, and he might as well carry a warning sign. Her favorite part of all was that, for her, he was gentle, sweet and kind. For her, he felt a lot like she imagined coming home would feel.

"And no one cares about the truck," he continued. "There's always another truck. There's only one you. What matters is that you're okay."

There was a new tenderness in his eyes. And it called to her in a way she couldn't ignore.

Katlin set a tentative hand on his chest as their gazes locked. She trailed her fingertips over his soft cotton shirt, enjoying the responsive flex of his pectoral muscles. He watched her closely, expression guarded, as she tested the physical boundaries between them. Katlin wondered if she was right to think he felt the incredible chemistry and unique connection between them, too.

His jaw clenched and his gaze darkened as she inched closer, flattening her palms against the hard planes and ridges of him. She glided her hands tenderly over his ribs and abs, then up and over his shoulders, exploring the nape of his neck before curling her fingers into the fabric of his shirt.

"Thank you for saving me," she whispered. "For protecting me. For coming to the hospital and keeping me alive. Thank you for being kind to me, even when I'm infuriated with myself."

He lowered his heated gaze to her mouth, and her lips parted in response. In request. She longed for him to close the distance and devour her.

A low moan escaped him as he reached for her. He latched steady fingers around her wrists and her heart skittered into a sprint. "Katlin, I can't," he said, and tugged her hands gently away. The expression of utter heartbreak on his handsome face was nearly enough to steal her breath. "I'm sorry."

"Why?" she asked stubbornly, allowing him to drop her hands into her lap. She lifted her chin and ignored the deep humiliation flaring inside her. She longed to run to her room and slam the door, but refused. She knew Jack felt whatever was brewing between them. She'd seen it in his eyes and heard it in his tone.

Hadn't she?

"It's my duty to protect you," he said, his voice gravelly and thick. "I promised Griffin as he died. I made a vow, and I owe him that. So I can't do this." He motioned between them before setting his hands against his thighs. "I'm sorry."

Defiance stiffened Katlin's spine. "That was what Griffin wanted. What do you want, Jack? Not Griffin. You." She waited, hating the conflict in his eyes. "I get that guys want their friends to stay away from their little sisters, but explain to me why. Why wouldn't he want the man he trusted most in this world to be with the woman he most wanted to see most cared for and protected? You're citing guy code as your big reason, but I'm calling your bluff. My brother trusted you with his life. Why wouldn't he trust you with me?"

She relented then, suddenly as disappointed in herself as in Jack. A small, humorless laugh bubbled to the surface, and she shook her head. "You know what? Red-hot chemistry or not, I don't want a man who puts anything ahead of me or ahead of us. So maybe you're right. We shouldn't do this."

Jack's gaze lowered to her mouth once more, and Katlin cocked an eyebrow in challenge. "What do you say, Jack? Friends?"

A low cuss rumbled in his throat as he reached for her, then wrapped his broad hands around her hips and tugged her close. His eyes searched hers a long moment before he pressed his firm, hot mouth to hers. The taste of chamomile lingered on his lips. His hands moved in tandem up her back, urging her closer. When he tilted his head and swept his tongue across her bottom lip, she yielded eagerly to him, parting and accepting as he deepened the kiss.

Katlin's arms wrapped around his neck, and she stretched one thigh across his lap to straddle him. Her breasts swelled and ached with need and a desperation to be touched by Jack. She imagined him rising and carrying her to his bed. Willed him to touch her more and everywhere as she met his tongue stroke for stroke. She gasped when his hands fell low again, gripping her backside and pulling her hips against him in one powerful move.

Kiss broken, their breaths were short and ragged while they evaluated one another. Her lips tingled from his kiss and every part of her wanted more.

She waited, unsure. She hoped he wouldn't tell her the kiss was a mistake, not when she was certain she had never been kissed like that before. Maybe no woman ever had. The touch, the heat and the connection had been perfection, and now he stared back, speechless.

What did it mean?

Jack leaned his forehead to hers and curled his solid arms protectively around her back, drawing her to his chest.

In the silence that followed, she could already feel him pulling away.

Chapter Fifteen

Jack fell asleep dreaming of Katlin's kiss. The scent of her skin and taste of her lips. The way her delicious curves fit perfectly against him, and all the ways their bodies could have fit together even better.

And he woke berating himself for the weakness.

Yes, Griffin would want his sister to be happy, safe and cared for, but he would absolutely not want the person meeting all her varied needs to be Jack. He'd made that clear when he'd nearly knocked Jack's head off for commenting on her looks in a photo. If Griffin could somehow know about half the thoughts Jack had had about her since they'd met, he'd be waiting for him on the other side of eternity with a rifle. Or a grenade.

Aside from the guilt of breaking a vow to someone who'd saved his life multiple times and in many ways, Jack wasn't sure how to justify getting physically involved with anyone who was under such duress and without her memories. What if she suddenly recalled she didn't date military men or that she preferred guys with suits and 401(k)s? He cringed internally at the thought. He'd never be a corporate drone. Never willingly push papers and put on thirty pounds while staring mindlessly at a screen full of statistics or client orders. That wasn't any kind of life for him. He grimaced as a far worse thought registered. What if Katlin was one of those women who liked docile, geeky men, not ones who'd survived foreign battlefields when most of their team members hadn't?

He forced himself out of bed with a grunt and headed down the hall for a shower. A cold one.

"Good morning." Katlin's voice rose through the quiet house, drifting to his ears from the kitchen on a whiff of fresh-brewed dark roast. "Coffee?"

"No thanks," he answered, bypassing the bathroom in favor of saying a proper hello to Katlin before getting on with his day. He told himself he was just being polite. He didn't need to see her now that he knew she was awake. It was simply good manners to greet her in person.

"Are you sure?" She stepped into view at the end of the hallway, a steaming mug cradled in her hands. An oversize gray T-shirt hung askew from her narrow shoulders like a nightshirt. Four large black letters stretched across the tempting curves of her chest. *ARMY.*

Griffin's shirt, he realized, feeling the reminder like a kick to his gut.

He lowered his gaze from her apparently braless breasts only to find a perfect set of slender thighs at the hem of the shirt. Bare thighs. And just like that, the fantasies returned. He wanted to greet her tantalizing mouth with a searing morning kiss, and satiate her sexy-as-hell body with gratuitous morning sex. And he wanted it more than he wanted his next breath.

He accepted the mug with a grin, dragging his gaze back to hers and admiring the heat in her deep chestnut eyes. "Thanks."

She bit the corner of her lip, honey-blond hair slightly mussed from sleep.

And he felt the familiar swell of his near-perpetual erection since meeting her. She knew she got to him, and damn if he didn't like it.

But he had to keep his head in the game. Before they could be more than just a protector and his charge, he needed to get her out of harm's way for good. That meant concentrating on his job. No more touching. No more kissing. No more moments of weakness. To do that, he was going to need a much colder shower than originally planned.

KATLIN CURLED ON the safe-house sofa with her e-reader, warm beneath a blanket and enjoying a fire in the fireplace. She'd opened a digital book from her library and was attempting to concentrate on the story line, but couldn't keep herself from imagining Jack's hard body in the steamy shower.

She glanced at the clock and frowned. He'd run off almost an hour ago and hadn't returned. Surely he was out of hot water by now.

She flipped the pages of her digital book, no longer seeing the words. Her gaze rose to the flag on the mantel across from her, and realization returned with a snap. Jack was still worried about what Griffin would say, and he wasn't taking an hour-long shower. He was hiding from her.

So much for enticing him with her oversize T-shirt and hot coffee.

She pushed onto her feet and headed down the hallway, hoping she was wrong. With everything else going so poorly in her life, she needed Jack to want her more than he wanted to please her brother. The chemistry between her and Jack had been present since the moment they'd met, and it had grown into something solid and comforting these last few days, not to mention something downright intoxicating. To deny that would be insane and heartbreaking. In fact, with all the awful things they kept facing, it only seemed fair that they should have a little fun. She wasn't trying to rope the man into marriage. It wasn't as if she was falling in love with him. She only wanted to explore what they had going already. Was that so wrong?

The sound of a slamming car door stopped her in her tracks. Her muscles tensed and her senses went on high alert as she imagined the shooter at their doorstep. "Jack," she called, moving quickly down the hall, past the empty bathroom and through the open door to his room.

He closed his laptop and pushed casually onto his feet. He'd dressed in jeans and a Fortress Defense T-shirt that clung to his sturdy frame. "Wyatt's here," he said.

Her shoulders sagged in relief. "Wyatt?"

"Yep." He gave her baggy shirt a cursory glance. "You should probably put on some pants."

Katlin crossed her arms over her chest as Jack slipped past her into the hall, completely unaffected by her yet again.

A moment later, she heard the front door sweep open. "Come on in," Jack said. "Thanks for coming."

The cold sting of rejection slapped her cheeks as she scurried to her room.

Jack had not only been hiding from her, but he'd also called in backup!

She dressed in a rush, sliding into a soft pair of jeans and even softer V-neck sweater. She brushed her hair and dashed her lashes with mascara, her lips with gloss. Whatever the men were talking about, she didn't want to miss it. She hoped the flush of embarrassment was gone as she hurried to meet them, following the sounds of their voices to the kitchen.

"We were able to confirm Dylan is police chief Peterson's son," Wyatt said as she joined them at the table. "Hey, Katlin. How are you holding up?"

"Okay," she said, lancing Jack with a stare. "He was hurt, not me."

Wyatt glanced at Jack, unmoved. "Still, you've had one hell of a week."

"I have," she agreed, not wanting to talk about it. "So we know Dylan is police chief Peterson's son, and that Attorney Fitch had a meeting with one of them on the day he died," Katlin said. Peterson wasn't an uncommon name, but based on everything else they knew, it seemed the sensible jump.

Wyatt nodded. "That's what I'm thinking."

"But we don't know how much the chief knows about the gambling ring or his son's involvement," she said. "Or even if his dinner meeting with Fitch had anything to do with either."

Wyatt rubbed a palm against his stubble-covered cheek. "Right again. I don't suppose you know how we can get our hands on the missing files? Maybe Fitch kept digital backups somewhere."

"Maybe," Katlin said. "I don't remember, but even if there are backup files, we wouldn't be able to access them legally." She tapped her thumb against the tabletop. "Maybe we should take another look inside my apartment. According to Maggie, a friend of mine from the newspaper, I keep the details of my research on a thumb drive Griffin gave me."

"I heard," Wyatt said, looking from her to Jack. "I can

go look around for it if you'd like. You'll be safer here. Any idea where you kept it?"

Katlin's head ached, and her jaw set. "No." That was the whole problem, wasn't it? She couldn't remember anything. If she had a clue of what was going on, she probably could have ended it by now. If she'd awoken at the hospital knowing who she was and who had hurt her, she would've made a proper police report and the criminals would be in jail by now. Instead, her inability to recall anything at all meant the person who'd tried to kill her on the highway had gotten several additional opportunities to take a shot. And the gambling ring was still going strong and her boss had been murdered. The frustration built in her like pressure inside a volcano, bubbling and brewing its way to the top. "Excuse me."

She slid her chair away from the table then made her way to the guest room in the safe house. Her temporary home, while she waited for her brain to work properly again.

Tears pricked her eyes, burning and blurring her vision until she reached her bed and fell onto the mattress in exhaustion. This stupid amnesia. This life. Jack's rejection earlier this morning after the most perfect kiss in history last night. It was all too much, and knowing how easily she could fix things with a single memory put her emotionally over the edge.

She wanted to scream and kick and throw things. She wanted to run until her limbs trembled from exertion and her mind cared about oxygen and nothing else.

She wanted Jack to hold her and tell her again that all these bad things were not her fault, and that very soon it was going to be okay.

"Katlin?" His voice pulled her into a sitting position,

and she swiped a few renegade tears as they rolled over her cheeks. Why did she have to be so emotional? Why did he always know the exact moment she needed him most? "You okay? May I come in?"

"No."

He narrowed his eyes. "No, you're not okay, or I can't come in?" He took a tentative step closer, then waited.

She chewed her lip, unable to meet his eyes.

Jack moved to her bedside. "I'd assumed it was all the talk about your awful week that sent you running, but now that I'm here, you look kind of ticked off." He took a seat beside her. "Since you barely know Wyatt, I'll assume I'm the one who made your hit list. I'm sorry."

She pulled her feet onto the mattress and shook her head. "I just needed a minute. Everything feels so overly complicated."

"Want to talk about it?"

"No. I just want my memories back, and I want you to stop avoiding me." She paused to let the accusation settle. In case he hoped she was too dim to have realized what he was doing today. "I can't control either of those things, and letting problems work themselves out isn't what comes naturally to me."

"I'm not avoiding you," he said, sincerity burning in his rich hazel eyes. "Your safety is my number-one priority. My feelings, however? Aren't even in the top one hundred."

"What about my feelings?" she asked, knowing the stubborn protector would likely tell her that feelings had to come second. She hated the rationale and the fact that she understood it even more. What good would it be to act on the frenzied passion that thickened the air between them even now, if the distraction cost them their lives?

"I care about your feelings," Jack answered gently. "That's why I'm here with you instead of out there with Wyatt. I need to know that you're okay. Are you?"

"No." She twisted her lips into a deep frown and held back the need to scream at the unfairness of life.

Jack dipped his chin in acceptance, then opened his arms.

And Katlin fell in. She wrapped herself around him, rested her cheek against his strong chest and let her eyes close, trying to hold the moment inside. His shirt was soft and warm. His arms strong and protective. She longed to be closer, to climb onto his lap and stay there until all the ugly things outside his embrace had long passed.

He rested his chin against the top of her head. "I'm sorry you're going through this."

"Thanks."

"But I'm glad you called me that night," he said.

Katlin pulled in a long uneven breath and tightened her arms around him. "You don't mind being bombed and shot at?"

"I'm getting in loads of cardio."

She laughed and heard his smile in the words.

"Anything for you," he whispered. The words came so softly, part of her wondered if she'd imagined them. Still, her heart ached for the statement to be true. It couldn't be, of course, because there was something he wouldn't do for her. He wouldn't break a promise to her brother.

Thinking of Griffin brought rise to an epiphany of sorts. She wiggled loose to stare at Jack. "I know why my decision to be an investigative reporter feels so unnatural," she said. "I think I did it for him. Not for me." Realizing the incredible pull her brother had on both

Jack's life and hers made her wonder if Griffin had been a magician or was just that loved.

Jack's brow furrowed. His eyes darkened. "Who?"

"Griffin," she said, taking Jack's hand. "Now that I can't remember him, I also can't understand why I'd ever have chosen this life. It feels like an act I put on. Pretending to be brave and courageous. I'm none of those things, but I probably wanted to be because it would've made my brother proud, and he'd clearly meant everything to me."

"You never had to try to make him proud," Jack said.

Her heart broke a little more. Because the only person she wanted to be proud of her right now was the man sitting there beside her.

Someone rapped against the open door, and Katlin sprang upright, releasing Jack and moving quickly away.

Wyatt looked at Jack with wicked curiosity, then turned his gaze on Katlin. "He's right, you know? I met Griffin in boot camp, and he adored you. I remember him talking about his little sister more than he talked about some of his girlfriends. He thought you were going to change the world, and he would've done anything for you."

"He'd have done anything for anyone," Jack said, a note of reverence in his tone. "He was one of the best men I've ever known."

"Me, too," Wyatt agreed. He watched Katlin closely, then added, "You'll get your memory back soon, but until then, we'll keep you safe."

She bobbed her head, unable to form words. A thick wedge of appreciation lodged in her throat.

"You like chocolate?" Wyatt asked, unexpectedly changing the subject. "My wife, Violet, baked brownies this morning and sent them over for you. She said people under stress need chocolate."

Katlin felt the tightness in her throat relax slightly and a smile bud on her lips. "I like chocolate."

"Good. Come on." He waved her to join him, then moved out of the room and into the hall.

Katlin followed with Jack on her heels.

"I know no one can replace your brother—" Wyatt said, casting a look over his shoulder "—but you can consider our team your brothers now. Maybe the four of us can fill some small piece of the void left in Griffin's absence."

Jack set a warm hand at the base of her spine, and Katlin felt her shoulders square.

It wasn't fair for her to want Jack to choose between a vow made to a dying brother-in-arms and her. She felt guilty for ever thinking it. She'd never know what it meant or felt like to be in Jack's position, but she knew what it felt like to be her right now, and she stepped away from his touch.

When she gave away her heart, the man had to be all in.

Chapter Sixteen

The sun was high in the sky as Katlin walked with her ridiculously attractive new "brothers," Wyatt and Jack, along the sidewalk outside her house in town. She appreciated the idea of having a team of capable men on her side, and more than one person in her life, but she sincerely hoped Jack didn't think of himself as her brother. That would be definite salt in the wound.

They'd swung by Fortress to collect a new vehicle after they'd finished making a plan for the day, then followed Wyatt to the cottage and gotten to work. They'd searched methodically through every nook and cranny of the older house, nearly taking the adorable home apart board by board in search of the Green Beret–logoed thumb drive where she kept all her research. Yet, they were leaving empty-handed.

They walked with Wyatt to the corner where they'd parked the trucks. They still wanted to give her part-time apartment another look and perform additional reconnaissance however they could. Maybe visit her car at the impound lot during business hours and ask to go through it. Or revisit her cubicle at the newspaper.

Wyatt crossed the street to his truck, then turned back before climbing inside. "Where to next?"

"We'll cover more ground if we split up," Jack said. "We got shot at while visiting the car and at her other apartment. Maybe you can try one of those first. No one will know you." He turned his eyes on Katlin. "We can talk to your friend at the paper again. You'll learn more from her than Wyatt will."

"Sounds good," Wyatt said, climbing into his truck without further discussion. He powered the window down and hung an elbow over the frame. "Touch base when you finish there and we'll choose our next destinations."

Jack beeped the doors unlocked on their new loaner and nodded.

Katlin climbed inside and buckled up, then began a mental list of random questions in search of a memory. Any memory. She'd begun the exercise two nights ago in what was so far a failed attempt to recall her life before the crash.

What's my favorite movie? Favorite color? Song? Scent? Food? Katlin took a silent beat between questions, waiting for an answer to rise from the enormous, endless void in her mind. She curled her fingers in frustration at her sides as she realized she had no idea what her favorite movie or song was, but her favorite color was the unique mix in Jack's eyes. Pale amber and brown irises flecked with bits of baby blue and every shade of green imaginable. Her favorite scent was his cologne. Her favorite food was the soup and toasted cheese sandwiches he'd made her. She moaned at her ridiculousness, then jumped at the sound of her phone.

"Is that you?" Jack asked, pulling away from the curb and heading toward the newspaper.

She wasn't sure if he meant the moan or the phone, but

both were true, so she simply said, "Yeah." She answered the call, catching Jack's eye as she spoke. "Hello?"

"Katlin!" Maggie was out of breath on the other end of the line. "Thank goodness. I called you like three times. Where were you?"

Jack glanced back at Katlin as he slowed at the next intersection. His eyebrows rose in question. "Everything okay?"

"I left my phone in the truck," Katlin told Maggie. She'd never dreamed anyone would call. So far, no one had, and everyone she knew or remembered, other than Maggie, was already with her. "Are you all right?"

"I think," Maggie said, the tension leaving her voice by a fraction. "I'm just glad you're okay!"

Katlin glanced at Jack again. "Why wouldn't I be okay?" Tension formed a constricting band around her chest as she waited for the answer. "Maggie?" she persisted, when her friend didn't respond.

"Sorry. I wanted to get a little farther away from the office before saying anything else." Maggie's breaths rasped through the receiver as if she was moving at an exerting pace. "The police are here."

"The police are where?" Katlin echoed, tilting the phone away and pressing the speaker button so Jack could hear her, too.

"At the paper."

"I'm with Jack, and you're on speaker now," Katlin said. "We're headed your way."

"I don't know if that's a good idea," she said. "When I came back from lunch, a bunch of officers were working their way through the room, asking everyone about you. They wanted to know who's seen you and where they can find you. I'm a terrible liar, so I turned tail and left. I don't want to say anything I shouldn't, and even if I manage to say the right words, my face would give me away."

Jack leaned in the phone's direction. "Maggie?"

The truck sped through the next yellow light as Jack's driving grew determined. Something bad was coming, and he felt it, too.

"You need to go back inside," he said. "Someone's surely told them Katlin was in this week and that she spoke with you. Leaving makes you look guilty, and you haven't done anything wrong. We'll come in and talk to the officers."

"I'm not going back," Maggie said, the panic returning to her voice. "They'll ask why I left."

Katlin watched the buildings grow taller in the distance as the downtown skyline came into view. "Where are you now?" she asked. "We'll meet you, then we can go inside together."

"I'm nearly at the corner outside the building. I'll meet you at the café on Main and Frank. You can give me a ride back." The sound of Maggie's heels clicking against the sidewalk grew louder as she increased her pace. "Is this about what happened at the docks last night? Gunfire was reported. That's where you were going. Right? To meet Dylan? Have you done something?"

"No. I haven't done anything wrong. And there was gunfire last night, but no one was hurt, and we left before the shooting began," Katlin said, feeling slightly guilty for the minor fib. She and Jack really had left before the shooting began. But she didn't think this was the time to point out they'd been the cause of those shots.

"Then why are the police looking for you?" Maggie asked. "I know you don't remember me, but you can tell me anything. You know that."

Katlin frowned, unsure she could trust anyone other than Jack and his team. "Why don't you go back inside and tell them we spoke? Tell them the truth. I have amnesia, and I didn't even remember you when I came into the paper."

Whatever the police wanted, it had nothing to do with Maggie, and Katlin hated to think of anyone else being dragged into her mess. "We'll meet you inside. We're only a few minutes away now. I remember that big glass building with the obelisk."

"The bank building?" Maggie asked.

Jack nodded. "Yes. Five minutes. We're catching a light."

"No," Maggie said. "I'll wait. I know where you were last night and why. I don't want to tell them. That's your information to share."

Jack switched lanes in the intersection and engaged his turn signal.

Maggie swore under her breath. "There's another cruiser up ahead. Looks like he's headed this way," Maggie said. "Change of plans."

JACK PRESSED THE pedal with more purpose and the engine roared. "Stay calm," he instructed. "Find a cluster of people and insert yourself, then tell us where you are."

"I'm going back to the parking garage," Maggie said, voice quivering. "I'll meet you in my car. At least I can lock the doors there. Are you still close?"

"Yes!" Katlin called. "We're at the light two blocks from there."

Jack pressed the mute button on the screen and frowned.

"What?"

"A cop patrolled the street last night before our truck blew up," he said.

Shards of ice sliced down Katlin's spine. "You don't think the uniforms at the office are dirty?"

"Or they could be fakes," he said, racing along the final block to the newspaper.

Katlin's stomach knotted. Neither of those options were good. "Do you trust Detective Reihl?" she asked, recalling the young female detective with her sharp blue eyes and soft, wavy hair. Was she dirty? Or was she an ally?

Jack pulled his cell phone from his cupholder in answer and dialed, pressing speaker as Katlin had done with Maggie's call. "This is Jack Hale," he began.

Katlin removed the mute feature from her phone and spoke absently into the receiver. "We're nearly there." Her attention hung on each of Jack's words to the detective.

Reihl listened quietly as he filled her in on the situation at the paper.

"If you don't feel comfortable speaking to them, you can speak to me," she said.

"Why do I have to speak to anyone?" Katlin asked, jumping in on the conversation. "Why are cops looking for me at my office?"

The pause that followed seemed to stretch on forever as Jack navigated the truck into the parking deck, passing rows of reserved spaces at ground level.

"You're wanted for questioning," Reihl finally explained. "In conjunction with a near-fatal attack on Dylan Peterson, a fellow Centre College student."

"What?" Katlin squealed, angling in her seat to stare at Jack's phone and nearly forgetting her own. "How could I possibly hurt that guy? He's half a foot taller and eighty pounds heavier!"

"Were you at the docks last night?" Reihl asked, her tone smug and self-important.

"You know we were," Katlin snapped. "We were also nearly killed by a bomb an hour later. So when exactly did I have time to beat up Dylan Peterson?"

"You tell me," the detective answered. "Really. Anytime you're ready. I can meet you at the station. Or how about a cup of coffee? You pick the place."

Katlin wet her lips as Jack set the phone on his thigh and took the spiraling cement ramp to the next level of the underground garage. "What does she drive?" he asked.

"Who?" the detective responded.

Katlin raised her silent phone to her mouth. "Maggie? We're here. What level are you on?"

Jack looked to her phone as he arrived at the next level. "Maggie?"

"What's going on?" Reihl demanded.

"Oh, no," Katlin said, her heart rate climbing. "Maggie!" She yelled into the phone and shook it, as if that would somehow bring her friend's attention back. The call was still going on. It hadn't been dropped or disconnected. So where was Maggie?

"We're looking for a friend of Katlin's," Jack said. "A coworker from the newspaper. She called us, worried, when she saw the police there after lunch."

Katlin searched the rows of empty vehicles for a sign of her friend as Jack drove them slowly around. There weren't any cars with a person in them. There weren't any people at all.

Jack cursed under his breath and slowed next to a red compact car with an open driver-side door.

"Is that her?" Katlin asked.

"No." He shifted into Park and climbed out, pressing a palm in Katlin's direction and leaving his cell phone on his seat. He set one hand on the butt of his sidearm as he approached the car.

Katlin felt the beads of sweat building on her brow.

"Empty," Jack called, jogging back to the SUV. "Reihl." He grabbed the phone off the seat. "Newspaper employee Maggie Franks has been abducted."

"Abducted," Reihl repeated flatly as Katlin's world tilted.

Katlin gripped Jack's arm, attempting to anchor herself before she was swept away in a current of emotion she couldn't come back from. "How do you know? Maybe she went inside the building. Maybe that's not her car."

Jack gave the small red car a remorseful look. "Small red hatchback on level two," he told Reihl, lifting the phone to his lips and shifting his gaze to Katlin. "Driver's door is wide open. No driver. Purse and phone are inside. Newspaper ID badge is on the floorboards."

Katlin clamped her lips tight to stop the vomit from coming.

Maggie was gone, and it was Katlin's fault.

Chapter Seventeen

Jack shifted into Drive and rolled slowly away from Maggie's car. Much as he wanted to stay and keep watch on the scene, instinct told him to get Katlin out of there.

Detective Reihl's voice rose from the cell-phone speaker in blunt, authoritative punches. She would send officers to the parking garage, but she wanted Katlin to meet her immediately. Katlin's expression was weary and skeptical, and she looked more unsure by the minute. More unsure, in fact, than he'd ever seen her, and something in his gut said the meeting with Reihl was a bad idea. Why wouldn't the detective have simply asked Katlin to talk to the officers in the newspaper building or have sent those officers to the garage? Or come to meet her here herself?

Jack circled the block outside the newspaper slowly, counting police cruisers along the south and west corners. Four cruisers in total. Why would it take so many lawmen to ask a few questions?

Katlin raised four fingers toward him and tented her eyebrows as she agreed to meet Detective Reihl at a coffee place near the police station in an hour. Katlin had noticed the number of cruisers, too.

And four was three too many.

Jack made a left at the next light and headed out of town, back to the safe house, where they could regroup.

He disconnected with Reihl. “Someone took Maggie,” Katlin whispered, tapping at her own phone screen. “I can’t believe it. How is this happening?” She scrolled and searched for something on the device while he kept watch on his rearview mirror.

He couldn’t risk being tailed to the only place that had been consistently safe for her. He wanted to gun the engine and reduce the commute time however he could, but being pulled over for speeding or being stopped for any reason seemed like a potential death sentence. At least until they figured out exactly what was going on and how deeply the police were involved.

“Oh, no.” Katlin gripped Jack’s wrist. “Listen to this. ‘Miss Andrews’s former employer, local attorney Nathan Fitch, was murdered on the night Andrews went briefly missing—’” Katlin said, attention glued to her phone “‘—only to return to the scene of Fitch’s murder on the night of an explosion. Andrews has since gone missing again, only hours after the near-fatal beating of Dylan Peterson, a Centre College classmate of hers, and police chief Peterson’s son. Local police are now in search of Andrews for questioning. If you’ve seen her or know of her whereabouts, please contact the station directly.’”

Jack swore and pressed the gas a little harder. “You’re being framed.”

“For all of it,” she said, stunned. “And it doesn’t make any sense. Why would I be shooting and bombing and beating people? I was just in a car accident. I only know like five people!”

“People believe what they read,” he said. “They don’t care if it makes sense.” If the article was right, and the police were really looking for Katlin, even the safe house wouldn't be safe for long. "Maybe we should talk with the doctor from the hospital," he suggested. "She can explain about your memory loss. That might help build your case."

"My case?" Katlin turned wide eyes on him. "You think I might really be arrested for all this?"

"Right now, I think anything's possible, and you need to be prepared. We should probably also contact an attorney and get your story on record."

Katlin straightened, her gaze darting around the world outside the truck. "Where are we going? We need to find Maggie."

"To the safe house," Jack answered, bristling at her angry expression. "I need to figure out how best to protect you while we get answers."

"Who cares if I get thrown in jail? Maggie is in serious and imminent danger. We have to look for her! Reihl barely acknowledged that she'd been abducted. All she cared about was meeting with me, and you're leaving town?"

Jack worked to remain calm. Katlin was clearly upset about her friend in danger, but he doubted that fear held a candle to the gut-wrenching, heart-slicing agony he was hoping not to show. Katlin was in danger, and he needed to protect her. To save her. He needed *her*. He swallowed hard and hoped his voice wouldn't betray him. "We'll find her," he promised, "but first we need to figure out where to look. And being arrested isn't going to help Maggie, so please don't say that again. Besides, if there are guilty cops looking for you, the last place you want to be is in their house."

Her skin paled in understanding. "Right. Okay. So, what first?"

He clenched his jaw, working through the tangle of emotions and possibilities. "I think speaking to your doctor at the hospital will help. She documented your situation, diagnosis and medical status. Those records could be important if things get any worse for you." He glanced in her direction when she didn't respond.

She'd turned her face away, scanning the scenery as it passed. "Maybe."

"Maybe?" His heart sank and his temper flared as a new realization hit. "You didn't tell her about your memory loss."

Of course she hadn't. The Katlin he'd met in that hospital room had been scared and anxious, desperate to get out. Telling the truth meant potentially being asked to stay, and she'd made it clear to him immediately, staying wasn't an option.

"I couldn't," she said. "I had to get out of there. I didn't know you then, but I had to trust you when I knew something was wrong. That someone wanted to hurt me. I'm sorry I lied." She turned repentant eyes on him. "I was scared and confused and I knew I'd die if I stayed."

Jack rubbed a heavy palm over his bearded cheeks and chin, then turned back to the road.

They made the rest of the trip to the safe house in silence.

Inside he spoke to Wyatt by phone about the missing woman, the police and Reihl while Katlin paced a small circle around the living room. He understood why she'd lied to the hospital staff, but he hated that she'd lied to him. And she'd continued allowing him to believe the lie, even after all they'd been through. How had she never found a moment to tell him? What if her head injury had been worse than they'd imagined, and no one knew because she'd kept such an important detail from the medical staff? And he'd whisked her away from the care she'd needed… What if something terrible had gone wrong while they were alone together, and he'd had no idea how to help her?

His heart and mind rejected the possibility of losing her. He'd loved and lost once and swore he'd never put himself through that again. The thought pulled him up short. Was that what this was? Love? No. He shook away the crazy thought. It was the complication of too many emotions tied to one human. Too many years of hearing her praises through the closest friend he'd ever had, then meeting her in person only to find himself powerfully physically attracted to her. To top that off, the time he'd spent with her had proven her to be all her brother had claimed and more. Katlin was strong and determined. Resourceful and smart. She was valiant, and he was honored to be useful to her at all. And if he allowed himself to think of the kiss they shared…

He couldn't do that. He also couldn't help wondering if he and Katlin would've hit it off at all if they'd met under other circumstances. He wasn't quite sure why she would possibly need or want him when she had complete control of her faculties. Because even without her memories, Katlin was a force to be reckoned with, and he was struggling to keep up.

He disconnected with Wyatt, then set his hands on his hips. "The team's looking into Maggie's disappearance. They'll reach out to her close friends and family and make certain a proper missing-persons report is filed." Just in case there was a reason that local PD didn't do that. "Sawyer's already on his way to the newspaper to take down cruiser numbers and find out if they're real or imposters. I sent Wyatt to meet Detective Reihl at the coffee shop. For what it's worth, I have a feeling she's one of the good guys, and I think Wyatt might be able to get her to see what we see. If the police force is contaminated, we need at least one ally on the inside."

Katlin stopped to stare at him, her face red with barely tamped emotion. "Someone nearly killed Dylan last night. Would the chief of police really hurt his own son?" she asked. "If Peterson is part of the gambling ring, then I can understand his determination to get rid of me. Breaking the story would ruin his side business and his career. He'd be humiliated and jailed. But why would he hurt his own son?"

Jack had considered those same thoughts and questions while driving back from town, but he didn't have any answers. "The chief can be involved without being in control." At least that was his best guess. "Maybe he was bought off or threatened. We just don't know."

"Yeah, well, abducted people rarely make it home, and they're usually dead within seventy-two hours. So we need to figure this out fast because Maggie's life depends on it."

KATLIN DRAGGED OUT her laptop and got comfortable at the small kitchen table. She pulled up the local news sites and scanned the articles in search of other shootings, bombings or gambling busts. Something else both violent and uncommon in the days, weeks or months before her car accident. What had gotten her started down this awful path? What had first made her suspect there was an illegal gambling ring at Centre College?

She stopped on an article from nearly a year ago. The reporter, A. Young, had declared an uptick in local busts and arrests consistent with what movies and television often referred to as evidence of organized crime. The article went on to warn readers that while authorities readily dismissed the reality of a modern-day Mafia, especially in central and northern Kentucky, the signs were all there. Furthermore, the reporter had shared the name and photo of one man frequently questioned and released by area police in conjunction with these crimes. Donald Rosch.

Her heart rate soared as she considered the possibilities. Was this the idea that had gotten her started? Could this reporter have more information on what she'd been up to? A few frenzied searches for the name Donald Rosch revealed a multitude of arrests and dropped charges, as A. Young had claimed. Money laundering, extortion and gambling, to name a few. Next, she searched for the brave reporter. She had a growing suspicion that if she could talk to A. Young, she'd discover it wasn't the first time they'd spoken.

She opened a new tab on her laptop, leaving her other searches up to show Jack when he came to check on her. Then she typed *A. Young name* into the search engine beside the name of the small newspaper that had published the article on organized crime.

"How's it going?" Jack called, arriving in the kitchen as she hit Search.

He stripped off his barn coat and toed out of his boots near the door. "It's getting cold out there." He rubbed his big palms together and puffed breath against them. "I added cameras to the mailbox at the road so I can monitor traffic in either direction, and set sensors about ten feet in to alert us if anyone is bold enough to use the driveway."

"Good. No surprises," she said.

He winked. "You got it. Tell me there's coffee."

"I made a pot." Katlin smiled, thankful to have Jack close once more. "We should order dinner in," she suggested. "You've been making every meal, and I've just found a thread I want to pull."

He poured a cup of coffee and set the steaming mug beside her on the tabletop. "Delivery sounds great. I can't eat anything else from a can or the freezer." His brow furrowed. "What kind of thread?" he asked, taking a seat in front of the mug.

"Here." She angled her laptop to give them both a good view, then clicked the first link in her search results and turned back to him. "A reporter wrote an article last year claiming an emergence of organized crime in the area, and I have a feeling it's what got me started. I want to see what you think."

"Katlin." Fear marred Jack's handsome face as his gaze trailed over the screen.

She turned for a look at the article and felt her stomach drop.

Rising Junior Reporter Dead in Single-Car High-Speed Crash

Chapter Eighteen

Katlin placed an order for two authentic Greek gyros, spanakopita to share and a double order of *loukoumades* from a restaurant named Acropolis. She'd found the menu, along with multiple others, in a folder on her laptop titled Heaven. She hadn't been sure what she'd thought she'd find inside when she'd first double-clicked the small manila icon, but a collection of downloaded carry-out menus hadn't been it. Still, she and Jack were both hungry, and they had a lot to think about.

She placed the order through the website after asking Jack what he liked, then guessing for herself. The food would be delivered in thirty minutes, and neither she nor Jack would have to risk venturing out again today. Also a solid win.

Jack finished another call and tossed his cell phone onto the table with a sigh. He ran his fingers over his freshly shaved head and raised warm hazel eyes to her. "Any trouble placing the order?"

"No. Any trouble with the reconnaissance?" she asked, trying not to admire the shape of his mouth or recall what it had felt like on hers.

He locked his fingers behind his head, showing off a set of impressive biceps. "Wyatt said Reihl wasn't thrilled to see him show up instead of you, but she heard him out, and she didn't push him to disclose your location right now. A good sign I was right to think we can trust her."

Katlin released a long, slow exhale, feeling the tension in her shoulders subside. "Good."

Reihl hadn't exactly given a warm or encouraging vibe when they'd met before, but maybe that was understandable. From an outsider's perspective, Katlin supposed she looked pretty shady, or at least of a questionable character. How else would anyone become involved in such a mess? Regardless, it was good to have someone in law enforcement on her side. "What about the police cruisers outside the newspaper? Real or imposters?"

He dropped his arms to his sides and collected his phone. "We don't know. They were gone when Sawyer got there."

Katlin rolled her neck as the tension returned. "What did Reihl say? Was she angry? Did she think he was just covering for me?"

Jack smirked. "I don't know, but you can ask him yourself. He's hungry and loves Acropolis, so he's on his way over."

Katlin smiled. "Perfect. I never know what's going to happen next around here, so I ordered plenty of extra food. I figured we could heat it up tonight or tomorrow as needed."

"Smart." He watched her, his gaze darkening as it dropped to her lips.

Katlin smiled, enjoying the flash of desire on his handsome face.

That damn undeniable connection, she thought. It was obvious that he had guilt over kissing her. A misplaced desire to be true to her brother. And he probably felt like he was taking advantage of her and the situation since she'd had a number of recent traumas and a head injury, but she doubted anything could change the chemistry sizzling between them. In fact, she had a feeling the bond that had blossomed between them at first sight, then bloomed at a breakneck pace, would've happened regardless of when they met, whatever the circumstances.

Jack's gaze snapped quickly back to her eyes. "We should probably turn on the news," he said, pushing back to his feet. "See if there's any mention of Maggie's disappearance and what local reporters made of all those officers at the paper."

Katlin set aside her laptop, then followed him to the couch. She could only hope there was more information available on the news than she'd been able to find online, which was nothing.

Jack powered on the television, then pumped up the volume when a man appeared behind a podium with the local police department's insignia. A banner along the screen's base declared: Thomas Peterson, Chief of Police.

Katlin perched on the cushion's edge, wishing she could read lips as the man on-screen began to speak. Dramatic breaking-news music played over his words, and a reporter's voice announced, "A press conference held earlier today revealed that an undercover team was assigned to Centre College after allegations of an illegal gambling operation were reported."

Katlin kneaded her hands, desperate to know what the outcome had been, and praying the chief hadn't named her as the criminal mastermind.

"Those allegations were thankfully proven to be nothing more than a hoax."

"A hoax!" Katlin squeaked. "Are they kidding me?" She looked to Jack. Surely this was a joke.

The regretful set of Jack's jaw said it all. He watched the screen carefully, evaluating, she supposed, and was likely seeing more than she could as frustration welled in her soul.

The reporter's voice was replaced by Chief Peterson's as the press-conference clip played on. "My love for Centre College goes back to my days as an athlete and student there, and it carries on through my son, Dylan, today. His dedication to the school, staff and student body is unparalleled. In fact, our entire family has an incredible sense of Centre pride, as do many of you, I know. I can only hope that you will all remain vigilant in your care and concern for our community. I would much rather have spent the time and resources to have my team determine the allegations a hoax than to have allowed something illegal to carry on in our beautiful town."

Jack leaned forward, resting his elbows on his knees. "He's sweating."

"What?" Katlin squinted, trying hard to focus while she mentally reeled over the public announcement. The gambling ring she'd been investigating, the one that had held an event she'd attended, had supposedly never existed. The camera angle changed, and a drop of sweat glistened on Peterson's temple. More gathered near his brow. "You're right."

"He's uncomfortable," Jack said. "He's saying the right words, using the right tone, but he's fidgeting with the notes on the podium and looking away from everything. The people and the cameras."

Katlin shot Jack a look. "Because he's lying?"

"Maybe." Jack didn't look so sure. "His body language

seems to say he's under duress. Maybe because he's lying publicly like this. There won't be any room for denial if he's caught. Or maybe he doesn't want to be there at all."

"The press conference wasn't his idea," Katlin said.

The press-conference clip ended, and the station cut to a commercial.

Jack muted the television and turned to her. "I don't think he had his son beaten up, or even allowed it. I think Dylan's beating might've been a warning from whoever's in charge."

"Rosch?" she asked.

"Maybe." The alarm on Jack's phone went off, and he pulled the device in front of him. "Someone tripped the sensors."

"Wyatt or gyros?" Katlin asked, hoping it was one or the other and not an ambush. She wasn't sure she could take that. Not here, in the only place she'd felt safe since waking in the hospital.

"Gyros." Jack handed her the phone and went to answer the door.

Katlin watched the screen, tracking a compact car with Acropolis logos on its hood, door and roof as it rolled slowly down the long lane. When the vehicle stopped near the porch, a man got out, secured his uniform ball cap, then pulled a number of white-logoed bags into his arms. The insignias on his button-down shirt and hat matched the advertisements on the car.

She met Jack at the door so she could take the food while he paid the driver.

At the door, Jack gave the man a long once-over before dropping his hand away from the gun in its holster at his back.

Minutes later, the delivery guy was long gone and Katlin had set the table for three.

Her stomach growled as the delicious scents of seasoned lamb, olive oil and thyme lifted into the air. The onions, feta and orzo called to her as she stared longingly at the steaming containers. "We should probably wait for Wyatt, right?" She bit her lip, hoping she was wrong.

"Nope." Jack handed her a plate and napkin. "Food's hot and we're hungry. He can reheat it if it cools before he gets here."

A smile split her face as she dug in.

They ate in companionable silence for several minutes, Katlin at an embarrassing speed, and Jack in a calmer manner. She hadn't realized just how famished she'd been until the first bite had hit her tongue. The folder from her laptop hadn't been a joke. The gyro really was heaven.

Her eyelids dipped, and she caught herself as her head tipped forward, as well.

"You okay?" Jack asked, the word slightly muffled from his mouthful of food.

She nodded, taking a quick internal inventory to be sure that was true. She was tired. That was to be expected given her level of continuous stress and lack of sleep this week. But it was more than that… She felt oddly, suddenly, fatigued. Her hands and face were slightly numb, like the warm buzz from a second glass of wine. Except, she hadn't had any wine. Her gaze dropped to the delicious meal before them. "Jack…" Her thoughts evaporated as the room dimmed and the floor rushed up to meet her.

JACK SHOT TO his feet as Katlin collapsed. "Katlin!"

He pressed a palm to the table to steady himself

when the world tilted slightly. The room shimmered as he lowered slowly onto the floor beside her. "Katli—" His tongue thickened and the word slurred. What was happening?

The floor spun as he reached for the cell phone he'd left on the table. The screen blurred before him as he pressed his fingertip to the unlock button. Beside him, Katlin was motionless and silent. A tidal wave of fear crashed over him. Was she dead? Had they been drugged? What had he missed? And how? His finger thumbed awkwardly across the number 9 on his dial pad. He blinked in concentration as he searched for the number 1. His eyelids drooped farther, felt heavier, and the world around him became a smear of colors.

Boom!

He started at the sound, unable to rise from the floor. Ears ringing, he rolled onto his back and watched as a set of legs strode into view, the front door swinging open behind them.

The delivery man crouched and smirked. "Enjoy your meal, Mr. Hale?"

Jack opened his mouth to cuss, spit and threaten. *Get away from her or I'll kill you. I love her, and I won't let you take her. My team is on the way. I have you on camera. You won't get away with this.* Rage built in his core, words piling on his useless tongue. The phone clattered to the floor, released by his numbing fingers. And the gun at his back was pressed securely against the floor beneath him.

The man scooped Katlin into his arms then tossed her headfirst over one shoulder. "I'll just take this and be on my way. I noticed the sensors in the drive. Nice touch—too bad they didn't matter." He tipped his hat and strode away.

Jack was left alone with his muddled thoughts, overwhelming fatigue and the sense of having watched his heart be torn from his chest.

He'd done everything right, and he'd failed her.

Chapter Nineteen

Jack's head pounded. A cacophony of sounds pierced his aching temples, and his gritty eyelids fought against him as he forced his eyes open. A groan spilled out as he worked himself up onto his elbows and forearms.

"Whoa!" a familiar voice boomed, distinguishable among the myriad of others. A heavy hand pressed against his shoulder, flattening him to the mattress. "Take it easy, cowboy." Wyatt's gentle drawl removed a bit of Jack's edge, but none of his confusion.

Distant beeping, ringing and footfalls echoed in his head. The squeak of shoes against a polished floor. The rattle of what? Metal carts? Wheels?

He tried again to get his squinting eyes open, despite the barrage of obnoxious fluorescent lighting. The effort paid off at a cost. Searing pain cut through his retinas, blasting straight to his brain. Sudden intrusive scents of bleach, stale coffee and bandages assailed his nose as his senses returned in full force. His stomach lurched in response.

He gripped the bed's edge and fixed one eye on Wyatt, allowing the other lid to droop. "Where's Katlin?" he groaned, his first words coming low and gravelly. "Is she okay?"

"Take it easy," Wyatt said, crossing his arms and scowling, a look Jack recognized as concern. "Get your bearings first. Then we'll work through the details."

Jack pulled his lips back in a feral show of teeth, unable to control the hostility brewing in him. "Talk."

Wyatt narrowed his eyes, but nodded. "The doc says you're going to be fine. The drugs you ingested were intended to immobilize, not kill. I'm just damn grateful I was held up in traffic downtown or we'd all have been knocked out. That'd be a real mess right now."

"What drugs?" Jack asked, the words raking from his dry, scratchy throat. He searched his mind for answers and waited for the memories to come. "The delivery food," he rasped.

Wyatt nodded.

Fear leached into Jack's skin like icy water through cloth. "Katlin," he murmured, sweeping his gaze around the stark white room. If he'd ingested enough drugs to lay him up like this, what had those same drugs done to her small and delicate frame? "Where is she?"

"We don't know."

Jack's gaze snapped back to Wyatt, his lips curling in rage once more. "Explain. Quickly." He winced against the noise of a busy emergency room. The hustle of staff and worried loved ones. The distant cry of a child.

"You ordered delivery," Wyatt began. "From Acropolis. Your delivery driver was knocked out and carjacked after leaving the restaurant. His attacker put on the uniform shirt, drugged the food then followed the GPS to your place. Stop me when it sounds familiar."

Jack cursed.

"Right," Wyatt continued. "The safe-house door was open when I arrived. You were on the floor. Katlin was gone. I called 911, and here we are. Sawyer's with the police at the farmhouse looking for leads. Cade's speaking with the driver and restaurant staff in town, hoping to get a bead on how this happened, but we think we have a good idea."

Jack levered himself upright once more, this time feeling less like a bag of sand and more like a soldier with a mission. He pulled the IV from his arm and thanked the powers that be no one had taken his clothes and dressed him in a cape that closed in back. "We've got to go."

Wyatt swung his arms apart like an umpire and widened his stance. "No, you don't. You need to rest while the drug runs its course, and you need those fluids to expedite the process." He pointed to the discarded IV. "You're not being admitted, but you're also in no shape to walk out."

"Get out of my way." Jack scanned the curtained-off area for signs of his coat and boots.

"Hey. We need you at full mast," Wyatt said, his voice smooth and placating. "Just lie down. Heal up and let us work. We've got this, brother."

Jack planted sock-covered feet on the floor. "Where are my boots?"

Wyatt crossed his arms, defiant for a moment, then wised up. "The nurse is going to have a fit when she comes to check on you and sees you're gone."

Jack shared a few expletives, and was handed his boots. "Thank you. Now help me up. I'll recover as we go."

Wyatt shook his head, curved an arm around Jack's back and helped him onto his feet. They moved steadily through the busy emergency room, avoiding eye contact and never slowing down as they exited the treatment area and cut across the waiting room toward the massive sliding glass doors.

A few people stared, but no one tried to stop them.

Smart. Because Jack was in no mood for nonsense.

A blast of icy wind beat against him as they exited the building, pulling yet another cuss from his lips.

"Sorry, I didn't think to grab your coat when they loaded you into the ambulance," Wyatt said.

Jack grunted, concentrating to keep his feet in motion.

Inside Wyatt's truck, Sawyer's voice boomed across the speakers, calling to check in before they'd made it out of the lot. "I've got something here at the safe house," he said as they barreled away from the hospital, into the painfully bright, cold day.

"You know who did this?" Jack asked, wincing at the snarl in his voice and pain that followed through his head.

"No, but I know how," Sawyer answered. "Cade said the folks at Acropolis told him you placed the order online. You didn't call or stop in. Your phone wasn't tapped, and you weren't being followed."

Jack circled a finger in front of the dashboard, wishing Sawyer would hurry up and get to the parts he didn't already know. "Yeah, and…"

"Cade called me, and I spoke with a crime-scene guy collecting evidence here at the farmhouse. He looked at her laptop, and guess what he found?"

"A bug." Jack's addled mind quickened as adrenaline burned through his veins. "Of course." They'd recovered the laptop from her cottage home in town, thinking it was a treasure, though nothing on it had been especially useful. "We brought it from her place. It's open all the time. She's been researching and trying to find answers."

"Yeah, well, someone's been watching and listening," Sawyer said.

Jack gritted his teeth. For all his efforts to keep her safe, he'd willingly carried a Trojan horse into their safe house. And someone with the know-how had infiltrated the device, accessing its microphone and camera features. "They heard us choose a restaurant," he said, putting the details of his tragedy du jour together.

"We think so," Sawyer said. "Then all they had to do was go down to Acropolis and wait for the order to leave the building."

Wyatt kept a steady watch on the rearview mirror as he switched lanes and made several unnecessary turns to be sure no one followed, a practice Jack also employed. "Why do you think they didn't kill these guys?" he asked, shooting an apologetic look in Jack's direction. "I mean, I'm glad they didn't, but they had a chance to finally shut Katlin up and didn't take it. Why?"

"Maybe they still need her for something," Sawyer answered across the line. "Any ideas what that could be, Jack?"

He scrambled for a clue, but didn't have one. "If they've been listening, they must know she doesn't have her memory by now. She's useless for information. If she wasn't, we'd already be building a case against whoever this is." Possibly Donald Rosch, he thought, recalling one of their last conversations. A possible local crime boss.

Wyatt hooked another right and headed for the highway, back to home base, Jack realized—Fortress Defense. "What's important," Wyatt said, "is that they still need something from her. That means they'll keep her alive until she can give it to them. And that gives us time to find her."

Jack curled one hand into a fist on his lap. "We've been looking for a thumb drive her brother gave her. Her friend Maggie said Katlin kept all her research on it. I'll bet they're looking for that, too. They probably heard us talking about it." Once Rosch realized she had evidence against him, it wouldn't be enough to simply shoot her. First, he'd need to destroy whatever dirt she'd collected.

"Maggie?" Wyatt asked. "From the newspaper?" His expression tightened, saying what he wouldn't. *The other woman who'd been abducted today.*

"That's her." Jack worked to steady his breaths and push past the pain ricocheting through his head to his heart and back. "If we find the drive and we get someone at the local PD to leave the computer compromised and available to us, maybe we can use it to communicate with whoever's been listening. We can offer a trade. The information they want in exchange for the women."

Wyatt returned his attention to the road. "All right, men. Sounds like we've got a plan."

"Roger," Sawyer agreed. "I'll catch Reihl and pull her aside. See if she can help."

Jack froze. "Reihl's there?"

"Yeah," Sawyer answered. "I think she's okay, man. We can trust her."

Wyatt nodded, and he hoped they were right. Because Reihl was suddenly their only hope.

Jack had to find Katlin and protect her the way he promised Griffin he would. Then he needed to tell her the thing he'd been stupidly, stubbornly, holding back.

He was deeply and completely in love with her.

KATLIN WOKE ON the ground, consumed by cold and darkness. Damp scents of earth and decay tainted the air.

Her mind struggled to make sense of her circumstances. Where was she? And why?

She rolled toward a distant shaft of light, high in the air, squinting and willing her stinging eyes to focus. The hard, gritty ground scratched at her arms and fingers as she struggled to orient herself in the space.

"Katlin?" Her name lifted in the darkness, so quietly she wasn't sure it was real. "Katlin?" The word came again, louder the second time and accompanied with short scurrying sounds.

She turned in search of her company, daring to dream that she wasn't alone, and that there might still be hope in this strange and terrifying scenario.

"You're awake." Maggie's tear-streaked face came into view, disrupting the stream of dust motes in the single shaft of light.

Maggie's hair was tangled and littered with debris, hunks of dirt and splinters of wood. Her eyes and cheeks were red and puffy, as if she'd been extremely ill or crying a long while. Her shirt, filthy and torn at the collar, was in worse shape than her hair. Desperation tightened the corners of her mouth and there were deep lines across her forehead.

"Where are we?" Katlin asked, forcing her body into a sitting position then cringing at the bullet-hot pain that exploded in her head. She pressed a tentative hand to her temple, then patted gingerly along her scalp in search of blood or injury.

"You were drugged," Maggie said, taking a seat beside her and pulling thin legs to her chest. She wrapped her arms around them and rested her chin on her knees. "I heard them joking after they left you here, and I saw the delivery uniform your guy was wearing. Acropolis," she added sadly. "You always liked that place. I thought you were dead."

"Back at ya," Katlin said, working on a smile. "Someone took you from the garage."

She nodded. "My guy knocked me out when I fought him. I didn't recognize him, and I haven't seen him since he left me here. Someone opens the door now and then to toss bottled water down the steps. Sometimes they add a box of crackers or dry cereal, but they never cross the threshold. I don't know if that's good or bad."

"How long have I been here?" Katlin asked, struggling to clear her thick, achy throat.

"They brought you in yesterday. I had to check to be sure you were breathing. You were so still. I sat with you through the night. I was trying to reach the window when you woke. You were shivering earlier, but there's nothing to cover up with."

At the mention of temperature, Katlin felt the chill return. She wrapped an arm around Maggie's back and rested her head on her friend's shoulder. "Thank you." She imagined Maggie attempting to reach the narrow window high above and realized they were in a basement. "I'm so sorry I dragged you into this." And Jack, she thought. She and Jack had been drugged. She and Maggie abducted. All of it was her fault.

Maggie snuggled close and patted her hand. "It's what we do, right?" she asked. "Reporters have to know the truth. Have to scoop the story." She sighed. "If we live, I'm getting a job at a wedding magazine instead."

"Fair," Katlin said, choking back a half laugh, half sob. "We're going to get out of here. Together. Any idea where we are?"

"Kind of," Maggie said. "We're on the west side. Not

far from where you crashed, I think. I saw the exit sign when I was being brought here. After that, I'm not sure. I was in and out of consciousness." She angled her head to reveal a large purple knot on the back. "Pistol-whipped. Not too many girls our age can say that. Maybe I'll put it on my résumé for the bridal magazine. What do you think?"

"Good idea." Katlin wanted to laugh at her friend's joke, but something about the room was eerily familiar. She stared at every brick and corner, letting the basement's menacing vibe curl deep into her aching head and twine with her thoughts. Slowly, an icy finger scraped at the place where her memories had been locked up for too long.

She twisted onto her hands and knees, then stretched slowly to her feet, ignoring the weakness in her limbs and the sway of her stance. She turned in a slow circle, taking in the dark, dank space and willing the icy finger in her head to slice through the fog.

"Donald Rosch," she said, the name rolling off her tongue before she'd made the mental decision to say it aloud. "Donald Rosch is a crime boss who has the chief of police under his thumb. He's using Dylan as leverage to force Chief Peterson into looking the other way while he carries on with business as usual. Rosch has pop-up gambling events all around town, specifically targeting coeds and highly funded private schools like Centre College."

She slapped a hand across her mouth to stifle the building cheer. "Maggie," she whispered against her frozen, filthy skin. "I remember everything!"

Chapter Twenty

Jack prowled through the safe house, scrutinizing every inch of the property, inside and out, while his team met with Detective Reihl for their marching orders. Fortress Defense had officially partnered with the young detective to find Katlin and Maggie as soon as possible. The collaboration should have made Jack feel better, but it didn't. He doubted anything would until he saw Katlin home safe.

He lowered to his hands and knees for the tenth time, running his fingertips over the floor where he and Katlin had fallen after ingesting their drugged meal. Whoever had taken her had left no trace. No sole marks from his shoes, no dropped receipts, ticket stubs or other pieces of investigative gold that always seemed to turn up on television and in movies.

His eyelids drifted shut, willing the memories to return. Instantly, he recalled the scents of the meal, heady and strong. Olive oil, seasoned lamb and feta. His head buzzed lightly in remembrance. He'd assumed the cause was fatigue or stress. Then she'd mumbled his name, gone limp and fallen. He'd dove for her, clumsily, limbs heavy as he landed in a heap at her side. He recalled the explosive sound of the front door being broken in and the steady footfalls that came for her. The delivery man had returned. The delivery man had been a criminal, and Jack hadn't had a clue until it was too late.

He rocked back onto his feet and scrubbed angry hands over his face and head. Hopefully his teammates were having better luck turning up something useful.

Wyatt, Sawyer and Cade had split up to check out Katlin's apartments, offices and car. Meanwhile, Reihl was reviewing surveillance footage from the newspaper, parking garage and Acropolis, looking for a clue as to who had abducted Katlin and Maggie. Reihl had already confirmed the four cruisers Jack had seen outside the newspaper were fakes. It was the reason she hadn't sent the officers to the parking garage immediately after discovering Maggie's abduction. They weren't her men, and she'd known with certainty then that Jack and Katlin's accusations were true. The information was as encouraging as it was disconcerting to Jack. There weren't eight bad cops, but there were eight criminals convincing and well-funded enough to fool everyone.

His phone rang as he made another loop around the space, glaring at the place where he and Katlin had been separated. "Hale," he answered, heart rate rising in anticipation of a solid lead and dreading the possibility of more bad news. It'd been more than twenty-four hours since he'd awoken in the hospital and initiated an all-out hunt for Katlin, his… The thought brought him up short. His what? Katlin wasn't *his* anything. And that was his fault. She'd been clear about her intentions. She wanted him and wanted him to want her. He'd been the stubborn one. The stupid one. Not seeing the truth for what it was. Griffin hadn't wanted Jack to lust after his sister, but Katlin was right—Griffin would never tell him not to love and cherish her. And the way his every fiber ached at the thought of losing her, he knew loving and cherishing her was exactly what he wanted to do. Every day of her life, if she'd let him. And he should have told her all that sooner.

"I'm on," Sawyer said, responding to Jack's greeting.

"Yep," Wyatt answered. "Cade?"

"With ya," Cade confirmed.

"All right," Wyatt said, taking the reins, as always. "Gang's all here. How are you holding up, Jack?" he asked.

Jack groaned. "That's going to depend on what you've got for me."

The long beat of silence that followed was a deafening answer to his question.

"Hang in there," Wyatt encouraged. "We've all been where you are. We get it. And we're going to help you get through it."

Over the course of the past year, each of Jack's teammates had fallen in love. Each man with a woman he'd been dispatched to protect, and they'd all nearly lost her at some point. Jack had been around for the terror and the aftermath every time. Never once did he think it could be him. He wasn't supposed to love again. Not after losing Cara. Not after the way that had changed and broken him. But here he was, lost for a woman he'd only had in his life several days and unsure how his world could turn without her. He was glad his friends knew, because he couldn't begin to put the torrent of pain into words. "Any new leads?"

"Nothing substantial yet," Wyatt said. "Reihl is canvassing businesses near the parking garage and restaurant right now. Her team is accessing local surveillance feeds and attempting to identify the imposter police officers. She's hoping that with enough footage she can track the cruisers as they moved out of town."

Jack rubbed a palm against his beard and neck. "How far has she been able to follow them?"

"As far as the highway."

Jack considered the information. "Highway cameras can track the plates from there."

"Maybe," Wyatt said. "She was only able to get partials, but it could be enough."

Jack collapsed onto the couch, willing his thoughts to sharpen. He was no use to Katlin if he was lost to emotion.

There had to be something he'd missed.

"We're going to figure this out," Wyatt insisted.

The other men grunted their agreement.

"Until she remembers what they want to know, we've still got time," Sawyer added. "Any ideas yet on where that thumb drive might be hidden?"

Jack released a long breath, centering himself. "None."

"Well, it was smart of her to hide it."

Jack's jaw locked at the unspoken completion of Sawyer's thought. It was smart of Katlin to hide the drive *because if she hadn't, she'd be dead by now.* He raised his eyes to Griffin's memorial flag, displayed on the mantel, and willed his friend to intervene and guide him.

Someone whistled long and slow into the receiver. "Hey..." Cade's voice rose through the line. "Any chance one of you guys have a Green Beret thumb drive like the one these guys want? Or can we buy one somewhere? Maybe we can use the compromised laptop to contact the abductors, then trade the fake drive for Katlin and

Maggie? We can coordinate with Reihl to set up a sting and grab the women."

Sawyer and Wyatt chimed in with feedback, opinions and logistics on the idea while Jack stared at the flag on the mantel. Griffin and Katlin had been closer than any two siblings he'd ever known. They were the best of friends. And she'd brought the flag with her even though she couldn't remember him. Why? Instinct? A sibling connection that even amnesia couldn't break? Or something else? Something *more*?

Jack stood and moved slowly to the fireplace. "She said she couldn't explain it," he murmured, as much to himself as to the men talking over one another on the call.

"What?" Wyatt asked, silencing the other voices with his question. "Jack? Who couldn't explain what?"

"Katlin," he said, taking the triangular display case off the mantel. "She brought Griffin's memorial flag from her apartment. She said she just knew she couldn't leave it behind." He turned the glass-and-wood contraption over in his hands, examining it from every angle before opening it.

"What are you saying?" Wyatt asked. "You think she remembered more than she let on?"

"No." Jack ran his fingertips reverently over the flag's material. He closed his eyes for a moment of remembrance, and in apology to Griffin in case he was wrong. Then, he slid his fingers into the neat folds of the flag until they bumped against something small, flat and hard.

Katlin had left the drive with her brother to protect, and it had worked.

KATLIN COUGHED AND gagged as an avalanche of dirt and rotten wood fragments rolled down from the small basement window and into her face. She stretched taller, up on tiptoes and undeterred. Her sore and swollen fingertips dug into the space around the ancient and deteriorating frame, where a few final shards of orange and amber light prevailed. Soon the sun would set, and they'd be cast into utter darkness, alone with the rats, according to Maggie.

Katlin hated rats.

"Here." Maggie tapped Katlin's arm with a nearly drained bottle of water. "Take a break. You're trembling."

Katlin fell back on her heels against the earth, muscles shaking from exertion instead of the cold. "Thanks." She sipped the water to clear her throat and relieve the cough.

They had to get out of there before anyone came to check on them. She'd heard voices outside the basement door earlier, but thankfully, the door had stayed securely shut while Katlin regained her faculties. It hadn't taken long for her to decide the window was the only chance of escape. Maggie agreed. She'd been digging at the decrepit frame when Katlin woke.

"I still don't understand why we're being held here," Maggie said. "I thought you were snooping on some frat kids and their side hustle. Now there's a crime syndicate?"

"Supported by our local police chief," Katlin said, returning the water bottle to her friend, and rising back onto her toes. "They'll torture me for what I know." And if that didn't work, they'd torture Maggie. They'd kill them both once they had what they wanted.

Katlin focused her fear and desperation on the work at hand, then tugged at the frame's edge until it broke. She gasped as the break sent her back several steps, arms pinwheeling and ankles turning.

"Whoa!" Maggie grabbed her shoulders to stop her fall. "What happened?"

"The frame broke." Katlin lifted a shard of jagged wood and grinned. "Now we're getting somewhere." She moved back into position, raising her new tool overhead. The sharp nose of the wood dug into the crumbling mortar.

"So you have proof about the police chief?" Maggie asked, resting a supporting hand against Katlin's back as she worked, steadying her in case she went stumbling again.

"Yeah," Katlin answered between tiny avalanches of dirt against her face. "Police chief Peterson and Donald Rosch came to a gentleman's agreement a few years ago. Rosch paid Peterson monthly, and Peterson looked the other way while Rosch and his people committed an abundance of petty thefts, some light racketeering, embezzlement, coercion and gambling. It went along smoothly for a while, then Rosch got greedy, power-drunk and belligerent with his crimes. Peterson was scrambling to cover for him, so he demanded more money for his efforts. That's when Rosch brought Dylan in on the gambling as collateral. He treated him like a king and told him not to let his dad know. Meanwhile, Rosch sent photos of Dylan to Peterson's home, implying that he'd better stay compliant or something bad would happen to his son.

"Eventually, Peterson confessed his sins to Dylan, hoping the truth would protect him, but Dylan was in too deep by then, and he owed Rosch money for gambling. So Rosch and Dylan struck a new agreement. Rosch would forgive the debt if Dylan kept his dad quiet. Dylan agreed, then Rosch stopped paying Peterson. He said the new deal was that he wouldn't hurt Dylan as long as his dad stayed onboard."

"Wow," Maggie whispered. "That's awful."

"Yeah. The bigger problem was that Peterson had become accustomed to the extra cash from Rosch, and it made things tight on his end. The reduced income caused questions from his wife, which made things even more complicated. So he came to see the attorney I was working for to talk it over off-the-record. All their discussions were protected under attorney-client privilege, but I was listening." Katlin shot a look over her shoulder. "I should have gone to the police then. I should have found someone to report this to, but I wanted the story."

Maggie rubbed her back. "At least you documented it all."

Katlin went back to work on the loose earth and mortar around the window. With a little luck, she'd be able to force the entire thing out onto the shabby grass and dirt perimeter of the home. Then she and Maggie could escape undetected. She worked furiously against the fading shafts of light on the horizon that would soon give way to moonlight.

"I recorded the conversations between Attorney Fitch and Chief Peterson from outside the closed office door, and I took everything I had to our editor. He wouldn't print it. Said it was unsubstantiated since I hadn't interviewed any of the key players. That recordings were easily and frequently manipulated. He said trying to break the case before it was foolproof could cause more harm than good, and the efforts could possibly be cast as another crooked reporter trying to make a name for herself. Ruining my career before it ever got started. Plus, I risked legal trouble for copying the files I had."

The chunk of wood Katlin had been using to dig with suddenly got lodged into the dirt and was now wedged there. Blood streamed from her hand where the opposite end broke through the tender flesh of her palm. "Argh!" She wrapped filthy fingers around the open wound, pressing hard against the flow of blood and biting her lip against the pain. "It's stuck," she said, rocking back onto the ground and working the sleeve of her shirt over the cut.

"You're bleeding!" Maggie squeaked, grabbing Katlin's hand and turning it in the fading light.

"I'm okay, but we're going to have to break the window if we want out of here before they come for us." At the pace she was currently working, she'd die of old age before removing the window any other way.

Maggie's grip loosened. "Okay. With what? There's nothing here but us and a lot of dirt. Believe me, I've searched. I couldn't even find a loose brick."

Katlin winced as the pain in her hand increased and her palm throbbed. Memories rampaged through her newly recovered mind.

She'd gone back to the law office to copy more files one night and seen Fitch inviting Rosch inside. Instead of sneaking in to eavesdrop, she'd seen an opportunity to check out an address where she'd suspected the gambling materials were stored between events. She'd reasoned that if Rosch was at the law office in Danville, he couldn't also be at a house on the west side of Campbellsville. So she'd come to the worst neighborhood in town and broken into the basement of the home where she was now being held captive. But that night the space hadn't been empty. The basement had been bursting with card tables, slot machines and roulette wheels.

She rested her head against the dirty brick wall, willing the memories to stop and her mind to focus on their escape. "I knew they used this place for storage," she whispered to Maggie. "So I came for pictures. For proof. I got everything I needed and was almost to the highway before I saw the headlights coming for me. I'll have to use my hand to break the window."

"What?" Maggie stepped back, eyes wide. "You can't. They'll hear, and how can you escape if you're all cut up and bleeding?"

Emotion pinched and stung Katlin's eyes. She squared her shoulder and shored up her nerve. "It's the only option we have left."

She'd have to take off her shirt, wrap it over her hand and hope she was strong enough to break the glass with a punch. She'd also have to hope the guards outside the basement door wouldn't hear the break. And that would be the easy part. She couldn't afford to injure herself any further in the process because they had no car or phone. Once they were out, they'd be on foot, at night, in the roughest part of town. Alone and hunted.

Chapter Twenty-One

Jack stood shoulder-to-shoulder with his teammates and Detective Reihl. They were all gathered in a semicircle around District Attorney Martin Weaver's desk. The Green Beret thumb drive was now plugged securely into the laptop before them. It was after hours—the building was nearly empty and they were asking a lot, but given the circumstances, and the fact no one knew who could be trusted anymore, this was where they'd landed. Weaver was mentioned as one of the good guys in a file on Katlin's thumb drive, and Reihl had called in a favor to get him back to the office after he'd barely gotten home.

"What do you think?" the detective asked, pressing her palms to the man's desk. "Is this enough to build a case and make it stick?"

Weaver raised his eyes to the group, pulling his attention from the computer screen with visible difficulty. "It's enough to put Peterson away, along with several officers and Donald Rosch for a long time. And this was all collected by one junior reporter?"

Reihl tented her eyebrows, dark waves of her hair falling over the shoulders of her black raincoat. "Yes, and she'll pay a steep price if we don't move quickly. We need warrants on Peterson, his lackeys and Rosch. If we can haul them all in, or at least get them on the run, it might remove Miss Andrews from harm's way long enough to locate and recover her."

He scraped a hand through thick salt-and-pepper hair. His gray suit was rumpled and his tie hung loose around his collar. He shook his head slowly, his expression pensive. "Heads are going to roll. The public is going to go crazy. A dirty chief of police with ties to local organized crime. It's going to be a PR nightmare."

"Let me worry about that," Reihl said, blue eyes flashing. "I just need to know you have everything you need. And that the charges will stick."

Weaver's weary eyes returned to the computer screen, scanning the files from Katlin's thumb drive. "There's a lot of information here. I'll need time to sort it all."

"But you can do it," Jack said, as much a demand as a question. They'd already been there for the better part of an hour, fielding questions and wasting time while Weaver evaluated the drive's contents. "Every minute we're standing here is a minute Katlin and Maggie could be being tortured. Or worse." His jaw tightened on the final word and heat rushed to his chest, neck and face.

Weaver released a heavy breath. "I can build the cases, but I can't guarantee protection for the women or guess how Peterson and Rosch will react to news of their pending arrests. Given the involvement of several members of the force, it'll be a miracle if they don't know we're coming before the ink's dry on these warrants." He moved his gaze to Jack. "They could decide it best to dispose of the women before the arrests."

Jack felt the world sway.

Wyatt set a steadying palm on Jack's shoulder. "We'll find her before word gets out."

"Will we?" Jack snapped, his hope slipping away. "We still have no idea where they're being held."

Weaver moved his mouse around the small pad and clicked a few times before the printer behind him rocked to life. "I might have a guess on the women's whereabouts." He turned to retrieve the paper from the printer, then placed it on the desk between them. "Rosch owns a number of properties, but there are three along the river near the exit where your friend had her accident. If I was you, I'd start with those. Each of these black dots represents one of the properties."

Jack leaned in, staring closely at the freshly printed map. An image he'd reviewed and dismissed on his ride over from the safe house. He'd assumed the marked locations were venues for previous gambling nights and hadn't given them another moment's consideration.

Now, those little black dots looked a lot like hope.

Jack turned to Reihl, renewed urgency tightening his limbs and fresh adrenaline brewing in his system. "We should split up. My team can cover two buildings at a time by breaking into pairs. I don't suppose you've got a partner somewhere we haven't met?"

"Or a team of lawmen you trust," Sawyer added, already moving toward the door.

Wyatt clapped Jack on the back and followed on Sawyer's heels.

A sly grin stretched over the detective's face as she liberated her cell phone from one pocket. "I might know someone."

Jack dipped his chin in thanks and acceptance, following his teammates toward the door. "We'll meet you there."

Reihl fell into step at his side. "Wait just a minute. You

can't make an arrest and these criminals are armed. You should wait for police backup."

Cade paused in the doorway and scoffed. "Pardon me, Detective, but we're also armed. Trained. And on a mission. If we run into trouble, we'll hold our positions until you arrive or for as long as we can. We won't fire unless fired upon, but, Detective, we will get those women back."

Jack's chest swelled with hope and pride as he stared at Cade. "Oorah," he bellowed, in homage to the former jarhead.

"Oorah," Cade echoed.

Jack smiled, then swung his attention back to the small brunette detective at his side. "We'll start at the westernmost property and move east. You and your team can start east and move west when you arrive. Together, we can have all three locations cleared in minutes."

Reihl nodded, already dialing and pressing a phone to her ear.

District Attorney Weaver followed them out, a grimace on his aging face. "Some days I wonder if my work matters. Nights like tonight, I remember why I ran for this position to begin with. Good luck to you all. I'll be waiting for your good news."

Jack turned to him and extended a hand. "Thank you." He offered a strong shake before breaking into a sprint to the parking lot.

If Katlin was in one of the properties on that map, he would find her.

Tonight.

KATLIN STRIPPED OFF her long-sleeve T-shirt, the frigid chill of the basement raising goose bumps over her exposed skin. Blood oozed from her wounded palm, the puncture deeper and more severe than she'd initially thought.

"Maybe there's another way," Maggie said, her small frame unsteady beneath Katlin.

"Just hold me tight. I'll count down." Katlin steadied her breath and secured the material around her closed fist. She'd climbed up to sit on Maggie's shoulders for added height and a better angle to break the glass, and hopefully not her hand, with the punch. "Ready?"

A low rumble of voices rose in the home above them, growing louder before stopping on the other side of the basement door. Katlin held her breath, temporarily frozen and staring across the dark expanse to the place where a fresh shaft of light bled under the door.

"Hurry!" Maggie whispered, her body swaying. Her fingers gripped Katlin's calves tightly enough to leave ten tiny bruises. "Now!"

Unable to think past her friend's urgent pleas and the men about to catch her in an attempted escape, Katlin pulled back her fist, twisted slightly at the waist, then snapped her hand forward, the way Griffin had shown her. The way he'd promised would flatten anyone bold enough to lay an unwanted hand on her. She could only hope the old glass pane was weaker than the average jaw.

The glass shattered upon impact, falling in blades over her tightly wrapped fist, raining down the wall and into Maggie's hair. And some landed on the blessed ground outside, reflecting the newly risen moon.

Before she'd breathed her first full breath of night air, Maggie had released her calves in favor of boosting her through the newly opened escape hatch. Katlin landed partially in and partially out of the window, her head and shoulders under the stars. She winced as glass dug into her bare stomach, arm and torso. Pain screamed through her.

"Go!" Maggie cried. "They're coming! Go!"

The door rattled, and a tall slice of light cut into the darkness behind her.

"Hey!" a man's voice boomed. "What was that? What broke in here?"

Katlin dug her fingers into the scrubby grass, broken glass and earth, pulling the rest of herself through the window while Maggie pushed and shoved her legs.

"Go!" she called, loudly now. "Run!"

Katlin spun on her stomach in the dirt and debris, thrusting blood-streaked arms back through the empty windowpane. "Not without you."

She and Maggie locked fervent gazes as blinding light flooded the room. Two men stood at the top of a rickety-looking flight of steps. A bulb on a chain swung before them like the pendulum of a ticking clock.

Maggie jumped for Katlin's hands and held on tight. Using their connection like a rope, she walked her feet up the old block wall until she was close enough to be dragged outside.

Katlin leaned away, feet planted in the hard earth, and heaved. Maggie's head and shoulders burst through the window, her legs kicking behind.

Slurs and curses burst through the basement as the men tore across the room, already down the flight of stairs.

A large hand hit the dirt beside Maggie's knees as she struggled to find her bearings. A second hand clutched her shoe and jerked her back by a foot.

Maggie's scream filled the night, and Katlin lurched after her, heart pounding and mind scrambling.

"I've got you now," he growled.

"No, you don't!" Katlin screamed back. She clutched her friend with her good hand, and searched the ground around her with the other. Her aching fingers curled over a palm-size stone and she brought it down on his hand with a stomach-tossing crunch.

The attacker fell back with a wail, releasing Maggie in an instant.

"Outside!" he yelled. "Get them!"

Footfalls hit the interior wooden steps at a run.

Katlin pulled Maggie to her feet. "Are you okay?"

Maggie nodded and gasped for air. "Yeah. Thank you."

"Good." She unwound the shirt from her hand and stretched the bloody fabric back over her sliced-up torso, then grasped her friend by the hand. She cradled her opposite, gashed wrist and forearm against her chest, fighting against the throbbing pain and burn. She sent up a silent prayer as the flowing blood seeped through her shirt and warmed her skin beneath. "Let's go."

Together, they stumbled down the dark and narrow alleyway outside the old home, ducking behind a dumpster when a set of headlights cut across the property's front lawn.

Maggie's teeth chattered in the darkness as the home's front door slammed open, and two men burst onto the aging and tilting porch, guns drawn. "More of them?"

"I don't know," Katlin said. "I don't want to find out."

A large black SUV appeared a moment later, roaring over the sidewalk and climbing half onto the craggy, unkempt grass. The vehicle's front doors opened and figures dressed in black took up position behind the barriers. Their guns were drawn, as well.

"Whoa." Maggie's grip on Katlin tightened. "We've got to move."

Katlin agreed, but following through was harder. Her body was weak, her head light and vision blurry. Her stomach rolled with each unsteady step as she bumbled along at Maggie's side, attempting to put distance between them and the pack of armed men.

"You're bleeding," Maggie moaned, tugging at her cradled arm. "Oh, my goodness, you're covered. Is that all from the cuts on your stomach and chest?"

"No." She opened her mouth to say she'd gashed her arm, was losing too much blood and needed to sit down, but gunshots rang out behind them, effectively silencing that story.

Maggie screamed.

Katlin's knees buckled, and her shins collided with the hard and broken asphalt.

"No, no, no," Maggie said, hefting Katlin upright and swinging her burning, bleeding arm around her shoulders. "We can't stop now. You need a hospital."

Katlin bobbed her head in agreement, her vision nearly gone. She trusted Maggie to guide her. She pressed on, forcing every awkward stride for the sake of the friend she'd unintentionally dragged into her mess.

"You can do it." Maggie whispered the words like a low and repetitive chant, whether to Katlin alone or for the benefit of them both, she couldn't say. She dragged as much as guided Katlin along the alley and into a dark and narrow space between buildings while the men on the lawn exchanged shots behind them. "Maybe we can find someone willing to let us use their phone," Maggie said. "Maybe someone will give us a ride, or we'll see a police cruiser on patrol."

"No…" Katlin choked on the word, struggling to work her failing tongue. "No police. We don't know—"

Her words were cut short once more. This time, as the broad beam of a flashlight landed on them and another man dressed in black stepped into their path.

He lowered the beam and reached for Katlin as her eyes rolled back and her legs gave out.

She'd never been so sorry. For the path she'd chosen. The decisions she'd made.

For putting Maggie in harm's way.

And for never telling Jack Hale that she loved him.

Chapter Twenty-Two

Jack's heart seized as Katlin's eyes rolled and her legs gave out. He lurched forward in the darkness, cursing the broken streetlamps and whoever had done this to her.

Maggie stumbled under Katlin's collapsing weight, a fierce and determined expression on her small, livid face. "Let her go!"

"I've got her," he said, working to keep his voice low and strong, even as Katlin's body fell against his, lifeless and limp. "I've got you, too," he vowed, locking gazes with Maggie in the moonlight. "You're going to be okay." He tugged the black balaclava below his chin, exposing his face from eyebrows to neck. "We're here to bring you home."

Maggie's lips trembled, and a small sob broke free. Her eyes were wild with terror. Her face and hair filthy. Her ruddy cheeks streaked with tears. "Jack?"

He offered a stiff, affirmative dip of his chin. "My team's here. Help is on the way. We've got to go." He swept an arm under Katlin's legs and raised her off the ground, cradling her body against his as a broad mass of clouds raced across the sky, blotting out the moon and stars. *Better cover for them*, he thought. *And better cover for their enemies, as well.*

"Stick to the shadows," he instructed. "I don't know how many of Rosch's men will respond to the gunfire." He turned back the way he'd come, scanning Katlin's face as he moved, straining for better sight in the darkness. Her breaths were short and shallow against his chest. Her skin cold to his touch. And a dark stain coated her shirt, hands and arm. He supposed it was too much to ask that she'd simply collapsed from dehydration, fatigue or fear.

"Are you hurt?" he asked Maggie, who rushed along at his side.

"No," she cried. "I'm fine. Katlin's hurt. She's cut and bleeding. She needs a hospital."

Jack's chest constricted painfully as he gave the woman in his arms another, closer look, willing the dark patches over her clothes and skin to be dirt, like the marks on Maggie. "What happened? How was she cut? When?" He changed trajectory, crouching slightly as he jogged closer to the nearest working streetlamp and into its light. He motioned for Maggie to follow. They needed to be careful not to expose themselves to any of Rosch's men.

Another nearby round of gunfire made Jack hunch his shoulders and hurry his steps. A heartbeat later, his stomach pitched at the revelation made beneath the streetlamp.

Maggie's sobs intensified at the illumination of Katlin's body, coated from her torso to wrist in blood. Her forearm was sliced to the elbow. The wound was jagged and deep. Similar cuts were visible on her stomach and side, where her shirt had ridden up as he'd carried her. "Get my phone," he barked, straining his neck for a look into Maggie's eyes. "Hip pocket. Dial 911. And try to keep up."

The moment Maggie retrieved the phone, Jack broke into a run.

Maggie followed, reporting the situation to a dispatcher as they ran. "She punched out the window to save us," she explained, detailing the horrific experience after noting their whereabouts and general situation. "One man grabbed my foot and she hit him with a rock. I think she broke his hand," she rambled. "She saved our lives, and now I think she might die!"

The final word nearly brought Jack to his knees. Katlin's skin was as pale as the moonlight, and losing her would surely stop his own heart. He couldn't let it happen.

Wouldn't let it happen.

Sirens raged in the distance, ripping their way through the night. Carousels of emergency lights wound high in the sky, drawing closer with each of his rampant heartbeats.

Cade was out of his seat the moment the waiting SUV came into view. "What the hell happened?" he yelled, breaking into a sprint for Jack and Maggie.

Jack opened his mouth to speak, but the words didn't come. Instead, he felt the heat and sting of emotion in his eyes, nose and throat. He couldn't lose her.

Would he lose her?

A riot of voices boomed through the night, rising on the air outside the home where Wyatt and Sawyer had been forced to open fire on a pair of men racing out with guns drawn.

Jack and Cade had taken the opportunity to find an alternate route of entry. The armed men at Rosch's property might as well have been beacons to Katlin and Maggie's location. Jack had taken to the alleyway, prepared for a stealthy extraction. Cade had remained at the wheel for a fast escape once the women had been recovered.

Katlin wasn't supposed to be hurt.

It wasn't supposed to turn out like this.

"On the ground!" Detective Reihl demanded in the distance, her voice strong and familiar.

Backup had officially arrived.

"Hands behind your back!" she demanded as the sound of doors being kicked open echoed through the night.

Cade darted into the road, playing chicken with the first ambulance on the street. He swung both arms overhead, shouting for the driver's attention. "Here!" He shoved the fingers of one hand into his mouth and whistled.

The ambulance redirected, bypassing the officers and arriving cruisers. Past Detective Reihl, who was cuffing men on the home's front lawn.

The EMTs piloted a gurney in Jack's direction. "What do we have?" the female asked, eyeballing Katlin as Jack placed her on the padded stretcher.

"Female, twenty-six," Jack began, fighting the tidal wave of fear and pain attempting to drag him under. "Multiple lacerations. Critical blood loss..." His ears rang as he ran down all that he knew about Katlin's condition, and let Maggie fill in the gaps he couldn't.

He watched, frozen and helpless, as they pressed an IV needle into her ghost-white skin, cut off her shirt, checked her vitals and cleaned her seemingly endless number of wounds.

He watched as they loaded Katlin into the bus, then pulled up Maggie with them.

And he watched as the ambulance drove away. Taking his heart with them.

KATLIN WOKE TO the blinding fluorescent light of a hospital. Her ears rang, and her eyes blurred as nearby voices spoke her name.

"Jack?" She'd parted her lips to speak. To ask how she'd gotten there. To ask if Maggie was okay. To request someone contact the police if they hadn't already. But the only thing her mouth and mind could manage together was that one precious word.

Jack.

The thought sent a spike of fear through her chest. Her gaze jumped from the myriad of blinking, beeping machines near her head to the door along the opposite wall. She'd been held captive. She'd gotten free. Gotten out with Maggie, and then there had been gunshots. "Jack."

"She's awake," someone whispered, drawing her attention from the closed door to a cluster of people at the end of her bed. Maggie beamed and covered her mouth, but didn't move. Instead, she slid her eyes in the direction of the most beautiful thing Katlin had ever seen.

Jack turned, eyes bright with relief and gratitude as he moved slowly in her direction. "Hey," he said, his voice as warm and light as the sun. "How are you feeling?"

Katlin felt her toes curl beneath the scratchy hospital blanket. "Better now." She bit her lip and did her best not to blush at the way he was looking at her. As if she was the most beautiful thing he'd ever seen, too. "Do I know you?" she teased.

Jack's lips twitched and curled at one corner. "Funny." The relief on his handsome face sent shivers down her spine, and when he came close enough, she reached for him.

He pressed his mouth to hers with such care and reverence that she turned to mush beneath his touch. Then he peeled her hands from his scruffy, bearded cheeks and planted a feather-light kiss on the bandaged palm.

Her fingertips curled over the warmth left behind

by his touch and tears swam in her blurring eyes. "I love you," she whispered, biting her lip and watching the flecks of green and gold grow more brilliant in his hazel eyes.

His mouth was on hers again in an instant. A long press at first, followed by a multitude of lighter ones. "I love you, too. I should have told you sooner."

Maggie squealed from her position at the end of Katlin's bed, and the Fortress men muttered things like "get a room."

"Katlin!" a familiar voice called, making her heart tighten in her chest.

Jack turned, giving view to faces she'd longed to see more than she'd realized.

"Mom? Dad!" she cried, unable to stifle the sudden punch of emotion. "How are you here?"

Her mother and father rushed to the bed, sending Jack out of the way.

"Baby," her mother wailed. "I'm so sorry we weren't here." She pressed warm palms to Katlin's cheeks, tears pooling in her brown eyes. "We've been on one plane after another since we got Jack's call." She pressed a kiss to Katlin's forehead, then rested her head against her daughter's. "We were so scared. What if we had lost you?"

"I'm okay," Katlin said, hearing the unspoken fear in her mother's words.

What if her parents had lost her, too? The way they'd lost Griffin.

"Jack saved me," she said, daring a look at her hero, who was shaking hands with her father while his teammates claimed their part in Katlin's saving.

Jack winked in her direction, and Katlin eagerly replayed his perfect words. *I love you, too. I should have told you sooner.*

Maggie bounced through the ring of brawny men, and threw her arms around Katlin's mom. "Hi, Mrs. Andrews," she said, stepping back with a wide grin. "Katlin cut herself saving me. She nearly died, but she's fine now. She's been out cold for hours, but before that she single-handedly broke up a gambling ring and took down a local crime boss and crooked police chief."

Her mom's mouth fell open. Her father frowned. Together, they turned to stare at Katlin.

"I had help," she said, waving an arm to the crew of newfound family before her, and a best friend she'd loved since college.

Her father moved in close and squeezed her unbandaged hand, then traded a look with her mother.

She turned her attention to the group gathered around Katlin's bed. "You were all there?"

Everyone nodded.

Her parents widened their eyes in wonder. "Well," her father said. "Let's hear it. We want to know everything. Including how we can ever repay you."

The room broke into a flurry of voices, each with their own tale of how the last week had gone down. Jack's teammates spoke of shoot-outs and corruption. The loss of Katlin's memory and the death of her poor boss, Attorney Fitch, killed by one of Rosch's henchmen. Maggie told of her capture and their daring escape. Jack ended the mash-up of stories with praise for Detective Reihl, her team and the district attorney, who'd made the arrests possible. "Thanks to them, it's safe for Katlin to live her life however she chooses again." He stroked her arm with the backs of his fingers and looked into her eyes.

He lowered his voice, turning his attention to her alone, and whispered, "I hope it will be with me."

She luxuriated in the sound of that. Living her life freely with Jack. Could there be anything better?

"What?" her dad asked, his voice sharp, bordering on harsh.

"Jack?" her mom asked, flipping her gaze from her husband, to her daughter, then to Jack.

"That nearly sounded like a proposal," her father said, crossing his arms and narrowing his eyes. "We talked about this."

Katlin's mouth sank open. "You talked about this?"

Jack nodded. "When I spoke with him by phone."

"I was on a plane en route from Libya," her father added. "I wasn't sure if I should give him a blessing or a beating, until I heard him out."

"Dad," Katlin gasped. The heat of embarrassment and anticipation scorched paths across her cheeks. "Stop."

"So, which was it?" Maggie asked. "Because he doesn't appear to have been beaten," she said out of the side of her mouth, wiggling her eyebrows at Katlin.

Katlin covered her face, a hodgepodge of emotions battling for the forefront in her mind. "I'm so sorry," she told Jack. "We don't have to talk about this right now," she whispered, casting a bashful glance over the quiet, painfully attentive guests.

But she hoped he'd still want to talk about it later.

Then Jack lowered to one knee and took her hand in his.

"Shut. Up," Maggie stage-whispered, linking her arm with Katlin's mother's and bouncing onto her toes.

A collective rumble rolled over the Fortress men as Jack fixed Katlin with a pointed stare. "I hadn't planned on doing this right now, but I also promised myself I'd never again put off telling you how I felt or how much you mean, so here it is." His voice cracked, and he cleared it before pressing on. "Katlin Andrews, you are the most fierce, resourceful and beautiful woman I have ever known. You healed and filled my broken heart when I was perfectly content with being miserable, and in doing so, you brought me back to life. I don't want to spend a minute of my future without you in it."

Katlin's throat ached and her eyes welled with unshed tears. "Jack," she croaked. "What are you doing?"

"Shhh!" Maggie exclaimed, and the group chuckled.

Katlin covered her mouth with shaking fingers, and filled her lungs with air.

"You trusted me to protect and fight for you the first night we met," Jack said. "If you'll take one more chance on me now, I promise that I will live a life dedicated to making you glad you did, every single day. For the rest of my life."

She sniffled, and a nurse passed her a box of tissues. A crowd of hospital staff filled the open doorway.

Jack rose to his feet and moved in close. "Katlin," he implored, leaning nearer still. "Marry me."

She nodded, unsure she could speak.

He stroked her cheek and kissed her nose, then raised her hand to his lips. "I'm afraid I'm going to need a verbal answer, for the record."

"Yes." Her laugh was interrupted by a fresh press of his lips.

And the room erupted in cheers.

The flash of a camera went off somewhere behind her closed eyelids, and she didn't care if the photo ended up in the paper or on the evening news. She loved Jack, and he loved her, and she melted deeply into the man who would be hers alone for the rest of their very long lives together.

* * * * *

COLTON 911: IN HOT PURSUIT

GERI KROTOW

To Mary Kerns
Thank you for your unconditional love

Chapter One

"This case has gone too far, Vikki. I think it'd be best if you ask to take your active-duty stint another time and do your part for our family business. Keep the Army out of this case." Riley Colton, CEO of Colton Investigations, stared at his little sister, Sergeant Victoria Colton, US Army Reserves JAG paralegal, his blue eyes bright with concern. Many people withered under Riley's scrutiny, but not Vikki. Strong, powerful men aiming their focus on her wasn't anything that bothered her. At Army JAG headquarters in Northern Virginia, she had often briefed general officers on legal cases and was used to taking her share of verbal volleys.

Vikki was even more accustomed to her older brother's intensity. Fifteen years her senior, Riley had helped raise his younger siblings after their parents had been tragically killed years ago. Riley knew her well, and it was difficult to hide anything from him. Except when it came to her job. While she worked as a legal consultant for CI, she was also a United States reserve soldier, a paralegal. Nothing trumped her duty to country. Currently a reservist on active duty, her orders were to investigate the death of an Army spouse at the nearby Fort Rapids base. The woman had been taking the RevitaYou supplement and died due to a toxic ingredient.

"I still can't tell you exactly what I'm doing for the Army with this case, Riley. Or any of you, as much as I'd love to put your minds at ease." She looked at the other four of her siblings who sat at the large dining-room table Riley insisted on using as a conference table, along with their tech expert, Ashanti Silver, and primary researcher, Bailey Chang. A half dozen other law enforcement officials occupied chairs in a second semicircle around the table. Colton Investigations was a multimillion-dollar operation and they used the table they'd all grown up with. Sorrow tempered with understanding pierced her musings when her gaze fell on her twin Sadie's empty chair.

"We don't want you endangered like Sadie." Kiely spoke up, and Vikki found the concern in her eyes heartbreaking. Kiely worked as a PI and was in high demand from law enforcement agencies at all levels.

Philippa, Kiely's twin, nodded in agreement. An attorney like their brother Griffin, Pippa missed nothing. Vikki trusted her judgment. Griffin sat across from her and stared at his legal pad, tapping his pencil. They were all worried sick about Sadie, even with her ensconced in a safe house Riley had found.

Vikki cleared her throat. "Unlike Sadie, I don't have an ex-fiancé who bankrolled a poisonous supplement." Her twin had been thrown when she discovered her ex-fiancé, Tate Greer, had been part of the major investor group at the top of the RevitaYou supplement's pyramid scheme. The epitome of a shark in dolphin clothing, he'd recently escaped custody and remained at large. His unknown whereabouts weighed heavily on the Colton siblings, as they wanted more than anything to keep Vikki's twin, Sadie, safe. "And remember, I'm trained to protect myself. I'm good. Trust me."

"It's not you we're concerned about, Vikki. It's Landon Street." Griffin yanked on his tie. "When I was in court for an adoption case earlier today, all the other lawyers were talking about was the legal case the Army could mount against the man who masterminded the RevitaYou formula. It's killed people after promising them the fountain of youth. The threat has to be a huge concern for Landon and his criminal cohorts. There's no telling what they'll be willing to do to keep the truth from getting out."

Vikki was set to interview Landon's half brother, a sergeant stationed at Fort Rapids. After failing to track down the suspect, her superiors at Fort Rapids needed to know Landon Street's whereabouts, and they figured his half brother, Flynn Cruz-Street, was a good place to start.

She looked at her fitness band for the time. "I'm already behind schedule. I need to get to Fort Rapids at the right time or I'm going to have to wait until tomorrow to start my investigation." She didn't want to wait. Finding justice for another dead victim of the tainted supplement RevitaYou, the promised youth elixir that for some unknown reason hadn't killed more people yet, was her top priority. She was tasked with collecting as much information as possible over the next twenty-four hours.

"Riley, have you heard from Brody lately?" Vikki posed the question before Riley ended the meeting. "The last I heard, he was still trying to avoid the RevitaYou debt collectors." Brody was their all-but-adopted brother, a disadvantaged teen whom their now deceased parents had taken under their wing. Recently, Brody got lured in by the lucrative promises of the supplement. He'd thought it'd be a great way to pay off his student loan debt. It enraged Vikki that he was the target of such lowlifes.

Riley waited for anyone else to speak up, then shook his head. "No. I'm afraid he's put himself undercover, not only hiding from the bad guys, but doing whatever he can to collect evidence against them."

"That doesn't surprise me." Still, it worried her. Brody was part of their family, too.

"Any chance you'll get out of the Army and join us at CI, sis?" Riley's countenance had softened and she saw the worry lines around his eyes. Since finding the love of his life, Charlize, Riley had mellowed, become more attentive to the lasting things in life: family, relationships, love. And they had a baby on the way, a true blessing for all of the Coltons.

Still, working at CI was the pivot point for their family. Vikki acknowledged that she and her five siblings were all so different, yet one thing they shared was their drive to be the best at whatever they found their calling to be. Luckily for CI, they were able to help out on various cases as needed, many on a volunteer basis.

Riley kept it all going, solving crimes that often the local law enforcement agencies struggled with due to case overload.

"Not if you're going to grill me at every meeting." That drew a round of laughs from the group and Vikki grinned. She'd missed them all so much. Army duty, even in the reserves, had taken her around the globe more than once, missing too many opportunities to bask in her family's affection. So much had changed for the Coltons in the last six months, including the addition of an entire new generation. Riley was about to become a father. Griffin was already a dad, as he and his love, Abigail, a noted scientist, were adopting her foster daughter, Maya. And Pippa and Kiely, also twins, had each found their fiancés in the midst of the RevitaYou investigation. Kiely was a new mom, thanks to FBI agent Cooper Winston's toddler son, Alfie. Pippa, long the intellectual heart of the family, had finally found a match in Grand Rapids PD detective Emmanuel. Everyone, except for Vikki and Sadie, was settling into their new families, enjoying the embrace of their partners. The pang of being away so much with several active-duty stints had hit Vikki harder this past year, since the awful betrayal by her cheating ex-boyfriend, Peter Stanley. Funny, she hadn't thought of him or how much he'd hurt her in a while. Her workload and concern over her twin had proved powerful distractions from her heartache. Hope sprang eternal that one day she'd forget him entirely. She prayed that would happen to Sadie one day. No matter how bad an egg any man proved to be, and in Tate's case, a criminal, it was still a loss.

Sadie mourned the loss of the relationship. Vikki felt her twin's grief deep in her heart, as if it was her own.

Riley stood, indicating the meeting was over. "Be careful on your drive back to post, Vikki. Weather reports show we may get a lake effect." Riley was always watching the weather, trying to control anything that could slow an investigation.

"This early?" She'd only recently put her few Halloween decorations away.

"It's November, sis."

"I brought a warm coat. I'll be home before a storm hits, anyhow."

She gave each of her siblings a quick hug, much as she had when she'd first arrived, with a promise to get together soon.

"'Bye!" With a quick wave, she walked out the front door toward her car. The air was replete with autumn, from the scent of the dry, crisp leaves under her feet to the swipe of frosty air. She relished the cold temperature, despite her shivers.

Maybe she should make more of an effort to spend more personal time with her siblings. But she'd been ashamed that she'd allowed Peter to take her for such a ride, making her think she was his everything. Until she'd come home early one weekday afternoon and found his cheating butt in her apartment with one of what had been several extracurricular affairs while they'd been together. The betrayal had been bad enough; for him to pick her apartment instead of his own hadn't helped.

It was a year ago. Move on.

She'd taken her time healing, but enough was enough. Vikki wanted to get back to being the woman she was before her heart had been crumpled and tossed in a waste bin. It was time to start living again.

After she dug in to the RevitaYou case.

The last of the day's light splayed from the skyline across Lake Michigan and lit up the view Vikki enjoyed from her small coupe. The westerly drive to Army Post Fort Rapids, on the other side of Grand Rapids, afforded her an unobstructed spectacle. Deep streaks of fuchsia and violet swept across the horizon, so rich they made her fingers itch for her watercolor brushes. A grunt escaped her throat, still scratchy from the eleven-hour drive. When was the last time she'd been able to take a day off, much less engage in her favorite hobby?

Her hands shook as she reviewed the meeting she'd just left. Vikki mentally went over her orders to gather all the information and potential evidence she could on RevitaYou, blamed for scores of users falling ill and now, in an awful turn, dying. Everyone at the CI table had been forthcoming with what they'd known. The team assembled around the Colton family table, also the CI conference table.

Riley had initially uncovered the pyramid scheme that had been established to distribute RevitaYou, at great profit to the criminal investors. Griffin was an adoption attorney by trade, but had been pulled into the RevitaYou mess when Abigail asked for help with Maya's adoption. Abigail's father was one of the original bankrollers of RevitaYou, but she had nothing to do with her father's illegal doings. In fact, it was Abigail who revealed that the sketchy supplement in truth contained a deadly, lethal substance: ricin. It was the by-product of castor oil that the chemist used in the formula.

Pippa volunteered to help CI draw out the loan sharks by going undercover, but was also drawn in by her bond with Emmanuel. Kiely worked nonstop as a private investigator and was working with the FBI when she at first butted heads with Cooper as they both became entangled in the RevitaYou case. The twins had each found love along the way, which made Vikki smile even while thinking about such a ghastly investigation.

Vikki represented the Army as her orders required, and when not in uniform, she helped her lawyer siblings, Griffin and Pippa, with whatever they needed for their portions of the case. Now she was under very specific orders from JAG headquarters in Virginia to collect information pertinent to the death of an Army officer's wife, due to RevitaYou. She shook her head as she drove, almost overwhelmed by the enormity of the investigation. What kept her focused was the desired endgame. Catch all players in the pyramid scheme gone wrong, and bring them to justice. All of the people and agencies they represented shared the immutable outcome.

She shut off her radio as she approached the post's main entrance gate, slipping into her Army paralegal role as easily as she'd served as a paralegal for CI at the earlier meeting.

Everything she knew before joining the Army, she'd learned in her home state of Michigan. The sole Colton sibling to join the military, she'd eschewed going to college, enlisted in the Army right after high-school graduation ten years ago. It was a decision she had zero regrets about.

When she'd enlisted, Vikki hadn't been stationed here right away. But after a two-year active-duty stint at JAG headquarters in Fort Belvoir, Virginia, Vikki had signed up for the reserves and been stationed at Fort Rapids ever since. Her immediate superior, a JAG officer, had asked her yesterday if she was interested in getting the latest information on this high-stakes case. Since she'd been working the case on the fringes for her attorney siblings, she hadn't hesitated to volunteer.

Stopping at the gate, she passed her ID and a copy of her TDY orders through the open window to the sentry. "Evening, Sergeant."

The guard, an MP, scanned her ID with his handheld instrument. Once he verified her identity, he read over her Temporary Duty orders. Handing her ID and paperwork back, he waved her through the gate.

Victoria had spent much of her high-school years on post, where the local small towns used the state-of-the-art fields and track for athletic events. She always enjoyed arriving back on base as part of her reserve duty. But this wasn't a time to reminisce. Time was her nemesis. The sooner she gathered the intel her boss needed, she'd have more time to work for CI again. And also, hopefully more time to spend with her family. She'd been contemplating the idea of leaving the Army reserves to more fully devote herself to the family business. But for now, she was 100 percent committed to her duty.

What a mess she faced in this current investigation. As she reread the facts, it was hard to reconcile the peaceful, law-abiding city she'd grown up in and its adjacent Army post as the scene of such deadly goings-on.

Ingestion of ricin-laced RevitaYou was the suspected cause of death for an Army captain's spouse, Teri Joseph. Right before her death due to mysterious symptoms, the victim had bragged to her friends that she'd felt younger than she had in years. Several other spouses had fallen ill, as well, but survived. The common denominator: they'd all attended the same home shopping party and taken the nefarious supplement several times after.

Captain Joseph, widower of the woman killed by RevitaYou, had been making threatening statements at work, not so quietly railing against the "Toxic Scientist" Landon Street, ever since his wife had died. Vikki's superiors wanted her to interview the widowed officer to try to determine if his threats were just grief gone haywire or worse. She wasn't a clinical psychologist, and didn't think it was up to her to figure out if the man was mentally stable or not, but orders were orders. She'd learned Captain Emerson Joseph's regular work hours, 0730-1700, from his administrative assistant. So far, the captain had ignored every phone call and message she'd left him, at work and at home.

The second person of interest was of more importance. Vikki hadn't attempted to contact him yet. She paused to read over the file of the sergeant she was going to be interviewing. Her boss had stressed that she shouldn't give him a heads-up. "Surprise is the best tool you have in a situation like this, Sergeant Colton."

Sergeant Flynn Cruz-Street, a decorated combat MP, was the half brother of mad scientist Landon Street, who had created the formula for the deadly supplement. If anyone knew where Landon was hiding out, Sergeant Cruz-Street would. He'd claimed to be estranged from his brother, but wasn't that typical of someone realizing they were in trouble for associating with a criminal? Vikki wanted to interview Cruz-Street ASAP. Since some of Captain Joseph's threatening statements had been directed at Cruz-Street, the sooner, the better. Before the aggrieved officer's words escalated to physical violence.

Vikki took a few minutes in the barracks parking lot to review her notes. As she skimmed the report again, she had a fleeting wish that Riley's suggestion that she leave this investigation to her siblings and other LEA professionals was possible. The case gave her the creeps. She'd been exposed to plenty of salespersons over the years in the Army Reserves, especially as she'd advanced in rank.

Her Army buddies included her in their family activities even though she remained happily single, and she was grateful. Several of their spouses were into various types of consumables sold in a home setting, from kitchenware to lingerie. It always tickled her when one of the spouses of someone she worked long hours with invited her to purchase yet another plastic container promising to keep her MRE fresher than ever. She didn't like the pyramid-scheme-y feel to them, though, which was another reason the RevitaYou case had jumped out at her. She often thought that civilian reps of these get-rich-quick-promise companies saw military spouses as easy marks. It was hard to make a separate career succeed when your active-duty spouse's career had you moving every two years to often remote postings.

A recent dinner party she'd attended had had a representative hawking vitamins, but Victoria had declined to buy any of the supplements. She wasn't against remedies, but the Army had a zero-tolerance policy when it came to drugs. Without knowing exactly what she was putting into her body, she ran the risk of popping positive on a random chemical analysis. Even though she'd be able to show proof of the vitamins, it wasn't worth the hassle. She noted that none of the alleged RevitaYou consumers on base were active duty or reserve, but rather Army family members. Was the Army's no-drugs policy the only thing that kept active duty from getting sick, or worse, due to RevitaYou?

With a final mirror check to ensure her hair was smoothed back into its bun and that she appeared every inch a US Army paralegal, she headed for the door. She'd find Captain Joseph first, saving what she expected to be the longer interview with Landon's half brother for a bit later. Sergeant Cruz-Street had better have some answers for her.

No one messed with her Army.

SERGEANT FLYNN CRUZ-STREET flopped onto the sofa in his barracks room and fired up his laptop. After a twelve-hour-duty shift, followed by two hours at the gym, and a huge, protein-rich meal at the chow hall, all he wanted to do was finish the paper for his British Literature class. One paper and two courses away from an online master's degree in English lit, he was determined to finish. He had another year left on his Army contract. His long-term dream was to earn a PhD in English literature and work in academia.

A ding from his phone reminded him that he had several unanswered texts, all from his Army buds and one from his mother, Rosa Cruz-Street. They'd heard the rumors about Landon. Who hadn't? Everyone knew his estranged paternal half brother, Landon Street, was suspected of creating a vitamin supplement allegedly responsible for scores of users falling ill—and now a death on this very Army post. He'd heard it was the spouse of an active-duty member, but so far no names had been released. Fort Rapids was like any other American town in that news and gossip traveled quickly. But with over twenty thousand active-duty and family members living on post, the particulars of any single incident weren't something he'd know about. His friends didn't believe him, though, when he assured them he had no idea how many people had been sickened, or if it was true that his half brother's supplement was to blame.

"Where the heck are you, Landon?" He spoke the words to his empty room, wishing he'd paid more attention the last time he'd seen his half brother, over two months ago, at their father's grave site. When reports of people being sickened came out, Flynn had tried to convince Landon to turn himself in, but Landon had insisted that RevitaYou was a "perfect molecular compound" that hadn't caused the illnesses. And then his sibling disappeared and had not been reachable since. If people had died because of Landon's crazy chemical cocktail, then how many more were in danger?

"Dang it." He opened the internet browser on his laptop, but not to find his favorite movie. Maybe if he put the last several places he'd seen Landon on a map, he'd be able to figure out how to find him now. Because this had to stop.

A large bang from the adjoining room cut through his concentration. All senses went on alert, a holdover from being in a combat zone, yes, but also an intrinsic part of his job as a military policeman. Another sound echoed through the room, and his gut tightened. He had his quarters to himself with no roomies, earned from long hours and a spotless performance record. The privilege of having not only a bedroom but an additional room with a kitchenette and work area seemed great when he'd been assigned it last year. But with the threat of an unknown intruder, it suddenly seemed not so great.

Silently and purposefully, Flynn rose and went to the threshold to his workroom. Incredibly, he heard breathing, and it wasn't his. Without preamble, he stepped in front of the entrance and yelled.

Into the face of his superior.

"Captain Joseph?"

"Bastard!" Without further warning, Emerson Joseph launched himself at Flynn, pummeling as if his life depended on it.

"Oof!" Flynn deflected the blows as they came at

him, but a right hook to his jaw landed square and he cursed. "Sir, stop! What's this about?"

Joseph kept swinging, never letting up. "Your brother killed—" jab "—my—" punch "—wife!" Captain Joseph roared the last word and, while it seemed to give his attacker more momentum, it made Flynn's defensive posture deflate.

This was the active-duty person who'd lost their spouse? His boss?

"Teri is dead, sir?" He managed the query between gasps, ducks and dives, swerving to avoid the captain's particularly painful left punch.

"Don't act as if you didn't know, Cruz-Street. Stop the innocent act. I'll never forgive you or your brother." Captain Joseph stepped back and Flynn waited, praying that the man was finally deplete of his rage, but when Joseph's right hand retrieved his sidearm, Flynn raised his arms.

"Whoa, sir, stop. This is insane. We can talk this out." Sweat trickled between his shoulder blades and Flynn forced all thoughts about Joseph being his superior officer aside. As long as the man had his weapon out, he was an attacker, the enemy.

"Teri's never going to talk again!" Flynn watched in horror as Captain Joseph pointed his pistol at him. Remaining thoughts fled as Flynn acted on years of Army training and instinct. Within three seconds that felt more like a lifetime, he wrestled Joseph onto the floor and held him down, gripping the right hand with the weapon with as much strength as he could summon. Though he held Joseph's wrist flat against the floor, the captain still managed to fire two shots. Plaster flew and glass shattered, but Flynn barely noticed. All he focused on was keeping himself out of the crosshairs.

VIKKI TRIED TO ignore the tantalizing smell of the half dozen cider donuts resting on the passenger seat as she pulled up to the enlisted housing area. It'd been impossible to resist a quick dinner of fish tacos from a local taqueria food truck on post after she'd had zero luck contacting Captain Joseph and his immediate superior, the post commander, hadn't had any helpful information about where Joseph went after duty hours. If he'd been home, he hadn't answered his doorbell. The house had been dark, but she knew if she'd just lost her spouse she might be sitting in a darkened room, too, unwilling to speak to anyone.

With the delicious meal behind her, she was back to business, determined to get at least one interview under her belt before she called it a day. Hopefully, Sergeant Flynn Cruz-Street had at least an idea of where his half brother was. Finding the scientist who'd created RevitaYou would be a huge boon and help close this case all the sooner.

Leaving her car in the Bachelor Enlisted Quarters parking lot, she entered the large building and quickly jogged up the stairs. As she placed her hand on the steel door to enter the third floor, two shots rang out. She didn't open the door right away, but took stock of her situation and reached for her phone.

Another shot, footsteps pounding. After calling post

security, she heard sirens, no doubt triggered by other callers who heard the gunshots, or the victim.

The victim.

Vikki didn't carry a sidearm unless in a combat area, but she knew enough first aid that she'd be able to help anyone who'd been hit. Moving very slowly, she inched the door open and looked into the corridor. A handful of men and women were standing in the hall, and she whispered to the nearest.

"Do you know which room it's coming from?"

A petite blonde turned to face her, looked over her uniform. "Who are you?"

"Sergeant Colton, JAG."

The woman nodded. "Right. It's coming from Sergeant Cruz-Street's room. We don't know any more and, frankly, shouldn't be out here. The MPs are on their way."

Vikki tried to keep her professional bearing, but at the mention of her much-needed interviewee, her stomach clenched. "Has he been shot?"

"I told you, we don't know. Are you okay?"

Vikki nodded. Before she had a chance to buck up, more shots rang out and she watched in horror as a man stumbled out of number 312, Cruz-Street's room. But he was wearing a captain's uniform, not a sergeant's. He turned in the direction of the stairwell and began to run.

"Anybody try to take me out, I'll shoot!" He swung his handgun up and down the corridor, the motion freezing everyone in place. He took slow, steady steps toward the stairwell. Toward Vikki.

As he neared, Vikki looked at his name badge, his insignia. *Joseph.* The widowed officer.

"Captain Joseph, I can help you." She stood in front of the woman she'd spoken to, determined to talk this man off the ledge and keep others from being hurt. "Please, put your weapon away."

He didn't say a word until he was past her, his hand on the stairwell door as he held it slightly ajar, ready to escape. "Who are you?" His weapon was still drawn but at least he'd lowered his arm. The gun hung at his side, pointed to the floor. His eyes kept moving back and forth, constantly monitoring the soldiers behind her. Sirens drew closer and she knew her time with him was short.

"I'm a JAG representative, sir. I'm so sorry for your loss, but this isn't how to handle it, sir."

He peered at her name badge for what felt like eons. Everything else faded away and it was just her and this captain, a widower, who'd just done something irrevocably wrong. She prayed he'd only fired warning shots. *Please don't let it be murder.* She hadn't met Sergeant Cruz-Street yet; he couldn't be dead.

But she'd heard the shots. If he was still alive, Cruz-Street must be in bad shape. Few survived that many bullets.

The sound of pounding feet, sure and rapid, echoed up the stairwell. Post security.

His eyes narrowed and he glowered at her. "Tell your boss that he's too late. And he'll pay for what happened to my wife, too. You all will." Spittle flew as he mouthed the threat, but before Vikki could react, he darted into the stairwell and up the stairs. There were three more floors—was he going to take hostages?

"Way to go. Who the hell are you?" Harsh words spoken with a deep voice boomed behind her. Vikki turned and looked into whiskey-brown eyes. Sharp, keenly intelligent. Focused on his prey.

"Cruz-Street, you okay?" An MP stood on the landing, looking straight at the man wearing workout gear who wouldn't take his gaze off her.

"I'm fine, Jimenez. Captain Joseph ran into this stairwell."

"He went up the stairs." Vikki pointed, still feeling the burn of Cruz-Street's stare on her cheek.

Without preamble, the MP motioned his team forward and disappeared up the stairwell.

"Who are you?" He asked the question again and she faced him. His voice reached out and pulled something in her middle taut, though his eyes revealed nothing but simmering anger.

"Sergeant Vikki Colton, JAG." She swallowed. "I'm actually here to meet you. Are…are you okay, Sergeant?"

Recognition flared when she'd said "JAG," as if he'd forgotten what was causing all of this chaos. RevitaYou. But when she asked about his welfare, a frown turned what she realized must be dimples into deep grooves on either side of his mouth.

"I'm fine, Sergeant Colton."

"It's Vikki." Eager to ease any tension, she forced a smile. "We're both soldiers. This won't take long. I'm here to help."

"I have nothing to tell you. If you don't mind, I have work to do." He turned toward his open room door, where they both saw a pair of MPs exit. The man in front nodded at Cruz-Street.

"It's clear, Sergeant, but we're going to need to take photos and samples for evidence. And you need to be checked out by the post clinic."

"I'm fine. The only thing injured by bullets was my wall. Can I get my laptop?"

"Not until we're done."

Cruz-Street swore a string of words Vikki hadn't heard since she'd been on a deployment. "Make sure you give me a signed statement for my instructor, who's expecting a paper from me by midnight tonight."

"You can use the post library." The MP wasn't taking any guff from his senior enlisted soldier. It was a matter of security.

"Me and all the high-school kids. Joy. Can I at least get my shoes and a jacket?"

Vikki bit back a smile. The situation was anything but humorous, yet Sergeant Cruz-Street's mannerisms bespoke a man who thought on his feet and made the best of a horrible situation.

Cruz-Street disappeared into his barracks room and she waited until he returned wearing athletic shoes, a civilian jacket and the same frown he'd given her five minutes earlier.

His expression deepened the moment he saw that she was still in the corridor.

"I told you I don't have any information for you."

"And I tried to explain that I'm here to help."

"The last thing I need or want is any help from you, Sergeant Colton."

Chapter Two

"Vikki. I told you, call me by my first name, Flynn. We're the same rank, for heaven's sake." Her face still had that professional expression, made harsher under the barracks fluorescent lights. But it didn't take away from her attractiveness.

Flynn sized up his opponent. Almost his exact height, save for an inch or two, easily attributed to her heels. Articulate, professional, thorough. She'd done her homework or she'd never have been able to talk to Captain Joseph like that.

"You're lucky Captain Joseph didn't take you out."

"As are you." She had green eyes that he'd bet had leveled a lesser soldier under her scrutiny. Civilians made the mistake that JAG officers were the driving force behind the Army's judicial system, but Flynn knew better. He'd worked with enough JAG enlisted in his tours to know that the paralegals did the heavy lifting for the JAG corps. He wasn't fooled by Sergeant Vikki Colton's sparkling green eyes or stunning smile. Her petite, curvy but Army-trim appearance belied the predator-like way a paralegal often had to act to get information. Nor was he distracted by her attempt to appear as a friend. She'd take anyone down she considered guilty. Plus, he suspected she was related to Riley Colton of CI. He'd worked with Riley on several cases pertinent to both Fort Rapids and Grand Rapids.

"I've got work to do, Vikki." She didn't even blink when he said her name on a long, purposefully drawn-out note. "I put in a full day at my command, and I have an online course paper due by midnight."

"So you won't mind if I walk with you to the library, then. We can talk on the way." She motioned for him to walk alongside her as they left the building.

"I'm driving myself there—the library's on the other side of the post."

Color rose in her cheeks. "I know where the library is. I mean, I knew that. I'd forgotten. I'm from here. I practically grew up on this post. My family is Grand Rapids through and through."

"Is your family any relation to Colton Investigations?"

She had the humility to nod right away. "Yes. Riley, the CEO, is my brother. I work for CI as a civilian. Have you ever worked with him?"

Anger stirred in Flynn's gut. "Yes. I'm so glad that a terrible situation that has cost a life and may contribute to more is working out for both your personal and professional gain. That's why I joined the Army."

"That's not true." She raised her chin and glared at him. "I'm a reservist, but I'm on active duty now, and I've been directed to interview you by my commanding officer. There is no conflict of interest here. I haven't discussed my Army orders with CI. As I see it, you have a choice, Flynn. I can have my CO call your CO and get your entire chain of command involved, or you can do the reasonable, right thing first. On your own."

He actually had to fight a smile. "I've never been accused of doing anything but the right thing, Vikki." She stopped in front of a modest red sedan. For some reason he'd expected she'd drive a decked-out SUV, courtesy of CI.

"Is this your ride?"

She nodded.

"How about dropping me off at the library? You can ask me all the questions you want on the way."

"No problem."

Five minutes later, they were driving in her car. The small but sporty Ford screamed practical. Vikki's claim about being a true-blue Grand Rapids citizen was reflected in her choice of make. Vikki turned onto the post perimeter road. There wasn't a more direct route to the library as the airstrip intersected the post.

"I'm surprised you drive a red car. Kind of stands out for your undercover work." He couldn't help teasing her.

She didn't take her gaze off the road, and he didn't blame her. Traffic violations on post came with heftier prices than civilian transgressions. Garner too many points and post driving privileges would be revoked.

"I'm a paralegal for the Army, not a private investigator, no matter what it looks like. When I'm working for CI, my work can include investigations, but usually I stick to the legal side of things." She slowed the car at a crosswalk and waited while a group of soldiers crossed the road. "You're looking a little cramped. Is your seat too close to the dash? There's a lever between your legs." He had to look at her then, to see if for the first time in his career a woman was being completely unprofessional with him. From the grimace on her face, she'd only heard her words after they'd left her mouth. Flynn couldn't make a joke about it, as he didn't want her to think he was being inappropriate. "I mean, *under* your seat." Her voice remained steady, but he wondered if her cheeks were red. Impossible to tell in the evening darkness.

"I'm not complaining. The seat's fine, plenty of legroom. Your heat works and—look at this—heated seats!" He flicked on the switch for his.

"Why do I feel as though you're slamming me for having my own car? Don't you have your own?"

"I do, but it's a little more…suited for the weather here." And he'd loaned it to his best friend, Josh, so that he could go north to hunt for a few days. He'd get it back tomorrow.

Vikki's face reflected the bluish glow from her dashboard's navigation screen. "When I came back to Michigan after being downrange for a while, during my last annual reserve duty, I splurged on a hybrid. It's small, sure, but it gets better mileage."

"That's wonderful, but not so great when you're dealing with a Lake Michigan snowstorm."

"I've managed so far."

"Where else have you served before coming back here?"

"Permanently? Only to Virginia, Army JAG headquarters. Staff duty. After a couple of years I came back here. I prefer the reserves. I don't like being far from my family."

"Rough duty."

She laughed. "Believe it or not, it was a lot of long hours. And I did deploy a couple of times along the way." Vikki maneuvered her environmentally responsible car into the library parking lot and chose a spot in front. She kept the engine running, for the heater.

"I need to ask you some questions. We can finish this tomorrow morning, but I need a few basics right now."

"Okay." He'd have preferred to keep talking about anything but the real reason she was here. He tried to dislike her, but Vikki Colton was proving to be more interesting by the minute. He tried to hide a long sigh. It was sad that a paralegal sent to ferret out information about his brother was a bright spot in what had become long workdays followed by intense studying. He needed to get out more, expand his social world. Date. Then he wouldn't be vulnerable to the likes of Vikki Colton. Landon's recent screwups had made the last couple of months insane, added to the pressure Flynn already carried to be his Army best and also finish up his master's degree.

She reached to the ceiling and tapped on the overhead lights. He squinted against the glare but didn't break eye contact. Flynn had nothing to hide. And nothing that would prove useful to this JAG soldier.

"Do you know where your half brother is?"

"No."

"No idea at all? Or are you saying you don't know where Landon is right at this moment?"

"Both. And I don't mess around when it comes to legal or security, Sergeant. Do you think I would have made it this far if I had?"

Emerald irises surrounded her pupils, made small by the inside light. He knew she'd turned on the lights for both of their protection, so neither could accuse the other of anything inappropriate. And probably to be able to read him better. He got it. But he didn't like it.

"You look annoyed, Flynn. We're on first names from here out. I hope I don't have to remind you again. I've got a job to do here and it won't get done as quickly as it can if you keep making me dig for answers. But make no mistake—I've got all the time in the world. I'm happy to make your life as miserable as I have to in order to get my job done."

"Define your job for me, Vikki?"

"I've been sent to interview Captain Joseph, and to find out if he's serious about his threats against Landon. After seeing him nearly kill you tonight, I'm fairly certain that he'll harm your half brother if he finds him. So now I have to find Landon first, to keep him safe from Captain Joseph, and hopefully to prevent Joseph from committing assault or murder. It's imperative that I find Landon.

"I also want to interview him about his supplement, RevitaYou. Several Army spouses have sold it and scores more have bought it during in-home, on-post retail events. Dozens of users have been sickened by the supplement, even as more swear by its rejuvenating properties. Now we have another death reportedly related to the concoction. I need to find Landon and get a verified list of all the ingredients from him."

"I'm aware of the reports. And I know Landon like you should hope you never do. He's a dangerous person, Vikki. He'll never give any ingredient list to you." The investigation wasn't his issue, but finding his half brother before Captain Joseph—or someone else—did was. In Flynn's opinion, the dangerous supplement Landon was peddling needed to be removed from the market ASAP. Let the forensic crime labs figure out what was in RevitaYou. Ricin had already been determined to be the deadly ingredient. How could anyone trust Landon to tell the truth, anyway? Vikki had to know her quest wasn't going to get her what she wanted, even if she managed to find Landon.

"My half brother is not the altruistic type, and the last thing he'll do is admit that there's something lethal in his product or turn over his criminal contacts to you. He doesn't know how to be honest, trust me."

"He doesn't have a choice. Not with lives still at stake. No one's safe until we get a full recall, and to do that most expeditiously, we need him to verify what we already know. Two people are dead from ricin poisoning. And there could be more lethal ingredients in the mix, too." She wasn't backing down and, while Flynn knew he was right—Landon would not give up easily—he respected Vikki Colton for standing her ground.

"He'd beg to differ. Before you ask again, no, I don't know where he is, where he's been since I reported him to the cops twice or where he's going to be next. For all

I know, he's left the state, or even gone over the border into Ontario."

"I'd like to think he'd be stopped by Customs at the border. He's a person of interest in this investigation and it's become part of a larger operation." Vikki wasn't giving an inch.

"Is there any chance it could still be Army business, with no civilian interference?"

Vikki didn't answer him right away. Instead she looked out the windshield at the brightly lit library building, the people coming and going. Was she looking for strength to break it to him that his half brother was a criminal? Wanted for possible murder? He quietly snorted. Nothing he didn't already know. Leaves swirled as the gusts off Lake Michigan intensified, and he thought he saw her shiver. Turning back to him, she offered a gaze that was compassionate at best, pitying at worst.

"It would have been Army business if everything had happened on post. People here were getting sick and the common denominator was RevitaYou. But a handful of people have died all over Grand Rapids… It's gone too far, Flynn. Your half brother is no longer looking at fines for some kind of production oversight that made people sick. It's bigger than that.

"If it's proved that RevitaYou is responsible for Teri Joseph's death, Landon will be charged with manslaughter or even murder, depending upon what we discover. And if you have any idea where he could be and aren't telling me, you'll face a trial, too. As an accomplice." Her eyes narrowed and he swore the walls she had around herself were nearly visible. She clearly thought he was a criminal, just like Landon.

It shouldn't bother him. So why did it feel like she'd just sucker punched him?

"I'm not going to defend myself when there's nothing to defend. I can tell you where and when I last saw him, what he was wearing. Since it was months ago, I have to think that's of no help to you now. I have no clue where he's gone or for what reasons. Landon's always had his problems and run-ins with the law, but murder? No, that's not my half brother. He wouldn't intentionally harm someone."

Flynn believed this, but he also believed Landon wouldn't stop until he gained what he felt was coming to him. Somehow his disturbed sibling had gotten the funds and resources to create a vitamin credited as the fountain of youth. "I know it appears as though Landon's product killed Teri Joseph, but we don't know yet—do we?—for sure. And I don't know about the other victims."

"You sound like you're defending Landon, Flynn. Are you?"

"Not at all. Trust me, I want him apprehended as quickly as you do, probably sooner. He's made my family's life a living hell these past several months." The sight of the sadness in his mother's face—Rosa Cruz-Street was also Landon's stepmother—and the thought of Landon's misdeeds smearing their deceased father's memory made him physically ill. Rosa had tried so hard to raise Landon as her own after she'd married their father, but his half brother had always been a tough nut.

Flynn didn't think anyone would have been able to save Landon from himself, from the inner demons that drove him to consistently choose the wrong fork in the road. Not that Flynn was about to share all of this with Vikki Colton. Not while she considered Flynn a prime suspect.

"I'm sorry. It has to be awful, seeing your half brother go downhill and hurt the ones you love most." Spoken without a hint of sarcasm. "But it doesn't change the facts, Flynn. Captain Joseph is after Landon with one intent—to kill him. I need answers about RevitaYou. We have to find him before anyone else dies."

At those words, Flynn's resolve to stay far away from Landon's troubles shattered. It wasn't Vikki's stunning jade green stare or being so close to her in the cramped confines of her car, where he caught whiffs of her tasteful but tantalizing perfume. He had to do the right thing, regardless of the consequences. It was in his DNA and reinforced by a decade of military training.

"I know where he likes to hang out."

"MY HALF BROTHER hangs out by our father's grave a lot." Flynn Cruz-Street spoke as if he'd been keeping a secret for too long. Vikki had enough experience interviewing persons of interest and suspects that she knew to remain quiet, to become the consummate listener.

Flynn stared at the darkness beyond the windshield, but she knew he was seeing something completely different from the well-lit post library, the sidewalks in front sprinkled with blue-tinted salt. A gust of wind rocked her tiny car and she turned the heat a few degrees higher.

"Do you visit your dad's grave, too?"

"Not as much as I think Landon does." Flynn had one hand on his left thigh, the other holding the dashboard as if he thought the car was going to crash. Compassion made her hand rise to place it on his shoulder in a signal of support. She snatched it back at the last moment, reminding herself to keep it professional. While Flynn seemed reasonable, it was always possible that he'd take it the wrong way, misinterpret her intentions. He didn't seem to notice her almost-touch and she was grateful for the dim light inside the vehicle.

"He's always been a bit off, my half brother. When I was little, I thought he was the coolest dude. We're eleven years apart and it was easy to idolize him. My mother married my dad after Landon's mother abandoned them. Landon always pushed everything to the limit. I was a little kid when he was a teen, but I still remember the fights between him and my parents. It was rough at times, but my parents kept him in line, provided what I realize now were opportunities to use his energy in more positive ways.

"Against all odds, based on his elementary-school grades, he pulled himself out of it and got top grades in high school. When he got into Michigan State, my parents threw a huge high-school graduation party. We visited him almost every weekend. That was more for me than Landon, I suspect. I was broken up when he left for college." His gaze flitted over her face, but she wasn't fooled by the brevity of the glance. Flynn was checking to make sure she wasn't judging him or thinking less of him for admitting such a private memory.

"That's normal. I was sad when each of my older siblings left, too, and I had a twin to keep me company."

"I know what you're doing, Vikki." His tone had shifted, his gaze suspicious. "It doesn't matter. I'm telling you the truth regardless."

"You mean—"

"Your interrogation techniques. Give me what seems like an intimate piece of information about you for one of mine. Do you even have a twin?"

She felt heat rush to her face, followed by what felt like ice take hold in her veins. She hoped he didn't notice her shivers. "It's true that what you described can be a method for getting a witness, suspect or client to open up." She couldn't deny it. But worse, she didn't want to tell him that she'd actually volunteered her family information.

You don't even know Cruz-Street. Watch it.

She needed to remember that, until she had several answers, Flynn was a possible suspect in her investigation. He possibly aided and abetted Landon.

"Save your skill set for the real suspects in this case. My half brother and now it looks like Captain Joseph are the people who need to be caught."

"Do you think the captain is more of a problem, other than the fact he's stated he wants to kill Landon and tried to hurt you? Is he involved with RevitaYou?"

His brow rose and she stifled a smile. "Isn't that reason enough, even for a JAG?"

"Hey, we'd better have an agreement right now to not mock each other's ratings." Vikki's tone was firm, no-nonsense. "JAGs do their part, and MPs do theirs. Although your job does seem Neanderthal in comparison to mine."

"Touché." He gave her the point. This time.

All of her internal warning bells clanged a cacophony of unease, and she wished she could turn back the last few minutes if only to keep herself from being drawn in by Flynn. The way he'd handled being attacked by his boss and the straightforward manner in which he answered her questions was impressive. Combined with his handsome looks, and the charm she caught glimpses of in his broad smile, Flynn Cruz-Street was exactly the kind of man she'd be attracted to. If he wasn't a suspect…

And if Peter hadn't cheated on you in the worst way.

Was her broken heart ever going to let go of the pain for good?

Desperate to change course, Vikki looked at the notes on her phone.

"It sounds as though you and your half brother are a lot closer, still, than you've let on. You've met him in the cemetery at least twice in the last several months—if you're telling the truth—yet you say you don't have a relationship with him any longer."

"'Let on' what to whom? I've only just met you, Serge—Vikki. And I reported each of the two times I've spotted Landon since we found out about his business scheme tipping into criminal activity. Both times,

I happened to run into him, and the last time I barely recognized him. He was wearing a wig and clothes he'd never normally wear." Flynn defended himself naturally. Without any kind of defensive posturing she'd experienced with other clients and suspects. Her training taught her that she couldn't go on her gut alone, but she'd learned it rarely proved her wrong. Flynn seemed honest, though, with nothing to hide.

Still, Landon was his half brother and RevitaYou had brought its creator millions of dollars. It'd be foolish on her part to ignore one of the main enticements that turned a good guy bad. Sex, power and money were the criminal temptation trifecta, in her experience.

"Did he see you at those times? Did you have a conversation?"

"The first time, as I've already reported, yes, we spoke. I said hello, as I hadn't seen him in months."

"Did he mention RevitaYou at that time?"

"No, but I did. Infomercials were on national television networks and music streaming services. It sounded as though he'd been able to expand his reach and, at first, I was genuinely happy for him. His graduate degree in chemistry was finally paying off."

"Have you ever tried RevitaYou?"

He grimaced. "Heck, no. I'm not big on any supplements, to be honest. I make myself protein shakes after a heavy lifting workout, but that's about it."

"Do you know anyone who has? Has your mother?"

"My mother? No, she's not the type to fall for gimmicky stuff. As happy as I first was for Landon, it was clear to me that the most this concoction did was allow folks to think they were doing something to turn back the clock. I don't believe any of the hype. And now it's proved lethal."

"I'm sorry. This has to be hard, seeing Landon take the wrong path." She'd already said it but wanted him to know she meant it. And ignored the part of her that was warning her to keep a professional detachment with Flynn.

"It's not me I'm worried about. My mother—she's the one I hate to see hurt again and again." The resignation in his voice spoke of a whole lot of sadness.

"Is Landon in touch with her?"

"No, not that I know of. I'm certain she'd tell me if he showed up or called her. He's dropped out of sight since the deaths occurred. She's worried sick about him, always has been, to be honest. I worry about her, as she lives alone in the house we grew up in." He confirmed that Rosa resided at the same address Vikki had uncovered, in a Grand Rapids suburb.

Vikki scanned her phone notes again, making certain she hadn't missed anything. Flynn's description of his mother tugged at her heart. It'd be wonderful to still have her mother and her father here to worry about her. Since their tragic deaths years ago, she'd learned what grieving meant, as had all of her siblings.

Focus on the case.

"That's all I've got regarding your half brother. If you'll spare me five more minutes, I need to know your take on Captain Joseph."

"He's been my boss for the last year. He's a hothead

and can be a little rough around the edges, but he's always been a good guy. And a devoted family man. His wife is everything to him. Was." Disbelief cracked the otherwise confident reply.

"How many times have you seen him since his wife died?"

"You mean since his wife was murdered by my half brother's poisonous, phony supplement?" He shook his head. "I hadn't seen him until tonight. And the man who broke into my barracks room, who fired his weapon like he did, the man who confronted and threatened you in the hallway, that wasn't the Captain Joseph I know. He's out of his mind with grief."

"Are you saying he wasn't trying to harm you?"

"No. I don't know. He sure had the look of wanting me dead. He definitely fired his weapon and would have taken me out if he could. He wasn't there, in his eyes. Do you know what I mean, Vikki?"

She stared at him, into his dark eyes that were no more than eighteen inches from hers. This was a man who'd seen a lot of what she had downrange, and probably a heck of a lot more. He deserved her honesty, even if she still had to consider him a suspect.

"I do. Sometimes people get too much thrown at them in too short of a time. We all have a breaking point."

"Have you ever been close to yours?" It was as if he'd read her mind about her parents.

"I don't think that's any of your business, Flynn."

A sharp rap on her window startled her, and she

turned to see one of the MPs from the barracks motioning for her to roll down her window.

"Yes, Corporal Hanson?" She read his name tag.

"Sorry to bother you, Sergeant Colton, but the security team is concerned that Captain Joseph is looking for you."

"Me? He doesn't know me."

"He confronted you in the barracks and several witnesses heard him threaten you. He's already assaulted Sergeant Cruz-Street, and he's known him for a long time. It'd be easier for him to harm you, as you're an easy target, without the emotional issues he may have toward Sergeant Cruz-Street."

"Holy moly, Hanson, you make it sound like the CO and I are buddies." Flynn broke the tension and they all had a brief laugh. "I'll keep an eye on Sergeant Colton while she's on base."

"That's not ideal, either, as Captain Joseph clearly has you in his sights, too, Sergeant."

She heard Flynn swear under his breath, but she kept her attention on Corporal Hanson, needing to maintain her autonomy.

"Corporal, I report to JAG headquarters. I'll call my command and see what they want me to do. I'm sure I'll be secure in my apartment, though. I work for Colton Investigations in my civilian life, and Riley—the CEO—has had the entire staff take extra security precautions. No one knows where I live unless I tell them." She had no intention of going anywhere but home after she was done tonight. But Corporal Hanson seemed very concerned. "You don't really think Joseph would come after me tonight, do you?"

"Actually, we do, Sergeant. There's no evidence that he's remained on post, and with him still at large, it's a risk we can't ignore."

"But you'll have the barracks and the post locked down, won't you? Sergeant Cruz-Street will be safe?"

A cold gust of wind blew through the window. She shivered, and she was inside a vehicle. "I'm sorry. You must be freezing, Corporal Hanson. We can take this in the library."

"No, Sergeant. I'm under orders to have you depart post ASAP and find secure lodging in town, not your apartment. There's a hotel we've used before when visitors need extra security. It'll be safer for you. We hope to have Captain Joseph in custody before the night's done, and you should be able to return to your home by the morning, no problem."

Her mind raced. She knew of several hotels nearby, but she could also stay with one of her family. Or at CI headquarters. But that would put everyone else at risk, if Joseph came after her. She didn't have a choice but to take the hotel option.

"I'm fine with that. I'll drive myself to a hotel and report where I am after I check in."

"You're not going alone." Flynn spoke up and she twisted back to face him.

"I am. I'm a soldier, same as you, Flynn. You need to go into the library and study. We'll finish my interview tomorrow. I'm sure they'll have Captain Joseph in custody by then, aren't you?"

Emotions warred across his well-proportioned face. His head went back, ever so slightly, as if her words had physically slapped him.

"Our unit is tops at what it does, Sergeant Colton." He spoke her name with a crisp staccato that underscored his ire. She'd offended him. What did she expect? He was an MP and Corporal Hanson's senior. And Captain Joseph's junior, one of his right-hand soldiers.

"I'm sure it is. I don't mean to suggest anything else. You agree it'll all be sorted by morning, right? I'll meet you in the chow hall for breakfast at zero-seven-hundred hours."

Corporal Hanson cleared his throat. "But, Sergeant Colton, you cannot go alone. I'm under orders. The CO ordered that you are supposed to be under MP protections, and Sergeant Cruz-Street has decided he'll do it. Since Sergeant Cruz-Street needs to stay off base for his security tonight, this works."

"Excuse me, Corporal Hanson, but with your boss on the run, who are you under orders from?" She knew it wasn't Sergeant Flynn Cruz-Street, who sat next to her.

"The post CO, Colonel Capuana."

Well, so much for her plan to talk a way out of this. If the post commanding officer said Vikki had to go to the moon, then she would. As long as an investigation was underway at Fort Rapids, the post CO was in charge and had jurisdiction over Vikki while she was there.

"Roger that, Corporal. I'll drive out now, and you can accompany." She turned to Flynn. "You can get your studying done now. See you tomorrow." Vikki nodded at the passenger door handle, her brow raised.

Flynn ignored her, leaned across her so that he could best see Hanson.

"I've got this, Hanson. It'll be better for both Sergeant Colton and me to be out of sight for the evening. We'll get rooms off post, and I'll make sure she's secure. Does that work for you?"

"Yes, Sergeant." The corporal nodded and walked off, speaking into his handheld as he went back to his vehicle.

"This really isn't—"

"You're on my turf now, Vikki. Do you want me to drive?"

"I'll drive."

Jerk. But an attractive one.

Chapter Three

Flynn wasn't any happier than Vikki about their imposed proximity, but orders were orders. She wanted to get the nearest, cheapest hotel available, but he didn't think staying in the places that most troops used was smart.

"Do you have a hotel in mind?" He waited until they cleared post security to question her. Unlike the usual quick drive-through, they'd been asked to stop the car, get out, and the entire insides were searched. The post was taking no chances to allow Captain Joseph to sneak off site.

"I'm going to pull into the nearest gas station and use my phone to find one and make a reservation. Unless you have a better idea?" Her words could have been harsh but instead he heard the resignation, the exhaustion. And he was glad to be helping her through this. It had nothing to do with how attractive he found her, or how he'd felt the deepest stir of his interest for the first time since losing his fiancée, Jena, downrange over two years ago. It seemed almost natural to be interested in Vikki Colton, as if maybe it was time for him to finally let the vestiges of his grief over Jena go. Losing her had been the hardest thing he'd faced since his father died, which had happened when Flynn was still in high school. He'd always wanted to serve in the military, even before his father's untimely death, but the unexpected loss of his fiancée had nearly done him in. If not for his mother's support and his Army buddies, plus lots of hours on an Army therapist's sofa, he wasn't certain he'd have survived Jena's loss.

"Flynn?" Vikki nudged him out of his thoughts.

"I don't think we should stay at any of the hotels remotely near the post. My suggestion is that we head into downtown Grand Rapids and stay at the Grand Hotel. They offer a military rate and it's the last place Captain Joseph would suspect two soldiers would escape to." Flynn's worry was that Joseph had been off the post long before the lockdown occurred, and while he had to trust his colleagues with it, he was going to err on the side of caution. He had a JAG soldier to keep safe for the evening.

"That's the most expensive place in town, if memory serves me right." She sounded wistful. Had she stayed at the undeniably romantic hotel with someone she cared about? A pull of emotion Flynn didn't want to name made him sit straighter, remind himself he was on duty until they found Captain Joseph or Vikki Colton was out of danger.

"It is, but the discount is sweet and we're not paying."

"We're not supposed to spend the taxpayers' dollars frivolously."

"I don't think avoiding a possible stalker or murderer counts as frivolous, do you?"

"No." She drove onto the expressway that led to Grand Rapids. "It'll be about twenty minutes." As she spoke, snowflakes hit the windshield. "No wonder it's turned so cold."

"The lake-effect storm wasn't supposed to blast in until tomorrow morning." He quickly checked the weather app on his phone. "Winter weather warnings are up."

"We'll get there before it gets that bad. How long does it say it's going to last?"

"At least twenty-four hours." Any other time he'd be stressed about missing his class deadlines, or having to work longer shifts if another MP couldn't make it on post in time to relieve him. It was interesting how perspective changed when faced with the possibility of having a full day with a fascinating soldier.

"That's not great for my investigation, but it will keep Captain Joseph from finding us, hopefully."

"Post security will have him in no time."

"I wish I were as sure as you. You realize he probably fled the post before they issued the lockdown order?" She vocalized his exact thoughts, which underscored that Vikki and he had more in common than their Army uniforms.

"Yeah, I thought that straight off. But he has no idea what you drive, and no one followed us off the post."

"How do you know that?"

"I'm trained to know that, Vikki. I'm an MP."

"Indeed you are." He saw her hands tighten on the

wheel and realized she was still in her uniform without the coordinating overcoat.

"Do you have winter gear with you?"

"Yes. It's in the back. But if the snow keeps increasing like this, we'll be stuck inside for the next day or so." They both looked out at the highway and the myriad red taillights that glowed through the heavy snowfall. In only twenty minutes the storm had rolled in, full force.

"Take the first exit into the city, and I'll tell you how to get to the hotel's parking garage." He looked at his phone, checking the weather warnings and traffic.

"It's not next to it?"

"Not since they did major renovations last year. You haven't seen it since then?"

Vikki shook her head.

"They kept all of the historical aspects of the building, but each room is equipped with state-of-the-art amenities. There's an indoor pool and solarium that's heated year-round. The garage was built on the land that used to be where Polska House restaurant stood." Michigan boasted a large population of Polish Americans.

"My sister told me it burned down. I loved that place. My family used to go and we'd order platter after platter of pierogi."

Flynn laughed. "That's not something you hear in the Army every day."

She laughed in response. The sound surrounded him in the small car and he fleetingly wondered how he'd never felt a woman's laugh so deep inside his chest before. He wasn't experiencing the usual grief he felt around women ever since he'd lost his Jena. There was something different here. Vikki's voice was of an average feminine pitch, but her laughter was deep and throaty, underscoring the fact that she was much more than a soldier. Vikki was an intelligent, beautiful, focused woman.

If he wasn't careful, he'd forget about the soldier part all too easily. Not good when they needed to maintain a professional relationship. Unlike his fiancée, Vikki and he were involved in the same investigation. That begged the question—if he'd met Vikki anywhere else, and neither of them had been in uniform, would he see her as a more-than-friend possibility?

There's nothing keeping you from her, Army-wise.

He knew this, as they were the same rank and not in the same command. But he also knew he wasn't looking for any kind of romantic entanglement. He'd put the worst grief over losing Jena behind him, accepted that he'd never get over her but it was possible to move forward. To know that she'd always be a part of him even as he found romance with other women. Still, a relationship with Vikki was best kept off the table while they were so entangled in the same assignment.

"Do I turn left or right, Flynn?" She'd stopped the car at a T intersection.

"Oh, uh, left. Sorry."

Her wheels crunched over the rapidly accumulating snow and he whistled. "This is piling up fast."

"Yeah, it's going to be a snow globe out here in no time." Vikki slowed the car to a crawl, matching the pace of the vehicles on either side of them in the downtown area. "Are we close? I remember the hotel being fairly close to the exit ramp."

"Except they've rerouted everything down here and what would be a short jaunt in a straight line now takes a bit longer. Go right at the next light."

They worked together, Vikki driving with expert caution and Flynn issuing directions, until she safely parked them on the third level of the garage.

"Great job, for a JAG." He couldn't stop himself.

"Funny, I was thinking the same thing. Your instructions were surprisingly accurate, without any extra hand signals." She teased him right back, and Flynn smiled at her.

"We make a good team." He wished he could take the enthusiasm out of his voice. He sounded like a new recruit, always stating the obvious.

"It's too early to conclude that yet." Vikki got out and Flynn followed, taking one of her suitcases off the carry-on bag that she pushed in front of her.

"I can manage my bags."

"I know you can. Indulge me. I need to feel as though I'm helping. It's the Neanderthal part." He bit his cheek to keep from laughing.

Her eyes narrowed, and under the fluorescent lighting, their jade depths appeared almost black. "You are a needy man, aren't you?"

His laughter reverberated off the concrete walls.

ENSCONCED IN A room far beyond what Vikki considered plush, she paused in front of the contemporary bathroom shower mirror to verify that she was still wearing a uniform. None the worse for wear, her Army blouse appeared far crisper and squared away than she did. The length of the day was catching up to her.

She began to pull the hairpins out of her French twist as she kicked off her heels and walked to the closet to hang her Dress Blues. Her phone pinged its warning alarm and she saw that the lake-effect storm was now predicted to bring up to thirty-six inches of snow within the next day. The amount wasn't a problem, as she knew Grand Rapids and, in fact, all of Michigan had the equipment, manpower and experience to tackle the fluffy stuff. But she also knew that it might mean she'd be stuck for the next twenty-four hours.

In a luxury hotel with Fort Rapids' hottest MP.

She shook her head and ignored her sad little libido, on hiatus since her ex so ingloriously cheated on her. Vikki wasn't even angry at him anymore—it was herself she was upset with. The warning signs had been all over the place. Peter had missed several dates, always blaming it on his taxing schedule as a local Realtor. She'd believed him because real estate in the Grand Rapids suburbs was constantly developing and Peter's drive was what had initially attracted her to him when they'd met at a holiday mixer two years ago. Everything she'd found so appealing, though, turned out to be the indicators of a womanizer.

While the hotel-room eight-head shower was appealing to her muscles after the long day, the sights of the soaking tub and lavender-scented bath salts won her over. She turned the faucets on and decided then and there to let go of the stress that she hadn't managed to find out all she'd needed to about Captain Joseph. No one was going to get anything done tonight. Certainly by morning, not only would Joseph be in either the post's brig or, if caught in town and off post, the civilian county jail, but Flynn would be ready to tell her the truth about where his half brother, Landon, was. Blame it on Peter, but she didn't trust Flynn was telling her everything he knew.

It would be too easy to trust Flynn, with his straightforward, no-nonsense manner and those brown eyes that were maddening in their intensity. As easy as sinking into the soothing scented bubbles.

"AND NOW FOR our Helping Grand Rapids segment. A local PI firm is warning consumers to not take any RevitaYou supplements until further notice. If you have already purchased the product, please do not dispose of them in the garbage. Please contact Colton Investigations and they will assist you." The contact information for Colton Investigations flashed up on the television screen.

"Screw you! What do you know?" Landon Street shut off the television for the fifth time in as many minutes. He hated the local news. They'd been the first to report when his university research project had failed, taking millions in government grants down the drain with it. But the project hadn't really failed—he'd walked away and used his knowledge to formulate the true fountain of youth, in one simple pill.

Except for several people sickened and one or two possibly related deaths, his formula had been a great success. He'd added the castor oil at a small enough dose that no one should have gotten ill. How was he to know that a percentage of the population had the genetics that would make any amount of ricin lethal to them? He was a chemist, not a geneticist.

Landon's cell vibrated and he saw Flynn's name light up. The fifth time since yesterday. Just as before, he flipped the phone over. Ignored it. Screw his little half sibling.

He had nothing to say to Flynn. He couldn't trust him anymore, not after he'd reported him to the police. Landon knew Flynn had reported him because when he'd returned to the cemetery the last few times, a patrol car had lingered not far from their father's grave.

If Dad were here, he'd know what to do. If only he hadn't died, Landon wouldn't be in this trouble.

"No, no, no. That's not the truth." He spoke to himself in the rat-hole apartment he was renting under an alias on the outskirts of Grand Rapids. He found it comforting to hear his own voice, and he liked to think aloud, too. "My life would be okay if my stupid mother had never left us to begin with. Then Rosa wouldn't have had to try to be my mother, and I wouldn't have had to compete with Flynn for attention." Truth was, though, that he liked his little brother. Had, anyway, until Flynn had finked him out.

His phone rang and he jumped. "Don't turn it over. It's just Flynn again." But his fingers, always curious, made for the laboratories he'd spent his life in, had their own will.

Melissa.

"I told you to never call me again." He should have blocked his biological mother.

"Honey, you're my only child. I'm going to call you again, and again after that. I care about you. How are you doing, sweetheart?"

"Don't call me that. I'm not your child. You left me. I haven't heard from you in over a year. Why now?" He couldn't stop the growling that came out of his mouth, or the sharp pain to his gut. Didn't she know that she'd called him "sweetheart" when he was a little boy, before he'd known how cruel life could be?

"My bad, Landon honey. You sound stressed, sweetie pie. What's going on? Do you want to talk about it?"

"No, I'm not stressed and I'm not going to talk to you about it. I just need people to stop saying bad things about RevitaYou."

"No one's saying anything really bad, honey. I believe in you." Melissa's voice was high and whiny, but it still sounded okay. Familiar. He curled into a ball and tugged on his hair.

"Are you sure?"

"I am."

He knew it was a lie, knew that she was a deserter, not one to be trusted. But he decided to believe her, just for tonight. If only he could sleep, he'd be able to think straight and fix this. He wasn't a criminal. He'd show them all.

AFTER A HALF hour in his hotel room, Flynn realized he'd better check in with his mother. The last thing she needed was to worry about him on top of the Landon chaos.

"Hi, Mom."

"Hey, honey. How are you doing?" Rosa Cruz-Street's voice reflected her joy at hearing from her son. Guilt swift-kicked Flynn in the shins.

"I'm good, Mom. How are you?" He'd meant to call her earlier in the week, but the days, as always, had gotten away from him.

"Not so great. Have you seen the local news?" Like many of her generation, Rosa still watched the news on television. Flynn found the local programming to be especially depressing, including so much crime that he couldn't do a thing about. His job was keeping Fort Rapids safe.

Except for now. He wasn't sure when he'd get back to post.

"No, I haven't. I told you I don't watch that stuff, Mom." He gently chided her. He wanted to protect Rosa from everything. She'd gone through so much, first when his father died and now trying to figure out what the deal was with Landon.

"Landon's vitamin may have killed some people. Lots of folks, mostly women, are very, very sick."

"I, uh, actually heard something about that." He couldn't break it to her that Landon's pill had indeed killed. Or that it had been his boss's wife and that his boss was now after him. Even with his mom being a veteran, there were things he didn't want to burden her with. "Mom, this isn't your fault. Landon will have to face the authorities and tell them what's in the supplement."

"Do you really think he'll make it that long? The last

time he went off his meds, he disappeared for weeks. If your father hadn't found him…" Her voice broke and so did Flynn's heart.

Rosa had adopted Landon the minute she and his father married. Landon's biological mother, Melissa, had abandoned him when he was only a toddler. Landon had been forever affected by the trauma. But Flynn wasn't so sure that Landon hadn't had some major issues long before that.

"But he did find him, and Landon did really well for a long while."

"Until that jerk loaned him the money. If Landon could have stayed at the university research center, none of this would have happened." Rosa had been heartbroken when they'd found out the university staff had kicked him off campus, for good. His moods were too volatile.

"Mom, they had no choice but to fire him. We can't second-guess any of this. Landon's always been his own person, and he needs more help than you or I can give him."

"It was one thing when he did things that only hurt himself. That was bad enough. But if any of these reports are true, if he's hurt innocent people or worse, I don't think I can live with this, Flynn."

"Mom, this isn't your fault. You've been the best mother possible to Landon."

"I'd feel better if I knew he was safe, even if it means going to prison. He needs to be caught, Flynn. Before someone else gets hurt."

"I know." And the plan he'd only begun to think

about gelled. He needed to go after Landon himself. "Look, Mom, I've got to go now. Are you ready for the storm?"

Rosa laughed for the first time in their conversation. "Please. I've lived in Grand Rapids for over three decades. And I've got the nice blower you bought me last Christmas."

"True. Sounds like we're both safe and sound." He prayed she didn't ask where he was. Let her assume he was on post.

"Good night, son. Love you."

"Love you, too, Mom."

Flynn set his phone down and stared outside at the wall of white, the streetlights mere glowing orbs through the onslaught. He wished he'd taken Landon in himself that last time he'd seen him. It wasn't Rosa's fault that Landon was still on the loose. It was Flynn's. He'd been the last to see him, and if he'd tried a little harder, he might have convinced Landon to turn himself in.

One thing the Army had taught Flynn was accountability. He might not be able to change a past mistake, but he'd for sure fix it. Before he could second-guess himself, he placed a quick call to his senior enlisted supervisor.

Five minutes later, Flynn was officially on leave from the US Army.

VIKKI CHECKED THE peephole and saw that Flynn stood in front of her hotel-room door. Her heart did a butterfly skip, the kind of reaction she got whenever she found a man attractive. But her mind—that was what gave her pause. Her professional and personal assessments of Flynn lined up. He was a hot, intelligent, thoughtful man.

And you're keeping it professional while you work with him.

She opened the door and waved him in. Like her, he was dressed in a warm sweatshirt and pants.

His warm eyes met hers without hesitation. She couldn't stop the immediate wish that they weren't on duty. "I see you're in the Michigan snowstorm uniform."

She looked down at her sweats and then back at him. His good-natured demeanor was infectious. "No matter how many years I've been away, when I come home, I want to be in the warmest, coziest clothing possible. Especially when it's storming. What's your excuse?"

"I grew up here, too, you know. The Coltons don't have the exclusive rights to Grand Rapids."

"You know my family, then."

"Not really, as it seems we grew up in different areas. Grand Rapids is a big place. That said, I know about Colton Investigations. Your family?"

"Yes. My brother Riley is CEO of CI. Have you worked with him?"

"Yes. Surprisingly, a lot of cases overlap in this area."

She nodded. "I saw them earlier today at a meeting about this case, but I can't say all that much about my Army business. They want me to go into the office and work the case with them. My twin sister, Sadie, just broke it off with her ex. Tate Greer—you may have heard of him? He's one of the silent investment partners in RevitaYou and an all-around horrible person. We're all worried about her, because Tate's made threats on her safety before."

"I'm aware of Tate Greer. I've had to get up to speed on the RevitaYou criminal activity as part of my MP duties. It's affected our soldiers on base." Flynn's attention was totally on her and it was so tempting to allow her mind to wander, to wonder how it would feel to be touched, kissed by him.

Nope, not going there.

"It's safe to say, then, that we both want the same thing—Landon captured. But first I have to find your boss."

"I have more than one boss. Captain Joseph is the big boss, yes, but my immediate supervisor is a master sergeant."

"Yes, I spoke with her on the phone before I came on post. I need to interview her, too."

"That's not going to happen tonight, or probably even tomorrow." He nodded at her hotel window, the blackout drapes drawn back so that she could enjoy this first storm in many years.

"You may be right." Vikki walked to the window, drawn back to the spot she'd been standing in for the last half hour as she'd pondered her next moves on the case. "I've missed this so much." The tip of her nose itched to be pressed against the cold pane, the way she'd watched snowfalls as a kid. "You probably think I'm nuts."

"Not at all. Whenever I've had to go downrange, whether it's overseas or to another state, for a few weeks or a full combat deployment, I miss it, too. It's hard to explain to anyone who's never experienced a Michigan winter, or who sees only the cold and not the frozen beauty." He'd walked up next to her and it was as if they were in their own snow-globe-within-a-snow-globe, hypnotized by the flakes violently pelting against the glass pane.

Flynn was close enough to touch, not that she'd thought of doing that. Of reaching out to lay her hand on his forearm, assure him that they were in this together and they'd work it out. His male scent, tinged with freshness probably from his soap or shampoo, made her want to close her eyes and sniff.

That made her giggle.

"What's so funny?" His dark eyes sparkled with interest, a light she'd longed for in her ex's but had never seen. Not really. Too late, she realized that she'd projected any true emotions she'd thought Peter had for her onto him. To maintain her stubborn insistence on a fairy-tale ending to their relationship, instead of the horror show it became.

Flynn's not Peter.

She broke their eye contact, walked to the glass-topped desk where her laptop sat. "Nothing. I'm tired, is all. I think we need to come up with a plan, a checklist to follow so that we don't waste our efforts."

"What do you think we're going to do in the middle of this?" His shoulder shrugged toward the window, to the view of the storm.

"As long as we have Wi-Fi and power, we're in business. We can figure out all of the places Captain Joseph might go if he stays in the area. And you can come up with a list of sites we'll search for Landon when the storm clears."

He took the few steps toward her to prevent them from yelling across the spacious room at one another. She sat in the desk chair and logged on to the internet. "No military discount here." The price for connection was exorbitant.

"We'll be reimbursed. We can use our phones as hot spots if we have to."

"That'll be too slow. I'm going to need to access Colton Investigations' databases."

"Don't you have to tell your siblings you're doing that?"

"I will, later. They know they can trust me. Our techie, Ashanti, will see me log in."

"I think your original suggestion is the best one. We get the rest while we can." Flynn's face lit up with the light of his phone screen as he read his findings aloud. "A blizzard warning has been issued for the counties in all of western and central Michigan, including the Grand Rapids metro area. Snowfall and blizzard winds are expected to last through noon on Sunday."

"Sunday?" It was only Friday, and the brunt of the storm was supposed to hit tomorrow night. That left over twenty-four hours of solid snowfall, something she hadn't been expecting in November.

"Like you said, this will give us time to come up with a plan, and then we'll be rested to execute it. Captain Joseph and Landon aren't going anywhere in this, either." He walked to her door and she remained seated, looking at him over her shoulder. She did not want to give the impression that this was anything more than a working relationship. If she got up and walked him to the door…it seemed too chummy. Or more.

Why did that tickle her interest?

"Should we set a time to meet in the morning?" She needed him to leave. Then she wouldn't have these distracting notions.

"Sure—how about at the breakfast buffet, when it opens?"

"See you then, Flynn." She turned back to her laptop.

"Vikki, lock the door behind me."

"Right." By the time she was up and at the door, he'd clicked it shut. She slid the dead bolt and flipped the door block. And did her best to ignore the fear that squirmed in her belly, reminding her that a man in shock and angry grief wouldn't let a snowstorm keep him away.

Maybe sexy thoughts about Flynn weren't so bad.

Chapter Four

Vikki's phone woke her up before dawn the next morning, and she sat straight, wide-awake, when she saw it was Flynn.

"Good morning."

"Hey, sorry to call this early. I know we were going to meet for breakfast, but I have a better idea."

"Shoot." She got out of bed and began dressing as he spoke, instinctively knowing that a fellow soldier didn't call with an "idea" for the heck of it. Flynn had an action plan.

"Let's get out of here and drive around to the places I last saw Landon. We have to go quickly, before the storm hits hard. I'd say we have another five hours or so."

Excitement simmered, the same as it did when she unearthed a valuable piece of evidence in a case.

"That sounds good to me. I'll be at your door in ten more minutes."

"Make it five, and I'm coming to you." He ended the connection and she shook her head. This was her investigation, her suspect to track down, yet Flynn acted as if it was his mission.

If this were any other case, she'd be thrilled to have a partner to work with. Vikki thrived on teamwork, and how each paralegal's and attorney's success was a win for the entire group.

Flynn Cruz-Street affected her. In ways another soldier or client shouldn't. It wasn't as if she hadn't been attracted to other men in uniform. She'd dated several, in fact, but always from another unit and definitely in a different chain of command. Vikki had worked hard for her accomplishments. She was proud to wear a US Army uniform in the JAG corps. She wasn't about to risk it for an inappropriate relationship.

Flynn was a person of interest in her investigation. True, he wasn't *the* person of interest, but rather, the half brother of the prime suspect. She wished she could blame her professional awareness on why she was so defensive around Flynn, but it was no use lying to herself.

Vikki knew she felt threatened by Flynn because he was lighting fires inside her that she'd thought Peter had extinguished. Worse, Flynn seemed to be able to tell what she was thinking, to anticipate what she needed from him. For the case, of course.

Images of him anticipating other kinds of needs of the more carnal variety had begun almost the minute she'd laid eyes on his attractive smile and felt the warmth of his undivided attention. The fact that this had happened when they'd been thrown together by the lethal actions of his very sick boss underscored the risk to her.

Vikki's heart had somehow become involved and was now in danger of entering into explosive territory again.

The rap at the door broke her self-involvement and she quickly gathered up her belongings, tossing all into a backpack. They'd be incognito, in civilian clothes, to avoid catching the wrong kind of attention as they searched for Landon.

She checked the peephole then opened the door.

"Hey."

"Hey, yourself. Ready?" His expression was pure friendly professionalism. No waves of sexual innuendo rolled off Sergeant Flynn Cruz-Street.

Vikki could learn a lot from a man like Flynn.

VIKKI DROVE, NOT only because it was her car but because, as she told Flynn, "You need to be free to see where we're going and if you catch sight of Landon."

He took them first to the cemetery where his father was buried. The visibility worsened as the morning wore on, and the wind that had been chilly last night had turned arctic. He noted that Vikki, like most soldiers, was an accomplished driver who wasn't afraid to let go of the GPS and take his direction. She also managed the steady snow with ease.

"Do you come out to the cemetery often?" She had her gaze fixed on the road and he wished for another glimpse of her eyes. He'd never seen such a deep, intense shade of green.

Focus on answering her question, man.

"Not really. I come with my mom at Easter, if the

snow's cleared, and we put in some lilies. Memorial Day and Veterans Day. Mom and I came last week and put a flag on his grave. My dad served in the Army, too. He met my mother in the Philippines, where she was serving and is also from. They were together for over ten years before my father died. It almost killed all of us, to lose him so young, but it affected Landon the most."

"What about Landon's mother? Is she still alive?"

"Yeah, but she may as well be dead. Melissa abandoned him and left him with my dad when he was small. As far as I know, he's not seen a whole lot of her since. My mother, Rosa, was the best thing that ever happened to my father and, in my opinion, to Landon." But it hadn't been enough. Rosa's love, as far-reaching as it was, hadn't kept Landon from becoming a criminal. A murderer, at this point.

"I'm so sorry, Flynn. None of this is easy to talk about, I'm sure. I regret having to hash it all up again."

"Don't. You're not at fault here. Neither of us is. Just for the bankrollers of RevitaYou and my half brother, and the rest of the scientists, who came up with the supplement—poison, actually."

"Is that the exit for the cemetery?" She pointed with a leather-gloved finger.

"Yes. Take the second part of the ramp, to the left." He'd driven this highway countless times. "My mom's home isn't far from here. She still lives in the house we grew up in."

"Did she retire from the Army?"

"Yes, she did. My dad's family was from Grand Rapids, and it was a natural fit for them both to be stationed here at Fort Rapids for their last assignment before retirement. I was five years old and Landon was already in high school, on his way to college."

"Do you remember much about Army life? I mean, before you joined up?" She decelerated and turned left, stopped by a red light at the entrance to the cemetery.

"No, not really. I have a vague memory of moving into our house, but I don't recall where we'd lived before that. We moved here from Washington State."

"Fort McChord?"

"Yes. Have you been there?"

She nodded. "Yeah, I had to fly out there to investigate a case last year. It wasn't too different from this one, actually. Except it was an active-duty soldier who'd come up with a steroid cocktail for his unit to use at the post gym. No one died, and it was a contained crime. Unlike this one."

The light turned green and she drove through the ornate gates, under a grove of trees whose bare branches had only recently lost their leaves but were laced with snow.

"I haven't been in this part of the city in a while. My grandparents are buried on the other side of the highway, in the older section."

"Where all the beautiful statues are." He, like so many locals, took pride in the artistic creativity of their city's historical venues.

"Yes. Although it doesn't seem so pretty when you're saying goodbye to the ones you love, does it?"

"No." He pointed. "See that big oak tree, the one with

the bench? It looks like a big white block in this snow. That's where I park."

"Sure thing." She followed his directions and turned the engine off after she parked a few yards from the tree, thankful the cemetery roads had been recently plowed. "Do you want to get out?"

"I do. Come with me?" His request took her by surprise and he saw it reflected in her expression. Vikki smoothed her hair back and shrugged on a ski cap.

"We might be smarter to see if you draw anyone out by going over there by yourself. I'll follow, promise."

"Good idea." How could he be so stupid, so needy? And since when did he need or want anyone but his mother with him when he visited Dad's grave?

He exited the car and walked through the several inches of snow to the grave marker. The flag they'd placed just a week ago was there, small but definitive in its claim, its tiny top spike poking through the snow cover. He leaned over and brushed the flakes from the stone.

Here lies a veteran. Looking at his dad's name, and his mom's—blank, thank God—made him still. It always did. Since he'd turned thirty a couple of years back, it was as though he'd left his youth behind him. In many ways he'd never had a childhood, not with Landon's constant demands on his parents and mother. Then, after their father died, Landon had consumed his mother's time. Even though Landon had been older, his emotional instability had required more attention than Flynn had as a grade-school boy.

"This is a beautiful spot, Flynn."

He turned to see her next to him. Instead of feeling intrusive, Vikki's presence was reassuring. Right.

"It is. My mom and I often stay for a while, sit on the bench."

"I, um, haven't seen another soul around." Her gaze checked out the surrounding land through the curtain of snowfall, and he agreed with her.

"No, Landon's not about to show now. He's running scared at this point, if I know him."

"How well do you think you know him?"

The wind whipped locks of her hair free from her knit cap and he fought to not help her keep it out of her face. Had he ever met a woman with such smooth, unblemished skin? With eyes so large, so knowing? Her generous mouth might be almost clownish on another woman, but on Vikki, it was sexy as all get-out.

"I never knew him, as in, was close to him. Landon doesn't get close to anyone. Would you, if your mother left you when you were still a toddler?" He heard the defensiveness in his tone and fought to back off.

Chill out, dude.

"You sound like you care for him. Or is it because your mother cares so much?"

"It's both. I know my half brother well enough to understand that he's not capable of a serious intimate relationship. Landon's love is for numbers, chemicals. He's a genius at chemistry and math, always was. But without being able to gauge whether someone's asking him to do something for the right reasons, he's gotten lost."

"So you don't think Landon's really to blame for the deaths caused by RevitaYou?"

"I didn't say that. Landon's no innocent. But yes, I think he got in over his head. I know that, at first, he enjoyed making such a large paycheck, after struggling through the often-impoverished academic steps needed to get his PhD. Think of it… If, when you get out of the Army, someone is willing to pay you ten times as much as you've been making—for doing the same exact thing?"

"I, uh… I can imagine that, actually." Vikki sighed. "But money doesn't corrupt most people to the point of murder. I see what you're thinking, Flynn. It's all over your face. You think nothing is as prestigious or worthwhile as being a soldier. And you're right—nothing is. But I'm older than I was when I enlisted, and I don't want to go to law school. I don't want to be a JAG officer. It's a natural fit for me to move home and work for my brothers and sisters."

"I had the impression that your brother runs that show."

"He's in charge, yes, but that's because he's such an old dog." She grinned. "Don't ever tell him I said that."

"I won't." He smiled back at her, and for a split second, it was just the two of them. Two newly acquainted people making connections, seeing what they had in common. Until her eyes shifted from his. And narrowed.

He followed her gaze. A car crept along the cemetery access road, no more than a quarter mile away.

"Do you recognize that car?"

He shook his head. "No. But that doesn't mean anything."

"I can't make out the person driving in this snow, can you?"

"No."

"I'm not feeling so great about standing out here in the open right now. We followed your protocol to make sure we weren't followed, but what if Joseph figured out he could find you here?" Vikki's voice went up a notch.

"He wouldn't know to come here." Flynn was certain about that. Captain Joseph was, had been, his trusted boss, his leader. Not a friend or confidant. "The only people who know that Landon shows up here are me and my mother. I never told anyone I work with." Although, Joseph had been privy to the police reports Flynn had filed on Landon.

"Could it be your brother?"

"Doubtful. He never shows up with a car. I don't know if he takes public transportation or parks in one of the closer neighborhoods, but Landon always walks here."

"That was before he was wanted for questioning in the deaths of RevitaYou users, correct?" Vikki's paralegal tone was back in her voice, wiping away the serenity bubble that had encapsulated them for that short, precious moment.

"I'm more concerned it's Captain Joseph." He quickly told her about when he'd reported his last sighting of Landon.

Vikki gasped. "He was unhinged at the barracks yesterday, Flynn. If it's him, we're sitting ducks." She shoved her sunglasses on her head and pointedly looked at the land around them. It was at least a several-second run to the car. If the person driving the strange vehicle wanted to, they could beat them to their potential escape.

They both looked at the car. When Vikki pulled her phone out, he grasped her wrist.

"Don't. If he sees you taking a photo, and it is Joseph, it might make him flip."

"Do you really think he can see us…?" Vikki's eyes widened. "Flynn, look. Whoever it is has binoculars."

He looked and, sure enough, they were being watched, closely.

"Forget what I said. Go ahead and take a photo, make sure you get the license plate."

She made quick work of getting the shots before they turned and headed for her car. A slamming door and tires on gravel reached them and they broke into a full sprint.

"Let me drive."

"Sure." She handed him the keys. "The lock is the top button."

Flynn was a good runner. Not fast, but lots of endurance. He had a hard time keeping up with Vikki, who made a beeline for the passenger side.

The other car was on them, one turn away from being right behind them. Within easy shooting range.

Flynn unlocked the doors and they slid into the seats in unison as if they'd practiced the move.

"You drive. I'll keep an eye on him." Vikki was twisted around in the passenger seat, taking photos with her phone. "Dang it. I wish I had a better camera."

"Can you see his face?"

"No. He's wearing a ski mask and sunglasses. It could be Joseph—he wasn't that tall, right? How tall is Landon?"

"Landon's tall with graying blond hair." The exact opposite of Captain Joseph's shorter, stockier frame and dark hair.

"It could be Joseph, then." As soon as the words left her mouth, two gunshots sounded.

"He's shooting, Flynn. I see a handgun."

"Just get the license plate and stay low. Hang on!" He turned the key and didn't wait to hear the engine turn over before he switched into gear and floored the accelerator. The car jumped forward, the wheels grinding and throwing gravel backward. The other vehicle was so close that he heard the small rocks hit its frame, the high-pitched pinging competing with the dull roar of Vikki's engine.

"Riley, we're being followed by someone, probably Captain Joseph." Vikki relayed their exact location in the city cemetery. "He's shot at us twice already." Vikki had called her brother using her hands-free app.

"Whatever you do, don't engage him, Vikki. I'm calling it in to 9-1-1 and the MPs at Fort Rapids." Riley's voice filled the car as Vikki's gaze remained locked on the shooter's vehicle. Flynn admired how quickly she'd acted. And was grateful—he was too busy driving to save their lives.

The back window shattered and they both shouted and ducked their heads. Flynn knew the lay of the land well enough to stay on the road, and made the quick left then sharp right, out of the cemetery and back onto the highway access road. He maneuvered around other vehicles, doing anything to lose Joseph.

"Okay?" He couldn't take his eyes off the road.

"Okay. I think we lost him, Flynn." Vikki spoke as she kept Riley on the line, updating both at the same time. "Riley, I'll reach out as needed."

"Stay safe, sis." Riley disconnected.

"I sent Riley all the photos I took and he's got Ashanti analyzing them. I hope he can get the license plate number." The sound of sirens reached them and a pair of police cars sped past, going in the opposite direction.

"I hope they can find him, but he's slippery." Flynn knew his boss. Captain Joseph was a security expert, with a long list of law enforcement skills. Trying to catch him was like trying to find a bad cop in the midst of the honorable ones.

"He either followed us from the hotel or was waiting for us." Vikki sighed. "I didn't even think about him stalking us, frankly, not after we've been so careful about not being followed."

"Don't even go there, Vikki." He heard the defeat in her tone. "It's impossible to predict the behavior of an unpredictable criminal. I'm okay with waiting. I made sure we weren't followed last night." Flynn had suggested all the turns and back roads that they'd taken from the post.

"You did, and I did my best, although I know I'm not the expert in this area like you." Vikki sounded energized, ready for the next hiccup in their plans.

"You're something else, Vikki Colton."

"How's that?" Good, he'd gotten her mind off the

no-win spiral he was all too familiar with. Blaming himself for not catching a bad guy before anyone was hurt. Thinking the entire world was his responsibility.

He waited to answer until he made certain Joseph wasn't tailing them, then began the drive back to the hotel on all side streets, no highways.

"Most persons would have been a little bit upset at what we just went through. We were shot at." As far as Flynn was concerned, it didn't matter if it was a combat zone or Main Street, USA; getting fired upon was life-changing. And too often, life-ending.

"I've been through worse, to be honest."

"Downrange?"

"No." She looked out the windshield, appeared to be collecting her thoughts. "Do you remember ever hearing about the DC shooter who struck right after 9/11?"

"The guy who randomly shot folks as they drove to work, or home, to the store, in places where you usually feel safe?"

"That's him. Well, there was a copycat shooter two years ago in DC. I was stationed there at the time."

"I heard about him, too."

"I was stuck in traffic on 495—DC's beltway—when he took out three drivers, all around me."

"That's awful, Vikki." If he wasn't driving, he'd reach over and hold her hand. But it was his duty to keep them safe from any reappearance of Joseph. And he sensed she needed to spill her guts on this. If he touched her, would she shut down?

Was it always going to feel this complicated around Vikki?

"It was. I figured out that the shots came from an overpass, and the traffic was moving there, so the shooter had to have been a drive-by." She paused. "After I called 9-1-1, I was able to help a couple of the victims who survived. But there was one who didn't."

"I'm sorry, Vikki." It seemed so inadequate.

"It was a nine-year-old child. In the back seat, doing her homework. Her mother was driving and her baby brother was next to her in a car seat. They both survived, but I'll never forget it, Flynn. It wasn't just the horror of the scene, but the reality that something so mundane but precious—picking your kid up after school—could turn into a nightmare with one random act. At least downrange, we know it's a risk. And we're ready to face it, as much as we can be."

"Kids always break the bank on any understanding I'll have in this lifetime." He double-checked the rearview and side mirrors, then pulled off into the parking lot of a large members-only warehouse store. It was packed with cars as people were stocking up before the big storm. Customers pushed oversize carts laden with economy packs of bread, milk, bananas and water.

"Are you planning on the storm lasting longer than a couple of days? I'm sure the hotel has plenty of food, Flynn." Vikki smiled at the crowds. "I have to admit, I've missed this."

"The early season snow?"

"The sense that everyone is on the same team. People are nice to each other when they feel there's something they need to protect themselves from. Does that make sense?"

"It does. It's why I joined the military, among other reasons. I love the camaraderie."

"That's it! Camaraderie. No one cares which side of the street you live on, but everyone's willing to help shovel you out."

Flynn couldn't have said it better himself.

"I thought this would be a safe place to stop and talk. I don't want to go straight to the hotel, and if Joseph is somehow miraculously following us, he'll have a hard time getting to us with all of these vehicles coming and going. We'll spot him first."

Vikki's phone dinged and he watched her read a message.

"It's from Riley. The police found Joseph's car, abandoned. The plates were traced to him."

"He's ditched it because he knows he won't get very far in it." Flynn drummed his fingers on the wheel. "Well, at least we know he's not able to follow us for now."

"Until he gets another car."

"He has a second, and a third car, come to think of it. His wife's car, and he drove a 1985 Mustang that he refurbished. It was his hobby and he always talked about it, explained that we all needed a hobby to help de-stress from the day job." Flynn wasn't a car guy, but he'd understood what Captain Joseph had been trying to tell them. The Army lifestyle, especially that of an MP, was prone to stress, to tearing families apart.

"Sounds like he needs more hobby time." Vikki's deadpan made a wave of mirth roll up from his middle and he let out a belly laugh. She joined in.

"You're a woman after my own heart." He gasped through his words.

"It's a sick sense of humor, right?"

They chuckled for a solid minute or two. It wasn't unfamiliar to Flynn, and he was pretty sure Vikki had experience with laughter as a good decompression tool after a traumatic event. Being shot at and chased by an aggrieved widower counted.

When Flynn and his battle buddies cracked up from crude jokes, they'd laugh until they couldn't, then maybe slap one another on the shoulder, do a playful punch to the upper arm.

He and Vikki grew quiet, and their eyes met.

And held.

Flynn saw intelligence, wit and strength in Vikki's jade depths. He also saw flames of interest and desire ignite. At least, that was what he was feeling in his gut.

The squealing carts, shouting kids, clang of trunk lids closing as folks finished loading—all melted into nothingness. All Flynn knew was this woman next to him. As if invisible threads were forming between them, weaving into an unbreakable cord.

A sharp rap on the door window startled them both. Flynn turned to see a man with beefy hands waving at him and rolled down the window.

"Yeah?"

"I wondered if you want my cart. We're done with it and there aren't any in the store. Also, don't forget to turn your lights off, buddy. You don't want a dead battery now." The man grinned in a "I see your distraction" kind of way and Flynn gritted his teeth.

"Thanks, man. We'll take the cart off your hands." He flicked off the lights, turned off the engine and got out of the car. He didn't trust himself to look at Vikki.

He knew he was blushing.

VIKKI FOLLOWED FLYNN'S lead and exited the car. It was serendipitous, as far as she was concerned, that the nice man had offered them his cart. She was ignoring the part about Flynn leaving the lights on. It was the law in Michigan, and most states, that if there was any precipitation that required windshield wipers, then your lights had to be on. Automatic headlights didn't always work well when the clouds were issuing only tiny light flakes of snow as they were now. Flynn had followed protocol, even in the heat of a dangerous car chase. It was an admirable trait and, in fact, incredibly attractive. Sexy.

But he'd been distracted by their conversation. So much so that he'd left the lights on. Did it mean he was feeling the growing attraction between them? She couldn't call it simply a need, or want, or even desire. But all of those things were part of it.

And they barely knew one another.

"Hang on. Why are we going in here?" She caught up to him, his back ramrod-straight as he pushed the cart and stared straight ahead.

"We may as well grab a few things. I doubt the hotel has the protein powder I like."

"Protein powder? You mean, for after a workout?"

"Yes. If we're going to be stuck and snowbound, I'm going to at least train. This hotel has the best fitness center of all of them, and a great junior Olympic-size pool."

"Good to know." She knew the hotel had been updated but not all the details.

Flynn flashed the salesperson his store member's ID and the man waved them both into the huge warehouse, its labyrinthine aisles swallowing up customers left and right.

"It feels odd to be shopping on Army time."

"I'm on leave, and you're supposed to be investigating me, right?"

Her insides froze. Flynn was only supposed to know about her looking to interview Captain Joseph and Landon.

"You are the half brother of one, and subordinate of another person of interest."

He stopped the cart in front of a stack of vitamin supplements that claimed to restore poor eyesight. Her stomach churned at the empty promise, and the parallel to the RevitaYou claims stirred her ire. People were dead because they had searched for answers in a pill.

When he faced her, Flynn's eyes flashed anger. "Spare me the legalese, Sergeant Colton. I know dang well that you think I'm part of the problem here. You think I'm involved in this RevitaYou scheme. Check all of my bank accounts, my Army records. You'll see I'm clean."

She'd already done all of the above, as per the investigation requirements, and knew his profile was clean. But Landon could be the one who kept the money for both of them. And reports she'd read estimated Landon's net worth at a few million dollars. A lot of money for an Army sergeant to share.

"I can't discuss all of the points of the case with you." She broke eye contact and walked away, toward a display of luxury towels. As she fingered the plush fibers, she wished she could throw herself into the pile. Anything to escape the constant keen observation that she realized was status quo for Flynn.

"I'm not asking you to tell me anything classified, Vikki. But ask yourself this. If I was part of the supplement problem, why would I be wasting time with you in this warehouse, hours before a storm, when I'm on leave and could go anywhere?"

Her physical response was so immediate that she didn't answer him right away. Heat infused her core, traveled to parts that had nothing to do with a legit investigation…and everything to do with how a woman responded to a man who had caught her attention.

"Everything about this case is ongoing."

He snorted, actually blew air out of his nose, and shook his head. "So we're back to paralegal baloney. Fine."

"No, wait. Flynn." She grabbed the edge of the cart, stopping him from stalking toward a woman handing out samples of plant-based, anchovy-flavored Caesar salad dressing atop butter lettuce leaves. "Thank you for having my back at the cemetery. And in the barracks." Belatedly, she realized that Flynn's quick thinking and the threat of his presence were probably all that kept Captain Joseph from harming or, worse, kidnapping her yesterday. "You saved my life."

Pride sparred with humanity in his gaze, in the way his jaw muscles flexed, his knuckles whitened on the cart handle.

"It wasn't personal, Vikki. I was saving both our skins."

Before she had a chance to try to break through his stony guard, he walked off.

Vikki thought she'd pretty much perfected her interrogation and interview techniques over her Army career to date. Flynn Cruz-Street was teaching her a whole new level of challenging client.

"Try our creamy avocado chocolate drink mix?" A woman in an apron and hairnet held out a tray of mini sips of what looked like burned pea soup.

"No, thank you." Vikki noted Flynn's spot by the protein powders and made a quick trip to the coffee-and-tea aisle. Maybe there was a huge quantity of chamomile tea. She sensed she was going to need help calming down around Flynn.

Chapter Five

On Sunday Flynn awoke at 0530 to a text from his boss. He saw Captain Joseph's name and had to verbally remind himself that the man wanted him—or at least his half brother—dead. "Not my boss anymore," he grumbled to himself, rubbing his eyes.

Tell me where you've gone with the JAG paralegal.

Flynn stared at the screen, concern chasing away the last of his slumber. He called in to the MP office and spoke to his master sergeant, reporting the text.

"I've gone on leave so that I can focus on finding my brother."

"I know you're officially in a leave status, Flynn, but I need your help. The community needs you. Stay in place and don't move even if the storm clears out early. We've got to be the ones to bring Captain Joseph in, if at all possible."

"Yes, Master Sergeant." The call was brief. It didn't need any more explanation. His senior enlisted boss wanted the military to capture Joseph so that he'd be tried under the military judicial system, the UCMJ. It might give the bereaved captain, clearly in mental and emotional distress, a fairer shot than if he got locked up by the local PD. While Fort Rapids relied on GRPD to return active-duty soldiers to the post and UCMJ, it wasn't a given.

Captain Joseph would be brought before the post CO and, if the Uniform Code of Military Justice determined he needed a full court-martial, he'd be judged by military peers who understood the depths of his commitment and sense of duty before his wife died. No matter what caused her death, it would have been awful, a tragedy in one so young. But the fact that it was from something sold as a scam vitamin that was supposed to make her feel better, more youthful, was all the worse.

He had over an hour until the breakfast buffet opened. The reminder of his appointment with Vikki had him wide-awake and fighting the attraction that had sparked between them. Flynn wasn't concerned; they both were professionals and he knew he, for one, would keep it in his pants. But he had to admit that if he'd met Vikki while off duty, in civilian clothes, he'd be wowed by her. From her sharp intelligence and warm demeanor, to her flat-out attractiveness, Vikki Colton wasn't a woman he'd ever miss in a crowded room.

But they weren't off duty, and he had to deal with his raging hard-on. The hotel had the best amenities, including a fifty-meter lap pool.

Nothing like a morning workout to keep the hormones under control.

He swam two full laps before he realized another person had joined him, two lanes over in the four-lane pool. Flynn immediately checked the swimmer out; it was part of his training to always practice personal surrounding awareness.

A slim female form sluiced through the water, her freestyle moving her legs and arms in pure harmony. While she wore a cap and goggles along with her modest training suit, he'd recognize her shape anywhere.

You are messed up, man.

So what? Each person had their own build. He happened to remember that Vikki had shapely legs and a long torso. And her breasts— Yeah, that was her.

Don't be a perv.

He forced himself to ease back into his strokes, allowed the rhythm of the movement to help him forget about Vikki Colton and how she made the one-piece swimsuit as sexy as if she'd been on a Brazilian beach, topless with only a thong.

His groan made more bubbles run out of his mouth and he sucked in water before he surfaced. Forced to stand and cough it out, he was grateful she appeared immersed in her routine.

Until she got level with him.

Fudge.

"Hey, Flynn. Wrong pipe, buddy?" She perched her goggles atop her silicone cap, and her eyes were a brilliant green in the overhead light as it reflected off the surface of the water. Huge picture windows, either steamed up or obscured by the still falling snow, surrounded them.

"Yeah." He continued to cough, gasping to get the one-syllable reply out.

"I've got some water with me—did you get any? They have it in the women's locker room." She splashed to the edge of the pool and retrieved the clear plastic bottle, waited to see him make eye contact, then tossed it to him. He caught it, gulped half of it down.

And felt like he was naked. Could she please stop staring at him?

"It happens to the best of us. Keep the bottle. We still on for breakfast at seven?"

"Sure."

Ten minutes later, he finished his laps and headed for the hot tub, where he immediately noticed Vikki sitting across from an older man.

"May I?" He motioned to the space next to her. Her head was against the rim and she let the bubbling water froth around her shoulders.

"Be my guest."

He slid into the water, careful to give a wide berth for their legs. The last thing he wanted was for Vikki to think he was coming on to her.

So, at last, you admit it.

"This is the best part of every workout." Vikki's expression showed pure bliss.

"Agree."

"Have you thought of anything new we need to talk about later?" Her voice was slightly raised over the hum of the water pumps. He eyed the stranger, but the man had his eyes closed and didn't appear to be paying attention to them. Still, Flynn's training precluded stupidity.

"I have, but I'll save them for our meeting." He waited for her to look at him. Once her eyes were aimed, he used his brow to motion toward the man.

Vikki nodded. "You're right. Did you sleep okay?"

"Until I got a text. Another thing I need to discuss with you later." She offered him a brief smile, her way of saying "Got it."

Warmth spread in his chest and through his limbs, a sensation that had nothing to do with the hot water or even his physical attraction to her. It was the sense of partnership that occurred with another soldier, the part of the Army he'd miss most once he left.

The man opposite them lumbered across the tub and hauled himself up the concrete steps. Flynn knew it wasn't his best judgment reacting when he silently cheered the departure. Time alone with Vikki was a good thing. They needed to develop a working relationship to strengthen trust in one another. She was still looking at him as though he had Landon's location in his back pocket.

"Do you swim regularly?" She kept her eyes closed, her head against the rounded edge of the hot tub. A bead of perspiration or spray from the bubbles dripped down her nose. The urge to reach over and swipe it took him by surprise, but it shouldn't have. Sitting this close to a woman as attractive as Vikki was enough to pique any man's interest.

Her eyes opened and she caught him staring. "Flynn?"

"Uh, yeah." *Keep it cool, dude.* "I prefer to swim, but I need to keep up my two-mile time, too."

Could he sound any more like an adolescent? What happened to the side of him that used to be comfortable with all women? He'd never been shy around the opposite sex. He credited it to being raised by a single mother and the close relationship they'd shared. As Flynn had matured, he'd appreciated what a wonderful, strong woman his mother had had to be, raising him as well as she had after his father died. And she'd always kept up with Landon, too—as much as she could, until Landon cut off ties with Rosa and Flynn.

"What is it?"

"What's what? Sorry, I drifted there."

"Yes, you did." Her eyes narrowed. "Your two-mile time, Flynn. Cough it up."

"I usually come in under eleven."

Her brow rose. "Were you a runner in high school?"

"You know it. This bod wasn't made for football." He was used to poking fun at his slimmer shape and had learned long ago that just because he wasn't over six feet tall, like so many MPs, he was just as adept at apprehending a suspect. His words seemed like a terrible come-on, though. Unless Vikki went for football players.

"Football's overrated."

"Really? I thought women liked the full-built, athletic type."

"That's pretty sexist. I'm all about the brain, myself. No brains, don't bother me."

"I'll keep that in mind."

Her gaze had remained locked with his and the heat on his face wasn't from the water. Vikki made him feel like he was the smartest guy ever. In fact, as he mentally reviewed the time they'd shared since their chaotic introduction, he'd never felt anything but acceptance from her.

Because it's her job. Careful.

"You're playing with me, aren't you?"

Vikki's cheeks flushed from pink to red. "I don't play with anyone, Flynn."

"I mean, it's your job, right? To make me all comfortable with you, to think this is offhand banter. Fun. Casual. Then you move in to get the information you want." As soon as he spoke, he wanted to slap himself upside the head. What had he been thinking?

"Are you saying that you have information? If you have any idea where Landon is, I suggest you come clean now. It's going to be a lot uglier for you if I find out you've been withholding evidence. Do I have to remind you what your half brother's suspected of, Flynn?"

He looked around the pool area, which had only one swimmer in a far lane. Still, sound carried, and he wasn't about to continue this with Vikki.

Flynn leaned in close to make sure she heard him.

"I have no idea where Landon is. I already told you this, and you can ask me ad infinitum. The answer's the same."

Shoot.

She'd angered Flynn.

Vikki watched him leave the hot tub, rivulets of steaming water trailing over and down his athletic form. His shorts were modest, but it didn't take a lot of imagination to see that he kept himself in excellent shape, well past what was required by Army standards. And Army standards were exacting.

He didn't look back and she didn't blame him. But it was her job to provoke, to push. She had to be absolutely sure that Flynn wasn't deceiving her. As his measured stride took him farther away, she sank down into the water and let the hot bubbles pummel her shoulders, her neck.

Way to go. You've alienated your one ally in this fight.

Because it was going to be a tough order to bring in Captain Joseph, if the MPs and police hadn't already. And Landon? He was the man they all wanted, hands down. Get Landon, and justice might be served.

Her finger pads were pruning. She got out of the swirling, steaming water and wrapped herself in one of the hotel's large thick towels neatly folded on a side table. Wondering if the snow had picked up, she slowly padded to the floor-to-ceiling windows, mesmerized by the snowfall. The storm had intensified, for sure. The flakes were indiscernible as the gale-force wind pelted the glass. She made out the grove of trees that surrounded the back of the hotel property. They were no more than sixty-foot arrows bending to the will of the storm.

Out of nowhere, a figure appeared, walking against the wind and toward the window. Vikki gasped and took a step back before she realized she was safe inside the hotel's pool house. And who said this person was a threat?

Still, her heart slammed out a beat of warning.

Who would be out in the middle of this storm? The person wore a parka with the hood up, covering their head as they made their way along what she knew to be a pathway that surrounded the hotel gardens. And led straight to the pool-house entrance.

Vikki took in a deep breath and looked around the room for another person to share her concern with. The person could be a hotel employee, perhaps a maintenance worker who needed to check on something integral to the building's operations. Or—

The figure turned and stopped, facing her, but she couldn't make out any features. Whoever it was was wearing a ski mask. Combined with the thickness of the pool-house glass and impenetrable whiteout, it was impossible to identify the person. Nevertheless, she strained to remember every single detail. The person looked like they were wearing a man's clothing; he was the same height as Captain Joseph, taking into account the slightly elevated path he stood on.

The outside exit door opened with a gust of wind, snow and danger. Her breath caught, her body tensed, ready to run if the man entered. All she saw enter the pool house were three men in maintenance overalls. The door slammed shut behind them and Vikki looked back through the window at the single person who'd stood in front of her. To find only the unrelenting storm. He'd disappeared.

"Excuse me." She walked toward the men. "Why did you risk the storm to get in here?"

The men looked at each other as they stamped the snow off their work boots.

"We're here to replace three of the overhead lights." The first man pointed to the ceiling, where three lights were obviously out.

"Oh, I thought it was dim in here due to the early hour." She looked back at them. "I just saw someone outside the window, down there." She pointed. "Is there a fourth person with you?"

"No, just us. We're only here in the middle of this storm because our offices are two buildings over."

"You're from Eberly Electronics Repair." She knew the building, the business. "I'm Vikki Colton."

"Colton Investigations. You related?"

"I am, in fact."

The middle man nodded. "We did more work for them last week. Riley's a good man to work for. How are you related?"

"Riley is my brother."

All three men focused on her. Vikki bit back a grin. Used to wearing her uniform and dealing with men day in and day out, she was shivering, in a wet towel, in no more than a swimsuit. Yet they all looked at her with a respect they hadn't shown before they'd learned she was a Colton.

"You think you saw someone else out there?" The man didn't want her to think she'd been ignored.

"I don't think—I did. But maybe they work for the hotel, too. It's probably nothing. Thanks, and good luck with the lights."

She walked away and wished she could convince

herself that she'd merely spotted someone who worked at the hotel or for a nearby downtown business. Someone who had to be out in the vicious weather, for a good reason.

Vikki had done a lot in the Army: deployed to a combat zone, dealt with cases she'd rather forget, especially those that involved sexual violence and child abuse. But she'd never been stalked, and whoever had been on the other side of the glass felt like some kind of predator. She swore she felt their focus entirely on her.

Calm down.

She'd been the only person here when the stranger had come up to the window, so it made sense the person had looked at her— If only the logical explanation would smother the fear that tugged at her.

Her stomach growled. It was her low blood sugar that was making her skittish. It had to be. The other alternative only stoked her pride, her anger.

She was letting Captain Joseph's threats get to her.

VIKKI SHOWERED AND dried her hair in her hotel room, planning to still meet Flynn on time. Her phone lit up with her oldest brother's number.

"Hi, Riley."

"When were you going to tell me that a dangerous man tried to hurt you?" His commanding tone rivaled any Army general she'd ever worked for. As the CEO of CI, Riley often ran the company, and their family, like a battalion. She didn't mind so much, except when he sounded like he expected her to tell him her entire life story. The only sibling she shared everything with was Sadie.

"I was going to call you after I got some more work done, and to follow up on the cemetery incident. How— Wait. Your Fort Rapids contact. I should have known you'd figure it out. Look, I'm sorry about the CI meeting. I wanted to tell you that I was working on the same thing as you are, but couldn't. I've already said too much. Except I know the reports filed by the MPs and local LEA have hit the news. It doesn't declassify what I'm doing, but I think you can put two and two together." She'd been stupid to think Riley wouldn't get word about what had happened in the barracks, especially since it involved RevitaYou.

"I get it, Vikki. And I would never ask you to break the law, for heaven's sake. But you're my sister. I don't like it that you were anywhere near Captain Joseph. The man isn't predictable anymore."

"I know. I mean, I realize that now. It all happened so fast. I'm thinking you've seen the report from the post MPs?"

"I have a summary of it." Riley was a former FBI agent. He also had cultivated military contacts all over the state and, while he wasn't privy to official Army matters, he always seemed to find out what he needed to. "We're working closely with the Army on this. They're eager to get RevitaYou behind them. It's terrible what's happened to Captain Joseph's wife and the other victims."

"Yes."

"Do you feel safe there, Vikki? I can—"

"I'm fine, Riley. No one's coming out in this weather." Except maintenance staff. And an unknown.

"You don't sound fine."

She let out a frustrated groan, making sure he heard it. Riley needed to know she could handle herself, but she didn't want to be coy or, worse, to keep what could be potential evidence from him. "I just was swimming and got rattled by a person I saw outside in the storm. It seemed odd, but then three other guys walked into the pool to fix the lights. They all know you." She relayed the conversation.

"Eberly is the best in town, for sure. But the other person you saw—they weren't with Eberly?"

"No. And whoever it was stopped in the middle of walking along that garden path—you know the one, where people get their wedding photos taken—and looked straight at me. It was creepy as all get-out. I'm being a bit paranoid, I'm sure. Captain Joseph is most likely hiding on post. If he did get past post security, he wouldn't stick around town, don't you think?"

"I think he's not in a good state of mind. If anything happened to Charlize or our baby, I wouldn't rest until I had answers. I understand his tremendous grief, but not the way he's dealing with it." He expelled a long breath. "Have you talked to Sadie yet?" Riley's words were tough, but his gruff tone told her all she needed to know. He was worried beyond reason.

"No. I was hoping to surprise all of you by maybe staying through Thanksgiving. But only if I get my job done."

"Sadie might still be in a safe house, Vikki. We don't know how long this could go on."

Shock ran over her. Sadie, her twin, was a part of her. "What? I mean, I know her ex has threatened her, but has more happened?"

"Yes. He's continued to harass her with texts and voice mails. With the unraveling of the RevitaYou empire that he bankrolled, I think Greer wants to bring her into it to use as a pawn against all of us." Riley's voice practically growled.

"Riley, I'm so sorry." Remorse hit her in the gut as effectively as if he'd kicked her. "I should have been there for her."

"The thing is, Vik, I need you. CI needs you. We've got to get Landon shut down."

"What report did you receive about Friday night?"

"That you were in the barracks when Captain Joseph lost it and attacked Sergeant Cruz-Street. I know that you confronted Joseph, and that you've been ordered to stay off post, since Joseph is on the run."

"Yup, you got the salient points. Because of Joseph's threats, the Army ordered me to not go back to my apartment. And before you say I should have stayed with you and Charlize, forget it. I couldn't risk bringing Joseph anywhere near her." No way would her brother argue with her logic to keep Charlize safe. "I'm at the Grand Hotel, and Flynn is in the room next to mine. We're stuck here with this storm, so we're going to come up with a plan to draw in Landon if we can. I still have to question Captain Joseph, but the chances of that are getting slimmer."

"You're on a first-name basis with Landon's brother already? I thought you'd be working on getting Landon's location out of Cruz-Street."

"He's Landon's half brother. And we're the same rank. He doesn't have any idea where Landon is, but he's seen him a couple of times over the last six months or so, at their father's grave site. You have that information, I trust?"

"I do."

"Look, I messed up by not telling you sooner, Riley. I'd never want to make you worry about me. I'm so sorry. What can I do?"

"Get your Army orders fulfilled, then take leave and help us solve this case. Or Sadie will kill both of us." The image of her high-energy, freedom-loving twin limited to a small home or cabin in the middle of nowhere until her loan-shark ex-fiancé was caught flashed before Vikki's eyes.

She laughed and was relieved to hear him chuckle, too. Riley always carried the weight of the world on his shoulders, and, to him, their family was his world.

"How's Charlize?"

"Good, thanks. The morning sickness has passed, and she's keeping both of us well-fed."

"Glad to hear it. I'm sorry I missed her on Friday. I look forward to seeing her in person again instead of on a computer screen."

"You will, soon. Listen, Vikki, I know you're a grown woman, but be careful. Sit tight in the hotel until the storm passes, and then come here and work with us, okay? You can do both of your jobs at the same time. I promise I won't press you for anything classified by the Army. It won't take more than a week or two to wrap this case with you on our team."

"I'll come when I can, Riley." There was no sense going over her Army duties—they had to come first at the moment. If Riley weren't so rattled by her and Sadie's circumstances, he'd agree. "Love you, bro."

"Love you, too, sis."

When they disconnected, Vikki felt the energy leave the room. Riley—and all of her siblings, for that matter—was a force of nature. The fact that he'd had to put Sadie in a safe house said it all. She was in danger, a danger Riley didn't feel he could save her from without drastic measures.

SHE HAD TEN minutes until she had to be in the hotel's restaurant. Enough time to check in with her twin.

Sadie picked up immediately. "Vikki!"

"I am so sorry that you're locked up, sis." She tried to tug on Sadie's funny bones, as the sad tone in her voice brought tears to Vikki's eyes. More than ever, she regretted not letting Sadie know she was in town.

"Yeah, me, too. But let's face it—it's all my fault."

"Stop it, right now. None of this is your fault. We all have our choices, and your ex made his." She couldn't bring herself to say his name. Tate Greer had financed the entire RevitaYou project, from the ground up, with an operation called Capital X. He'd tried to use Sadie's position as a CSI at GRPD to gain insider information on the law enforcement efforts against RevitaYou, in addition to bankrolling what he knew was a misleading product.

"If I'd not been blinded by his sweet-talking ways, I'd have figured it out sooner. Just think, Vikki. If I was smarter, I'd be the one who got into his business and we'd already have them all locked up, RevitaYou shut down. But enough about me. Tell me all about your Army life and what you're up to. Have you found a new Mr. Sexy yet?"

Vikki laughed at the nickname they'd invented as teens to describe their current crush. It had carried into their adult lives.

"Ah, no." The image of Flynn climbing out of the hot tub flashed and she shook her head. "Definitely no."

"Aha! I hear a hesitation. Spill it, Vikki."

"Actually, I just talked to Riley. He's a little upset with me."

"Why?"

She relayed the previous two days. "I drove on post Friday, thinking that my sole job was to interview Captain Joseph and Sergeant Cruz-Street, to get information. Maybe to get information on Landon's location that I could turn over to my bosses on post and at JAG headquarters in Virginia, plus GRPD." They both knew that included Colton Investigations. Although a private firm, CI had gained community trust and worked closely with local law enforcement. Federal LEAs, too, when called for.

"Vikki, are you safe? From what you've said, Captain Joseph is out of his mind with grief. He's looking for a point of blame and Landon's the logical target.

But without getting him, he'll settle for Sergeant Cruz-Street. You could end up in between them." Sadie's law enforcement training shone in moments of stress and crisis. And, Vikki knew, Riley had to be feeding her information to keep her in the loop.

"You're right, but I'm hoping they'll catch Captain Joseph soon. At least after this storm passes."

"That's the only good thing about an early snowstorm. No one's coming for me in this safe house, not through this."

"Do you have any reason to think you're not safe, Sadie?" Fear clutched at Vikki's heart. She and her twin were emotionally and spiritually inseparable even when miles apart.

"No. You know Riley would only put me in the best place possible. The FBI is involved now, too, as RevitaYou crossed state lines ten times over."

"You're right. It sounds like we're both stuck right now."

"So tell me about this sergeant you're snowbound with, sis."

"Don't even go there, Sadie."

They finished the conversation as Vikki had to head to breakfast. She wished that she felt more certain that they were both safe. Losing their parents as they had, the sense that something awful could happen at any moment had taken years to fade. It seemed a lot more than coincidence that they were both being stalked by men related to the RevitaYou case. Men on opposite ends of the ugliness: one who'd caused it and one a victim. Yet it didn't matter which side either was on. They were coming after them.

As she left her hotel room to meet Flynn, Vikki had to face facts.

She couldn't shake the sense of danger that surrounded this entire case. Now that deaths were attributed to the big moneymaking supplement, the risk to her was nothing less than life-threatening.

Chapter Six

"You didn't have to wait for me." Vikki spoke as she slid into the seat across from him in the bistro-style restaurant. "Is this coffee?"

"Yes. Let me pour." He filled her mug and swore he felt anticipation coming off her in waves. He wished it were for more than caffeine. "You're a coffee person, too?"

"Absolutely." Her eyes closed as she breathed in the scent.

"I didn't wait—this is my second cup."

"I need to eat. Swimming always makes me famished. We help ourselves?" She added two healthy dollops of half-and-half to her brew and stirred.

"Yes. Go ahead. I'll keep the table till you get back."

Vikki's eyes widened and she looked around the mostly empty dining room. "Um, I don't think we have to worry about anyone taking our stuff." She leaned over and looked at the chair next to him. "I see you brought your laptop, too."

"Never leave home without it."

"That's right—you're in school. I should really think about going back."

His stomach grumbled, but he didn't want to break the spell of seeing more of Vikki as she revealed herself over her first cup of coffee.

"What would you go back for?"

"That's just it. I finished my bachelor's two years ago, in criminal justice. But I have no desire to go to law school or to be a cop. I think, truth be told, that I'm interested in getting out of the Army and working at my family's firm."

"Another CI investigator."

She nodded, poured herself another half cup of coffee. "Yes. I have three more months before I have to re-up, so there's some wiggle room. I plan to talk to my brother about it when I see him. By the way, CI has the full lowdown on what happened Friday on post. No one's seen Captain Joseph since. That reminds me…"

"What?" His gut tightened, the way it did when a battle buddy gave him the signal that trouble was imminent.

"I've already spoken to my brother about this, but since it's still bugging me, I'd better let you know. I'm concerned that Captain Joseph is nearby." She explained what she'd witnessed from the pool house and her sense of being watched. "I've dealt with enough in my career to know that this could all be explained away as my sympathetic nervous system going into hyperdrive. Even though I didn't feel unhinged at the time by Captain Joseph on Friday, he was being a jerk and did threaten me. It's normal to be on edge for a bit."

His back molars ground as his jaw clenched. If Captain Joseph was anywhere near them, he would be looking for Flynn. The fact that he'd scared Vikki infuriated him. And triggered another emotion he didn't want to look at.

Protectiveness.

"I'm the person he's after. Maybe I need to make myself more visible, walk around the building."

Vikki looked across her mug. "That's not wise. I know that, like me, you're from here and know how to deal with the cold. But let's say Joseph is out there, lying in wait. You won't be able to identify him in the first place, with all the cold-weather gear he'd have on, and calling 9-1-1 wouldn't help, as the police have their hands full with keeping citizens off the streets until the storm passes."

He liked that Vikki was able to dissect the simple, logical truths of what they were up against and still maintain her composure.

"You've done a lot during your Army time, I can tell. Why don't we both get breakfast, and then we can talk about it?"

"Sounds good."

As they loaded their plates from the heated chafing dishes on the buffet tables, Flynn took extra measures to look around the room, reinforce the exit point locations, notice where someone could look into the wide windows that spanned one wall, not unlike the pool area. He silently praised the updated security technology; cameras were evident in every corridor and he counted four in the dining room alone.

Back at the table, they dug in to their meals. Flynn relished his eggs Benedict and noticed that Vikki was enjoying her French toast and scrambled eggs just as much.

"It feels kind of weird having all this space and food to ourselves. I'm used to eating in the chow hall and living in the barracks."

She smiled and he watched as it traveled to her eyes, making her irises sparkle under the chandeliers. "Same, although I have a tiny apartment off post. It's like we're in a fairy tale and can have whatever we want."

He couldn't agree more, except that her words made heat rush to his groin. The mental image of what he'd love to do with Vikki Colton had him reaching for the goblet of ice water.

She didn't miss the invisible arcs of attraction that her comment triggered, either, judging by the dark blush on her cheeks.

"I didn't mean it that way. I mean there aren't many other guests than us, and we have everything to ourselves." She fussed with her napkin, a heavy linen number that was bigger than some tablecloths.

Fudge it.

Flynn reached over and covered her hand with his, waited for her gaze to meet his again. "It's okay, Vikki. I know what you meant. This is a bit unusual, being marooned in a snowstorm in a fancy hotel. But we'd get through it if we were downrange, right?"

She nodded. "Except we'd be in air tents instead of a grand ballroom. Or in a dugout."

"And we'd be eating whatever the mess had on hand, till the sandstorm died down."

"I'm sorry. I know I'm probably making you think I'm a rookie at something like this. I'm used to working with a team on the bigger cases, believe me. This has exploded in what feels like an instant." She withdrew her hand and began to eat again. "I thought I'd find you, interview you until you told me where your brother is, then maybe get a chance to interview Captain Joseph. I never in a million years would have expected things to turn south this quickly."

"Trust me, I never thought my commanding officer would barge into my barracks room and assault me, either. And then he fired his weapon—that doesn't happen on a regular Army day." It felt good to talk openly with Vikki.

"Unlike the movies." She looked at him. "Something's still bothering you about me. You're looking at me as the enemy and not a colleague."

"More like you think I know where Landon is. I have no idea. Don't you think I'd want him caught, too? He's caused nothing but pain and heartache for my family."

"I do believe you, Flynn. Please understand that I had my marching orders, and it was easy to assume that you were hiding Landon from justice. I have a twin sister I'd do anything for. I'd give my life for any one of my five siblings, in fact." Her obvious love for her sister made something in his heart region constrict. It'd be wonderful to have a sibling he could trust. An impossible concept, with Landon for a half brother.

"But I'd guess your twin hasn't concocted a bestselling supplement that is suspected of sickening hundreds and now has killed someone."

"You'd guess correctly. As I told you, I spoke with Riley earlier. He's been working close with the post to keep the RevitaYou distribution and effects to a minimum. You probably already know this, as an MP. He's concerned about Joseph coming after me. He's already worked up about having to put my sister in hiding over *all of this.*"

"How so?" He knew the Coltons were well connected in Grand Rapids. CI had a stellar reputation and, matching his impression from the few times he'd worked with Riley, he'd heard nothing but good things about Vikki's brother. The private investigative firm was known for its effective methods and excellent track record, without being overbearing to local and federal law enforcement. His office, as well as the CID—Army Criminal Investigative Division Command—shared information with CI on various cases as needed.

"Sadie was engaged to the scum who ran the loan-shark operation that took money from investors in the project and enabled Landon and his lab team to come up with the supplement as fast as they did."

"That kind of bank can make magic happen. But RevitaYou's initial success came at a much higher price." It reminded him of the diet-pill tragedies he'd heard of from his mother when he was young and she was a senior enlisted soldier. The Army was strict about soldiers not taking certain supplements and over-the-counter medications for a reason. Personnel readiness began with keeping a soldier healthy and alive.

"Yes. Now we know there's a secret ingredient, all right. Ricin, a by-product of castor oil." Vikki's sober expression made something inside him want to do back-flips or tell a joke. Anything to erase the deep concern from her features.

"That's what I heard, too."

"But it's worked for people, Flynn. Lots of users have had zero side effects except softer, wrinkle-free skin. Or so they say. They're not willing to turn over their supply.

"Not unless," she added, "the creators and distributors behind it are stopped in their tracks. That's why catching your brother is critical."

"Half brother. If we're going to trust each other and work together, you've got to understand that while my parents really tried to make us a cohesive family after they married and I was born, it's never been that way. Landon never accepted my mother as a parental figure and missed his mother, always."

"Tell me about Landon's biological mother. How often did he see her?"

"Never. Wait—that's not true. Maybe two, three times over the course of ten years, that I can remember. Melissa is a piece of work. Abandoned her family on what seemed a whim. Now I wonder if she doesn't suffer from mental illness, too."

"Like Landon?"

Flynn nodded. "Yes. My mother took him to psychiatrists all through his college years, way after our dad died. One said that Landon suffered from delusions of grandeur. That makes sense, with his agreeing to come up with this supplement. I always saw him as more of an inventor. I never expected he'd get into the pharmaceutical industry. And not an illegal product like RevitaYou."

"I'm sorry, Flynn. It sounds like Landon's issues put a lot on your family. How is your mother now?"

"My mother, Rosa, is great. She's worried about Landon, but learned that she had to have a healthy detachment from him. My mom's worried about me, always. Even though she served in the Army and understands more than anyone what it's like to be a soldier."

Vikki smiled. "It's a mother's job to worry, I think."

Her wistful tone reminded him that she'd lost her parents when they were still relatively young.

"Your brother Riley… Is he a lot older than you?"

"Yes, by fifteen years. He held all of us together when our parents died. It was an awful time." Her eyes reflected her stormy past and his hand moved to hold hers again, but he gripped the side of the table instead. She'd think he was some kind of needy weirdo.

"You're all still close, it seems."

"We are, which makes it hard when one of us is hurting. I'm gutted that Sadie has to be in a safe house. We're used to clients at CI needing to be protected, and I've dealt with that in the Army, but when it's my twin, it hits home."

"I'm sorry, Vikki. Let's get our plan formulated so that we can put an end to everyone's stress ASAP."

"You're a man after my own heart, Flynn." Vikki's words were offhanded as she pulled her laptop onto the table, but there was no denying what Flynn's conscience was communicating.

He wondered what it'd be like to be the man who had Vikki's heart.

Don't do it, man. Stay in your lane.

FLYNN WAS EASY to work with and they stayed at the breakfast table for another couple of hours. The service staff were hospitable, and since they were the only two in the restaurant, Vikki and Flynn had all the coffee and snacks they wanted.. The few waiters on staff during the storm brought them an endless array of pastries, cookies and, once it approached noon, sandwiches.

"This feels wrong, using government funds to work in such fancy surroundings." Flynn shut his laptop and looked around the room for the umpteenth time.

"Do you ever stop checking the egress points?" She couldn't help teasing him just this little bit. He was so serious.

Brown eyes rested on her and she recognized surprise. "It's that noticeable?"

"Maybe to me, because I've been around enough MPs to know that your training goes bone-deep. You can't help yourself, can you?"

A slow grin formed across his features. A shiver of awareness caught her off guard and she looked away. "I'm sorry. It's not my place to make fun of your skills. You save lives every day by doing what you're trained to do."

"Stop going back into your head, Vikki."

"My head?" She shored herself up to look at him again, and those eyes, his bright smile, his pure confidence, hit her in the solar plexus. And rushed to all of her sexiest parts.

"Yeah. You're retreating from an accurate observation by becoming all logical about it. Going back into whatever you've decided is your job description."

"You mean what the Army gave me as a job description."

"No, this is about you, Vikki. It's clear to me that you're excellent at your job. But do you ever take a break, let your hair down?"

"I could interpret that as a sexist remark." Her hand jerked to her ponytail and she wished she'd blown her hair all the way out, left it down, since she was in civilian attire.

"If you stay in your head, yes. But if you listen to your emotions, to the attraction that's happening here, you might see that I'm being exceptionally aboveboard, considering our circumstances."

Her breath caught somewhere in between her lungs and throat. Flynn, a man she'd known for barely two days, had seen past her most polished defense mechanism. Her identity as a soldier and paralegal. Peter had thrived on her being the professional, even in civilian clothes and at his work parties or with his friends. Flynn saw past it all, right to her soul.

"'Our circumstances'? You mean being stalked by your boss and trying to figure out how to draw Landon to us?"

He leaned in and she was aware of the texture of the linen tablecloth under her palm, the scent of the fall flower arrangement in the middle of their table. But what she'd never forget was the heat that flickered in Flynn's eyes, the curiosity that she shared. Wondering what it'd be like to take their mutual attraction and do something more constructive than wait out a snowstorm hunched over their laptops.

"No, Vikki. I mean…maybe we both need to take a break from this case and do something beneficial for one another. I'm offering this as a suggestion and with intention of it not going any further than you'd want it to."

She couldn't take her gaze from his, as if it were her lifeline to the real Vikki, the woman she never let show in uniform. The woman who longed for a relationship where she could be 100 percent herself, with a man who completely understood her commitment to country, too.

Vikki had known this assignment was going to be challenging. She'd been thrown off guard when Captain Joseph had threatened her. Having to go off post to be safe from him had been a stumbling block, too.

But Flynn Cruz-Street? He was the hurdle she knew she wanted to clear.

Just not now. Her heart was too raw after the way Peter had mashed it, like potatoes in a blender. And the case. She had to keep the case first.

HE SAW THE confirmation in Vikki's eyes when her irises deepened in their green intensity. It was at the same time that she let go of a long sigh, as if she'd been lost for hours and in need of a cold drink of water.

But when the clouds came back and turned her gaze stormy, he knew he'd overstepped.

"I'm not taking your, um, offer the wrong way at all, Flynn. The truth is that, besides the obvious—" she waved her hand over their laptops and stacks of papers "—I'm not ready to get involved with anyone right now. I'm coming off a pretty sucky breakup."

An instant flash of hate for whomever had hurt her made him unable to reply right away. Vikki seemed to take it as a signal that he was upset with her.

"I'm sorry, Vik."

"I don't want this to change how we work together on the case. We've accomplished a lot in the past few hours, and I like working with you so far." Her eyes were clear pools of honesty. Integrity.

"Hold on. I'm not going to start acting like a jerk because you turned me down. What kind of guy would I be?"

"Not the man I'm beginning to know." Her gaze didn't waver and Flynn knew he was on a path to destruction. Vikki's words, her calm demeanor in the face of a monumental case, her solid nature, were rare qualities in a person, and then add in that she wore the uniform, too, able to understand his line of work. Vikki was his dream.

She was also his colleague and a fellow sergeant.

"Thank you for that. May I suggest we take a break, go over our notes individually, then meet back for dinner?" He needed some time alone to lick the minor wounds her refusal had caused. But, dang it, Vikki even made turning him down something sweet, between her straightforward honesty and dedication to duty.

He got it.

And he hadn't missed the one thing he'd bet she wished she'd not revealed. She hadn't denied the gauntlet he'd thrown down, that they were experiencing a shared attraction. Vikki was just as attracted to him.

They gathered their belongings and walked to the bank of elevators. Flynn waited for Vikki to enter, holding the door for her.

"You first."

"Thanks." He caught a whiff of the hotel shampoo when she passed. Mingled with Vikki's scent. Soft and feminine but with a spicy edge. His desire raged and he fought to keep from getting a hard-on in the dang elevator.

They didn't look at one another as they waited for their floor. Alone in the brass-trimmed space, the mirrored doors reflecting two figures intent on getting to the next destination, he couldn't think of anything but how her skin would feel under his hands.

Back off, buddy. She said no.

Had he been too quick? Maybe she would have regretted being with him when the snow cleared. He looked at her, found her staring at him. With a wide grin to boot.

"Ask me again after the case is wrapped, Flynn."

"All right. Will do."

No, she wouldn't regret their being together. He might, though. Vikki was different from the women he usually dated. Not in anything he'd be able to name off the top of his head, but deep down, where it counted, he knew Vikki was a woman who could bring him to his knees.

The elevator bell dinged and the doors slid open. Again he nodded for her to go first, then walked alongside her to their adjoining rooms.

"I'll make sure you're locked inside." Hers, 707, was first. His was 709.

She waved her phone in front of the keypad and the green light flashed. Her slim hand turned the handle and Flynn prayed she'd please just go inside. *Don't turn around. Don't prolong this.* He needed to be alone in his room, ASAP.

"Flynn?"

"Vikki."

"Can you come in for a minute? I have one question I need an answer for, before I go back over my notes."

Relief sluiced through his muscles and he almost laughed. "Sure thing." Work. She wanted to talk about work. Vikki had already forgotten their conversation and her elevator suggestion. He could work with this. As long as they kept things about business.

"After you." She waved him ahead this time and he acquiesced, figuring she wanted to be the one to lock the door behind her. As soon as he stepped inside her room, he felt like a wild animal caught in a domestic backyard, lured into a trap by a tasty treat. But the cage was worse, because it hit him with Vikki's essence from all sides. The bath-product fragrance, her scent, her luggage left open and revealing a pile of panties and bras in several shades of red and pink.

Awareness slammed right to his crotch once again.

Her hand on his shoulder startled him, more so when she tugged and turned him around to face her. Her expression was not one of Sergeant Colton, but of Vikki, the beautiful woman who'd walked into his life Friday but felt like she'd been there all along.

"Um, Vikki?" He took a step back but she followed, until she was inches from him. Her breath fanned the base of his throat and he thanked the heavens above for this moment. But what was Vikki thinking?

"Flynn, listen to me. I know I just said no to being with you in any capacity other than Army business. And I'm certain that we can't—or rather shouldn't—get involved. But I can't help but wonder..."

"What?" He could barely breathe.

"Can I kiss you?"

Chapter Seven

Vikki didn't have a problem being the pursuer. In fact, it felt more natural to be going after Flynn than it should, considering their situation. She might regret this later, but she'd regret it more if she didn't ever experience the taste of him on her lips.

"Have at it. As long as you're sure?" The timbre of his voice stroked her in every sensitive place and she hadn't even reached up to kiss him yet.

"I'm sure." She wrapped her arms around his neck, stood on her tiptoes. "Wait. You're shaking, Flynn. Are you okay? Or you're laughing at me?"

She scrutinized his expression. Man, Peter had really left a mark on her self-esteem. Here she was, with a hot guy who clearly wanted her, had said he did, and she was worried he was making fun of her. Instead of appearing like a man holding back laughter, Flynn looked…in pain. "What's wrong?"

"Do it, Vikki. Kiss me."

She leaned in a little closer, closed her eyes and pressed her lips to his.

In a hot nanosecond Flynn wrapped his arms around

her waist, hauling her up to him with zero space between them. His mouth moved over hers with a skill she matched, tongues tasting, lips savoring. As the kiss deepened, she felt his hands move to her bottom, squeezing it, and her knees melted when he ground his erection into her softest parts. They were both in blue jeans and she had never been so irritated with the stiff fabric.

"Vikki." He breathed her name and she clung to his shoulders, held on for sanity's sake as he trailed his tongue down her throat and back up again, swirling and sucking under her ear. When he nipped on her earlobe, she groaned.

"Oh, wow." She held his face in her hands and urged his mouth back to hers. "Please don't stop kissing me."

Flynn obliged. Vikki's skin was ultrasensitive to his every caress, and she breathed in his male musk as if it was oxygen at high altitude. Necessary. Life-giving. Life-changing.

"Vik, hang on." He lifted his lips from hers and she heard a whimper. This was dangerous. She'd never met a man who'd made her sound like a needy kitten before. "We should talk about this. A few minutes ago, you said it wasn't a good idea while we were working on the case."

"That was before I kissed you."

His slow smile made the sparks between them intensify and it was as if she were a teenager again, not knowing what to do with the hormones raging through her system.

As a twenty-eight-year-old woman, she knew very well what would calm her down.

"Babe, this is what I was trying to communicate. We've got something here that's extra special. Have you ever been this turned on so quickly?"

"No. Are—are you turned on like this all the time?"

He laughed, let go of her waist and reached for both her hands. She liked how they fit together perfectly, how his hands were just a bit larger than hers. And he wasn't so tall that she had to tilt her head way back to look at him; his direct gaze was always right next to hers.

"No. I can honestly tell you that no other woman has ever fired me up as fast as you do. I'm sure I can be a dog with the best of them, but I'm not wired to play that way. When I get involved with someone, I'm all in. Not that I haven't casually dated, but it's not my favorite way to know a woman." The flame in his eyes tempted her in the worst way.

"Explain something to me, Flynn. Why did we stop kissing again?"

"Because I don't want either of us to have regrets. And you were right about the case—we have to keep it as the priority."

She nodded. "It's way easier if we keep this all to business." But his kiss. His touch. Unlike other attractions that had caused an itch, this one wasn't going to be scratched out with one time together. Or two. As much as she knew one of her superpowers was her ability to get the most intimate information out of witnesses and clients, Vikki knew that Flynn could have a significant spot in her life. Her heart.

"You've been hit on by dudes all the time at work, I'd think." He caressed her cheek with his finger and she turned to kiss its tip.

"It's inevitable with the close quarters we have to work in, and then live in downrange. Most soldiers are professional and allow me to be, too, but yeah, there have been times when it's a bit much. It's the ratio, you know? So many men, not as many women yet, proportionately."

"It's also you. You're a stellar paralegal and you happen to be an incredible woman."

"You've only known me for two days, Flynn." As she spoke, her words were the cold shower she needed. "And I've only known you that long, too." She let go of his hands, stepped back. He didn't follow her, but his gaze held zero recrimination. Yeah, Flynn was a man of integrity. That was her Achilles' heel, especially after Peter.

"You had a great idea in the elevator, you know."

"I did?" Her brow quirked, as did a corner of her luscious mouth.

"We can wait to see how we feel after the case is closed. It'll give us a carrot to work all the harder."

"You're taking this awfully well, Flynn."

"Like you said, it's only been two days. We can—"

His words were cut off by a huge bang, the floor reverberating with the percussion. Vikki and Flynn dived for the ground at the same time, except Flynn managed to land on top of her back, protecting her from the ceiling plaster that fell all around them.

Vikki's Army training kicked in and she tried to move, to get under the bed.

"Stay down," Flynn growled in her ear, in full MP mode.

"Under the bed. It's safer."

"They're platform beds."

As she figured out they were stuck between the queen beds, the shaking stopped and the room grew quiet. She felt Flynn's body lift, but his hand remained in the center of her spine. "Stay here until I check things out. Here—" he placed a pillow on her back "—in case more plaster falls."

He got up and she could hear his sneakered feet on broken glass and plaster. The sound of the blast had receded to be replaced by the howl of the wind. The air lowered in temperature by the second and Vikki realized the window had been blown out.

Her mind tried to grasp what they'd just experienced. It wasn't unlike the few rocket strikes she'd witnessed in Iraq, in how they'd had zero warning and how the blast had crumbled more from the percussion than the actual strike. But they were in downtown Grand Rapids, USA. It could have been a bomb. But what terrorist would strike an almost-empty large hotel in the middle of an incapacitating storm?

Unless her gut was right and Captain Joseph was still on the loose. Stalking them, seeking a way to take them both out. Did he cause the explosion?

"I'm going with you, Flynn." She was on her feet and next to him before he had a chance to reply. With a curt nod, he stopped being the protector and let Vikki be the soldier she was trained to be.

They were a team.

VIKKI CALLED THE front desk while Flynn called in to MP headquarters to let them know what they were dealing with. Some impact or explosion had caused Vikki's window to shatter, her ceiling to crack in several places. As soon as the calls were placed, they regrouped by the door.

"We'll move into the hallway, nice and easy, okay?" He made certain Vikki heard him, was prepared for each step. She'd had a lot of training, much the same as his, but she wasn't an MP. Just as he'd defer to her in the courtroom, she needed to trust him with this part.

"Yes, your call, Flynn. You're the MP." Her immediate trust and the echo of his own thoughts reaffirmed that they already shared more than a working relationship. But now wasn't the time to let his mind wander. At all.

He looked through the peephole and the corridor was empty. He looked at her. "You sure the front desk said they were sending security up?"

"Positive."

"There's no one here yet. The elevators may be out or the stairs blocked. Let's go check it out."

They entered the hall and he drew his weapon, grateful he'd had the presence of mind Friday to bring it with him.

The elevator doors opened as they approached and Flynn pushed them both against the wall to avoid being so vulnerable. His arm was across Vikki's chest, his protective instinct in high gear, but she'd moved with him, not needing to be coached.

Two hotel security officers stepped out and Flynn lowered his arm and the pistol. The officers spotted him, then Vikki, and stopped.

"You two okay?"

"We are, but her room isn't. Do you have any idea what it was?"

The first security guard, older than the second one, who looked to be just out of high school at best, nodded. "We think it's one of the old water towers on the roof. You're on the top floor, and when they renovated the hotel, they turned the roof into a garden bar. But they kept the hundred-year-old water tower for historical reasons. It's not filled with water anymore, though."

Flynn knew the wind could have blown the tower over, but thought it highly unlikely. "I'm pretty sure whoever left the tower there would have secured it in anticipation of storms."

"True, but the winds from the storm might have blown the top off, and if it filled with enough of this snow, it's possible it tipped over. Mind if we take a look at the room?" The security guard looked at them for acquiescence.

"Not at all," Vikki answered.

The tension eased from Flynn's muscles as he processed what the guards reported. They walked past them and he turned to Vikki.

"Are you thinking what I am?"

"That Captain Joseph got up on the roof and made

that thing fall over our heads? As in, pushed it over? That seems almost impossible to do."

"Never put anything past an Army soldier with enough motivation."

Vikki nodded. "It's possible, Flynn—but improbable. He'd have to be off the post for certain, have made it through the storm to the hotel and then climbed to the roof during the storm. He'd need to know where our rooms were. How would he have gotten up there?"

"As easy as we could have if we'd tried. Taken the elevator up to this floor, then walked down to the roof elevator."

"Let's go check it out."

"Wait a minute, Vikki. We're not going up on the roof in the middle of these winds. Especially if it was the water tower, there might be loose pieces of metal waiting to pull free and do more damage. I'm not going to have either of us risk getting injured."

"I agree with you," she said. "But we don't have to go outside. I saw online that the rooftop bar has these huge custom automatic doors. We'll be able to see enough from inside."

"Okay, fine."

They walked to the end of the hall, where they found two doors identical to the hotel's main elevators but a bit smaller.

"Wait—I don't know if we should use the elevators or the stairs." Flynn paused, his hand midair in front of the button.

"Let's use the stairs to go up. They're over here." She

pointed. "We can take the elevator down if we think it's safe."

The stairwell smelled of new paint and fresh welding. "This must have been built just for the new renovations." Vikki turned on the landing, her head tilted back as she checked the basic structure.

"These don't just go up, though," Flynn noted, "like the roof elevator." He looked down, down into the rectangle the stairs circled through. From how dizzying it appeared, he was fairly certain this smaller stairwell reached to the ground floor at least, if not the parking garage below street level.

"They spared nothing for this old building. I'm glad they kept it, though, instead of razing it. It gives the riverfront way more character."

Flynn didn't disagree, though his mind wasn't on the building but on who was in the hotel with them. His hackles were up and he'd been in enough tight spots to know to pay attention. Drawing his weapon again, he stepped around Vikki and took the lead up the steps. "Stay on the first landing until I clear the next one, and then again when I get to the top."

"Roger."

Once more they fell into soldier mode, working the situation they'd been dealt with professionalism and almost two decades of Army training between them.

Flynn cleared the last step and confirmed the cold air a flight below was due to the gaping hole in one of the automatic doors Vikki had described. A large bent piece of metal lay on the floor amid the pellets of safety glass. Frigid air blew straight in, snow piling up on the corners of the rooftop bar's inner lobby. Flynn couldn't make out much in the snowy landscape, but he did see a giant receptacle on its side.

"The security dudes called it. It was the water tower." She stood next to him.

"You were supposed to wait for my okay."

"When I didn't hear voices or a gunshot, I figured you'd forgotten about me."

Forget Vikki Colton? Never.

VIKKI STOOD NEXT to Flynn, shivering in the face of the harsh wind. "I don't love this part of living in Michigan."

"You said you loved the snow."

"The snow. Not the cold. Holy icicles!" Her teeth clattered together and her lips were tinged with blue.

"Look over there. See the water receptacle?" Flynn pointed to what she'd been trying to figure out from the fuzzy white mess on the other side of the broken door. The water tower lay on its side, a hole torn through the aged sheet metal.

"An explosion that created that hole, Flynn. We're lucky we're still alive."

"We are."

"It's hard to believe the hotel construction company didn't weatherproof everything on the roof." She noted a larger section of the building that seemed to stick out, its doors secured by padlocks. "Look, that's where I'd guess they store the patio furniture and bar supplies out of season."

"Copy that." Flynn started to walk toward the opening, but she held him back, her hand on his forearm.

"Wait. Let me get photos for evidence before we change anything."

"Fine, but hurry up. It's freaking freezing!"

She laughed and used her phone to capture every image she thought might be pertinent, from the metal piece that had shattered the door glass to the carpet and the snow that was falling inside now. As her flash lit up a spot of the carpet, the outline of footprints made ice crawl down her spine.

"Flynn, look over here."

He was next to her, and both lowered to their haunches.

"Son of a—"

"Yeah, those are footprints." Some kind of boot, she estimated, and the size was larger than her foot. She and Flynn were both in athletic sneakers, typical Army running shoes. "Someone else has been up here."

"And they've gone."

She looked at Flynn. "It's looking like Captain Joseph is more resourceful than we gave him credit for."

"We don't know it was him for certain," Flynn pointed out.

"True, but it's highly suspect that I saw that man look at me through the pool windows, and now this." Vikki wasn't taking any chances. "We should move to another hotel ASAP."

"There's an APB out on him. He'd have been recognized downstairs."

Flynn was a trained MP and she respected his view,

but he wasn't seeing this for what it was. Joseph had escaped the post but hadn't left Grand Rapids or Michigan. As she'd feared and suspected, he was here.

"He'd have been recognized by the hotel's security officers, yes, but not by the front desk. Not if the receptionist hasn't been watching the local news. And while the hotel's mostly empty, there's enough distraction and entrances that someone could have sneaked in. We're going to have to look at the security footage." Vikki never lost sight of their objective. Impressive, since they'd just been targets of a malicious event.

"Everyone's been watching the local stations, with the weather. It'd be awfully hard for Joseph to walk around out in the open, even in a storm." Flynn hated the thought that Joseph got past them so easily.

"Flynn, we have to assume he's in the area."

"We do." He nodded. "I just wanted to make sure we looked at this from all angles. I agree about a new hotel, but there's no way we're driving in this, not yet."

Her stomach sank. He was right. "We can hike it."

"We could—or we can get two new rooms, stay here tonight and leave at first light. The storm is supposed to be out of the area sometime over the next twelve hours."

She looked at him and tried to stay professional. To not stoke her fear that Joseph remained nearby, stalking them. But looking into Flynn's eyes, all she saw was security. A port in the storm, literally.

"You're the security expert. I'll defer to you on this."

FLYNN WANTED TO shout at Vikki to *Run, quick. Get away.* He hadn't been able to save Jena from boarding that Apache, hadn't been able to stop the crash under enemy fire that had taken his future with him.

There was no reason Vikki should trust him. In fact, it would be better if she still suspected him of aiding Landon's disappearance. Then maybe he wouldn't have to face the truth.

That Vikki was the first woman he'd been so compellingly drawn to since Jena died. He'd tried to tell himself it was just attraction, maybe one he'd follow through on with a fling. He wasn't anywhere near ready to commit to anything serious.

"I don't like that we're staying here an extra night any more than you do, Vikki."

They sat opposite one another, each on a queen bed, in the room they'd decided Vikki would stay in. He'd had the hotel put their rooms under assumed names, giving himself a female moniker, Vikki a male. If Captain Joseph was going to hack the system, he'd have a harder time finding them. Thankfully a group of stranded high-school basketball teams had arrived earlier in the day, before the brunt of the storm raged as it did now, which would complicate it even further.

"I know. And I said it before, but I meant it. I trust you. The police are probably right—Joseph risked his neck to get up to the roof, place the explosives and loosen the bolts on the tower.

"But he had it fall, then detonate, right on top of our rooms. That's what's got me the most riled up."

"I don't think he hacked into the systems. If he has, we've taken the right precautions with fake names and switched rooms."

"Then why would he go to all that trouble?"

"To scare us. Or to see if we're here. You're not even certain the man you saw outside was him, so there's a good chance that whoever that was didn't know for certain it was you in the pool. Your hair was wet, slicked back, and he'd only seen you once, in uniform." Flynn left out the part about how beautiful she was, how her every curve and the strength of her toned body were incredible turn-ons for him.

"I hadn't thought about that." Relief played over her features. He wished his fingers had smoothed her worry lines.

"We've taken care of all the logistics. Except..." He needed her complete attention, needed to see her reaction.

"Except what?" She arched one pale blond brow, her head tilted, as she leaned toward him.

"I think I should stay with you in this room tonight. Not because of what we were about to do earlier, but for security. We can finish up the plans we began to search for Landon, pack and be ready to split as soon as the storm's over."

"Do you really think we'll stay in this room together and not end up in the same bed?"

"Come on—give me some credit. Like you, I assume, I've been in situations downrange where I had to bunk in coed situations. It happens, and when the bullets are flying, no one's thinking about sex."

"There aren't bullets here—at least, not for now. And to be clear," she said, "I'm not doubting your ability to keep it on a professional level."

The green gaze sliced past his defenses and shot a bolt of desire through him.

"Vikki, you've had a scare."

"So have you. And we're here, alive, with a blizzard raging outside."

Flynn didn't hesitate this time. He stood and hauled her to her feet. Vikki's body was smooth, soft and everything he dreamed of when he thought of the perfect woman to be with. In a single motion, he cupped her face and lowered his lips to hers.

Her moan reverberated through his mouth, down to his erection, which he pressed against her as he dipped his tongue in to taste hers. This wasn't just a strong attraction or a reaction to the shock they'd both been through. This was explosive, a meeting the likes of which he'd never experienced before.

Flynn knew he was in deep.

Chapter Eight

Vikki didn't hold back as they kissed. She responded as Flynn's hands expertly stroked her throat, allowed his hands to wander down to her waist before climbing back up and cupping her breasts. When his thumbs brushed her erect nipples through her sweatshirt, she leaned into him, half hoping he'd tumble backward onto his bed.

He lifted his head and she cried out, needing his heat, his touch.

Fingers through her hair, along her back, pulling her pelvis against his hard length as it pressed through his jeans.

"Don't stop, Flynn. Please."

"Oh, babe, we're just beginning. But I want to do something special here. Can you hang on for five minutes? I'll be right back. Trust me, it'll be worth it."

Every inch of her woman parts screamed *no* at the thought of him leaving the room, leaving their embrace. But the twinkle in his eyes tugged at her curiosity.

"Five minutes, Cruz-Street. Don't be late or you'll face the consequences."

His low, rich laughter rumbled through her. Flynn pulled her to him again, kissed her hard. "Wait here."

She followed him to the door, though, to dead bolt it behind him. Peering through the peephole, she watched him make a beeline for the elevator and she smiled. What was he planning?

Condoms. He was going to get protection. She usually carried some with her, but hadn't planned on recreational activities when she'd started this mission.

But she did have some sexier underwear that she'd packed, just in case. She looked through the peephole again. The corridor was empty. She was safe and Flynn had the key—they'd gotten two for each room, one for each of them.

Before she lost any more time, Vikki undid the dead bolt so that Flynn could slip back in, and raced to the closet and her suitcase. She dug through her neatly folded uniform blouses, her stockings, socks, and found her silk zipper bag where she kept her nicer panties and thongs. Her hands shook, her excitement at being with Flynn making her like a crazed teenager. This wasn't the time to wonder how she'd gotten to this place so quickly with a man she'd known for a short time; there would be plenty of time to psychoanalyze herself later.

Vikki was tired of looking at everything, every man, every relationship, with her head. Since being burned by Peter, she'd heightened her defenses so much that she'd been missing out on life.

It was time to lead with her heart.

She went to the bathroom to brush her teeth and change into the sexy thong. As the water ran, she heard the door click open and wished she'd donned the black lace first. But Flynn would wait—she had, after all.

"I'm in the bathroom. Be right out." She kicked the door closed and rinsed her toothbrush.

The door burst open, catching her on the shoulder. Why would Flynn be so rough?

"Ouch! Wha—" Her words halted with her breath, in her throat, as she stared at the man hovering in the bathroom doorway.

Dark, glittering eyes, as if fevered, stared at her from under a hoodie.

Vikki screamed as loudly as she could, until her throat caught on an inhalation of toothpaste foam. Cold, strong hands had her by the throat, pushed her back, back, twisted her around and held her against the wall. His breath was an awful rush of everything putrid.

Captain Joseph.

"Stop fighting and it'll go easy for you."

Vikki crossed both arms at her waist then raised them quickly, breaking Joseph's hold on her. She ducked down and made for the door. A sharp, painful tug on her hair stopped her, and drawing upon her hand-to-hand combat training, she stomped her heel down on Joseph's shin.

"Ow!" His howl confirmed she'd hit her mark, but he tugged on her head again, this time slamming it against the tiled bathroom wall. Vikki fought to stay conscious, but immediate dizziness and nausea assailed her. It was impossible to keep the moans of pain quiet, her discomfort annoying and frightening at the same time. She had to stay alive, keep Joseph there until Flynn came back.

Her hands tried for purchase on the sink, the wall, the doorjamb, with no luck as Joseph dragged her out into the sitting area beyond the bedroom. He shoved her onto the desk chair, which she noticed he'd already moved to the center of the room. Cold fear shot through her at the sight of wires and what she knew had to be a bomb. She opened her mouth to scream again, but his hand was over her mouth, his face in hers. Her vision was wavering and pain pounded in her temples.

Flynn. She needed his help ASAP.

"Shut up or I'll put a bullet between your boyfriend's eyes the minute he comes back." Joseph quickly gagged her, bound her to the chair and then placed the small deadly box on her chest, using a rope to hang it around her neck.

Stay here. Stay focused. Memorize every detail.

Her Army training broke through her incredible discomfort, the focal point enabling her to not wet herself in fear. Joseph looked haggard. His sweaty face reminded her of soldiers when they experienced anxiety and panic attacks at different times during bomb raids. Except he'd been in this state since losing his wife. His ranting and mumbling underscored the shaky state of his mind.

"No one will tell me where Landon is... Fine. I have to take matters into my own hands... Twelve years in the Army and this is what I get. Nothing. I've lost the love of my life, all because of secrets and greedy moneymakers." His voice cracked and he shot Vikki a furtive glance.

She was too slow to look away, her reflexes still not back after the hit to her head.

His face was back even with hers as he crouched in front of her. "I didn't want it to come to this. But you and your lover boy won't give me the information I know you have."

She moaned "No" through the cloth tied around her mouth but couldn't risk shaking her head—she'd definitely vomit. The spinning room had just begun to settle as she sat utterly still in the straight-backed chair. If not for the zip ties that bound her to the furniture, she'd collapse on the floor, she was certain.

"Don't waste your words on me, Sergeant."

He definitely remembered her. And now she knew he'd somehow followed her and Flynn out here, at least close enough to narrow his search to their hotel. She confirmed that his hoodie and pants looked like those she'd seen through the window and driving snow at the pool. The hoodie was a muddy green and his slacks khaki. She'd bet his hiking boots matched the prints on the roof.

Joseph fiddled with a couple of wires that led to what she thought was a wireless transmitter he'd placed on the desk. Vikki wasn't trained in EOD—explosive ordnance disposal—and had no idea how to construct or defuse a bomb, but this looked like one to her. Joseph was going to kill her if Flynn didn't lead him to Landon. Why else would he go to such elaborate measures?

"That's it, sweetheart. I'll be sending further instructions to Cruz-Street. When he comes back, tell your lover to cooperate or you're going to be no more than a pile of ashes." Joseph left the room without a sound, yet the chill of his sneer remained. Vikki began to shiver uncontrollably. No wonder they hadn't detected his presence sooner—the man had the foot tread of a cat.

Vikki didn't know whether she should pray Flynn returned quickly or not. There was no sense in both of them being killed. Tears spilled down her cheeks as she realized she'd have really liked to get to know Flynn better. Facing her death, it was clear that he was special, maybe the exact right kind of man for her.

She might not ever get her time with him, but she could pray he'd survive to fight another day.

FLYNN TOOK THE steps two at a time as he carried the champagne bottle like a football. Thank goodness the hotel bar had been willing to sell him a bottle of their best bubbly. Vikki had inspired him to celebrate their time together to the best of their ability. If she turned out to be the woman for him, he wanted to do this right.

The hallway was empty and he made a beeline for the room.

The door wasn't locked shut, as he'd left it. It was ajar, a coat hanger propping it open. His heart stopped then sped up as he put the bottle down and pulled his weapon. Without preamble, he raised his arm and entered the room.

The sight of Vikki bound to the chair with a bomb hanging from her neck filled him with a sense of dread and rage that was all too familiar. It was the same sense of powerlessness and helplessness he'd experienced when Jena's helo went down.

Think, Flynn. Fast.

He had to compartmentalize if he was going to get them both out of here alive. Her head was lowered, her eyes closed, her skin so pale he feared it was already too late for her.

No.

His cell pinged and he looked at the message. It was from Joseph.

Give me your brother's location, and he'd better be there or I'll blow her up. Choice is yours. After I kill Landon Street, I'll defuse the bomb.

Flynn looked over the device and the attached transmitter, and quickly used his voice-activated phone to call the post and 9-1-1, giving the specifics of the equipment. They'd have a bomb squad here ASAP, but in the storm, he knew it'd be at least fifteen minutes, if not more. He checked the countdown timer and saw that there were twenty minutes left. He knelt in front of Vikki.

"Vikki? Babe, I'm here."

Her lashes fluttered and she moaned. "Head hurts. Go find Joseph. He did this." She gasped between each phrase, her pain evident.

He touched her cheek, examined her as best he could. "I know, babe. I need you to stay with me. Can you raise your head?"

Vikki did as he requested, her mouth parted in a soft

O of pain. "You need to leave, Flynn." Her words were clear, so that was a good sign. She was aware of where she was and the situation.

"No way. We're both going to walk away from here, free and clear. Now, I need you to stay still. I'm going to undo your ties, but you can't move. Can you stay in the same place?"

"Yes." Her eyes opened, and he knew he'd seen their jade hue for the past two days, but the way they reflected her emotions had never struck him as they did now. Soul-deep pools of green promise. He pulled out the multipurpose knife that he always kept in his back pocket and sliced through the plastic zip ties. Her skin had been broken and bruised in several places, but that was the least of their worries at the moment. He had to let his rage toward Joseph go, for now. The best revenge would be to get out of this alive.

"Sure we're going to survive this. I'm JAG, remember? Can't put one over on me. At least you can go on, Flynn. Leave me."

"We have the best EOD on post and the local PD has a superb bomb demolition team. They'll both be here before long."

"Can you call CI for me?"

He saw the intent in her eyes. Vikki wanted to talk to her brother and as many siblings as possible. She really thought she was going to die.

"Right away." He already had the number in his contacts, as he did a lot of networking and coordinating with CI for cases that involved military personnel.

"Riley Colton. What's going on, Flynn? Is Vikki okay?"

"Ah, actually, no." He thought Riley would have already heard the police chatter, but when it came to explosives, the lines were often kept tight, secure. "I'm here with Vikki, and she asked that I call. Are any of your other siblings present?"

"Not at the moment. I'm the only one here until the winds cease. Stop stalling and tell me what's going on, Flynn."

Flynn filled Riley in.

"Let me talk." Vikki spoke up, her face still pale but the fight evident in her manner.

"Riley, the phone's on speaker. Vikki wants to talk."

"Vikki?" Riley's concern reverberated through the tiny speaker.

"I'm okay. Listen, tell Sadie I love her. I love you, and Kiely and Pippa and Griffin. And Charlize—tell her to love that baby for me. I can't thank you enough for supporting all of us after Mom and Dad died, Riley. Because of you, Riley, I was able to find myself. I've had a job I love, both in and out of the Army and with CI. You saved me, bro." It took her every ounce of strength to tell her brother what she needed to say, and Flynn had to stop from screaming for her to stop. He wasn't going to let her die. Not like Jena.

"We're going to get you out of there, Vikki." Flynn heard Riley's fingers on a keyboard, as well as his string of swear words that was low but loud enough to make out. "Do whatever Flynn tells you to. The demo team is thirty seconds away."

"Wait. Riley. One more thing."

"Anything, sis."

"Kiss Pal for me."

"Will do, Vikki. Flynn, I'm disconnecting. You need your line for the LEAs."

"I do." Flynn ended the call and looked at Vikki. "Who's Pal?"

"Riley's dog. We love her. So much." Tears streamed down her cheeks and Flynn sucked in a breath. He'd never felt anyone's pain more acutely. Not since Jena died, and all at once, the familiar fury swamped him.

No. This was not happening. Vikki wasn't going to die. Not today. Not on his watch.

"How are you doing? Do you want some water?"

"I don't want to risk moving too much."

"I understand. But listen to me, Vikki. You had basic EOD training before you went on deployment, didn't you?"

"I did, but nothing very involved. I'm a paralegal, remember?" A ghost of her usual grin teased her lips. Normally pink and plump, they were now gray and drawn in a straight line. Her forehead was shiny from the cold sweat he knew had to cover her entire body. He'd been in scary situations during combat that had caused the same reaction.

"You haven't lost your sense of humor. That's good." He bent over and kissed her lips, gently, so as to not force her to move more than she should. "I've got you, babe. We've got this. You've got this. You've done so well. You're so strong—"

Heavy footsteps sounded, followed by steady vibrations as the extended team of Grand Rapids PD, Army

Post Fort Rapids MPs and the Michigan Regional Response Team Network's Certified Bomb Technicians arrived.

"Sergeant Cruz-Street!" The first member in, a woman, wore full tactical gear.

"Yes, ma'am." Flynn always addressed his civilian counterparts with "sir" or "ma'am," no matter their rank. He was a military soldier, and he served the civilian population, not the other way around.

"What do you know?" She motioned for him to step back to brief her. A half dozen more officials in tactical gear swarmed in, around the equipment and Vikki.

"Not much, ma'am, but I know who did this." He told her all he knew, the entire time fighting the urge to knock the police away from Vikki, to keep her safe, all to himself. It was a primal reaction, he knew. Because he had no idea how to dismantle the kind of bomb Joseph had hooked up.

"Thanks. I need you to clear out. Help with the hotel evacuation."

"No. I can't leave her."

"Sergeant..." She looked at him, her visor up, then at Vikki, whose gaze had never left Flynn's figure from across the room. She sighed. "Okay. You can stay right here, but no closer." She leaned into him, lowered her voice. "If we can't stop this, or get any indication that Joseph's going to detonate this, you'll dive for the door. That's an order, soldier."

"Yes, ma'am."

And so he waited, standing in place, his focus entirely on Vikki.

Chapter Nine

Vikki would have sobbed if she could, but it was as if everything in her had shut down once she'd spoken to her family and Flynn had kissed her. She knew that fear and abject horror awaited in the recesses of her heart and mind, but she ignored them for the pure strength she'd never found before.

The steel in Flynn's gaze kept her sane, present, trusting. Gave her hope. The tactical team appeared to know its job, and she knew from her minimal experiences with bomb squads that they were highly trained and capable.

"We're three minutes from killing it, boss." One of the officers spoke as two others worked wires and used measuring equipment on the explosive box attached to her chest.

Flynn's gaze left hers for a split second and she followed it. He was staring at her chest, but she knew it was the timer he was looking at. She wanted to know how much longer she had. But why? It'd only make her risk hoping that she had any chance of surviving.

"Eyes on me, Vikki." Flynn's voice reached out to her, drew her back to him, the one sure thing in this room.

Besides the bomb ticking away atop her breasts.

His eyes held the world for her. The gravity of her lethal situation, the warmth of what they could have shared together, the tiny flicker of hope that this nightmare would end with something other than total annihilation.

"Cruz-Street, everyone, we need you to clear. Now." The officer in charge of the Spec Ops unit entertained no alternatives.

"Stay strong, Vikki. I'll be waiting for you, babe." Flynn's use of her name and the endearment, combined with the way his voice broke at the end, gave Vikki what she needed. Comfort. If she had to die, she knew Flynn wished they had had more time together, too.

Her eyes devoured the image of Flynn departing, followed by five other fully outfitted officers. It was only Vikki and the senior bomb expert, his fingers working over the box on her chest as if performing open-heart surgery.

"You're doing great, Vikki. Just another thirty seconds and we'll both walk out of here." Officer Robert Hartman spoke as if they were having a latte and not fighting to stay alive. She'd seen his name tag when he'd first knelt in front of her, and then heard the others call him Rob.

"Okay, Rob." It didn't seem right to be formal. They were going to die together or, if lucky, survive a horrible threat.

She sat, frozen, as sweat poured down her face, mixing with the tears that came unbidden after Flynn left. She didn't miss the irony of a ticking bomb over her heart. It was how she'd felt since she'd met Flynn in the barracks, his intelligent yet compassionate gaze drawing her to him even as her mind fought the instinctual pull. Her once shattered heart and broken trust had been healed, if not in that moment, then in the hours that followed. There were still good men on the planet and Flynn was one of them.

Perhaps the one for her.

Rob's forehead glistened with sweat. He'd taken his headgear off and was working with bare hands. Sometime during the last few minutes, he'd laid the timer on its side, and the numbers glared at her, daring her to hope.

Forty-five seconds remained. Forty-four. Forty-three.

Something snapped against her chest and Rob tugged at the bomb, bringing her with him. Vikki was afraid to lose any contact her body had with the device, in case that set it off.

"And…we're done! You made it, Vikki!" Hartman grinned at her and she could only stare, uncomprehending. Transitioning from stark terror to unrelenting relief took her a few seconds. But when she looked at the timer and saw that it had frozen on twenty-eight seconds, she let out a long, deep sob.

"We're clear, boss," Hartman said into his mic. "Bring in Disposal."

Five that felt more like sixty minutes later, two officers came back into the room, still in protective gear.

It hit her that they'd all evacuated the area of the bomb blast. They had expected the worst.

Within seconds, they had the device off her chest and one officer held out his arm for her to grasp. But before she could stand, Riley and Flynn burst in.

"Hey, gentlemen, take it easy. There's still a lot of C-4 in this room." The team leader kept Riley and Flynn from going farther than the threshold. "We'll bring her to you."

Vikki took the officer's arm and was grateful he looped his other arm behind her as her legs quaked—from residual fear, relief or fatigue, she had no clue and didn't care.

She was alive, and Flynn was still here. Without hesitation, she fell into his arms, soaked up the tender words he murmured into her disheveled hair, her ears, the soft kisses he used to wipe away her tears. No man's embrace had ever been so right.

"Vikki, why don't you sit for a bit?" Riley's parental tone broke through her pink cloud of joy and she nodded and pulled a tiny bit back from Flynn.

"Okay. I'm okay." Both men helped lower her to the floor and she rested her back against the wainscoting. "My legs, they're not listening to me."

"That's normal. You'll bounce back quickly." Flynn smiled then turned to Riley. "How did you get here so fast?"

Respect for her older sibling vibrated off Flynn's demeanor.

"I have my ways." Riley, ever the former FBI agent,

didn't crack a smile until he looked at her, his expression softening. "How you doing, sis?"

"Fine, but I could use some water."

As she spoke, two EMTs approached, and both Flynn and Riley moved aside to allow her the necessary medical attention. The EMTs placed her on a gurney to allow for a more thorough examination. She couldn't help but wonder what Flynn and Riley were talking about in the corner, engrossed in something serious.

It didn't matter. All that mattered was that she'd survived and now had time to spend with the man who'd somehow captured her heart.

RILEY COLTON WAS a formidable opponent and a great ally. Flynn wasn't sure where he stood yet with Vikki's eldest brother.

"You, of all people, know how unpredictable someone like Joseph can be. He's unhinged at the least, and now we're going to add 'homicidal' to the list. Why did you leave my sister alone?"

"No excuse, sir." Flynn purposely called him "sir." Riley was former FBI, the head of a private civilian investigative firm. He didn't report to him. But Riley was Vikki's brother. Had been there for her after their parents died, so his investment was even deeper.

"Dang right there's no excuse. Where the heck were you when Joseph broke into the room?"

"In the hotel lobby bar, buying a bottle of champagne."

Riley's scowl turned into a threatening menace, and

Flynn, not shaken by a lot, fought to stand his ground. "Champagne. While my sister—"

"Was waiting for me to return, yes. I messed up. I'll never let her out of my sight again." Flynn's heart seemed to stop beating, then begin again, racing to catch his thoughts.

He'd meant what he'd said. Literally. He never wanted another day of his life to be without Vikki. It didn't make sense, but then, when did anything related to heart matters? His mother still hoped that Landon would come around, see the error of his ways, admit to his part in the RevitaYou development and production.

"Why do you need to be around her at all again?"

"We're working on finding Captain Joseph and also my half brother, Landon. Both related to RevitaYou, as you know. And, Riley, you have to know that there's nothing you could say to me about leaving Vikki alone that's worse than what I've already told myself."

Riley's countenance shifted from protective older brother to compassionate colleague. "We both care for her, apparently. And I'm the last one to judge whatever's going on between you two, no matter how quickly it's transpired. When your life is at stake, it can make a relationship form much more quickly."

Flynn nodded, not willing to share everything with Riley. The man knew enough, and Flynn and Vikki needed time to talk things out. Heck, he didn't even know if she felt the same as he did.

"What's with the bruise on her temple?"

"She told me that Joseph knocked her head into the wall." He grimaced as he looked back toward the EMTs.

One was shining a flashlight in Vikki's eyes while the other was hooking her up to an IV. A solar blanket enveloped her form. "She had signs of shock and it looks like they're treating it. I won't be surprised if she has a concussion."

"Did she lose consciousness?"

"Not that I know of, but as you've already pointed out, I wasn't there when Joseph assaulted her."

"She's not staying here any longer. The storm's about to break, and she needs to be in a safe spot. So do you." Riley wasn't asking; he was telling Flynn what to do.

"I take orders from my military commander."

"The same guy who just tried to kill all of us, most of all, my sister? Besides, you took leave."

Dang Riley Colton and his ability to ferret out information, no matter how secure or classified. It made for a great investigative business, but being on the receiving end made Flynn feel…vulnerable. Flynn didn't do vulnerable.

You'd better get used to it, with the feelings you have for Vikki.

Son of a puppy. His growing connection to Vikki had shoved him into the deep end.

"Where should we go?"

"Let's go talk to Vikki." Riley walked over to Vikki, who was alone on the gurney as the EMTs filed notes on their respective laptops and phones.

"How are you feeling now, sis?"

"Better. A lot better, in fact. I must have been dehydrated." Her color was returning and she seemed more herself, albeit exhausted.

"In shock is more like it. Listen, Flynn and I have been talking, and you both need to go to a safe house ASAP. You can't stay here with Joseph on the loose." Riley looked at the EMT who'd walked back up. "Can she go with us or does she need a hospital?"

"She should get a CT scan to rule out a concussion. That's a nasty lump on her head. There's no outward sign of a major problem, but we can't rule it out."

Riley nodded. "Can you take her in your ambulance?"

"Hey, I'm right here. And I don't want to waste time going to the ER. We need to get out of Dodge. Let us go join Sadie."

"You're not going where Sadie is. I'm not exposing both of my sisters like that."

Flynn knew Vikki wanted to be with her twin, but his instincts railed against it. He had to agree with Riley; they were safer split up. If Joseph didn't find them, the loan sharks for RevitaYou would. They'd kill everyone in the vicinity if they did.

"You're being ridiculous, Riley. Sadie's my twin, and she needs me right now."

"You need a head X-ray, and you and Flynn need a safe place far from here. We know that Joseph must be tracking you, either via your phones or another device he somehow attached to your belongings. It was most likely him that you witnessed outside of the pool room. CI is providing you burner phones, and don't take anything that you have in the hotel rooms. Everything you'll need is at the safe house."

"How many safe houses does Riley have access to through his contacts?" Flynn's curiosity was piqued.

"That's proprietary information." Riley and Vikki spoke in unison and Flynn laughed.

"I'm so glad you're part of the CI team. And I get that the Army needs you now, too. Just come back to us in one piece." Riley leaned in and kissed her on the cheek. "I'll have a vehicle waiting for you when you're done with the ER." He looked at Flynn. "Go with her in the ambulance. Take only your weapon and what you're wearing. I'll get both of your personal effects and we'll store them at CI headquarters until this is a closed case."

"What are we supposed to do in a safe house?" Flynn needed to get out and look for Landon.

"You'll still be able to search for your brother—no worries. Trust me, we all want Landon and every one of his cronies behind bars."

Flynn tried to be relieved that the mission could continue as it had begun, but as he rode alongside Vikki in the ambulance, he knew that nothing was as it had been.

He'd fallen for Vikki Colton.

VIKKI WASN'T A fan of small spaces, but her Army training had her keep her eyes closed through the CT scan. The procedure showed a clear brain, if what she overheard from the techs was true.

Thank goodness.

The scan and tests took the rest of the night to come

back, and the sun was rising on a new week as the attending physician briefed them.

"All the tests are in. You're going to be fine. No concussion."

"You're certain there wasn't any subdural bleeding?" Flynn questioned the trauma doctor as if he knew more about emergency medicine. But she caught the protective tone in his voice. The emotions of almost dying would make it easy to think that what was going on between them was something more. But not when she saw how he listened to the doctor's instructions, keeping notes with one of the tiny burner phones Riley had supplied them.

"Positive. I know it looks ugly, but that's what's saved you. The swelling is on the outside of your skull instead of in your brain. I'm going to make a few more notes in your chart. Then I'll need you to follow up with your general practitioner in ten days. Sooner if you experience any sudden dizziness, loss of consciousness or a severe migraine-like headache. You're going to be sore for a few days. That's normal. Stay ahead of the pain. I've prescribed hydrocodone."

"Thanks, but I'm not going to take any opioids. They make me nauseous, and I'll be fine with ibuprofen and acetaminophen." She tried not to smirk. This civilian doc had no clue how tough a soldier was. She'd had far more soreness after long hours of physical training in preparation for deployment. Even a paralegal had to be able to pull her own weight, and possibly her fellow soldier's, in a combat zone.

"As you wish. Good luck."

"Thank you, Doctor." Vikki was eager to get out of the hospital and out of Grand Rapids. She felt like a sitting duck in the hospital bay, which, though behind a secure entryway, could be breached by someone with the right weapons. She had to assume Captain Joseph was prepared to find her and Flynn again, whatever the cost.

As the doctor left, Riley came in. "What's the verdict?"

"I'm fine is what the results are. We just wasted an hour and a half of solid getaway time." And risked that Joseph would find them, sitting in the hospital for so long.

"Good to know. Your ride awaits you. Let's go." Riley turned and left.

"Take it easy." Flynn was right at her side, helping her off the examination table when she began to move.

"I'm okay, Flynn." She stopped, grasped his forearm. "Thanks to you." Tears flooded her vision and her throat expanded as if she'd swallowed a wad of cotton. Even if she could speak, she wouldn't. Just being with Flynn, alive, both of them okay, was enough.

He turned to her, and Riley kept going, momentarily not realizing they'd stopped.

"You did it, Vikki. You. I've never been prouder of anyone in my life. And I have no right to be proud of you—you're not mine. If anything had happened to you, I'd have never forgiven myself for leaving you alone."

"You were able to get there and do what had to be done in the moment. If you'd been there when he'd broken in, he might have killed both of us. He's off base, Flynn." Fear still shook her voice and she hated it.

"I'm with you, Vikki. I'm not going anywhere."

"About what you said—that you don't think you have the right to be proud of me? We need to talk—"

"What are you two waiting for? We've got to get you both out of the hospital and settled in the safe house." Riley had returned. His tone was commanding but his eyes reflected a deeper emotion, and Vikki knew her brother thought he understood what was happening between her and Flynn.

"We had some details to work out." She let go of Flynn's arm. "Let's go."

The three of them exited and Vikki squinted at the sun. When had the long nightmare of last night turned into a new day? And the snow had stopped, leaving a quickly melting blanket of white on the ground. Riley nodded at a large pickup. "There you go." He handed Flynn the keys.

"But this is yours, isn't it?" Vikki knew how proprietary Riley could be with his vehicles.

"Exactly. Joseph's smart and we have no idea what he has on you. By not renting a car today, we're helping keep you off the grid." Riley handed her a thick envelope. "This is yours for any necessities, but don't stop except to get gas. You shouldn't need to, as I just filled the tank and your destination is within range."

"Okay. But this seems like a lot of money, Riley."

"You may have to move on short notice. Also, you'll need groceries."

"Thanks for taking care of all of this." Flynn held his hand out and Riley shook it.

"It's my job. And you know yours."

Vikki looked at Flynn, but he simply nodded at her brother.

"If my head wasn't hurting so bad, I'd be rolling my eyes. You two are ridiculous. It's not Flynn's job to take care of me."

"Let me be your big brother just this once, will you?" Riley leaned over and kissed her cheek. "Love you, sis. Check in when you get in."

"Love you, too. Will do."

Chapter Ten

"You look uncomfortable in this truck." Flynn drove her brother's Ford F-250 through Grand Rapids and out into the open countryside, wincing every time he took an unplowed turn. The snow was melting but there were still icy patches. "Have you ever driven a truck before?"

"Yes. I happen to have one myself, a Jeep Gladiator. It's a much smaller profile. I don't want to mess this one up at all. Can you blame me? It's your brother's. I'm lucky he let you leave with me."

She laughed and winced at the same time. "It's a truck. And it's impossible to mess it up."

"You're kidding, right?" He motioned at the console, equipped with the latest technology. "These seats are more comfortable than regular furniture."

"Riley wouldn't have given you his truck if he didn't trust you." It wasn't a platitude; she knew her brother. "He's giving you a hard time over me and what he thinks is going on between us, but you've worked together before, right? If he didn't respect you, you'd know it, trust me. He'd be the one taking me to the safe house. He'd make you stay at CI headquarters and guard you round-the-clock until Joseph showed up. Or Landon. Or both."

"You're probably right." Flynn's gaze flickered from the road to the clock and back to the highway. "We've got another few hours. There's something I'd like to get worked out between us, if you're up to it."

Her stomach had flutters against its lining, and it wasn't from her hit to the head. "I'm good to talk, Flynn." Would now be when he admitted they weren't going to explore their feelings any further, even after the case was closed?

"Okay, great. Let's do this. What do you think is going on between us, Vikki?"

"Whoa." She carefully leaned into the leather headrest. "Give a girl time to settle before you toss out a whammy like that." She closed her eyes and let the rhythm of the road soothe her. The relief that he wasn't building up his defenses against her was a balm, and she recognized how concerned she'd been that they were over before they'd even begun. Not ideal timing, but when was anything that had happened in her life?

Flynn swore. "Sorry, Vikki. You've been banged up and almost blown up. Forget I said anything."

"No, it's a fair question. We're at—what?—forty-eight, almost seventy-two hours. Three days of working together." And wanting to make love. No, not love. She wanted to have hot, no-holds-barred sex with Flynn. It was too early for that.

That's not what you thought while wearing a bomb necklace.

"Yeah. Crazy, right?"

"It feels more like a year. Longer. Never in my life have I been through almost dying, an explosion or an almost-explosion." Never had she spent so much time with a man like Flynn, either. Sure of himself, with no need to flaunt his power in the business world. Like her, Flynn had picked the uniform, to serve and defend.

"Me, either. Scratch that. I did have a day like yesterday, over two years ago. Only, it didn't end as well."

Her curiosity was piqued. She didn't want to push him, though. "Neither of us is going through any of this alone, Flynn. That's for certain."

"I wanted to make sure I'm not the only one who's thinking this way. I've been around the block and know when something's special. And I know how quickly things can disappear. I'd hate to lose a chance on something just because it's what I'd usually think is not enough time. Does that make sense?"

"Yes. It's exactly what I've been grappling with. In between us getting shot at and the like." She couldn't help but try to bring humor to their conversation. "We've each faced enough scary stuff to last a lifetime."

FLYNN DROVE THEM farther from Grand Rapids, on a winding road that would take them far out of the city and into practical wilderness. The question of whether he'd tell Vikki about Jena gnawed at him. As did how long they might be gone together. The sense of intimacy between them could come from close proximity. He wouldn't know until they returned to their normal routines, had some space between them and this case.

Riley assured him that his command would understand if he needed to extend his leave, as he was fleeing for his life. Until Captain Joseph was caught, all means to keep Vikki safe was his priority. He'd been hoping against hope that he'd find Landon and put an end to all of this in time to take some actual leave days before he used up his stockpile of vacation, but it seemed like a frivolous desire now.

Was he ready to share his broken heart with another woman?

His memory dredged up images from what had been the worst day of his life since his father died.

"What is it, Flynn?"

"It was downrange. Two years ago."

"We don't have to talk about it if you're not ready."

"I've talked about it a lot, actually. To the command psychologist, several times, and to my mother."

"You're close to her, your mom."

"I am. It's been her and I for a long time, since my dad died. She's never given up on Landon, not completely, but he's been out of the picture in terms of our family life for at least ten years."

"Landon sounds like a very troubled man."

"He always struggled, but now he's crossed the line into the criminal. It's a damn shame, but nothing I could have prevented. I didn't cause it, either."

"Did you ever think you did?"

"Sure, as a kid. It was easy to think that by having me, my parents upset Landon's until-then perfect life. That I was the troublemaker. He wasn't a fan of mine, that's for sure."

"That's a lot for a little boy to carry."

"I was in middle school when I thought it, and it didn't last long. My mother was always quick to unearth my troubles. She set me straight."

"I miss my parents, but Riley's morphed into that parental figure for me. I think of him as a brother, but for a long while, he was more of a parent to all of us. He had to be."

"He did a great job, I'd say." Flynn risked a quick glance at her and it was worth it to see her smiling at him.

"Thanks. You haven't met my other siblings, though."

"Why? Are they that much different from you?"

"Actually, yes. But we're all pretty close, even though we're very much individuals. Going through tough times has cemented our bond in the best way. I know it doesn't always do that for all families, but for us, it did. And I had Sadie, which made a huge difference for both of us. There's no one who knows me better than my twin."

"Are you still worried about her?"

"Yes and no. I hate that she's had to put up with so much from Tate, but I'm grateful she's protected, safe. If she weren't in the safe house, she'd be raining down fire on her ex and anyone else she could get her hands on. It wouldn't be a pretty sight. I'd die if anything happened to her."

Exactly how he'd felt when he'd seen that bomb around Vikki's neck. "We've taken a very long, circuitous route from the original question. What's happening between us?" As he mentioned it again, a warmth spread through his chest and headed south. He shifted in his seat. Him getting an erection wasn't what either of them needed at the moment. One glance at Vikki's bruises and the pallor of her skin underscored that.

"We have. But you were about to talk about—"

"My worst day. It was downrange, but not in combat. We were having an ordinary training day. One of our choppers went down, pilot error. My fiancée, Jena, was aboard. Of six crew members, she was the one who didn't make it."

"I'm so, so sorry, Flynn."

"Me, too." He let the sadness wash over him, as it always did. But it wasn't the soul-crushing tsunami it once was, the weight of the wave more of a small crest than the kind that had brought him to his knees day after day for the first year or so after Jena's death.

"We don't have to talk any more about it."

"No, it's okay. I'll never forget Jena. She'll always be a part of me. But I've learned that life moves on, and sometimes good things can happen even when you think your world is over."

"I feel like a dolt for whining about my breakup. Sure, it sucked, but I didn't have to see Peter die. Not that I didn't fantasize about some kind of revenge."

"It's all relative. Pain is pain."

"You must still miss her. A lot."

"Sometimes. At least, I did." Funny thing was, he hadn't thought of Jena as much these past few days. And he didn't feel the guilt that he once had when he'd noticed an attractive woman or thought about dating again. Not with Vikki.

"Have you been with anyone since her? I'm sorry. I'm being way too personal, aren't I?"

"Babe, we've just been through some of the most personal emotions any two people can have. All that's left is to— Crap." He'd almost said "make love." No matter what his heart was telling him, it was too early to use the four-letter word with Vikki, wasn't it?

"I know what you were going to say. All we have left to do is have sex."

He didn't like how he wanted to correct her, tell her that it'd never be just sex between them, no matter whether they ever shared physical intimacies.

"Is your straightforwardness something you've always had or is it part of paralegal JAG training?"

He was rewarded with her laughter. Softer, less boisterous than usual, but that had to be due to her injuries. Healing bruises hurt.

"My family says I'm the most stubborn. And I wanted to be a journalist for the longest while."

"Why didn't you do that?"

"Probably the same as you. I wanted to prove myself sooner than waiting to finish a four-year degree would allow me. When I joined the Army, I could have gone into journalism or communications, but the law always interested me, too. I'm glad I did JAG, too, because being a paralegal has taught me I don't want to be a lawyer."

"What do you want to do?"

"Come back here, most likely, and work for my brother, as I told you before. Investigation seems to be in our blood."

"That's interesting, because I've thought about getting out and earning my PhD in English literature locally."

"What do you want to do?"

"Teach, preferably at the university level. But I'd be happy anywhere, as long as I'm giving back."

"Serving others."

"Right."

A comfortable silence descended and he thought she had fallen asleep. He looked over at her reclining form, her profile a beautiful line of simplicity.

"I'm not asleep, you know." Her murmur triggered a laugh and he returned his focus to the road.

"What's so funny, Flynn?"

"We're already finishing one another's sentences, and you just read my mind. I'd say we have something to talk about—this thing between us—but maybe neither one of us is ready. Not yet."

"I think you're right." Sleepiness flowed through her words.

"Rest. We'll be there soon enough."

And they'd have time to figure things out. Or would they? Flynn caught himself up short. This wasn't some kind of fun weekend getaway he was taking with a beautiful woman. They were being stalked by a madman, and in search of another. Hardly the setup for a sexy affair.

That was good, because he was feeling a lot more than just attraction toward Vikki.

And it scared the devil out of him.

THE SAFE HOUSE was a small cottage behind a large house, and he parked the truck in a small clearing. Flynn had to admit, it wouldn't be easy to find them unless they'd been followed, which he'd made certain they hadn't been.

Vikki was sound asleep and he knew her body needed it. She hadn't even stirred when he'd left the highway or when they'd driven over the graveled drive. He was loath to wake her, as watching her sleep was as close to heaven as he'd been in a long while.

The sappy thought made him laugh.

"What are you laughing at now?" She was instantly awake, a trait he commiserated with. You didn't go through the kind of training and lifestyle the Army handed you without learning to fall asleep standing up and waking up ready to fight. It was part of the soldier package.

"Myself, truth be told. I seem to be discovering new sides of myself since we've met."

She blinked, peered through the windshield. "We're here."

"We are."

"I hear you, Flynn. I'm considering things I thought wouldn't be on my horizon for many more months, if not years."

"What kind of things?" He thought he knew, but wanted to hear her say it.

"Why don't we continue this conversation inside? I take it that's our place, and not the bigger place over there?" She nodded at the cottage and pointed at the full-size home.

"You'd be correct. At least, that's what he told me." Flynn let himself out of his side and jogged around the truck's front to reach Vikki before she got out on her own. He wasn't being polite or chivalrous; he was taking care of his partner. She'd taken a blow to her head and who knew how many other hits from Joseph. He didn't want her risking a senseless fall because she'd temporarily lost her balance.

He opened her door and reached up for her. "I'm here, Vikki, and we've got all night. Take your time getting out."

"I'm banged up but I'm not helpless." Her grumbling hit his funny bone but he thought better of letting loose with laughter. Her hand was small but firm in his grasp, and while she leaned on him to step out of the truck, she didn't seem weak or unsteady. Still, she moved gingerly from the truck.

"Whoa." She paused on solid ground and gripped his other arm, too. "Give me a minute, babe." Her eyes focused on his chest and she breathed in and out. Flynn had been here before, needing time to let his body catch up to what his mind was used to making it do. He tried to remember how he'd reacted after the repercussions from a rocket grenade, but the way Vikki called him "babe" had him struggling to contain his baser emotions. Lust. Need. Desire.

You know it's more.

"Okay?" He caught her gaze.

"Yes. I feel myself mostly, except for when I switch

positions. From sitting to standing—who knew it could make me dizzy?" She stamped her feet in the several inches of snow that covered the ground but was quickly melting. Her cheeks had color again, as did her full lips. "Hard to believe this was probably twice as deep just yesterday."

By yesterday at this time, Flynn knew he was getting in over his head with Vikki.

"Ready to go? I'll come back out for our things."

"Sure. But I'll need you to stay with me until I'm inside—I need something to lean on."

I'll always be here for you.

He wanted to say the words, wanted to remind Vikki that he'd meant the endearments he'd used with her, that he was the real deal. But logic warred with the warmth in his chest.

And he couldn't allow himself to forget how close he'd come to blowing it completely—losing Vikki to Joseph's sick stunt. He hadn't been there for her when she'd most needed him.

Flynn wouldn't make the same mistake twice.

"THIS IS SO SWEET!" Vikki knew she sounded vacuous, but after having a live bomb attached to her chest, she could not care less. She allowed herself to coo over the sweet safe house.

The cottage was a darling slice of country life. From the lace curtains over the kitchen sink to the all-white wood trim set against pale blue and ivory walls, the small residence was the epitome of a guesthouse. The bedroom was off of the main living area. Its brass-framed queen-size bed had a patchwork quilt made of the same shades as the walls and trim, giving the tiny building an overall sense of cohesion and airiness. She noted the refrigerator was fully stocked. CI thought of everything.

"This looks like it's usually a guesthouse. How did Riley find this?" She spoke to herself as much as to Flynn as she walked into the kitchen area and inspected the contents of the refrigerator. Her nausea was gone and her stomach rumbled.

"As a soldier, I've never been involved in setting up safe houses for personnel. As you know, the military doesn't conduct operations involving US civilians. I have friends who were hired by FBI and CIA after they got out. I imagine that their work involves stuff like this."

"I don't know enough about the ins and outs of our family's business to be able to comment, but I'm sure you're right. Riley's pretty good at cutting me in where he can, but frankly, I'm not around enough to help CI much at all."

"I heard Riley. He seems intent on you coming to work for him."

"He is."

"What do you think?"

"I've said 'no way' for so long that I can't believe what I'm thinking now. It's getting to the end of my enlistment and, like you, I've been going to school almost the whole time I've been in. I have my degree in criminal justice. I used to think I'd want to go to law school, but I really enjoy the part of my job that involves interviews and data collection. Evidence collecting."

"You're more of a detective."

"I am. I think I am. And Riley doesn't treat me like a little kid sister or daughter anymore, despite what it looks like. He's just worried about me now, but after we catch Joseph and Landon, he'll chill out."

Flynn laughed, and she thought she'd never heard anything sexier. Standing next to him in front of the refrigerator, it was such a domestic scene that it should have revolted her after all she'd gone through with Peter. Instead, it struck her as oddly comforting. Solid and right. As if they'd done this before and would do it again and again.

Was this what people meant when they said they knew the love of their life from the first glance?

"You're drifting. What's on your mind?" Flynn's directness brought her back.

"We're remarkably in sync for only knowing one another a couple of days."

His expression sobered and the lines that crinkled at the edges of his eyes in mirth smoothed out, the furrow between his brows deepening.

"I'm not the man for you, Vikki."

Like a gut punch, his words hit hard, as if Flynn wished he was anywhere but here with her.

"Hey, wait one minute. I'm not proposing we get married or anything. I was referring to how much we've accomplished in such a short time." Her lie hung between them and she wished she was feeling more herself, so that the shakiness in her voice didn't betray her crushed heart.

Crushed, not broken.

A heart she hadn't given away again couldn't be broken. Could it?

"We have done a lot, but it's smart for both of us to remember this is about finding Landon, at the end of the day. And staying low until Joseph is caught."

"At the end of the mission, you mean. You don't have to worry about me mixing up professional compatibility with anything else, Flynn. I can do this without making you squirm." She shut the refrigerator door after grabbing a few slices of cheese, noting it was fully stocked. Riley had taken care of everything, and still given them funds in case they ate through this stash. "I'm going to make use of that fancy bathroom, if you don't mind."

"You're not taking a shower yet. Not until you know your equilibrium is one hundred percent."

"No, I'm taking a bath." Five minutes ago she might have volunteered that bubble baths were a personal weakness, but not after Flynn's freeze-out. What had she done or said that had triggered him to turn so defensive?

Why do you think it's you?

"I'm not sure that's a great idea, either."

"The thing is, Flynn? As you've been so clear about, we're working together, nothing more. So unless you want to come in and watch, I suggest you mind your own business and let me take care of mine. I need a soak after all my body's been through. We can discuss our plan of attack to find Landon when I'm done."

She walked away, hoping her shaking insides weren't visible to his gaze. Flynn missed nothing, as she'd witnessed, but neither did she. Talking about Jena had made him realize that she wouldn't ever measure up to his fiancée, even after this mission. Fine. Better to know now than after she made a huge mistake.

Chapter Eleven

Vikki had finally convinced Flynn that she'd be okay to take a bath on her own. She'd all but cried when she'd seen the shelf over the claw-foot tub in the small but quaint bathroom. A full assortment of naturally scented soaps, salts and oils had been arranged on an antique white shelf above the brass spigot. She opened the faucets and poured both Epsom salts and peony-scented oil into the stream of hot water.

As the tub filled, she checked out the medicine cabinet, the shelves of freshly scented towels. And laughed when she recognized a large box of condoms. CI thought of everything, indeed.

Disrobing wasn't so easy, with all her sore spots and tired muscles, but she decided it was more than worth the effort once she sank up to her shoulders in the water. The tub's edge was the perfect height for her to lean back against, and she reveled in the heat as it warmed her bones.

She prided herself on being from Michigan and used to cold weather. Yet it seemed her blood had thinned a bit over the years. So much so that a quick snowstorm had her longing for hot sunshine.

Her mind wandered over the case to date, and she allowed her hands and arms to float in the water, making mini whirlpools with her fingers. There was no way anyone could have predicted the two major occurrences. First, Captain Joseph's behavior her first day, in the barracks, had been completely unexpected. She and Flynn should have been more receptive to the possibility of him doing something dangerous, even lethal, when he'd escaped the MPs at Fort Rapids, which had resulted in the second major incident at the hotel.

There had been two red flags. One, when the captain had come after them in the cemetery, and the other when she'd spotted him outside the hotel pool house. They wouldn't make the same mistake twice. She made a mental note to tell Flynn they should maintain a military watch schedule, meaning one of them would be awake and responsible for the cottage's surveillance at all times. He'd have to trust her with his weapon, too, because if Joseph showed up, she figured they'd need lethal force to counteract his latest scheme.

That brought her to the topic of Landon. Flynn had originally been defensive about his involvement, or lack thereof, with his half sibling. It was to be expected, as she'd assumed that Flynn had known Landon's whereabouts. Or at least had a way to get in touch with him. But now that she'd finally accepted that Flynn had no idea about his half brother's location and had admitted she was having feelings disproportionate to the amount of time they'd spent together, he was pulling the crusty soldier routine again.

She had to keep her mind on the case and off her more-than-attraction to Flynn.

A slight rap on the door stilled her hands in the water, and her thoughts.

"Yes?"

"Just checking to see if you're okay." His voice came through the door, strong and purposeful, sending tiny shock waves of awareness over her skin.

"I'm good. But, Flynn...?" She waited for him to reply.

"Yeah?"

"I might have a rough time getting out of this tub." She couldn't stop the words if she'd wanted to. Was it her head injury, making her more willing to yank his mental peace-of-mind chain? Or was it more? Did she want to break through the walls he was so intent on rebuilding, to discover who was hiding in there?

"Are you ready to come out now?"

Was she? The water was rapidly cooling, and her fingers were wrinkled. Yeah, it was time to get out of the tub. But was she prepared for what might happen, or worse, not happen, between her and Flynn? Could she handle another rejection, no matter from a man she barely knew, after the emotional battering she'd taken from Peter?

Screw Peter. Screw being afraid.

"I'm ready now."

The door opened and she half expected Flynn to enter with his hands over his eyes. Instead, he grabbed one of the large, fluffy pale blue bath towels. He held it up in front of his face and she bit back a grin.

"I'll come to the edge of the tub, and you can hold your arms up. I'll lift you and wrap at the same time."

Vikki didn't think she'd be able to keep from giggling. Seeing Flynn come toward her like a Halloween ghost was too much.

And not enough.

With a start, she realized that no amount of time would ever be enough, not with Flynn Cruz-Street. The man who was unlike any other.

The man she wanted to make love to.

FLYNN FELT LIKE a dang fool with the too big towel hanging in front of his head, his hands clutching the edges like he was about to swaddle a little kid. If he were smart, detached enough from Vikki as a woman, he'd be able to walk the two short steps to the tub and haul her out. But his need for her grew each minute, and he knew that if he saw her naked, the hold he had on his desire would snap.

"You okay, Vikki?"

"Yeah, sure, I'm fine. Okay, you can come over now. Let's do this."

There was a weird note in her tone, and he couldn't shake the feeling she was toying with him. But she'd agreed to keep this professional, had given him no reason to think she was still willing to take their bond beyond the constraints of their mission. Who could blame her? The one time they'd almost made love had turned into a freaking nightmare with a bomb around her neck.

His face heated as he relived the horror of finding her so vulnerable, with him unable to do anything until the bomb experts arrived. It had been the worst few hours of his life to date. And all centered on a woman he'd known less than a week. Yet he was certain he knew her better than most. Go figure.

"Uh, Flynn? Are you going to get close enough to help me out?"

"Yes, sorry. Okay, ready?" He inched forward until his knees hit the porcelain-on-iron rim. "I'm here. Give me your hands."

"I think it'll be easier if you go around to the front of the tub, Flynn." Again, she had that inflection of teasing.

He complied, circling around the oval tub to the front lip. "This better?"

"Much."

He held out his arms again, the towel in front of his face. He felt like a class-A dork, but this was for her modesty.

Wet hands in his, which he immediately grasped. "You okay, Vikki?"

"I'm fine, but you seem too…too—" In a complete surprise move, she tugged on his hands, hard, and Flynn found himself tipping, falling through the air and into the tub with a loud splash. He caught the tub's edge with his hands to avoid hurting either of them. Vikki's laughter broke through his surprise and anger, but his ire was short-lived. The moment she pulled the towel from his face and looked at him, his resistance washed away.

"Vik."

"Flynn. I'm sorry about your clothes."

Clothes? All he felt was white-hot heat as he stared at her eyes, her plump lips, felt the give of her body under his, her most feminine spot plastered against his erection.

"Screw my clothes." He lowered his lips to hers and proceeded to kiss her the way he'd wanted to in the hotel. He thrust his tongue into her mouth and staked whatever claim she'd allow, needing to be one with Vikki in all ways possible. She groaned against his mouth, moving her pelvis with tiny thrusts up against his, making the water slosh around them and onto the tiled floor with soft splats.

His hands reached for her breasts, but the towel, wet and heavy, was in the way. "We need out of this bath ASAP."

She giggled. "We do."

He gingerly levered himself by the sides of the tub and pulled the drain plug. They'd worry about the towel and cleaning up the mess later. "Wait a sec." He grabbed another towel off a hook and handed it to her. "I want to dry you myself, but I need to get out of these wet clothes."

Vikki's eyes widened and he saw the dilation of her pupils, the high color on her cheeks, the way her moist lips parted in anticipation of more kissing. His hands shook as he stripped out of his clothes. He never took his eyes off Vikki, needing to see her every reaction. His gut clenched with the fear of this never happening had she not made it yesterday.

"Flynn, stop." She stepped out of the tub onto the

bath mat, then wiped her breasts, her stomach, her legs. "I can see it in your eyes—you feel guilty about yesterday. Stop. It was both of our faults."

He stood and took the towel from her, quickly drying his front before allowing her to see him the way he did her. Completely naked, aroused, and in the spell of the chemistry that had enveloped them both since they'd sat in her car outside the post library.

"I don't want to talk or to think about anything right now except you and me, babe. This is about us."

She smiled and he saw the shimmer in her eyes. It wasn't from pain, or pain meds, or her knock to the head. Vikki wanted him. Maybe as much as he did her.

Flynn reached for her, cupping her face in his hands, and kissed her with all the need he'd tried to keep on a leash.

He might regret this later, but he'd regret not being with her more. One thing the Army had taught him was that life was short.

Make love when you can.

VIKKI COULDN'T GET enough of Flynn's musky scent, the way his hands kneaded her shoulders, her hips, her buttocks. He pressed her up against his erection and she leaned her head back, the goose-egg-size bruise all but forgotten in the heat of their passion.

She looped a leg around his hip, grinding her pelvis against his, unable and unwilling to hide her impatience. She'd waited her entire life to be with a man who turned her on as intensely as Flynn.

"You sure you can handle this so soon?" he asked her against her throat, his tongue swirling just under her jawline.

"Yes, yes." She reached down and grasped his length, delighting in his gasp, the way his body stiffened and then leaned against her. "Let's move to the bed."

"Absolutely." He bent over, lifted her into his arms, and she threw her arms around his neck. The small cottage proved its worth when just a few seconds later they were on the bed, kissing, touching, stroking.

"Babe, I've got to taste you." Flynn didn't wait for her response as he kissed his way down her abdomen to her pelvis, her mound.

"Oh, please don't stop." Her words came out between breaths and she opened to him, needing his tongue all over her, inside her. Flynn's heat on her soon made the contact unbearable in the most delicious way. As she reveled in the intimacy with him, a climax rocked her, exploding from her center and sending waves of sensation through her core, her limbs.

"Beautiful." He breathed over her exposed femininity, and before she came down from the rush, he licked her again, providing the right pressure to make her come again. Her screams were full of joy and pure delight as they ripped from her at the onslaught of pleasure.

"Flynn, I could do this all day." But she wanted to please him, to help him let go, as he had her. She rolled to her side and got up on all fours. "It's your turn."

"Babe." He lay back, but instead of allowing her to

reciprocate in the same manner, he grasped her wrists. "I can't wait that long, not this time."

"Give me a sec, babe." Vikki left him only to obtain a foil packet from the bathroom shelf and returned with a grin.

She held the condom up with a flourish. "I'll let it go this one time, as long as you promise to let me go down on you the next time."

"Deal." He spoke through gritted teeth and a thrill rocketed through her at his obvious desire for her.

As soon as he donned protection, Flynn carefully flipped her to her back and raised himself to his elbows, hovering over her. His heat radiated across her breasts, her belly, her sex, her legs. But it was his gaze that held her taut, the dark brown sparking with amber notes of need and want that she'd never experienced from any other man she'd been with. Her heart's pounding echoed in her ears, and just as she knew there was something tangibly fateful about her connection with Flynn, she knew this was going to be the most significant joining of her life to date.

"I want you, Vikki."

"I want you, too, Flynn."

He pushed into her in one sure stroke, and the sheer power of his body had her on the edge again, as if they'd been engaged in foreplay for hours. She tried to grasp at her thoughts—he was unlike any man, he was so big, he filled her perfectly—until it was futile and all she wanted was to soar again, but this time with Flynn.

Thrust after thrust joined them in the most elemental way until his shout mingled with hers and they flew together.

Afterward, with no new information on the case, they fell into a much-needed slumber.

Chapter Twelve

The next morning Flynn slept soundly on the bed, and since she didn't want to wake him, Vikki very slowly eased off the mattress to stand. She gave herself a few more minutes to watch him in the dawn light. Sooty lashes fanned over the shadows under his eyes, and while his face was relaxed, the worry line between his brows remained. Even in repose, Flynn's brain was working out problems.

Vikki's heart skipped as she acknowledged she had a big problem on her hands, a personal relationship problem. This wasn't how she usually ran an investigation or case evidence collection. For starters, she didn't get personally involved with clients or suspects. She didn't believe for one moment that Flynn was in cahoots per se with his half sibling, but it wouldn't be unusual for him to have some idea, at least on a subconscious level, of where Landon was located during times of stress. Flynn had taken on the responsibility to care for Landon enough times as an adolescent that it was easy to see how Flynn would still feel responsible for his half brother. At the very least, Flynn wanted to protect his mother from the fallout of Landon's nefarious activities. The time she'd spent making love to Flynn could have been time spent seeking more information on Landon.

She couldn't ignore that her personal feelings were influencing her professional opinion of Flynn's role as Landon's half brother. At least in terms of all that had passed between them since she'd walked up to his room in the barracks. She and Flynn had survived a gamut of emotions couples together for decades might never encounter. Her spine went straight, rousing her from her musings. The most recent development withstanding, when had she started thinking of them as a couple?

She shook her head. It was time to reach out for help.

There was only one person who understood her well enough that Vikki was willing to talk to. She quietly went into the bathroom and phoned Sadie, who picked up immediately.

"Vikki! I've been worried about you."

"Me? You're the one in a safe house."

"Aren't you basically in the same predicament, but in a nice place with a man with a hot bod? Riley told me you had to move. And I read the situation report. I'm so glad you're okay, sis."

Heat crept up Vikki's throat, but she refused to look in the mirror. No way could Sadie know what had just happened, twin or not.

"Me, too." She bit her lip, unable to address her twin's comments about Flynn. Whom she'd just made love to.

"Vik? You there? You've slept with him, haven't you?"

"How can you possibly know that?" Exasperation replaced her reticence. Really, there was no use trying to keep anything from her sister.

"I knew it! We always have our twin sense. You know that." Sadie's tone glowed with satisfaction.

"True." She'd known Sadie was in trouble before Riley confirmed it by telling her that her twin was at the safe house. "But just because I may have had some fun doesn't mean it's anything to worry about."

"I didn't say it was something worrisome. Don't kid yourself, Vikki. You're not the type to get this involved, so quickly, unless the guy's really worth it. I know you. You've never jumped in so soon."

"Which is why I don't think I should—"

"Stop with the 'shoulds.' Enjoy it, Vikki. You deserve it as much as anyone, even more so. After that rat you were with for way too long, you deserve to meet a good guy for a change. Trust me, I know the difference, thanks to Tate."

"Stop beating yourself up about Tate. He's going to meet his own justice." Silently she prayed this would happen. "I'm not a total loss at picking out a good man. I've been with other decent guys."

"Um, not really. Unless you count that boring dude you saw for a few months five years ago."

"Chuck. I'd forgotten about him." Nice guy, nice plans for the future, but a yawner at meals or anywhere requiring conversation. And that was pretty much everywhere.

"That's it, yes. It was Chuck. Forget about all of your exes. Tell me about Flynn."

Vikki opened her mouth to do her usual guy breakdown with Sadie, but was stopped by a huge tug from her conscience.

"Vik? You're worrying me. You're never this quiet."

"I'm in the bathroom, trying not to wake him."

"Oh, I get it." She could almost see Sadie's eyes widening, the matching grin. "And something else just clicked for me, about you and Flynn."

"What's that?"

"This time it's different," Sadie said. "With Flynn, I mean. No, not in that way. That's none of my business. But you're usually quick to give me the lowdown. You don't want to because you're still trying to process what Flynn means to you."

"How is it that you're the one hiding from a criminal ex, yet you're giving me love advice?"

"Hey, I didn't say I had a good picker, did I? Besides, that's in my past. Or will be, for good, once they catch Tate. Be grateful Peter isn't a wanted felon."

"I'll keep that in mind." Vikki heard rustling on the other side of the door. Flynn was awake. "Look, I've got to go. You sure you're still in a good spot?"

"I am. I hate being here and not living my life as usual, but I'll take staying alive over just about anything else." Sadie's positivity reverberated through the connection. "You take care of yourself, okay?"

Tears welled and Vikki swallowed. "I am—don't worry. You, too."

"Love you, sis."

"Love you, too."

She disconnected and this time looked in the mirror.

Instead of her polished Army paralegal self, a woman with sex-mussed hair, flushed cheeks and bright eyes stared back at her. Most significant, her eyes had something they hadn't had in a long time.

Joy.

FLYNN WAITED WHILE Vikki finished in the bathroom, wondering if she was having any second thoughts about their lovemaking. She'd been as eager as he to explore their unexpected and powerful attraction, but it didn't mean she wouldn't have regrets. They were in the middle of a case, after all.

And he was charged with keeping Vikki safe, even if she was trained and able to protect herself. As far as Flynn was concerned, having Riley Colton entrust his sister to him was as official as could be.

Guilt sucker punched him and he sat up, leaned against the brass headboard, ran his hand over his face. If Joseph had shown up again at any time over the past hour, he'd have caught Flynn and Vikki off guard. In the throes of a passion Flynn had never experienced before. It was one thing to desire a woman, but the need he had for Vikki was far more, something extraordinary.

And nothing he could afford to contemplate with two bad guys out there. His phone buzzed and he picked it up, looked at the screen. *Riley.* The guy must be psychic.

"Flynn."

"Are you and Vikki doing okay?" Riley's impatience underscored the high stakes of the op.

"We are. I made sure no one followed us, and it's

a perfect spot. I thought you'd put us in the middle of the woods."

"Hiding in plain sight works just as well." Flynn thought he detected some angst in Riley's tone, underscored by his extended pause. "The local and federal agencies want to capture Joseph ASAP. With Landon still on the loose and in need of being brought in, Joseph is a distraction we can't afford."

"Understand." Why did he feel a "but" coming?

"Is Vikki within earshot?"

"No, she's in the bathroom." He left out the part about why the cute cottage bed was a mess, how he'd just had the most life-altering sex with Riley's little sister. Big brothers didn't need to know everything.

"They want to draw Joseph out and you're the one to do it. We'll need your help, but I don't want Vikki involved because she'll insert herself and this isn't her gig, as much as she thinks it is because her superiors sent her to interview Joseph."

"They also sent her to try to find Landon and interview him. She's doing what she feels is best for the case, sir. I don't think it's realistic to keep her out of this. Nor is it fair. She's been a part of how far we've all come in only four days."

"Understood, but since you've now spent some quality time with my sister, you no doubt see how stubborn she is. And how excellent her detective skills are. She'll be on to us and taking over the entire op in a heartbeat. I'd rather avoid that."

"She is exacting." Flynn grinned. Vikki was right; Riley knew her very well.

"Exactly. Vikki won't rest until she feels she's gotten every point, every bit of evidence, collected. She'll have all of that when she can talk to Landon. Joseph's a distraction from what we all know is the focal point of this case."

"Landon."

"Right. I'm thinking the captain has a contact on the Grand Rapids PD who must be feeding him all the latest information. That's how he tracked you both to the cemetery to start with, then to the Grand Hotel. I've told Detective Emmanuel Iglesias my suspicions, and he's agreed to do whatever he can to bring in Landon, too."

"That makes sense."

"It makes our plan easier. We'll make sure that same inside contact finds out that we're using you as a lure to draw Landon out. We'll get a Landon look-alike, have you on the spot, and lure Joseph in."

"Look, Riley, I appreciate that you want to keep Vikki safe. I do, too. But she's fully capable of figuring out what she can and cannot be involved with. This is as much her case as ours. I'm not keeping this from her. I can't. We're a team." He hoped using Vikki's brother's given name would underscore his belief. "Tell me where to be and when." How he was going to convince Vikki to keep a safe distance was another matter. He couldn't hide any of this from her. Plus, he trusted her abilities.

"As soon as I have it, you'll know. In the meantime, continue your planning with Vikki, about Landon, so that she doesn't suspect anything."

"Got it."

They disconnected as the bathroom door clicked open. Vikki stood wrapped in a towel, her wet hair hanging around her shoulders. She usually kept it up, and being able to run his fingers through it while they made love had been a heady treat.

Their gazes met and the answer to his question was in Vikki's eyes.

"Who was on the phone?"

"Your brother. Riley." He clarified automatically, trying to treat her as his professional partner. Because if he didn't stay focused, he'd bring her back to bed and they'd never capture Joseph or find Landon.

"At least he waited until morning to call." She walked over to him. "Flynn, we need to talk." She sat on the bed and leaned close to his face, her hip next to his.

"Wait." He gently grasped her shoulders—her smooth, soft shoulders—and pushed her back. "We let our emotions get away with us."

She blinked. "What? I was about to ask how we were going to move forward, through the investigation. I was hoping we'd be able to do that and explore this other side of our partnership." Her blush combined with the shyness in her voice all but undid him.

He ignored the way his body immediately reacted to her. If he hadn't had the sheets bunched around his middle, he'd never be able to convince her that he thought they'd done the wrong thing. It'd be too clear that all he really wanted was to roll her onto the bed and take her in every way possible, all day long.

"We can't do anything but find Joseph and Landon, Vikki. They have to be our priority." He watched the pride and hurt play tug-of-war across her face and wished it could be different, but it couldn't. This was about keeping them both alive to serve again. And if his heart had its way, to love again.

Impervious detachment cloaked her expression, and she rose and walked to the bathroom door. "I get it. I do. I don't have a choice, do I?" She tugged at her damp hair. "I need to get dressed." The door closed. Not a slam but not a soft close, either.

Flynn allowed himself a second to silently curse his crappy timing—his error in judgment. Why couldn't he have waited until the case was closed to make a move on Vikki? Because this was more than a sexual attraction. With the sound of her dressing on the other side of the door, he gathered his clothes and waited to use the shower.

The Vikki who came through the door was the woman he'd met in the barracks a few days ago, but with greater resolve and zero openness in her gaze. His heart thumped, heavy with remorse. He wanted her eyes to sparkle for him again.

"I'll take a shower and we'll go over what's next, to find Landon. Riley has a plan in place already for Joseph, but it's at a standstill until he gives the go-ahead."

"Absolutely." She pulled her laptop out of her backpack and walked toward the small kitchen area. "I'll get a pot of coffee going."

Flynn didn't reply but instead bolted for the bathroom before he threw all caution to the wind. One more second in her presence, with the aura of hurt and disappointment radiating off her, would be all it took for him to go to her, beg her forgiveness, explain why he had to be so detached. But Vikki understood, too. He hoped it was at least partially why she was back to being über-professional, and not because he'd just made a colossal mistake, placing a mission before what was proving to be the most significant relationship of his life.

As soon as he closed the door between them, he let a deep breath go.

Coward.

VIKKI MEASURED OUT the coffee and tried to be nice to the coffee machine, but it was so satisfying to slam the filter into the holder, toss the coffee in, slap the switch on.

Flynn had done what every other soldier she'd ever dated had done. It was all great until reality came back that they had work to do together. She got that, in truth. And if she was being really honest with herself, she knew that at least one of them needed to keep the mission as priority at all times, or they'd risk blowing it all. And her real reticence with men stemmed from Peter's cheating ways. No matter how angry she was at this moment, she knew beyond a doubt that Flynn wasn't anything like Peter. Not by a long shot.

Think.

Flynn hadn't shown any signs of being a genuine jerk. In fact, he was clearly doing his part to salvage their working relationship and allow them to move forward with the case. So why did it seem that he'd dropped her?

The brew dripped and she opened the fridge to select a creamer. Riley had remembered, or given an assistant the information, that she preferred an almond milk creamer. This particular one was pumpkin pie flavor—her absolute favorite.

The sweet addition to her coffee didn't take the sting off of Flynn's apparent rejection, though. As she'd showered and dried off, she'd heard his low voice through the door and figured he was on the phone. To find out it was Riley made sense. And raised her little sister red flags. Was Riley keeping something from her?

She grabbed her phone and dialed CI.

"Riley." He picked up right away.

"What did you discuss with Flynn?"

"What do you mean?" Riley never, ever, played coy.

"Aha! I knew it. You may as well tell me what you're planning now. You know I'll figure it out."

"Flynn agreed that he'd fill you in, Vikki. What's this really about?"

"Stop treating me like a kid, Riley. What the heck is going on? One minute Flynn's all cool with me and us working together on the case. The next he's all stone-cold soldier again, stiff as a board. What did you say to him?"

"Calm down, Vik. Yes, I talked to Flynn about the case today, mostly MP and security stuff. I'm not sure what you mean by 'stiff,' as he was nothing but professional with me."

"That's my point, Riley. Please stay out of my part in this. I get that the local authorities call you in to consult, but my work here has nothing to do with CI. You need to trust me that I'll tell you anything I find out that could help your efforts."

"I'm not going to agree with you on this. RevitaYou has everything to do with CI. Our sister, your twin, is in a safe house because of her ex's involvement in the poison. You've been attacked by a RevitaYou widower. People have died, Vikki. It's going to take all of us working together to stop Landon and his cronies before someone else is killed."

The bathroom door opened and in her peripheral vision she saw Flynn come out.

"I get that. And I need you to get that I know how to do my part of the teamwork."

"I have the utmost confidence in you, Vikki. As does Flynn. Why else would I want you to leave the reserves and work exclusively for CI? Speaking of which... This might not be the best time, but have you thought about it any more?"

"There hasn't been time." And no matter how irate her older brother could still make her with his overprotectiveness, she knew she wanted to always be part of the CI team.

"We'll table it until we have both Joseph and Landon behind bars."

"Sounds good to me. Speaking of which... I need to go. Flynn and I are coming up with a plan to lure Landon out."

"Sounds good. Talk to you soon." Riley disconnected, a little too quickly. She eyed Flynn, who'd helped himself to coffee. His white T-shirt was tucked into cargo pants and she forced her gaze to his face, away from the body that had brought her such exquisite pleasure. The afterglow of their lovemaking was still in the air, for heaven's sake, but they were looking at one another as if they'd barely met.

"Was that your brother?" He sipped his brew.

"Yes."

Flynn's direct gaze cut through her attempt at casualness. "I told you that I'd fill you in on our conversation. Don't you trust me?"

"Of course I trust you." She clenched her teeth, making her head pound. "You have to understand that Riley has a habit of overstepping appropriate boundaries at times. He's my older brother by several years and can too easily see himself as my parent. It's annoying, and if he said anything to you about you needing to take care of me, forget it. I can take care of myself."

He met her gaze without hesitation. "I've no doubt in your abilities, Vikki. And we need them to close the case. I suggest we get to work."

Their eye contact continued for a split second longer than it needed to, and the same thrill that had tickled her stomach since they'd met was back. But then Flynn moved to the kitchen table, laptop in tow. And the moment shattered into the shards of regret Vikki was too familiar with. She had the emotional scar tissue to prove it.

"Here, let me fill you in on CI's plans to lure Joseph out. Riley didn't want you to know at first, but I told him you and I are a team." Spoken with quiet conviction, his words eased some of her concerns over how easily he'd shut down their sexy times.

"His plan makes sense to me. And for the record, I won't get involved unless it's called for. I know when it's time to observe and when I need to act." It still stung, that he'd flipped over to a professional stance more quickly than she had, but she got it. Darn it.

Relief shone from Flynn's eyes for a split second. "I know you do, Vik."

They sat opposite one another and again went through their various plans to both find Joseph and then Landon. As she listened to Flynn outline Riley's proposal, she couldn't let go of one belief.

The man she'd made love with was still here. But he wasn't letting her in. He couldn't, just as she had to make sure she was operating as a soldier, not a girlfriend. Anything less could prove deadly in the wrong situation.

Chapter Thirteen

"There's one unknown that we haven't addressed about my half brother." He and Vikki sat at the pinewood table painted to match the kitchen trim, the remnants of their lunch resting between their laptops.

Vikki took a sip of her iced tea. "What's that?" Her expression remained neutral to the point of droll and he wanted to kiss her until she laughed, until the Vikki he'd become so close to came back. But it wasn't his right.

Flynn's relief that he and Vikki had both made a silent pact to stay professional until they caught their suspects proved that he was right to stand up to Riley's original idea to cut Vikki out. As long as Vikki knew the plan, she'd stay safe. And he had to protect her at all costs.

"Landon's biological mother, Melissa, is still in the picture. That is, when she wants to be."

"You said she abandoned him along with your father when Landon was still very young?"

"Yes. And even though my mom and I have repeatedly told Landon that she's not worth his time, he never says no to her. Melissa's called him over the years for financial help to pay her bills, find a place to live. After she left him, she took up with a bad crowd, lived in a remote, hippie-type commune."

"The place out in the woods north of here, near the Canadian border?"

"Yes." Native Michiganians knew the place well. It was both feared and a source of humorous remarks at cocktail parties. "But she left the compound about ten years ago and, as far as I know, she's still living in a trailer park." He mentioned one of Grand Rapids' most impoverished suburbs.

"Maybe it's good that Landon has been able to help her out. To give both of them a sense of family. You said that he's not particularly close to you or your mother, and that he was always a difficult child. Besides the obvious, his mother abandoning him, could it be something else?"

"My parents had him tested for everything. He has issues, that's certain, but to be honest, I never discussed them with my mother. It's Landon's business now, anyway. He's an adult. I don't believe he ever meant for his supplement to cause problems, much less hurt and kill people, but he's accountable."

"So are the bankrollers." She knew firsthand, with Sadie in hiding.

"Have you spoken to your sister recently?"

Her face wrinkled in concern. "I did, earlier today. She's still at the safe house and will be for the duration. At least until her ex is captured."

There were too many bad guys looking to hurt others, as far as Flynn was concerned. Vikki tapped on her keyboard and he saw the familiar lines on her brow furrow in concentration.

"What are you writing about now?"

"I'm trying to figure out if there's a connection between Landon and Sadie's ex, Tate Greer. If they've ever worked together."

"They know one another, I'd think. Landon needed millions to launch the prototype. He didn't get the resources from his family, that's for certain."

"They may never have met in person." She dropped one hand to her side and closed her laptop with the other. "I was hoping we'd figure out a way to draw all three of our madmen out at the same time. The widower, the scientist and the money guy. Apparently the odds of it happening aren't much more than nil. At least Riley's plan might work, for Joseph."

Both their phones beeped simultaneously.

Vikki gasped. "It's from Riley. He says—"

"That another victim has been identified. She died earlier today." Flynn read the texts they'd both received. And the second one, just for him.

Leave the cottage in ten minutes. Drive to the old grain warehouse on the lake pier. Solo. Do NOT bring Vikki.

"You got a second text." She was peering over her phone at his screen.

"I did."

"And?"

"It's time to move in on Joseph. But you need to stay here. Please don't argue with me on this." As soon as he said the words, her face fell, her anguish from having nearly died no longer a question. Vikki was hurt. By his words.

His resolve to remain detached from Vikki blew up.

"I'm sorry, Vikki. That was stupid of me."

"Not stupid—honest. You're right. Joseph needs to be caught, and I do have a history of sticking my nose in where I don't need to. But me following you isn't going to hurt. I'll stay back, as we went over. Honestly? I've had enough drama to last an entire investigative career." Her admission fueled his resolve to protect her.

"It was the bravest thing I ever saw, babe. You handled yourself as if you'd done it before, as well as any Army EOD expert." He reached across the table and grasped her hand. "It's normal to have a lot of anxiety after an event like that, you know. You do know it, don't you?"

She nodded, but he saw how she bit her lower lip, kept her gaze on her computer, her handwritten notes; anywhere but on him. "Sure. And I know I'm okay. I'll look back on it like any other bad memory, with time. It's just a little tough right now."

"I'm sorry, Vik. It isn't easy." He longed to stay with her, to hold her, to make love to her again. Take her mind away from that ugly day. "Tell you what. After we get through this next part, I can pick up anything you'd like for dinner tonight. What's your choice?"

"Did you see our refrigerator? It's stuffed to the gills with food. There's even wine and beer in there—that's Riley's MO."

"He must think we'll be here for a while. That's why

we need to take advantage of getting something cooked for us when we can."

She ran her fingers through her hair. His own fingers twitched as if the muscle memory of stroking her hair while he kissed her hadn't let go. Who was he kidding? He'd never let go of any memories of Vikki.

But he had to remember that Vikki wasn't meant to be in his life for any longer than this not-so-brief moment. She was the woman he fought alongside to defeat some very bad guys. That was all she could be. And he couldn't offer her what she deserved—far more than what he'd present.

Vikki would never settle for the quiet life of a college professor, his dream job. Not that he'd ask her to. He feared she'd never fully trust him with her emotions again since he'd pulled away.

VIKKI WATCHED FLYNN pack extra ammo into a backpack as her mind raced with possibilities. He still hadn't agreed to her plan to go with him.

"Let me go with you, Flynn."

His eyes sparked with steely resolve. "No. This is something Riley needs my expertise for. Stay here. The only reason you'd need to move is if you feel this spot is being compromised. If it is, then take the truck and go. I'll be in the vehicle Riley suggested I use, in the barn next to us. If you need me, text me on one of the burners." He nodded toward the small living area, where a basket of burner phones sat on a coffee table. It was signature Sadie, who helped Riley and CI with security details.

Sadie. She was a victim of the entire RevitaYou scheme, too. Stuck in a safe house and unable to fully use her skills in person that would undoubtedly bring the criminal group down sooner.

"Vik? Are we on the same page?" Flynn hadn't missed her drifting off.

"Yes. For sure. We are. We both want the same thing, right?"

He looked at her for a prolonged moment and then nodded. "Right." He slung the backpack over his shoulder and she moved to follow him to the door. Instead he threw her off guard by stepping toward her and swooping her up against his chest.

"Whoa." She wasn't complaining. Never would she resist Flynn embracing her.

"We have a lot to talk about when this is over." He kissed her. She closed her eyes, pressed closer to him, relished his scent. This wasn't a sensual or provocative gesture. Nor was it one of the blazingly passionate kisses they'd shared in the bed on the other side of a thin wall. This was a kiss of pure need, and something Vikki wasn't willing to acknowledge. If she did, it'd forever change everything between her and Flynn, and she couldn't risk it, not yet. Not ever. His moods were too changeable.

He lifted his head and let her go.

"I want you to stay safe and tucked in tight here, Vik. But I know you better. If you're going to follow me, take it easy. You had a rough day Sunday."

"I'm capable of staying out of the op, Flynn." And she almost believed herself.

Flynn walked out the door and she threw the dead bolt, sure she was okay with all of this. But her trembling hands and shaky knees revealed how much his kiss had moved her. And made her realize how close she was to giving herself away to another man again. Could she do it, after all she'd been through with Peter?

Peter. She couldn't help the giggle that erupted from deep in her chest. Being with Flynn these past days had turned Peter into nothing more than a shadow memory. If only she'd met Flynn first, she'd never have been attracted to a man like her ex.

Flynn had all the qualities she'd admired in her friends' partners. The ones who were happy. That was why he, and whatever it was that was blossoming between them, scared her. And what she'd just felt in his kiss underscored her concerns. Besides the unique intimacy that Flynn elicited from her, the kiss had triggered a sense of belonging. Flynn had somehow claimed her as his.

Could she give herself completely to one man again?

She shook her head and looked out the window to see Flynn driving a modest blue sedan out of the garage. This wasn't the time to worry about her heart. Two criminals were at large. She and Flynn were a team; he'd said it himself. There was no way she could allow him to proceed to the docks without her. The odds of him needing her backup were slim, but enough.

She grabbed the truck keys and left the cottage.

Chapter Fourteen

Flynn used all his energy to focus. Focus and drive off the property and onto the highway. He'd never allowed a relationship, a woman, to interfere with his mission. Ever. And he wasn't about to now.

Sure you aren't.

For her safety, for the chance to return to Vikki to make love again—that had been the singularly hottest romp in the sack he'd ever had—he had to get this part of the job done. Alone, without the worry of Vikki being hurt. Not from her inability to defend herself but from the evil that he knew lurked in Captain Joseph's mind, not to mention Landon's. He knew she'd follow him to the lake, or she wasn't the steely soldier he'd made love to.

The op, man. Stick to the goal.

He sucked in a deep breath, reminded himself of what Riley had run down with him and he'd shared with Vikki.

They were going to lure Joseph out by making him think that Flynn was to meet Landon at the warehouse. The local police and Riley had agreed that Joseph had to be intercepting GRPD comms; he'd shown up in places the Grand Rapids Police Department was investigating related to RevitaYou. Add to that Joseph's close following of the entire case even before his wife's tragic death, and it wasn't a big leap to figure the captain had put as much of the puzzle together as any of them. He wouldn't fall for anything other than the chance to face Landon in person. To kill him, as he'd threatened.

The traffic was heavy closer to the city and Flynn checked his rearview and side mirrors. With a jolt, he knew he'd messed up. He hadn't scanned for followers like he normally would have. Flynn's grip tightened on the wheel. This wasn't how he'd wanted to walk into a potential shoot-out, distracted.

The slow crawl until he exited onto the pier road gave him the time and space he needed from Vikki and what she was doing to his state of mind.

It's more than your brain, dude.

He identified the pier and exact warehouse, taking care to drive around to the back as Riley had told him. A glance in his mirrors revealed that he, indeed, had a companion, and it wasn't GRPD or Riley, who'd told him he'd be in a black SUV.

Vikki had followed him.

Of course she has.

He bit back a smile and prepared to follow through with the plan. He had to ignore the protective side of him that wanted to swaddle her in Bubble Wrap. Vikki was a soldier. Like him, she knew how to take care of herself. He'd trust her with his life; it was time he trusted her with hers.

It didn't negate the need for the silent prayer he sent up, that they'd both make it through whatever Joseph or Landon threw at them.

VIKKI WATCHED FLYNN park and followed on the other end of the warehouse. She wasn't sure what he and Riley were up to, but it reminded her of a takedown CI had coordinated a few years ago. She'd been home on leave and Riley had asked her to help out with the communications part of the operation. The person of interest had been an abuser who'd refused to honor a restraining order and had repeatedly taunted his ex-wife and two daughters. He'd always eluded apprehension, though, and gone on the lam for several months at a time. CI had helped GRPD and the family to capture the man by having the woman pretend to want to meet him to talk things out. As soon as he appeared close to the property, he'd been arrested.

Vikki's imagination went into overdrive as she watched Flynn walk toward the warehouse. Regardless of how protective Riley, and probably Flynn, was, she'd been assigned this case. She had every right and, in fact, obligation to be in on it.

She wished she wasn't on Army duty and able to carry a weapon as she normally did when working for CI. Since this was official Army business—as a paralegal, her job didn't require a sidearm unless in a combat zone—she had to go into this unarmed. But not unprotected. The body armor that Riley had stashed in the F-250's truck bed fit her perfectly.

Flynn moved toward the single entrance door visible

to her. She hunched behind the truck, waiting to make her move. No doubt he'd spotted her; it was his job to know if he'd been followed. When a large semitruck had crossed in front of her on the highway, it'd looked like she might lose Flynn, but luck had been on her side with the traffic jam right before the pier exit.

The warehouse door was opened by a man she'd know anywhere. Riley. A fraction of the tension she carried in her shoulder muscles eased. Riley and Flynn were the two men she'd pick to get her through a firefight, whether combat or civilian. The first she'd known her entire life, the other only the last few days. Neither Emerson Joseph nor Landon Street was a match for these two highly trained professionals.

Still, the thought of Captain Joseph being anywhere near her again made her skin crawl. The man was out of his mind with grief, and he'd already strapped a bomb to her chest once. Vikki had no doubt he'd take her out if it furthered his desire to get to Flynn and, in turn, his half brother. The man saw Landon as the murderer of his beloved wife. Vikki and Flynn were just flotsam.

The reminder that they were all here for justice for the victims of RevitaYou steeled her and allowed her motivation to gel.

The murders and illnesses stopped here, if she had anything to say about it.

Without further hesitation, she bolted for the warehouse door.

"You found it," Riley said as he let him in and Flynn gave his eyes a minute to adjust to the dim insides of the humongous building. It appeared to be little more than corrugated metal held up by I beams. Row upon row of commercial-grade shelving filled the center portion, with larger access aisles surrounding the circumference. Three banged-up forklifts sat forlornly in one far corner, highlighting the emptiness of the facility.

"It wasn't hard, only the traffic. And I was followed."

"By whom?"

"Your sister."

"Dang it, Flynn, I told you to keep Vikki at the dang cottage. Where is she?"

"Still in the parking lot." Flynn's conscience pinged with guilt. "She's not one of us, as far as operations go, but Vikki knows how to take care of herself, Riley."

Riley's swift curse stunned Flynn, and as a soldier, he thought he'd heard it all. "The last time you thought she could handle herself, she ended up with a ticking bomb around her neck."

Flynn allowed the accusation to sink in. He deserved it. "You're absolutely right. I messed up. I told you, it won't happen again." He trusted Vikki, but not her enthusiasm. He prayed she'd hang back and wait for the outcome of this attempt to draw Joseph in. The last thing anyone needed was for her to insert herself into the op.

Riley shook his head. "If I wasn't concerned that it'd tip Joseph off, I'd go out there now and tell her to stay put. But we're running out of time."

"You've already sent the messages?" Flynn was impressed. Riley didn't mess around.

"Yes. We know Joseph has the capability to intercept all of the Grand Rapids PD communications, and we opened up one of the CI frequencies that his equipment will also pick up. The story went out that Landon's meeting you here—" Riley looked at his phone "—in five minutes."

"Where's the Landon look-alike?"

"Look over there." Riley pointed to the far end of the warehouse, where a tall man in a wig and glasses waved at them both. Then he exited the building through the door Flynn realized he'd use as soon as they knew Joseph was close.

"That really looks like my brother. Who is it?"

"A rookie cop. He's fully dressed in body armor. He wants to work in undercover, so this will give him a taste of how an op is run."

Flynn shook his head. "No, but I'm impressed."

"Wait." Riley's phone pinged and he held up his hand then tapped on the screen. "Our spotter on the west side of the building just saw a car drive up. Hang on."

As Riley scrutinized his screen, Flynn waited, his pulse steady. This was what a soldier trained for. Combat skills transferred to all sorts of civilian settings, law enforcement in particular.

"I saw the spotter on the roof, but other than that, great job with concealment."

"Agree. GRPD knows what it's doing." Riley was quick to give credit. "There's considerable LEA interest at the federal level, but if we can get Joseph, it'll allow the FBI to put all their energy toward Landon. He's got the information we're all looking for." Riley's phone pinged again.

Flynn held his breath and sent up another prayer that Vikki was lying low.

"It's Joseph. He's parked his car on the other side. There are six additional cruisers parked out of sight, and they'll move into position now. You're up." Riley's eyes reflected determination and something else that made Flynn pause. Trust. Riley trusted Flynn to not screw this up. He felt the weight of having to prove himself with Riley. It was an onus he put on himself.

"Roger." He nodded at Riley before he walked to the far end of the building, to an exit diagonally opposite. If all went as planned, he'd be out that door in ten seconds and within another few minutes Joseph would be under arrest.

He reached the door and pushed it open. The bright sunlight was expected after the dim interior, but it still took him a couple of seconds to regain his vision.

"Landon, where are you? Don't make me wait any more. I've searched the warehouse. There's no one here." He shouted toward the perimeter fence, pretending not to notice the SUV in his peripheral vision, parked a couple hundred yards to his right. He saw Joseph get out of his car. The shooter on the roof would have his rifle aimed at his boss, and while Flynn appreciated the backup, he hoped the chance to apprehend his CO wouldn't cost the bereaved widower his life. Flynn had no illusions that Joseph was in his right mind, or still his superior, but still, he'd gone into a combat zone with the captain once.

The Landon look-alike shuffled along the fence,

dragging his hand against the chain link as if still undecided as to whether he could trust his "brother."

Flynn cupped his hands to his mouth, keeping his peripheral vision on Joseph, who'd walked around to the front of his vehicle. "Landon! Come on, man. It's me." He held his hands out to his sides, facing the decoy, his weapon tucked into his waistband at his back.

The look-alike stopped and began to walk toward Flynn.

Joseph moved closer and then stopped, as if afraid he'd spook the man he believed to be Landon Street. Flynn was painfully aware that Landon was the one Joseph wanted to kill, but he couldn't tell if Joseph carried a weapon or not. He was too far away. He assumed Joseph had come armed, as he'd already shot at him and tried to blow up Vikki. He had to trust the rooftop shooter and surrounding GRPD officers to back him up.

"Let's talk, Landon." He didn't have to shout as loudly since the decoy was within fifty yards.

"Landon" took a few more halting steps as if still not sure if he should turn and run or meet his half brother across the asphalt. The wind kicked up and the river churned just yards beyond them. Flynn focused on staying put as Riley's plan played out. His job was to act like the brother who was carefully bringing his mad scientist sibling in for a meeting, so that the police could then apprehend Landon for his part in the RevitaYou scheme.

Flynn had been here before, in the middle of an op where time took on its own dimension and waiting became the true test of a man. Where things like his growing need and affection for Vikki could distract him.

Instead, he took comfort in knowing she was nearby. Vikki knew how to keep herself safe in the midst of chaos, and that relieved what otherwise would be constant concern for her welfare. If he needed her, she'd act. He had no doubt.

It seemed like an hour, but he knew it was only a few minutes that they all waited. Joseph seemed to vacillate, taking one or two steps forward, then returning to stand at the front of his vehicle. The look-alike mirrored the captain's maneuverings, only coming closer to Flynn as Joseph appeared to make his final choice and walk toward them.

There was still no way for sure to tell if Joseph was armed or not; Flynn had to rely on the rest of the team, but most especially the rooftop sharpshooter. His only hope was to get through this so that he could hold Vikki one last time. Before they each had to go their own ways.

That was definitely a first for him, to trick his mind through the agonizingly stressful last minutes of an op with a woman as his carrot. He'd never even done that when he was engaged to Jena.

If Captain Joseph wasn't the death of him, Vikki would be.

VIKKI WATCHED THE drama unfold from the northwest corner of the warehouse, behind a pile of wooden pallets. She'd texted Riley to let him know she was there, only to receive a definitive reply from her brother who wished she'd remained at the safe house.

Do not interfere in the op.

It couldn't surprise Riley that she wanted to be here. It was a bit beyond what her job description required, sure, but she hadn't made rank as quickly as she had without pushing boundaries, stretching herself.

She watched Flynn remain in a very vulnerable position, with one man walking toward him from the edge of the pier as another approached from a parked SUV at the other end of the warehouse. He was a little too far away for her to visually ID him for certain, but the make and model of the SUV matched Joseph's. An unfamiliar sensation clawed at her from the inside out, sending waves of anxiety through her. Terror. For Flynn. She hadn't texted him, only Riley. The last thing she wanted to do was to distract Flynn from whatever this crazy dance was that was unfolding in front of her.

But what if she'd made a huge mistake? If she never had another chance to communicate with him?

No.

Her thoughts could not go down that dead-end, rutted road. Flynn knew what he was doing, Riley was tops at what he did, and she was certain there was an entire team of officers and agents surrounding the building. Especially if that was Landon walking in to meet Flynn.

In a flash she realized what was going on. The pieces all clicked into place. The man dressed like Landon wasn't him; if it had been Landon, the officials would have already apprehended him and taken Joseph out. No, this was a setup. To capture Joseph.

With all of her other cases, she'd remained professionally detached, searching for evidence that would help make the Army's legal position stronger. Rarely had her assignments involved life-threatening situations, but RevitaYou was its own maelstrom, one they were all caught in.

And Flynn was in the epicenter of it.

"Come on, Landon. Let's talk, man." The Landon look-alike was no more than ten yards from Flynn. When she saw Joseph begin to stride toward them both, she kept her head, didn't panic. Flynn had this; he'd been in combat.

But she couldn't stop her hands, her body, from quaking.

When Joseph drew a weapon out of his jeans' waist that he'd concealed with the side of his body and his baggy pants, true panic set in. She quickly ascertained that running in front of Flynn wouldn't help—she'd never get there in time—and in fact would only make things worse. The captain didn't want Flynn; he wanted Landon. But Flynn stood between Joseph and his target.

Joseph was no more than twenty yards from Flynn, closing in, yet Flynn didn't make any move to defend himself. Didn't he see the other man? A scream formed in her throat that had nothing to do with her being a soldier. It was primal, a call to the man she'd inexplicably become attached to.

But as she opened her mouth, shots rang out in the clear, crisp November air. She jerked, flattened behind the pallets, no longer in observation mode, but survival.

"Man down! EMTs requested ASAP." Flynn's command was in the form of a shout, and she looked back up to see the Landon look-alike and Flynn crouched next to Emerson Joseph's limp form. She eased up and carefully walked toward them, knowing from experience and training that she'd become a target of Riley's shooter if she moved too quickly, didn't announce herself.

"Sergeant Victoria Colton. I'm Riley Colton's sister." She spoke loud and clear, with her hands up, made a full 360-degree turn.

"She's clear." Riley's voice rang out and she saw that he was at the entrance to the warehouse, watching the entire scene. Puzzlement hit her. Why wasn't Riley helping with Joseph?

The grim truth revealed itself as she drew closer.

Captain Joseph had joined his dead wife.

Vikki sent up a prayer that they'd both have peace finally. She opened her eyes, looked in the direction Riley had shouted her credentials and saw the sniper, still in place on the roof. Thank goodness, or Flynn would not be standing next to Joseph, hands on his hips, absorbing the reality that his boss had gone from a decorated war hero to criminal in less than twenty-four hours. And now he was dead. Flynn would have been that body, not Joseph, had the sharpshooter not done his job.

Flynn's gaze found hers and she didn't think, didn't take into consideration the setting or need to remain professional. Vikki let her heart lead as she ran to Flynn and threw herself at him, wrapped her arms around his waist and squeezed tight as she laid her head on his chest. It was impossible to hear his heartbeat through his body armor, and she hated that her vest kept her from feeling his heat. But they were both alive, and he'd survived a deadly situation.

"Hey, babe." His voice caught and she hugged him even more, tears spilling down her cheeks. Flynn was okay.

"I thought he was going to take you out." She pulled back and looked into his face. Flynn's eyes were bright, his mouth a grim line. He knew how close it had been.

"He didn't. And you are supposed to be at the safe house."

"I know you knew I was behind you."

"Actually, I didn't, not until it was too late to stop you." He let go of her and took a step back. It felt as cold as it had been two days ago in the middle of the snowstorm, yet they were standing in bright sunshine and air that was twenty degrees warmer. But the chills on her skin didn't come close to the frigid glaze over his eyes as he watched her. He remained silent.

"There's no doubt you spotted me, Flynn. You're telling me that you, a trained US Army MP, didn't know that I, a JAG paralegal, was tailing you here?" Maybe a little jesting would draw him out.

The lines on his face tightened and she saw a look she'd never experienced with Flynn before, even when she'd thought he was a suspect and he hadn't trusted her enough to open up yet.

"Look, I never thought about anything but our time together until I hit the outskirts of Grand Rapids. The traffic jam is the only reason I caught a glimpse of you to begin with. I was distracted, Vikki. I can't do my job around you."

"But we have to finish this together. I need closure as much as you do with Landon. Do I have to remind you that I'm here on Army business, Flynn? This isn't some cops-and-robbers thrill for me. It's my job."

"And my job is to find my half brother before the same thing that happened to Captain Joseph happens to him." The tone of his voice made her heart trip, and not in the sexy way it had back in the cottage's bed.

She wasn't welcome in Flynn's life anymore.

Chapter Fifteen

Vikki had no choice but to go back home. Heading to a hotel on her own wasn't necessary, as she had a perfectly good place to stay in her apartment, but she wanted to be in her childhood home if she couldn't be with Flynn.

Riley and Charlize were gone overnight and had taken their dog, Pal, with them. Riley had told her they were going to check on Sadie at the safe house. She'd wanted to go but was too exhausted and still had reports to write up. It hurt to not be with her twin, but she wasn't good company for anyone right now.

Seeing Flynn standing out in the center of the lot behind the warehouse had unnerved her. Not the fact that he'd taken on the challenge to bring in Captain Joseph. Nor the fact that she'd watched a man—Joseph—die today. Right in front of her. It was grim, sad and awful, for sure. Yet none of it had shaken her to her core.

Not until she'd seen the flash of Joseph's weapon and for one split second thought he was going to kill Flynn on the spot. Flynn was wearing body armor, like her, but had nothing on to protect his head. Joseph, like any MP, was surely an excellent shot.

She shivered and tried to shake the images of what had happened, and what she'd feared could have happened, from her mind.

Her old room, once shared with Sadie, wrapped around her like a warm blanket. There was now a comfortable queen bed in the center, where once they'd shared bunk beds. A futon against the wall served as an extra bed. Tonight, however, Vikki needed the comfort of the larger mattress. She dropped her backpack and single suitcase on the futon and headed to the kitchen to make a cup of tea.

The phone in Riley's office rang and she paused. It was the CI headquarters line, rarely used during off-hours. If their clients needed them, they could be reached on their mobile phones.

It was probably nothing. Still, she paused and waited to listen to the message that would be left.

"Riley? Anyone? It's me, Brody. I lost my phone and…and it's really bad out here. I can't hold on—" The man who was all but an adopted Colton sibling sounded lost, scared.

"Brody, it's Vikki," she said, scrambling to put the receiver to her ear. "Where are you?"

"Vik." His gasps were harsh, as if he'd survived a fight.

"What's going on, Brody?" She cursed herself for not following up on Brody over the past several days. She and Sadie had promised to handle keeping tabs on him for CI, but ever since she'd driven into Grand

Rapids, the RevitaYou case had enveloped her every waking hour.

"I owe them a lot of money, Vik. The Capital X loan sharks. They've taken all I have." He sobbed and she wiped at her cheeks, her tears unable to help Brody. Only her quick action would save him.

"You've lost your phone? What are you calling on?"

"It's a burner. I paid cash for it at Walmart."

"I've got the number. It came up on caller ID." She wrote as she spoke, then began texting Riley.

"I'm sending your info to Riley."

"Thanks so much, sis. I'm sorry I haven't been around."

"I could say the same. I meant to reach out to you more, but I've gotten caught up in a case." Her words sounded pompous, uncaring. She bit her lip. "I'm so sorry, Brody. Please let us get you out of this."

"Riley's calling me. 'Bye, Vikki." He disconnected and she stared at the receiver. Then checked her texts. Riley had replied.

Got it. Calling him now.

She felt superfluous. CI didn't need her on this case.

Guilt tugged at her. Sure, she'd messed up by not following up on Brody's whereabouts and status, but she'd also been embroiled in a mess of her own. Brody meant a lot to her. She should have tried harder.

As the water in the teakettle rumbled, she considered what had to be done over the next few days. She was still keen on wrapping the JAG file up, sending in her reports and going on legit leave status so that she could help CI full-time and also enjoy her family.

But it wasn't up to her when the RevitaYou case would end. With Landon Street still on the run, all involved LEA were stymied.

The front doorbell rang and a shiver shook her. It wasn't yet eight o'clock, but the early nightfall made it seem much later, as did the long day behind her. The security system for CI was robust, and she looked at the screen on the kitchen monitor.

Flynn.

Anticipation immediately took root in her gut and she forced herself to breathe. He was probably here to talk to Riley about the case. He had no way of knowing she'd come here, although it wouldn't be difficult to figure out.

"Flynn." She opened the front door, usually reserved for clients, and waved him in.

He stood rooted in the spot. "Vikki. What are— I didn't expect you here."

"Clearly. Come on in." There was no use pretending. If he'd known she was there, this was the last place he'd have come.

He walked past her and turned around in the space, peering into Riley's office.

"Where's Riley?"

"Out. Why do I feel you've been here before?"

Dark eyes on her. His guard was still up, but she sensed his unease. As if he struggled over what to say to her, how to say it.

"Riley's had me here to go over information a few

times. But not since this case broke. What are you doing here?"

"I grew up here, remember?" She'd told him about her childhood that night in the hotel, during the storm. "Although maybe I didn't explain that Riley uses the home we grew up in as CI headquarters."

"You may have, but I was distracted." The glitter of heat was back in his eyes, and she couldn't stop her body from responding. The key was to keep from acting on what Flynn's presence was doing to her. He'd already made it plain that they were going their separate ways. If she gave in, she wasn't sure she'd come back from it.

"I'm about to make tea. Would you like some?"

"Sure." He followed her into the kitchen and stood too close, his energy too intense. Her skin prickled with every motion he made, from resting his hips against the counter next to where she poured the boiling water.

"Peppermint okay?"

"Fine."

She added another bag to the pot and put the ceramic lid in place. "Riley and Charlize usually have cookies here somewhere." She opened and closed a couple of cupboards. Anything to ease more space between them. It was unbelievable, the way Flynn inflamed her deepest desires from the inside out. And he hadn't even touched her.

"I don't want any sweets."

"Well, I do."

"Vikki." The plea in his voice made her stop. She gripped the counter and turned to face him. Pain etched lines across his forehead, and she stopped breathing.

Flynn had gone through a lot today, too, and she'd been so wrapped up in her reaction that she'd never stopped to think that maybe he'd had his own reasons for being so cold. Detached.

"Flynn, I'm so sorry. I didn't take what you've been through into account. Have you had dinner?"

A curt nod. "I ate on post. Went back to fill in my team, even though I'm still officially on leave."

"You need to rest."

"There is no rest, not until Landon shows up and is in custody." He shoved his hands into the front pockets of his jeans. "It's got to happen, but it still sucks that I have to help put him away."

Compassion pierced her reluctance to touch him, and she went to him, laid her hands on his upper arms. Tried to ignore how cut his biceps were. "You've tried. Your mother has tried. I know you care or this wouldn't hurt so much. You're a good man, Flynn. You could have called off on this case at any point. Why haven't you?"

"It's personal to me. My half brother has caused my mother nothing but grief since she married my father. I need to be part of this. If I'm not the actual person who puts the cuffs on him, I can at least help get to him. Landon's chemical concoction has killed people. It was one thing when his quirky behavior hurt my mom's feelings or upset his teachers and then professors. But now…now it's bigger than any of us. He needs to face justice."

She rubbed his arms, then reached up and framed his face with her hands. "You're not at fault here, Flynn. You know that, right?"

He closed his eyes, nodded. “Yeah.”

She pulled her hands away, but he caught one and raised it to his lips. When his mouth opened on her palm and his tongue made a swirling caress, she knew she was lost.

“Flynn.”

“I need you, Vikki. Today, when I stood there, knowing it could be my last seconds here, all I thought about was you. Us.” He pulled her finger into his mouth and sucked. She sagged against him, her breath coming in pants.

“Y-you said we were done…working…together. Flynn, stop.” She pulled away. “We keep going back and forth with one another. The middle of a case isn’t a time to make relationship decisions. Are you certain this is what you want?”

“I can’t promise you what will happen long-term with us, Vikki, but I can tell you that right now I can’t think of anything but being in your bed. If you need me to leave, God help me, I will. Your call.”

There was no “call” for her. She’d take Flynn any way, any how. Oddly, it wasn’t at all how she’d thought it’d be, needing a man this much. She’d not let a man into her heart, but with Flynn it was easy to let him in.

Until he shuts you out again.

She ignored her scared self and threw her shoulders back.

“Stay, Flynn.” She reached up, pressing into him with her breasts, her pelvis. One leg wrapped around his as she clasped her hands at his neck. “Be with me tonight.”

He lowered his head and gave her kisses that promised fire but delivered soft touches. She groaned and pressed her mouth closer to his. She needed all of Flynn.

"Babe."

"Yeah?"

"What about your other siblings?"

"They're all gone tonight. We're alone."

"Babe."

"What now?" Annoyance had her opening her eyes, when all she wanted was to get lost in him.

He grinned, his brown eyes stunning under the kitchen lights. "You're telling me we have this entire house to ourselves, all night?"

The thrumming in her center took on an insistence that required they stop talking ASAP.

"Yes."

"Relax. That's all I needed to know." A flash of white as he grinned again, wide and slow. Vikki stared at him, wondering what was going through his mind.

"Then why—"

His finger was over her lips. "Shh." His hand moved from her nape, down her spine, to her lower back. Vikki had never felt so turned on as she waited to see what Flynn would do next. When his other hand made the same journey but detoured to her front, slipping inside her pants, moving her underwear aside, she closed her eyes.

"Flynn. Please. Don't tease me."

"Eyes open, babe. Look at me."

She looked into his eyes, the contact making what his fingers were doing in her wet depths all the more erotic. "I can't..." Words left her as an orgasm hit hard and fast, the wave of pleasure as strong as it was unexpected. Before she was done crying out, his hands were on her waist and he lifted her onto the counter.

Flynn's mouth met hers without a whisper of the softness from earlier. They weren't strangers to one another's bodies any longer, and he remembered every single spot that aroused her. She wanted to reciprocate, to touch him, to hold him, to make him come. But his mouth required her full attention as he communicated pure passion with his lips, his tongue. For the first time in her life, Vikki let herself totally go in a man's arms. She gave in to their attraction full throttle, pushing her tongue against his with every mutual thrust. When his hands cupped her breasts, she wrapped both legs around his hips and pulled his pelvis into hers, stroking his erection through his jeans.

"Vik. Where's your room?"

"We're not going to make it to my room." She shoved at his shoulders and slid off the counter. "But that's where the condoms are."

His hand went into his front pocket and he retrieved a foil packet, his brow raised in challenge.

"What were you saying about not making it upstairs?"

"I'll show you." She shucked off her pants, lifted her top over her head.

"Stop." His voice was ragged, his face flushed. "Let me look at you."

She laughed. "This is my least sexy underwear, Flynn." If he looked too closely at her modest pink bra-and-bikini set, he'd see the tiny heart print. While the set was one of her favorites for every day, it wasn't what she'd have worn for a hookup.

This is more than a hookup.

The thought shook her as much as her desire for Flynn. As she stopped her sexy twirl, the air thickened between them. As if he hadn't made her come only minutes earlier, as if they'd waited years for this. Maybe they had.

She took a step toward him and he held up his hand. "Stop." As she watched, he undressed, and she fought to stay in place. It took every last bit of her restraint. When he was down to his underwear, he shucked it off and his erection made her pulse inside, needing him there.

"No more talking, Flynn." She reached for him and he was ready, kissing her with a force she'd only ever dreamed of. Flynn wanted her. Only her.

With zero fanfare, he unhooked her bra and impatiently tugged her panties down. "How do you want me, Vikki?" He breathed the words into her ear, swirling the tip of his tongue along its edges, making her shudder with pleasure.

"Here." It was all she could do to speak, but she managed to get to the bench window seat in the corner of the kitchen and knelt on the cushion that spanned the long length. She nodded behind her. "Take me this way."

Flynn didn't speak until his legs were against hers, behind her, his erection pressing into her most private spot. He leaned over her, his chest against her back, and as one hand held him in place, he used the other to cup her breast. His lips trailed down her spine, to the base, and his hand left her breast for one of her hips. When his other hand grasped the other hip, she arched her back.

"Please, Flynn."

He entered her in an excruciatingly slow glide, making every inch of her light up with ecstasy. The feel of where they were so intimately joined mixed with the scent of their lovemaking, and Vikki knew that this was what she'd compare all other intimate experiences to for the rest of her life.

"Babe, you're so hot, so wet for me." He began to move faster, and when it got to a place where she thought she'd never come down from, he reached under her and touched her exact spot for maximum effect.

Vikki screamed, the second orgasm even more intense than the first. It was like some kind of out-of-body experience, to be flying with the sensations yet feeling so grounded, so connected, to another.

To Flynn.

Flynn's shout followed hers, and she smiled into the seat cushion. There was nothing as satisfying as knowing he'd taken pleasure from this, too.

"Babe." His cheek was against her back again, his heartbeat reverberating through her rib cage.

"That was incredible." She soaked in the moment, allowed her body to float as long as it needed to.

"The night's still young."

FLYNN SHOWERED AFTER their third round of lovemaking. Vikki was asleep in the bedroom and he couldn't wait to join her. But he needed to think about what this meant. Where they might be going.

If there wasn't a potential for him to face down his unstable half brother in the near term, he'd suggest they see one another for at least a while. He knew that Vikki thought she might stay in the Army or join CI. But he also knew that she was so good at what she did, the Army wouldn't give her up without a fight. And it was hard to say no to something you loved doing. Like him, Vikki loved being a soldier.

And what about him? Would he ever consider moving from here or even following a woman around the globe as she pursued her active-duty career?

The answer came before he was done thinking up the question. He'd follow Vikki anywhere. But did she even want him to? Was Vikki anywhere near where he was, thinking that what they shared could go the distance?

As he toweled off with the fluffy pink towel in what must have been Vikki and Sadie's bathroom, he knew what had to happen. The smart thing. The right thing.

But tonight, he'd sleep with Vikki in his arms. Just this one last time.

Tomorrow would come soon enough.

VIKKI WOKE TO an empty space beside her where Flynn had held her through the night. He'd covered her with the comforter before he'd left, and she vaguely remembered him kissing her and telling her he'd be out of reach for the duration of the op.

Military speak for ghosting.

She cursed Flynn's sense of duty, his need to detach from her in order to face the battle ahead. As she yawned, stretched, she longed for his body heat. The sated weight of her bones, her muscles, was incomparable. Until the reality of what they'd shared, and what they were both giving up, crashed in. It wasn't a matter of "if" she'd regret losing Flynn. He'd be a cherished memory.

Memories were all they had, all that remained. He'd made that clear before they'd drunk one another in last night. No matter how much her heart wanted her to find him, convince him that they had to somehow make this work, she knew better.

Best get moving. There was no telling when Landon would appear. And when, in turn, she could finish this up and leave any reminders of Flynn in her past—before they leveled her flat.

LANDON HEARD THE knock on his crappy apartment's crappy door. It had to be the gun guy. It better be, because he'd forked over thousands in cash to get the unregistered weapon. No way was anyone going to issue him a handgun legally, not with his history, even though he was certain he was completely stable. What did the medical doctors really know, anyway? No better than the Capital X jerks, who were through with him since the word on ricin in RevitaYou had gotten out.

He looked through the side window and confirmed it was a teen with a take-out bag from a local restaurant. The reminder that he hadn't eaten since who knew when made his stomach hurt.

He opened the door and the kid peered at him from under a baseball cap. "You Landon?"

"Yeah." He shouldn't have used his real name. What

had he been thinking? The police were already crawling all over Grand Rapids, searching for him. But he couldn't leave town. He had to stay close to his dad. The fact that Major Orlando Street was six feet under didn't matter to Landon.

"Here you go." The boy shoved the bag at him and took off, running into the night. Landon locked up and sat on the cigarette-burned sofa, the bag on the upturned cardboard box from a case of RevitaYou.

To think, he thought he was going to live a life of leisure after the supplement hit the market. Sure, he knew that adding castor oil to the recipe had the slim risk of producing ricin, which might not agree with some folks, but they were adults. They knew the risks of any supplement, didn't they?

He pawed through the bag. It was his lucky day. The kid had taken precautions in case caught and there was also real food, a hot meal's worth, in the sack. Landon took out the few containers and placed them on the box, not leaning back until he pulled out the prize. A .45-caliber handgun and a box of ammo. Relief stopped the chattering in his brain for a nanosecond.

He had protection. No one was going to hurt him, or keep him from visiting his father, anymore.

Chapter Sixteen

Flynn cursed for the third time in five minutes as he stared at the map of Grand Rapids he'd hung in his barracks room. He was still on leave from duty, but he'd needed a place to stay and the base was his home, on duty or off. He hadn't seen Vikki in two weeks, not since he'd given in to temptation and gone to her in the bedroom she'd grown up in. As much as he wanted to beat himself up over making the choice to make love to her again, he couldn't. They needed something as a final memory that had nothing to do with their case, with the awful scene in the back of that godforsaken warehouse.

Everything in his life felt as though it was on hold, until he was able to help bring Landon in to the authorities. His half brother had chosen the last two weeks to go silent on all fronts, including Rosa's and his. Neither of them had heard from Landon.

His focus should be completely on finding Landon, but he struggled to keep from spending all of his time going over what he'd shared with Vikki.

He'd done nothing but think of her since, wishing he could have couched his words more gently after Captain Joseph had been killed, not caused the pain and then defensive anger that had contorted her face. Only moments earlier her expression had been filled with concern and relief. For him. And after he'd made love to her that last time—they'd made love to each other—he'd shut her out again, let her think he'd only done it for some kind of release from the pressure of the case.

His phone rang and he picked up, needing yet another distraction from his dire emotions.

"Hi, Mom."

"Flynn, have you seen what Melissa's posting on social media?"

"Landon's mom?" He had little contact with Melissa Street, his father's first wife and Landon's mother. "No. I don't even know the last time I checked my pages, Mom. You know I don't keep up with it." He kept his social media accounts current enough so that if anyone needed to contact him they could, but he didn't make a habit of posting due to operational security. Besides, the people who really mattered to him could always send him a text or call.

"She's lost it, honey. I mean, it's scary." Rosa's voice trembled, and it got his attention. His mother was a retired Army E-9, the most senior enlisted rank. Few things rattled her.

"What's going on?"

"She's saying that she's going to take a huge dose of RevitaYou and, Flynn, it'll kill her. You know it will."

"Hang on, Mom." He had his laptop open and waited for Melissa's page to load. The barracks' Wi-Fi chose this moment to run more slowly than usual and he drummed his fingers on the back of the monitor as if it would increase the speed of the connection.

"I'm going to her, Flynn. She needs us to help her." Resolve was back in Rosa's voice and it scared the heck out of him. Almost as much as seeing the bomb around Vikki's neck had.

"Mom, no. Please. Let me handle this. I'll call Grand Rapids PD, CI, and inform my unit on post. We'll get to her before she does this. Trust me." He hoped his reassurances didn't turn out to be empty promises.

"You do that, son, but I'm still going over there."

"Whatever you do, don't carry, Mom. You don't want to be in the middle of a firefight with LEAs."

"I think I can handle myself." Rosa's veteran traits reflected in her tone: strong, clear-minded, prepared. "Melissa's a sweet soul who never had a chance. Her intentions are well-meaning, but she's clueless. We both know that."

"Right. So why do you think you have to be the one to save her, Mom? She's never done anything for Landon, and only caused more stress for you when she showed up."

Flynn knew that he owed his sense of belonging in life, and his emotional stability, to his mom. She'd raised him right. If only Landon had allowed Rosa to be more a part of his life… If Landon had accepted Rosa's mothering, they all wouldn't be facing another life-threatening situation, thanks to RevitaYou.

"I'm going in fully protected and armed, Flynn. If Landon shows up, we have no idea of knowing where his mind's at." He heard the sounds of a zipper opening and closing, sure signs that Rosa was packing up the supplies she referred to.

"Mom, please listen to yourself." As he spoke, he texted the link to Melissa's social media accounts to his colleagues on post, Riley at CI and his contact at the Grand Rapids PD. "How would you feel if I was the one who'd called you? Would you still think it was a good idea to show up on my own at Melissa's?"

"If it meant saving Landon—"

"Think, Mom. There may be no saving Landon at this point. I'm sorry, but that's what we're facing. Landon's responsible for a substance that's killed at least two people. It's sickened scores more, many gravely. Is it worth any more people dying? Please let the authorities handle this. You can be there for Melissa afterward."

"You mean 'be there' for Melissa and your brother, don't you, Flynn?" Rosa's challenge dripped with icicles born of fear. Fear that she'd messed up in raising Landon. That someone else was going to suffer or, worse, because of it, that Landon might get killed. At the very least, he was looking at a lifetime behind bars.

"You know exactly what I mean, Mom." Flynn struggled to remain detached from his heart. Except that if he gave in to his emotions, his mother's pleading, he'd be effectively giving up any control he had over her welfare. It was little enough as it was. He couldn't live with himself if he didn't do everything to protect her.

Not unlike how you feel about Vikki.

"I'm going over there, Flynn. If I see you there, great. If you can't meet me, I understand. I was active duty once, too." She disconnected and he swore, staring at his blank phone screen. It was as if his heart had been ripped out of his chest. And the sad thing was, it wasn't unfamiliar, not since a certain Sergeant Vikki Colton had walked into his life.

Vikki.

Nothing had been the same since the last time he'd seen her, two weeks ago. He'd been in dangerous situations before, said what he knew could have been his last prayers. It wasn't that he wanted to leave the planet before his time. He loved life and all that went with it.

But he'd found something, someone, he cared for more. In his line of work and during the middle of a lethal case. This case seemed unending. Captain Joseph was no longer a threat, God rest his soul, but Landon remained at large. While he wasn't particularly concerned about his half brother harming him, Landon had surrounded himself with a criminal element that had zero appreciation for individuals. For the Capital X investors, the dollar was the bottom line. RevitaYou and its profits in the face of dead bodies proved their motive.

Flynn threw together what he needed and headed to his car. And willed himself to not even think about reaching out to Vikki. Their professional collaboration was over. As was any personal involvement.

Liar.

VIKKI POURED HER first cup of coffee from the pot in the CI kitchen, looking forward to moving back into her apartment as soon as Landon was caught. She hoped against hope that today would be the day she'd shake off her most inconvenient attachment to Flynn. He'd made it clear the week before last that they were done working together, that it was time for them to each carry on with their respective assignments as they pertained to RevitaYou. Then he'd proceeded to rock her world through a night of lovemaking she still hadn't let go of. How could she?

She put the old, chipped mug with the happy face down, a relic from before she'd left home, before their family had been torn apart by her parents' deaths. It had been her mother's favorite, according to Riley. As she looked at the mug, it came to her with alarming clarity that she recently hadn't felt any of her usual nostalgia for how her life had been before her parents died. No "what could have been" thoughts had come to haunt her as they'd done every year of her life since that fateful day.

Flynn had changed everything.

She took a minute to regroup, have a moment of quiet in the kitchen. It was predawn and she liked to be up before CI got buzzing, which it had been all week. With Charlize and doggy Pal back, the house was rarely silent. Sleeping in the room that she used to share with Sadie had given her little comfort. All she'd thought of was how it felt to have Flynn nearby. And then, next to her.

Her phone lit up. *Sadie.*

"Hey, sis." She willed her heart to slow down, stop pounding. If Sadie were in trouble, Riley would already know about it.

"Hey, yourself. You're already up, aren't you?"

"Well, if I wasn't, you would have woken me. Everything okay?"

"Yes. No. I can't handle staying in this house for much longer, Vikki. Maybe you can talk some sense into Riley and have him talk to the FBI. I need out." The desperation in Sadie's voice made Vikki's insides ache, more than how they already were from knowing her twin was in jeopardy, and from the onslaught of emotions Flynn had released in her.

"You need to stay alive, Sadie."

"Don't you think I know that? But here's the deal. Tate is a man with a lot of resources. If he wanted to find me, don't you think he already would have?"

"Two things." She took a sip of her coffee and promptly burned her tongue. "Dang it."

"What's going on?"

"Nothing—I didn't let my coffee cool off. Listen. First, Tate has unlimited monetary resources. I get that. But he has to hire the right people to utilize those capabilities. And I'll put Riley—all of us—and CI up against any corporation at any time. We're the best. Even the freaking FBI comes to us for consult."

"All right." She heard the cautious acceptance in Sadie's voice. "You're thinking that Tate is waiting for CI to break its chain of security just once, and then they'll get me?"

"I'm thinking Tate is a man who doesn't take no as a complete sentence, ever. I'd bet my GI Bill that Tate's not going to stop until he finds you, which means he's putting pressure on his team, pouring money into the effort. That is the first reason you need to trust Riley and stay put. The minute CI gets a whiff that Tate is closing in, we'll move you someplace else."

"I need out, Vikki. I can help myself and this entire matter a lot more effectively if I'm at CI headquarters." Sadie's nerves reflected in her trembling voice. Like Vikki, her twin rarely displayed emotion while actually working a case.

"Honey, I'm so sorry. I know this is hard. But we'd never forgive ourselves if something happened to you." Especially something they could have prevented.

"You said you had two points to make?"

"Yes. Second, it's gotten volatile at this point. Meaning, the federal agencies like Treasury are looking to freeze all of the RevitaYou-related accounts. This is making Tate and his cronies liquidate like crazy, stashing cash who knows where. I know it's hard, but you're so near the end. You'll be home soon. I'm certain of it."

"In that case, tell me something to distract me."

"What?" Sadie's sudden change of subject threw her.

"Tell me what's going on with you. I know you're back at the house and working eighteen-hour days on your Army reports, but what exactly happened between you and Sergeant Cruz-Street?"

"Flynn? How do you know so much about the time I spent with him?"

"I don't. That's why you're going to tell me. Come on, Vikki. Throw your sis a bone. I'm dying in here."

Vikki couldn't help but laugh at Sadie's dramatic portrayal of the last couple of weeks. "You're nowhere near death. Riley said the house has everything you need, including your favorite streaming services."

"There are only so many vintage television series a

girl can watch at a time, Vikki. Now stop changing the subject and tell me about your sexy sergeant."

"He's not 'my' anything. We had to work together at first, and the snowstorm prolonged it. But then he didn't want me around any longer. Said I was too much of a liability."

"But I thought he had no choice but to obey your orders?"

"Not exactly. We're the same rank, so I can call BS on him when he's not helping me out. But he's not obligated to include me in his ops. Not at all. It's okay, really. I don't need the ego stroke, and that's all it would be, working with the Fort Rapids MPs on this case."

"The last time we talked, it sounded to me like something bigger than this case was brewing between you two."

"Yeah, well, no. Not anymore."

"Aha! So there was something. What happened?"

Vikki looked out the kitchen window to the backyard their family had spent hours in during the Michigan summers. It soothed her spirit to allow her mind's eye to wander, reminisce over each memory, exactly where it was planted.

"I don't know, Sadie. Sometimes you meet a person and there's instant chemistry, a sense that you've known them forever. But do those relationships ever really last? Can you name one couple who told you they were excellent together from the get-go?"

"Mom and Dad. From what I remember, anyway."

"They're our parents. There's no way of knowing for

sure." Vikki didn't want to continue this subject with her twin. It was too painful.

"He hurt you. How did that happen so fast?" Typical of her twin, Sadie cut to the chase. She must have heard it in Vikki's voice, the way she didn't want to talk about Flynn.

"I let myself get hurt. It's a miscommunication. I thought we were starting something, which was ridiculous."

"I'm the first one to tell you to do what you want to do, what's better for you. But you know you can't judge what's going on with this new guy while you're both carrying the weight of the RevitaYou case on your shoulders. Riley's counting on you to come back and work at CI. We all are. With your skills, CI will become the best PI and security firm in North America."

"Wow, that's a tall order. Nothing like letting me figure things out on my own, then ease into it." Vikki ignored the part about Flynn. The mere thought of how he'd looked at her on the warehouse pier still stung. He'd shut her out.

Sadie laughed. "Riley's afraid that if he pushes too hard, you'll never come back home. But he's desperate to have us all working together. It's a balance thing, you know?"

"I do." She didn't deny that it took all personalities to make CI run well. "And the times I've helped out, when I've been on leave or when Riley's called to ask for advice, have been great. But I'm not sure I'll be as happy back here as I would at the base." It was impossible to tell Sadie how complex Army legal cases could become, and the amount of responsibility she was charged with. In fact, the law prevented her from sharing anything classified, which most of her cases were.

"Well, just think about it. Please? Meantime, I'll stay here and go over what we've come up with so far. I'll call if I figure anything out."

"Same. Thanks, Sadie."

"No, thank you for taking my call. I'm on the verge of serious cabin fever, is all."

"Sure thing. Sit tight, sis. Love you."

"Love you, too, Vikki."

Sadie was right.

After a quick meal of toast and an egg, she sat at the table where she'd once enjoyed family meals, and still did, when everyone was home. It had become her desk this past week. Opening her laptop, she entered the world that never let her down: the Army.

Her hard-won reverie was short-lived when her phone lit up for the second time predawn.

Flynn.

"Flynn."

"Vik—babe."

"What's going on, Flynn?"

"I'm almost done with all of this, Vikki. And I was thinking, maybe we should talk after it's all wrapped up."

"Anything you can share with me?"

"I don't have time to go into it. You'll know soon enough. I'm in the car and can't talk much longer. But, babe, I want you to know that I've been thinking of you. I had to let it go after that night."

"I know."

"No, you don't. You deserve someone who can be there for you all the time, Vikki. As long as I'm a soldier, I'm not that man. And once I'm out of the Army, I have plans to continue my education. I have no idea where that will take me."

Surprise, concern and a good dose of excitement washed through her. Flynn was talking to her about the future? Their future?

"Flynn, we'll talk about it later. I, um… I'm thinking about making some geographical changes."

"Not for me, Vikki."

"I didn't say it would be for you." The friction that sparked so easily between them hadn't subsided during the time they'd been apart. In fact, she wished they were together so that she could do something with the tension other than talk on the phone.

"Sit tight and keep your head low for the next day or so. I'll be in touch."

The line disconnected and she allowed a grin to ease the tension she'd been holding. Another woman might be miffed that Flynn hadn't been more expressive with his words. That he hadn't declared his feelings for her. But she didn't need that. Flynn was a soldier. She knew firsthand that a guarantee to reconnect wasn't a casual commitment.

It meant that during a pivotal turn in this mission, Flynn had thought of her, reached out to her. It left

Vikki with a sense of calm, as well as a desire to know more details.

Where was he going, and how soon could she get there?

"VIKKI." RILEY'S VOICE shook her from the summary she was compiling, the work she'd tried to escape into after Flynn's call.

Riley stood in front of her, waiting for her to focus on him. She sighed. It was pointless doing anything else until more information was revealed. She'd spent the last week compiling evidence and information related to RevitaYou. She had everything except to report that Landon had been captured and the operation had been totally shut down.

"You're up early. What's going on?" she asked. Her papers were splayed in front of her laptop and she'd claimed a good amount of the CI conference table.

"Flynn's reporting that Landon's mother, Melissa Street, is threatening to take several RevitaYou pills at once. She's doing it now on social media. At last count, just about a thousand followers are watching her live feed." His words triggered relief, immediately followed by worry. This was what Flynn had been talking about.

"You've got to be kidding." She quickly called up the site and entered Melissa's name. An image of the older woman holding the familiar green bottle of supplements appeared. "No, you're not." She noted the viewer counter in the lower right-hand corner of the frame. "There are fifteen hundred followers."

"It's going to blow up now that the day's beginning and users are logging in."

"Riley, this is the best kind of promo if we want smart people to not even try RevitaYou. It's the worst kind of promo for Landon and Capital X investors, though. If people look it up, they'll see all the people who got sick and the ones who've died."

"It won't prevent them from taking it. Especially if Melissa Street is one of the lucky ones who doesn't have any side effects."

Vikki continued to stare at her screen, at the woman who had abandoned her son so long ago. Did she feel an iota of guilt for how Landon had turned out? For his years of suffering before he channeled his pain into producing a substance with such deadly potential?

"I've got to go there, Riley. If there's a chance Landon is going to show up in person, I know that—" She stopped herself.

Riley slid into the chair across from her.

"I know, Vikki." Her brother's expression was so kind, it brought tears to her eyes. The jig was up.

She was in love with Flynn.

"You do?" She gulped. "How can you know when I have no clue?" She blinked back tears. Talking with Sadie had made her more emotional than normal.

"I saw what was going on between you and Flynn. And while I'm more comfortable being the protective older brother, I don't want you to miss out on a chance for something special." Riley's eyes shone with what she knew was his love for Charlize and their unborn baby. Love had changed her big brother, the hero of her childhood. Heck, her adulthood, too.

"Wait a minute. Who's talking about love?" She

wasn't ready to admit it to anyone but herself. Shouldn't Flynn be the first to know how she felt?

"Love? I never said anything about love, Vikki. That's all on you." His grin infuriated her. The downside of all big brothers—they knew you too well.

"I hardly know him. You and I have talked about this already." She grumbled, tried to distract herself with Melissa's social media feed. "We've only got another hour before Melissa Street's going to pop the poison pills."

"I need your help in this. With Sadie out of the fold, we've been shorthanded. You can ride shotgun with me in the armored SUV. But you have to promise me one thing, Vikki."

"Name it." If he was willing to let her go into the middle of this, where she knew Flynn would be, she wasn't kidding. She would do just about anything to be there. As if, by her presence, it would keep Flynn from getting hurt.

She really needed to get a grip.

"You do exactly as I tell you, and no interference. Especially with Flynn. He can't be distracted when it comes to Landon. Got it?"

She nodded. This was a promise she could keep. What she couldn't guarantee was that she'd stop herself from doing whatever it took to save Flynn, if need be.

It was time to face the devil that had been eluding them all.

Chapter Seventeen

Flynn cursed after he disconnected with Vikki. What had possessed him to call her now? He'd had two weeks to reach out again and he picked moments before he was going to be face-to-face with an old childhood monster.

Melissa Street.

She wasn't his stepmother, or a blood relative in any way. But Melissa had always been the bad guy to him, the woman who'd made his older half brother sad. And when the sadness wasn't enough, it turned into a bottomless pit of anger that had helped turn Landon into the person he was today.

You know why you called Vikki.

Yeah, he did. Vikki was the one person who'd been with him through the toughest parts of this case to date, and it felt odd to not have her at his side. And yet he didn't want her anywhere near Melissa.

He glanced at the car dash. Forty-five minutes until Melissa took the pills. Did Landon know? Would he be there? His half brother was so unpredictable. Definitely not a man who spent any time on social media, but he assumed Melissa had texted or called Landon, or both. And Landon had never been able to resist his biological mother.

His hands-free phone rang.

"Flynn."

"It's Mom. I'm a block away from Melissa's. There are already police surrounding the building, Flynn. I'm going to need you to help me get in to talk to her."

"Wait until I get there, Mom. I'm five minutes out." No way was Rosa going into that house. He'd make sure of it.

"I don't have a choice." Her voice trembled.

"Mom, this isn't your fault. We'll get it taken care of. Landon's not going to hurt anyone else."

"I don't want Landon to end up like your boss, Flynn."

Flynn's gut felt the icy grip of fear and he held on to the wheel. He couldn't promise his mother anything. Just like with Vikki. Two for two this morning. There was no way he could guarantee either of the women in his life who mattered the most that they'd all come out of this alive.

"Mom, I'm closing in. Stay where you are until I reach you." He knew the police line wouldn't allow her inside the danger area, and he wasn't planning to meet up with her until the showdown was over.

Because it was clear that this wasn't going to be easy. Melissa and Landon were never a good combination, and Flynn didn't want his mother anywhere near it.

He pulled up to the line of Grand Rapids PD vehicles, mixed in with SWAT vans. Several agents were scattered around, their backs imprinted with ATF, FBI,

GRPD in letters that reflected the increasing daylight. He got out of his car and donned his protective armor, placed his knife in the ankle holster and handgun in the holster at his waist. It was overkill, most likely, with all these trained officers around him, but Flynn was trained to be prepared in all situations.

It did seem a bit of a dream, though, and not a good one, to be potentially facing his half brother and his mother so fully armed. Flynn was used to the enemy being a terrorist nation, not his own family.

He flashed his ID to the officer guarding the perimeter and called out to Riley, who stood in the thick of the group. Riley motioned for the officer to allow Flynn in.

"Thanks for giving us the heads-up, man." Riley's relief was evident. "I don't know if we would have found out about it in time."

"It wasn't me. It was my mother, Rosa Cruz-Street. She's a retired MP."

"I know. She's over there." Riley motioned toward the area where two ambulances were parked, and Flynn saw that his mother was being attended to by EMTs.

"What happened?"

"Nothing. I told them to keep her talking, and under no circumstances can she get any closer to the action."

"She's going to be pissed at me." Both men laughed, a break in the tension that hung over the crowd.

"Any sign of Landon yet?"

"No, but we'll know the minute he shows up. We've got every inch covered."

A Grand Rapids PD lieutenant walked over and nodded at each of them. "Riley, Flynn."

"Hi, Tripp." They both greeted Lieutenant Tripp McKellar, a powerful force on the local law enforcement scene. Never afraid of what a situation might bring, Tripp's dedication to duty was legendary.

"Good to have you both here. Any idea when your brother will show?" His blue gaze scrutinized Flynn. Flynn knew he passed Tripp's muster; they'd worked together in the past. Still, the other man's attention made him stand straighter.

"None. He could decide to keep hiding, but I do believe what Melissa's been saying will anger him enough to come out. It could get dicey. I don't want anyone shooting at him. I need to talk to the lead."

"Already did. It's the FBI agent over there, Agent Gordon." Tripp pointed.

"I know her. We've worked together on a few cases." Relief that he knew the key players on the team was short-lived. "But does she agree that there's to be no shooting?"

Riley nodded. "Everyone wants Landon alive, Flynn. We need his testimony when we get to the Capital X henchmen. Agent Gordon wants you to go forward and talk to Landon if she needs you, but otherwise, we're to stay out of it."

Flynn looked at his watch. "Do we still know Melissa hasn't taken the pills yet? For sure?"

"Not yet. At least not visibly. She's still ranting on social media." Riley pointed to the seventeen-inch laptop an agent monitored from the back of a comms van. Flynn made out Melissa's face, saw that she was still talking to the camera. As he continued to watch, his heartbeat tripped.

Vikki was the "agent" working the laptop.

"Vik." He left Riley and walked to her, unable to stop his legs from carrying him toward the person he cared the most about in all of this.

She knew he was there before he'd spotted her. He could tell by the way she gave him a casual—too casual—nod. How she kept her arms folded across her chest when she wasn't working the keyboard.

"Hi, Flynn. Melissa's still talking, encouraging Landon to come forward." Her gaze was on him, but she had her professional mask firmly in place, her mouth a straight line.

"Yeah. Riley told me." He swallowed, tried to keep his bearings. "You're not getting in the middle of this, right?"

Challenge flashed in her eyes. Then she looked somewhere past his shoulder and her resistance dimmed. "Since Riley will have my hide if I do, no. And in truth, it's not my op. These folks have all been working the case far longer than I have…than we have."

Her acknowledgment of their partnership in this meant more to him than if she'd declared he was her personal hero. Vikki Colton was a woman of strength like none he'd ever known before, and she was on the same page as him. They were together in this. And if it was up to him, they'd be together a lot longer afterward, too.

But first, they had to capture Landon.

He stepped closer and leaned in next to her so that

he could whisper in her ear. Her scent assaulted his nostrils and he pushed past the emotions that elicited, shoved them into a safe place for later, after they made it through this.

"Don't give up on me, Vikki."

Without waiting for her reply, he headed back to Riley. After a quick dialogue, Flynn walked toward the woman who'd ruined his half brother's childhood. He'd be damned if she'd do any more ruining today.

VIKKI'S TRAINING WAS all that got her emotions, not to mention her hormones, under control and allowed her to focus on the social media page. Riley had given her one assignment, and it was up to her and the FBI agent on the other side of the house to monitor Melissa's activity.

Melissa's constant pacing, coming in and out of frame, along with her, at times, nonsensical chatter, kept her attention off Flynn. For the most part. She still heard his and Riley's voices, along with Lieutenant McKellar's, as they were all on the same wireless connection. Hcr headset buzzed with activity, from LEAs to Melissa's performance. But Vikki was the only one who had direct eyes on the social media feed. The others had to be prepared to act at a second's notice. From her. Vikki relished the opportunity to play a real part in the takedown. Especially if Landon appeared.

Melissa came back into the camera frame.

"Look, I still have not one, not two, but three of these miraculous babies in my possession." She held up a juice glass, empty but for the three capsules at the bottom. "These are the fountain of youth. Do not believe anything you're hearing on the news. It's all lies. The people who claim to have been hurt by RevitaYou were already ill by other circumstances. Look at all the thousands, millions, of people who've taken RevitaYou and not only lived, but reversed the aging process! We can all live so much longer with the aid of science."

Melissa refocused the camera and then sat in an easy chair. She placed the juice glass and ricin-laced pills on the table next to her and folded her hands, prayer-like, in front of her ample bosom. Vikki noticed a large bottle of water on the side table, too. Melissa had everything she needed to make her threats a fait accompli. But Vikki also saw something else on full display. A mother's love for her son. Melissa really believed Landon was going to show up, stop her from taking the dangerous substance. She also counted on her son watching this live feed. Vikki and the rest of the LEA knew there were no guarantees, but she had a sixth sense that Landon would show.

"Vik, where we at with Melissa? She still talking?" Riley's impatience jolted her.

"Yes. She hasn't stopped. I hope Landon's planning on making his appearance soon, though. She's all set up with the pills and plenty of water to chug them with."

"We're all looking for him, trust me." Her brother's reminder to stay in her lane.

"Roger. I'll let you know."

Melissa continued her soliloquy. "I know my son Landon—that's Dr. Landon Street to you. He was destined for greatness as a young child and always had the intelligence to match. He'd never, ever, create something to harm anyone. Landon is a pussycat."

Vikki snorted. If the fact Melissa was doing this at all didn't trigger Landon's concern, this would blow the lid off his anger. What grown man wanted his mother, especially one who'd abandoned him as a child, calling him a "pussycat"?

Before she had a chance to express her observation to Riley and Flynn, Melissa jumped up from the easy chair and darted to the window behind her. Vikki knew this was the front living-room picture window.

"Got him." Flynn's voice confirmed Melissa's strange action.

"Confirmation of Landon Street's ID by his brother." Riley's voice sang in her ear. Finally, this would come to an end.

Strangled screaming rent the air, dissolving any short-lived satisfaction that Landon was present.

Since Melissa was no longer on screen, Vikki looked around and noticed that all the LEAs were moving in, closer to the house but not passing the safety perimeter that had been established when they'd all arrived. The others were hunkered down behind their vehicles. Flynn's mother, Rosa, was being pushed into the ambulance, a good place to take cover. Vikki felt for her—if she had the training Rosa did, she'd want to be front and center with her son during all of this, too.

But Landon was unpredictable, and a mother's love could be, as well. As evidenced by the source of the nonstop shrieking.

Melissa stood on her front lawn, her wild arm gestures making the flowing sleeves of her thin dressing gown flap like a trapped bird's wings. She wore what looked like a shirt and athletic pants under the gown, and her hair was out of the ponytail she'd worn while streaming her video.

The source of her distress was a man who stood at the front lawn's edge, straddling the line over the sidewalk and grass. He was dressed in a large neon-orange hoodie, baggy pants and bright yellow tennis shoes. Vikki wondered if Landon thought he had disguised himself by hiding in plain sight with such a getup. Before she could analyze any more of his outfit, a familiar figure walked purposefully and carefully toward Landon.

"Landon. It's Flynn." Flynn's voice was so clear on the headset it brought tears to her eyes. *Please, please, let Flynn be okay.* Let all three of them make it through this. She didn't see that Landon held any kind of weapon, but she was too far away to be sure. The officers around her didn't draw arms, but she saw the rifles trained on Landon in the first ring of police who surrounded the house.

A muffled response was all she made out of Landon's words as Flynn's mic was engineered to pick up his voice first. Melissa's screams made everything else sound like white noise.

"Hold it right there, Landon. You've got several weapons trained on you. They won't fire, and you won't put Melissa at risk, if you turn yourself in now."

More muffled noises. The officers holding the rifles didn't move, but she saw the almost-imperceptible movement of their hands as they maintained their target. Landon. But now Flynn was between Landon and the sharpshooters.

The bullets would have to go through Flynn first.

"TAKE MELISSA WITH you and get out of here, Flynn. You're no help to me. They all want me dead anyway." Landon stood closer to him than he had in months, save for that time at the cemetery. Next to their father's grave, Landon always seemed smaller, a shadow of himself. In his current getup, he appeared taller than usual, formidable.

Landon hadn't spent a lot of time with this disguise straight out of a horror flick; all Landon was missing was the hockey goalie mask. He wore a dark-haired wig, but Flynn saw the wisps of his graying blond hair at the temples, recognized his usual silver wire-framed glasses. He wore an oversize neon-orange hoodie, baggy work pants and bright yellow sneakers. It was the exact opposite of his usual pullover sweaters, T-shirts and sweatpants. Even in his lab at the university he'd always dressed for comfort, his white lab coat covering everything but pajamas. A pang for the man Landon had been, or the hope for the man he could have become, assaulted Flynn.

Eye on the prize. Get Landon out alive.

"Don't you have anything to say for yourself, Flynn? I'm surprised you're even here. I know you've been working with them all along." Landon's eyes were empty behind the glasses that he'd had for at least ten years.

"Who's 'them,' Landon? Because it isn't me, or any of the police. We all need you to tell us your story, the real story. No one here wants you or anyone else to get hurt today. You have to trust me on this."

Landon replied with a blistering cluster of words that Flynn usually heard in a military setting. "I'll never trust you, Flynn." The depth of his bitterness was encapsulated in his words. They hit Flynn like bullets, shattering any remaining optimism he had for his half brother's redemption. Landon had chosen the dark side.

"Don't hurt my baby. Let him go!" Melissa's screams were becoming more strident and she took several steps toward Landon.

"Melissa, stay put or you risk getting Landon shot. He's going to be the first to be hit." Flynn didn't mince words. The woman had frightened him as a child, and now, while she didn't pose a threat to him, she had the capability of causing Landon's harm, or worse. If she made one move that Landon responded to by either drawing a weapon or running away, a rain of bullets could end them all. As much as Flynn trusted the officers and agents holding weapons on Landon, he knew that there was always a chance of missing a target. Especially a moving one.

Vikki needed the information only Landon could provide. They all did. This was their chance to bring down the entire network of poison distribution.

"There's no reason for all of this!" Melissa yelled and motioned in a half circle, encompassing the myriad LEA who were all trained on her tiny front yard. Flynn was equidistant from both Melissa and Landon, ready to take on either or both of them. He felt the tension between all three of them, knew the next few moments would decide the outcome. High-stakes scenarios often came down to a timeframe that was a fraction of the time that had been spent preparing for it.

Flynn had prepared his entire life to confront his half brother. No longer did he need to be the peacemaker or the little kid who looked up to an academic genius. But he had to be a brother, and a good brother brought his criminal sibling in alive.

"Landon, this is for keeps. Nobody's doubting your capability or trying to take away your professional reputation." He lied easily. It was what this was going to take. "We need to talk to you about RevitaYou and what you put in it and why. Only you know all of the ingredients and how they interact."

"I've already been labeled a murderer. No one wants my side of the story."

"Keep him talking, Flynn, and try to give more clearance." Riley's voice came over his earpiece and he ignored the "clearance" part. He knew what that meant. There was no reason to take Landon down—yet. It didn't appear he had a weapon. But if he did, all bets would be off.

"You can't believe the news, Landon. You know that. Remember when it was reported that my unit was hit by a roadside bomb eight years ago? It wasn't true, and I was fine." But it had given Rosa the scare of her life.

"People have died because of something else. I'm telling you, my formula didn't kill anyone."

"I know it didn't, baby. I took it! Look at me. It's like

I was when you were little!" Melissa proclaimed what Flynn didn't know for certain. If she'd taken the pills, it had been off camera.

"We have no confirmation that she took the pills, folks." Vikki's voice. "Her phone camera is still on, live feed, but the glass she had the pills in is out of the frame."

"Watch her for signs of poisoning, Flynn. Three pills is enough to kill if it is the first time she's taken it, but she could get nauseous or pass out without warning." Riley again. Flynn longed to talk back but had to stay present with Landon. And Melissa.

"Riley's correct." Vikki again. Her way of letting him know she was there, hadn't given up on him.

"Vik, keep the chatter down." Riley, being the natural rule-follower that he was, wanted the line quiet. Flynn was grateful for the sound of Vikki's voice. It grounded him, gave him a sense of purpose.

"I appreciate the info. Keeping it steady." He spoke low, so that neither Landon nor Melissa could hear him. They were each still a good ten feet from him.

"Are they telling you to shoot me now, Flynn? Or do you have to ask some questions first? Want to know how the ricin got in there?" Landon spoke through clenched teeth and his hand went under his hoodie, to his waist.

Flynn's mental warning bells went off.

"No, they're actually asking if Melissa took the pills. Did you take them, Melissa?" He spoke to her but didn't take his gaze off Landon. If his half brother had a weapon, there was nothing he'd be able to do for him or Melissa. The officers would open fire.

Melissa would lose her son and her entire reason for luring Landon here would be moot. She'd wanted to protect him, to prove his innocence. Once she accepted he'd taken the criminal path, she'd only want him caught alive.

"I did not, but I'm not afraid to. I have them here." She pulled her hand out of a pocket and revealed the three pills on her palm. Melissa faced Landon, tears running down her cheeks. "I've always believed in you, baby. I know you're not a thug like those men you work for." Her summarization of the Capital X loan sharks was spot-on.

"I've never been good enough for you. Or my father." He left Flynn out of the equation.

"That's not true! I had to leave you when you were small. I had no choice. I would have been a terrible mother to you. Rosa did a great job raising you."

"No one raised me. I raised myself. I don't need you. Or you—" Landon spared Flynn a withering glance. But Flynn wasn't concerned about his half brother's hatred. All that mattered right now was defusing this situation so that the arrest could be made.

"Landon, be respectful to Melissa." He knew that Landon had always fared better with an authoritative tone. "Turn yourself in. Give yourself the chance to explain your side of the story."

"I'm not wasting my time with you, Flynn." Landon's hand pulled out a handgun, but it caught on the too long zippered hoodie. Flynn saw his window and went for it.

Chapter Eighteen

What was Flynn doing? Vikki wanted to scream "No!" over the comm system but couldn't risk distracting Flynn or any of the other agents and officers on the line. From her vantage she saw Landon grow increasingly edgy, fidgety. He moved from foot to foot, scratched his nose, and his face reddened.

It took her a full second to realize that Flynn was practically airborne, his movements were so quick. Gunfire rent the air and she was on her feet, running toward Melissa's front lawn.

A gunshot rang out.

"Vik, no!" Her brother's order rang in her ear. She ripped the earpiece out, unwilling to listen to Riley, needing only one thing. Flynn. Alive. Unhurt.

"Flynn!" The scream left her mouth, unimpeded by her usual military bearing. This was a matter of her heart, something greater than anything she'd ever experienced. As she ran, she saw Flynn wrestle with Landon, who had at least three inches and thirty pounds on Flynn.

Please don't fire again. She knew the shooters were

exercising extreme restraint to not take Landon out. They were close enough and had the experience to do so without hesitation. But it put Flynn at risk. Melissa stood to the side, sobbing as the brothers wrestled. Flynn got Landon into a facedown position, holding his arm behind his back.

Thank God.

Two sets of hands grabbed her at the same moment she saw Flynn raise his hand, holding a pistol. Landon was disarmed. Vikki's forward momentum halted midstride and she struggled against the restraint.

"Stay back. Everyone's okay. They have to take Landon Street into custody." The officer to her right spoke first.

"You going to stay here if we let you go?" The GRPD chief, Andrew Fox, gave her a long glance, as if to determine her mental state. She was out of breath, much like when she'd run the two-mile PT test and beat her colleagues. Yet she'd only come a half dozen yards or so.

She nodded. "Yes."

"You can go in after Landon's apprehended." The officer nodded toward the scene. Law enforcement moved in on Flynn, Melissa and Landon in practiced steps. Tripp McKellar was in the middle of it and she watched as he cuffed Landon, who remained facedown on the ground.

"Okay. I'm fine." She shook off the officer's hold, hugging herself tight. It was over. Landon was being led off to a cruiser. Flynn talked to Melissa. Vikki would wait until Flynn peeled off. She didn't want to interrupt whatever he had to do now. All she cared about had transpired. He'd lived.

Flynn is okay. Alive.

"You must be Victoria Colton." A pretty older woman with dark hair and sparkling eyes—Flynn's eyes—stood next to her. The same worry that Vikki had experienced was on the woman's expression, and her cheeks were still wet with tears. Vikki wiped at her own cheeks, stared at her wet hands. The stealth tears had fallen as she'd waited to see if Flynn was okay.

"And you're Rosa." Vikki held out her hand, which Rosa swatted away.

"Come here." She opened her arms and Vikki stepped into a tight, warm hug. "We're family, honey." She spoke into Vikki's hair and Vikki didn't have the energy to argue with the woman. Flynn's description of his mother was correct. She was a force of nature.

Just like her son.

VIKKI MADE HER way through the crowd that had formed around Melissa's front lawn. Landon had been taken to the county jail for processing, and Melissa was being addressed by a woman with a clipboard. Vikki thought she might be a social worker.

The only person she wanted to see was Flynn. He was listening to Rosa, who was speaking quickly to her son, her hands holding his tightly between them, her stance purposeful. Vikki waited a few feet away.

"Good job, sis." Riley gave her a playful knee to the back of her knees.

She shook her head but couldn't stop the grin from erupting. "I was going to smack you back there."

"You were going on about chemical composition and crap. We didn't need that."

No, but Flynn needed to know she hadn't given up on him.

Riley's brow quirked at her silence. "Oh, I get it. You did it so that Flynn would hear you. He was never in any danger, Vik. He made it."

"No danger? Landon fired his gun at him."

"Only after Flynn had him in a lock, his arm pinned down. The bullet went right into that tree." He nodded at an overgrown maple, its remaining leaves a burnished red and ready to drop with the next gale.

"Thank goodness." She was still in grateful mode. This entire case could have taken a wrong turn at any number of places. "It's over, Riley. We caught Landon. And Joseph."

He nodded. "Yeah. Not exactly how we wanted it to fall out, but Landon should be able to give us the gauge on Capital X and their ops."

"I hope so. Do you think Sadie can come home now?"

"Nope. In fact, we're moving her. She's not safe in the same spot for so long. And after we realized how easy it was for Captain Joseph to intercept our comms, I'm concerned that Capital X can do the same. I'm not taking any chances, Vik."

"I don't want you to. But she's not going to be happy about it." Sadie was already climbing the walls. Vikki would call her as soon as she got home.

"No." Riley's gaze was over her head and she turned. "I'll see you later, sis." She barely registered his words as she looked up into Flynn's face.

"You did it." Her words were a mere whisper in the face of the emotions rolling off him. Battle-ready intensity, satisfaction, sadness. And a glimmer of relief.

"We did it together." He reached out and pulled her in. Unlike the passionate we-made-it-through-hell-babe embrace and kiss she'd expected, this was more the kind of bear hug you'd give your battle buddy after surviving a firestorm. Sincere. Heartfelt. But not romantic in the least.

She stepped out of his arms and looked at him with fresh eyes. This was the Sergeant Flynn Cruz-Street she'd met almost a month ago, when she'd rolled into town and found him under fire in the Bachelor Enlisted Quarters. An Army MP, conditioned to take on whatever the mission threw at him.

"I've got to get back to CI headquarters." She didn't know what else to say and bit her lip against the tears that welled. Why had his mother acted as if she were going to be part of their family? Worse, why had she believed a woman she'd only just met, under duress, no less? So much for Flynn's plea for her to not give up on him. People did a lot of unusual things under stress, when they thought their lives were at stake.

"I imagine you're relieved to have this behind you."

He nodded, ran his hand through his hair. He opened his mouth to speak just as Riley walked up. With a start, she realized he'd been patiently waiting several feet away, giving them privacy.

"Riley." Flynn held out his hand.

"Flynn."

They shook hands, gave one another pats on the shoulder. Typical bro love stuff. Vikki saw her exit. This was too painful, and it seemed the only person hurting was her.

She turned and wove her way through the cops, agents and all their associated vehicles. A woman in need of a good cry required solace.

One last cry over Flynn and then she was done. It was time to think about her life after the Army and it wasn't going to include him.

"YOU DID IT, Flynn." Riley rocked back on his heels, his hands in his pockets, oblivious to the fact that the love of Flynn's life had just walked away. When had he realized she was his love? The One?

You don't deserve her.

"We all did, Riley." His gut churned and he didn't have the usual relief or sense of accomplishment that he'd experienced after other takedowns. "Tripp moved in at the right time. Landon's strong—I was afraid he'd flip me over."

"Save your modesty." Riley assessed him with his gaze. "What's going on between you and Vikki?"

"That's a really good question." Flynn thought he knew—they'd had several intimate moments together, worked well as an Army team, end of discussion—but the way his heart was hammering as her figure disappeared into the crowd told him otherwise.

"Can I give you a suggestion, Flynn?"

"Can I stop you?"

Riley nodded. "Fair enough. My sister is a tough customer. She's made of steel, and I'd trust her with anything, including my life."

"But?" He sensed the big brother of not just Vikki but the entire Colton clan had a lot more to say.

"But." Riley blew out a breath. "Did she tell you our family history? About our parents?"

"Yes. And how it might be related to the entire Capital X group. I'm damn sorry about that, Riley."

"You and me both. What I'm trying to tell you is that underneath all of her solid soldier bearing is a woman who has had her heart crushed more than once. My parents' deaths and then that dirtbag she was with for a while."

"She mentioned that."

"Well, then, there's the answer for you."

Flynn wasn't aware he'd asked a question. "What question is that an answer to?"

"Vikki trusts you. That's huge. I'm her oldest brother, and she doesn't tell me stuff. Sadie, her twin, knows her best, but she didn't open up completely to her, either. Not about that jerk who cheated on her, or what Vikki's thinking about whether she'll stay in the Army or not. If she's talking to you, telling you her deepest thoughts, you're the one. Don't screw it up."

"Roger." Flynn got it, loud and clear. Riley walked away, called over by one of the FBI agents. Flynn stood alone in the middle of organized chaos as Melissa was tended by EMTs, Landon was put in the back of a police cruiser, and several officers and agents combed Melissa's property for evidence.

Only a few minutes ago he'd had the woman of his dreams standing in front of him. How had he let her walk away again?

More important, why?

Chapter Nineteen

"I haven't seen you this upset since Dad died, Flynn." Rosa Cruz-Street sat across from him at her small kitchen table. His mother had purchased the modest townhome after her Army retirement, declaring that she wanted to be financially independent and knew it wouldn't happen if she stayed in their family house. His dad, Orlando Street, had left her what he'd had financially, and Rosa had her own Army pension and health-care options. Yet without careful planning, her monthly stipend wouldn't be enough.

"I messed up, Mom." He had so much running through his heart, now that the path between his brain and heart had opened up. Unfortunately, he'd shoved aside the woman whom he really wanted to share his revelations with.

"Are you feeling guilty over helping to turn Landon in? He needed to come in, honey. You know that. And you were the soldier I've always known you are. Your father would be so proud of you."

"Thanks, Mom." Her praise would normally buoy him. Not today. "I appreciate that. But I haven't been a hero where it matters—with someone I care an awful lot about."

"Vikki Colton." Rosa said the name with warmth. "Honey, I knew from the minute you met her that your life was in the middle of change. And you've been different these last weeks. You're in love, sweetie pie."

He'd let Rosa know he was working with another Army sergeant on the case, but he certainly hadn't filled his mother in on the more personal details. He shook his head. "You always know stuff about me, even before I do."

She laughed and patted his hand. "It's a mother's instinct, honey. As much as my attention seemed to be on Landon for your entire childhood, I have always had a special bond with you. Not that I didn't spend so much, maybe too much, on Landon's well-being." Rosa's eyes brimmed with tears. "If I had known what would have made a difference for him, I'd have done it."

"I'm so sorry you've been through all of this, Mom."

"Don't be. It's life. While I care deeply about Landon, it's your father that I always worried about. Can you imagine? He was left with a tiny tot in the middle of a deployment. He picked up the pieces and made it as good as he could for both of them." She wiped at her cheeks where tears streamed. "I miss him."

"Wherever Dad is, Mom, he's proud of you, too… You did so much for our whole family. And you never stop caring."

They sat together in silence for a long while, allowing one another to process their emotions.

Rosa wiped her eyes and smiled. "Enough. We've

done our part, me when Landon was young and now you. He's in the safest place for him, and he'll face the consequences of what he's done. No one else is going to be hurt by him, which is the best we can hope for. It's time for you to live your life, Flynn."

He wasn't about to remind his mother that the Capital X loan sharks who'd funded the entire RevitaYou mess were still at large and were bound to cause trouble until they were caught. Or that Vikki's twin was at risk until the apprehensions happened.

"I do, Mom. You're right. You're always right. I'm afraid I've messed up but good this time, though."

"Nonsense. Where there's love, there's always hope. Get out of here and go take care of your future, son."

As he hugged his mom and took his leave, Flynn recognized the topsy-turvy nature of his gut wasn't from fear or the constant vigilance the past several weeks had required.

Hope was still struggling to get a foothold in his life. It wasn't a familiar feeling.

FLYNN CHECKED HIS appearance one last time in the barracks' mirror. He'd struggled between wearing his Dress Blues or civilian clothes, and picked civilian. He hoped like heck that Vikki would be willing to hear him out.

The bouquet of flowers he'd ordered was almost too big to fit in his passenger seat. Ridiculous, but he had to go over the top with his gesture or go home. Vikki deserved so much more than what he had to offer her.

The least he could do was give her spring flowers when winter was closing in.

Thc drive out to CI headquarters, and where he knew she was still staying while on leave, was no more than fifteen minutes from the post, and yet it seemed to take eons. Then he blinked and he was parked in front of the house.

What if she laughed at him, threw him out? He didn't think she would, not after the passion they'd shared, the life-threatening situations they'd fought to get one another through. Would she believe him that he was willing to follow her around the world, wherever the Army sent her?

"Only one way to find out." He spoke quietly inside the car before getting out and rounding the front to grab the flowers. His sweaty palm almost dropped the blooms. He hadn't been this nervous since waiting to find out if he'd passed all the required exams to enlist in the Army and join the MP corps. That had worked out for him; he had to keep the faith that this would, too.

Or his life would never be the same. Vikki was his life, his love, his reason for getting up in the morning. All he had to do was convey it to her.

"YOU SAID YOU were thinking you'd re-up for another five years." Sadie looked around the small room they were packing up to move her to the new safe house. It was a lousy reason for a reunion, but Vikki was thrilled to have this brief time with her twin.

"I know I did, but I changed my mind. I love my Army job, and I've enjoyed the reserves. But it's time to focus on CI without being concerned about my monthly weekend and annual two-week active duty. This way I can support Riley and CI without always feeling so torn between my active-duty time or working for CI." Vikki placed the clothes Sadie had piled on the bed into a small suitcase.

Sadie laughed. "I never looked at it that way. You really haven't had a break in a long time, have you?"

"No, but I get fun in where I can." Immediately images of Flynn laughing, Flynn touching her, making her… *No.* She'd had a heck of a time this past week since Landon had been arrested, training her thoughts to stay away from Flynn. Thanksgiving was days away. She'd known him for almost a month. What a different woman she was from the one who'd driven into Grand Rapids four weeks ago.

"Speaking of fun… Have you heard from Flynn since last week's takedown?"

"You know I haven't, and I won't. I already told you all of this, Sadie." Her impatience made her feel guilty; Sadie was stuck in limbo, moving to another safe house, and deserved a little more compassion.

"You did tell me, but I still think I'm right. Landon was his half brother, for heaven's sake. That's a huge family deal. I'm sure Flynn needs time to process, and to do all the Army paperwork for why he was involved in the apprehension while he was on leave. Then you'll hear from him. When he knows it's right for you both." Sadie was a hopeless romantic, and this was what had gotten her in too deep with her criminal ex. Vikki stood straighter. Just thinking about Tate Greer and his threats against Sadie made her bristle.

"Um, it's the twenty-first century? Flynn could have called or texted me, at the least. No, it's over, Sadie." She fought the tears that welled.

"You sound so certain, Vik."

"I am." Not about her feelings, for she knew she'd never love another man as she did Flynn. But he'd withdrawn from her twice, both after major events. He'd only come back because it had been rough for both of them, and they'd needed the stress relief. A lot of soldiers had consensual, mindless entanglements to relieve the anxiety of drawn-out missions. She couldn't believe that Flynn believed that was all they'd shared, a quick hookup, but without talking to him in person, she wasn't sure.

"You also sound sad, Vikki." Sadie handed her a tissue.

She swiped at a tear. "I am sad, I suppose. I let myself have dreams of being a professor's wife. That's what Flynn wants to do, after the Army."

Sadie's laugh was compassionate. "I know you really care for Flynn if you even contemplated such a quiet life, after being on the go with the Army for so long. Don't give up on Flynn yet, sis."

"It doesn't matter at this point. I'm moving on. What are you going to do to keep busy, Sadie?" She was worried about her sister's mental state. It was hard being stuck for so long.

"This! I had it shipped to CI. It was in the box you brought." Sadie held up two different knitting kits, one for a complex multicolored sweater and the other for socks. "Remember how much we used to love to knit when we went to the lake?"

"I do." Those had been simpler times, when they'd been teens and their parents were still here.

"Time to go, Sadie." Riley walked into the room and surveyed the boxes and luggage. He shook his head. "You sure have collected a lot of stuff for being locked down the past several weeks, Sadie."

"We'll get it in the car ourselves—don't you worry." Vikki swiped at her older brother, making them all laugh.

"I'd rather wait until the FBI gets here. Give it five minutes. I'm going to do a quick sweep of the house and use the restroom."

After several minutes, the sound of vehicles outside prompted Vikki to pick up a box. "That's our cue."

"I'd love to have the truck packed before Riley's out of the bathroom." Sadie's lighter self shone through the stress she'd been, and continued to be, under. Vikki let out a long sigh. Her twin was going to get through this. It'd be all right, for all of the Coltons.

Vikki stepped outside first and held the front screen door open with her foot so that Sadie could wheel two suitcases through.

"Don't move or your sister's dead, Vikki." Cold metal pressed against her temple and Vikki dropped the box, stunned at Tate Greer's voice in her ear.

"Either of you make a sound, you're all dead." A man she didn't recognize stood in front of her and Sadie, pointing a machine gun at them.

"Take her. Now!" Tate's words shot from Vikki's ear to her breaking heart. No, no, no! Not Sadie. When two additional henchmen, wearing ski masks, hauled Sadie from the entrance and began to drag her across the front lawn, a whimper left Vikki's lips.

Sadie turned her head and gave Vikki one last glance, and with their twin intuition, Vikki knew her twin loved her. She hoped Sadie knew how loved she was.

"Sadi—"

A harsh tug on her shoulder, the barrel pressed harder into her head. "Last warning, princess."

Vikki was helpless as Tate's goons dragged Sadie away, then shoved her into the back of a windowless van and shut the doors.

Tate waited for the van to screech off before he shoved her to the ground, facedown, and placed his foot on her head. "Stay here until we're gone."

She heard his footsteps retreat, the sound of a slamming door and then more revved engines as Tate and his entourage escaped.

Vikki began to stand, her body shaking. She had to get inside and tell Riley, call the police. Where the heck were the FBI and promised backup?

"Vik, what—" Riley walked through the open door with a box, then threw it to the side and rushed to her.

"She's gone, Riley. Tate came and took Sadie. Sadie's kidnapped!" The sounds she'd been forced to silence let go in one long wail of anguish.

A WEEK LATER, Vikki finished dressing and grabbed her laptop, a constant companion as she'd finished up the last of her JAG reports. She was due at CI headquarters in thirty minutes and wanted to grab a cup of coffee along the way. The coffee maker in her apartment had refused to work upon her return and she'd not had time to replace it yet.

RevitaYou was still an ongoing police investigation, until Tate Greer, Wes Matthews and the Capital X loan sharks were captured. And Sadie was returned to the Coltons in one piece. Vikki held on to her belief that Sadie would not only survive being kidnapped by Tate, but come back stronger for it. It was still very odd for Vikki to have to wrap up her case and consider it over. None of the RevitaYou issue would be finished for her until her twin was home safe. But as far as the Army was concerned, the case was closed. Vikki had been able to visit and interview Landon in the county jail. He'd been forthcoming with information and she knew this was the best work she'd ever done for the Army. It was a good way to leave her enlistment, at the top of her game. A lighter heart would have been nice.

Vikki was so looking forward to Thanksgiving with all of her siblings at home.

Home.

She enjoyed being back in her apartment, on her own, no question. Even when the sad thoughts of Flynn and what they'd shared, and lost, overwhelmed her. But maybe it was time to think about finding a town house or small house to buy. She wasn't getting any younger, and clearly, her life was just that—hers, solo.

Hot lattes for herself and the entire team in hand, she entered Riley and Charlize's home through the back kitchen entrance. Only when she walked into the dining area, with the conference table, did she feel she was in CI headquarters. The house had been a safe place in the midst of the Joseph and Landon cases, and she'd stay here again if she needed a temporary place in between leaving her apartment and moving into a new place. But Riley and Charlize, and the baby, would need their own space. Maybe she'd call a Realtor later today. She'd saved enough for a down payment on a modest place. The riverfront condos in Grand Rapids looked inviting.

"Hey, Riley, Tripp, Charlize." Lieutenant Tripp McKellar sat with the others at the table, and she noticed Ashanti was sitting with a cup of coffee and smiled when she saw the covered paper cups with the known logo.

"Finally, some real brew."

"Yeah, I brought the fancy stuff." Vikki put the beverage carrier down and took a seat. And tried to ignore her aching heart. First Flynn, and now Sadie's kidnapping, had taken the oomph out of her step. She was grateful for work, which proved a distraction.

"Any news on Sadie?" She always asked this first, unable to wait for Riley to give a rundown on the latest.

"No, but I promise you, Vikki, and all of you, I'm going to find Sadie, and Tate Greer is going to face justice." Tripp's statement matched the determined glint in his blue eyes, an attractive counterpart to his silvering hair. Vikki wished Sadie would fall for someone like Tripp, instead of scum like her ex, Tate.

"I know you will, Tripp." Vikki nodded, then turned her attention to Riley.

The next hour was spent going over Tripp's plan to lure Wes Matthews out of hiding and shut down the entire RevitaYou scheme for good. Ashanti agreed to serve as a decoy, much as the GRPD rookie had done to lure Captain Joseph out. This wouldn't go down at a warehouse but on the dark web, where Ashanti would pose as a financier looking for a health product to invest money in. The plan seemed solid.

Several GRPD officers and detectives were searching for Sadie, and Vikki tried to take comfort in the concerted search efforts.

Vikki took notes but her mind kept going back to Flynn. Shouldn't she be totally focused on her twin? Because she wasn't, the truth stood out in harsh lights to her. She'd never get over Flynn.

"Don't give up on Flynn yet, sis."

Was Sadie's intuition correct? Would he come around, eventually?

No. No more fairy-tale fantasies.

Vikki was relieved when the meeting broke up. She wanted to get going on her house search. Anything to distract her from Sadie's welfare and Flynn's departure from her life. Tripp departed, as did Riley, promising to call in with any news on Sadie. Ashanti and Charlize had disappeared into the tech room at the back of the house.

The doorbell rang as she carried her second cup of coffee to the table. "I'll get it," she mumbled to herself as she walked to the front door.

The side glass panes revealed a tall figure and she froze. She knew that silhouette, the profile.

Both were forever burned upon her heart.

She opened the door. "Flynn."

"Vikki." He held out the most humongous bouquet of pale pink peonies. "For you."

"Thank you. They're beautiful. I had no idea the florist could get peonies in November." She accepted the bouquet, her ridiculous chatter evidence that she was gobsmacked that Flynn stood in front of her. With flowers.

Do not do this to yourself.

"Can I come in?" He looked as shaky as her hands.

"Um, sure." She turned and walked into the house, unable to allow him to pass next to her. Keeping her distance was the only way she'd get through this, whatever "this" was. "If you're looking for Riley, he's gone."

"I know. He's looking for Sadie."

"He told you?"

"Yes. We've spoken each day since last week. Since three weeks ago, actually. The base MPs are helping with the case when they're off duty. As thanks for finding Captain Joseph before he hurt anyone."

"Oh." Flynn's phone did work, after all. "Did you get in trouble for working the case while you were on leave?"

He shrugged. "Not really. My superiors were less than pleased with me, but happier that we caught Landon. Captain Joseph's death required an investigation, and everyone's still sad. But once I gave my statements and my bosses spoke to everyone involved, I ended up with a promotion. Go figure."

"That's wonderful, Flynn! Congratulations." Warmth

filled her and it wasn't forced—she really was happy for him.

"I didn't come here to tell you about myself, Vikki." He looked uncomfortable. As if his shoes were too tight.

"What's going on?"

"It's what's not going on. I can't sleep. I can't eat. Everything is gray. Nothing is the same without you, Vik."

"You'll get over it. It's normal for us to form deep attachments during an op. The op's over." Boy, she was doing well. If she could keep from crying or screaming, she might fool him.

Flynn took a step closer and she backed up…into the dining-room table. "I don't want to get over it, Vik. I want you. I want me and you. Tell me you've been able to forget the way we fit together."

She sucked in a deep breath and couldn't tear her gaze from his. Her resolve to keep her distance waned… and then completely failed. Tears fell, plopped onto the peony petals.

"I can't forget any of it, Flynn. I'll never forget you." She moved to wipe her eyes, but Flynn was there, taking the bouquet from her, placing it on the table, taking her face into his large, capable hands. And kissing her with his soft, sexy lips, moving his mouth over hers, using his tongue to take her breath away.

He raised his lips enough to whisper, "I love you, Vikki. Marry me."

"Marriage?" She kissed his jaw, his throat. "Isn't that rushing things?"

"We've done nothing slow, babe. Why start now?" Their mouths met and they shared a kiss that Vikki knew was a promise. For today, tomorrow and forever. Flynn was her other half.

"Vik." He pulled away and lowered himself to one knee in front of her. "Will you marry me?"

"Yes, Flynn Cruz-Street, I'll marry you."

He stood and kissed her again. "I'll follow you wherever your career takes you."

She told him what she'd already decided, what she'd discussed with Sadie. "So maybe it's me who's following you around."

"No, babe. I'm getting out and going to school at the University of Michigan."

"Really?"

"Yes. I've been accepted to the PhD program. English lit."

"It seems we're meant to be—in Michigan. And Ann Arbor is only two hours away, so we can come back often."

"There's something else that's meant to be, babe." He kissed her, this time with more heat, until she had to lean on him as her knees were caving.

"We're not alone, Flynn. Ashanti and Charlize are in the back."

"Dang." They both laughed. Flynn's phone chimed with a text and he pulled it out from his pocket.

"It's Riley. Let me call him back. It might be about Sadie."

She listened to Flynn's voice as he spoke to her brother, and it filled her with tremendous strength. Comfort. Love.

"Got it. Yes, I'll tell Vik." His gaze was on her, making her want more than kisses and hugs. He put his phone down and took her in his arms again.

"Babe, it's okay. We'll find Sadie."

"Flynn, I'm sorry. Our first time admitting we love each other, and your proposal, and this is how we're going to celebrate. Finding my sister."

"Hey, babe." He lifted her chin and she saw the love shining from his eyes. "We're a team."

And she knew that it would be all right as long as she and Flynn were together.

* * * * *

NINA SINGH
MICHELLE MAJOR
MILLS & BOON
True Love
KATE HARDY
MELISSA SENATE
MILLS & BOON
True Love
THERESE BEHARRIE
STELLA BAGWELL
MILLS & BOON
True Love